Also by Robert Repino

Culdesac
D'Arc
Malefactor

MORT(E)

A NOVEL BY ROBERT REPINO

Published by
Soho Press, Inc.
227 W 17th Street
New York, NY 10011

Library of Congress Cataloging-in-Publication Data

Repino, Robert.
Mort(e) : a novel / by Robert Repino.

ISBN 978-1-64129-293-1
eISBN 978-1-61695-428-4

1. Human-animal relationships—Fiction. 2. Monsters—Fiction.
3. Imaginary wars and battles—Fiction. I. Title.
PS3618.E76M68 2015
813'.6—dc23   2014030185

Interior illustrations by Sam Chung@A-men Project

Interior design by Janine Agro, Soho Press, Inc.

Printed in the United States of America

10 9 8 7 6 5 4 3 2 1

For my family,
and my families

Then the LORD opened the mouth of the donkey, and it said to Balaam, "What have I done to you, that you have struck me these three times?" Balaam said to the donkey, "Because you have made a fool of me! I wish I had a sword in my hand! I would kill you right now!" But the donkey said to Balaam, "Am I not your donkey, which you have ridden all your life to this day? Have I been in the habit of treating you this way?" And he said, "No." Then the LORD opened the eyes of Balaam, and he saw the angel of the LORD standing in the road, with his drawn sword in his hand; and he bowed down, falling on his face . . .   —Numbers 22:28—31

God is love, they once said, but we reversed that . . .

—Margaret Atwood, *The Handmaid's Tale*

PART I **WAR**

CHAPTER ONE
THE STORY OF SEBASTIAN AND SHEBA

EFORE HE TOOK his new name, before the animals rose up and overthrew their oppressors, before there was talk of prophecies and saviors, the great warrior Mort(e) was just a house cat known to his human masters as Sebastian. It was a time that now returned to him only in dreams and random moments of nostalgia that disappeared as quickly as they arose. All of it except for Sheba. The memory of her was always digging at him like a splinter under a nail.

Sebastian's mother, a nameless stray, gave birth to her litter in the cargo bed of a pickup truck. If he tried hard enough, Mort(e) could see brief flashes of those days spent suckling with his brother and sister. He could recall the warmth of his mother's fur, the rough surface of her tongue, the sound of her cooing, the smell of his siblings as they climbed over him, the wetness of their breath.

He could not, however, remember the circumstances that separated him from his family. There were no records for him to consult once he became sentient. All he could do was imagine the truck driver—most likely a friend of the Martinis, his eventual owners—discovering the destitute brood while loading the vehicle one morning. Sebastian's mother probably hissed and scratched when the humans removed her kittens. But in the end, she must have been grateful to be relieved of them. Instinct told her that she had fulfilled her evolutionary role and was still young enough to have more kittens.

From that morning on, the days dissolved into one another for little Sebastian. Janet and Daniel Martini were a young couple then. The newlyweds spent their first year together renovating their house for the children they planned to have. Left to himself, Sebastian believed that he owned the place. He crept into the rafters and slunk through the newly constructed ceilings and walls. The workmen covered up the wooden beams, shooing Sebastian away from his favorite hiding spots.

Once the living room was complete, Sebastian would recline in the square of sunlight on the carpet, drifting in and out of sleep, watching the dust motes floating around him. During the day, while the Martinis worked, the house was quiet. At night, Sebastian would visit his masters at the dinner table, sometimes reaching his paws up to Daniel's lap. The man wore jeans that carried the scents of his print shop: chemical cleaners and metal and ink. The manufactured odors would sting Sebastian's nostrils if he inhaled too deeply. Daniel would then lead the cat to the basement stairs, where he kept the water and food, along with the litter box.

Sebastian rarely thought of his siblings or his mother, until one morning when a family of strays marched in single file across the front lawn. The mother led two kittens who obediently hopped behind her. Sensing they were being watched, the mother stopped and pointed her tail in the air. She eyed Sebastian, who stared at her in return, his paws propping him up on the windowsill. She hissed. Sebastian hissed back, mimicking her. Then she extended her paw, and three sharp claws emerged from the tips. Sebastian flinched. Satisfied, the mother cat kept walking. Her young ones gave Sebastian a final once-over before following.

A dog's bark sent them scurrying out of sight. The dog was Hank, a brown mutt who lived across the street. Hank seemed to have no purpose in life other than barking until he was hoarse, while his red nylon leash strained to keep him at bay. He often focused his anger on Sebastian, who slept on the windowsill when he wanted to feel the cool glass on his side. On this day, Sebastian let Hank holler for a little while before stepping away from the window. It was an act of mercy.

Sebastian gazed at his own paws and noticed for the first time that the toes were not as long as those of the other cats. The digits had been sheared off. That seemed impossible, for he should have remembered such an incident. Regardless, this observation produced a moment of clarity for him. There were probably many things he did not remember about his past, living by himself in this house, sleeping away the time. Moreover, there were cats and other creatures beyond the walls, and he had been one of them. But now he was here, separated from others like him. He knew there was no way out, even though he had never searched for one.

Though it may have been terrifying, the moment drifted away, along with most other memories. There was warmth and food here, along with other wonders and distractions. A new plush carpet in the living room was even softer than his mother's furry belly. An enormous gaudy mirror took up nearly an entire wall of the living room, leaving him baffled for weeks after its installation. Not only was there another room, but another cat! This stranger had a white chin with an orange streak that draped over his forehead, extending along his spine to his tail. Though Sebastian was relieved to discover that the other cat was an illusion, he still had to remind himself of this fact every time he walked by the mirror.

He dedicated entire days to the new television, with its

flickering screen, endless looping wires, and whirring circuitry. When the Martinis left the attic door open, Sebastian had a new world to conquer, filled with toys, cardboard boxes, holiday decorations. His first expedition lasted from one sundown to the next. From the window he could see gray roofs, green lawns, streets that glistened in the rain, and a never-ending stream of cars rolling along the horizon, the edge of the known world.

And then Janet brought home a young one of her own. A few days later, Daniel picked Sebastian up—something he never did—and carried him into a bedroom where the baby boy lay on a towel on the mattress. Daniel spoke softly to Sebastian, rocking him gently before placing him on the bed. Sebastian sniffed the baby's soft, clean skin. The baby gurgled and waved his arms. Daniel let Sebastian sit there for a long time.

Sebastian liked the child, whose name was Michael. And he was happy when, perhaps a year later, Daniel brought him another infant, a girl named Delia. These were his people, and he belonged with them. This was home. He was safe here. There was nothing else to life. There didn't need to be.

FOR MANY ANIMALS, things began to change when they were first exposed to the hormone. For Sebastian, the real change began when Janet started sleeping with the next-door neighbor.

The neighbor appeared out of nowhere in the Martinis' driveway one day. Janet chatted with the man while the babies were asleep upstairs. Sebastian observed from the window. The neighbor was tall, with long hair that flopped behind his ears and a pair of round glasses that reflected the light in brief flashes. Beside him, fidgeting at his knees, was a dog. Large brown eyes. A white coat with an orange patch extending from the hip to the shoulders. Mysterious and exotic, a creature from another world. The man would occasionally grasp her collar in order to hold her still.

Sebastian was convinced that the dog was about to attack Janet. He pawed at the window in an attempt to warn her. If only he had those sharp claws like the stray cats, she would have heard the scratching. The neighbor gave the dog a whack on her side, and she sat down and remained still. This animal was clearly the man's property, and posed no threat. The use of force to subdue the dog surprised Sebastian, for the only time he could recall being disciplined was when he sat in the recliner. Janet had swatted him out of it so many times that he began to believe that the chair was somehow connected to the woman, and could summon her instantly.

It wasn't until the neighbor was saying goodbye that the dog finally spotted Sebastian. She cocked her head, trying to figure out what this little creature was. The man yanked her collar one more time, and she left with him.

Her name was Sheba. A few sunrises later, the man and the dog performed an odd ritual in their yard. He tossed a fluorescent green ball, which the dog would chase down and return to him, over and over. Both of them seemed so pleased when the task was completed that Sebastian again wondered if the dog somehow ruled over the man. But then the man dangled a piece of food until she sat and waited for it.

Sebastian once dreamt of the dog invading his house and taking his family from him. He saw himself on the other side of the window, in the forbidding cold, while the dog stared at him from his spot in the living room.

Some time later, the Martinis invited another stranger to the house. A teenage girl named Tanya. The couple dressed up in new clothes—Janet in a long silvery dress, her sandy hair tied in a bun, and Daniel in a jacket and tie. They kissed the children goodbye and left the house together for the first time since Delia had arrived. Tanya sat on the couch watching television. She smelled weird, like candy, flowers, and mint. Every once in a while, she would go upstairs and check on the children. Sebastian kept his distance, spying on her from behind a chair or underneath a table.

Something had happened to the family. Tanya had split them up somehow. She was clever. She said hello the way all guests did, with a smile and a gentle hand. Sebastian ran away from her. She could not be trusted. A predator was in his house. Sebastian was on his own. He had to protect this place by himself.

Each time Tanya visited the children's room, Sebastian stayed on her tail while still remaining far enough away, in case she pounced on him. In case she had claws. It went on several more times until he could barely stand it.

She went in once more, and he waited in the hall. He could hear the girl speaking softly, her palms sliding down the fabric of the sheets. The lights dimmed. Something was happening.

Furious, Sebastian charged, butting the door with his head. The sound of the collision was like an explosion. Tanya was the first to scream. Sebastian began screeching as he never had before. He pawed at the door. Inside the room, both children were crying. Tanya whispered in response, trying to soothe them. Sebastian would have none of it. She was trying to trick them, the same way she had tricked the Martinis. *Don't believe her*, he tried to say. *I am here to protect you.*

Eventually, the Martinis' car pulled into the driveway. Sebastian stopped yelling, relieved that he was able to summon them so quickly. While the children continued to cry, the babysitter stuck her head out the window and called to the Martinis for help. She was loud enough to get Sheba barking from next door. Janet arrived first. Sebastian let her walk by, proud that he had held off the intruder long enough for his masters to see. She tried to open the door, but it was locked from the inside. She banged on it for a few times before Tanya let her in. The girl's face was slick with tears, her eyes red and raw. Janet hugged her, then went to the children's cribs and rocked them to sleep. Defeated, the girl sat in a chair and wept.

Sebastian walked downstairs, where he found Daniel leaning against a wall. The man's tie was undone, his skin yellow and wet. Sebastian noticed a new scent on him, a putrid version of Janet's perfume. Daniel stared at himself in the great mirror, a line of drool hanging from his bottom lip. Sebastian went to him, hoping for some kind of explanation, but the man nudged him away with his foot. Sebastian stood there, stunned. Meanwhile, Janet walked the traumatized girl to the door. She and Daniel exchanged angry words. Years later, Mort(e) imagined her saying something to the effect of, "Your cat showed more concern for your children than you did." And then she must have said something about his drinking. She ignored his angry reply. Tripping on the first step, Daniel managed to drag himself to his room, where he promptly fell asleep.

The house fell silent. Sebastian was alone to contemplate what had happened. It was he who was the enemy, the intruder. He was a prop for this house, not to mention its prisoner. They had mutilated him so that he could guard the house in name only. He pictured the days stretching endlessly before him. He realized that he would die alone in this place.

When the moment passed, he wandered over to the window. Tanya was gone, and Janet stood in the driveway speaking to the neighbor again. The dog was with him. This time, Sebastian did not have to wait for the dog to make eye contact. She stared at him, her tail wagging. Dogs seemed incapable of controlling their tails. Minutes later, the neighbor and the woman sat at the kitchen table sipping tea and laughing the way the Martinis used to years earlier. Sebastian did not have the energy to stand up to yet another stranger. Besides, he was content to stay by the window. Sheba remained in the driveway, her leash tied to the doorknob.

The glass separated them. Sebastian drew closer. Sheba pressed her paw to the window and licked the glass in a vain attempt to get to his face. Sebastian sniffed the trails of saliva but could smell nothing. This continued into the night, while the two humans shared stories and jokes. It was not long until all the evening's events were forgotten, replaced with Sheba's warm brown eyes and lapping tongue.

A NEW RITUAL began. Several nights a week, Daniel left for night classes at the local community college. Janet would put the children to bed. And then the neighbor would sneak across the yard, Sheba in tow, sometimes mere seconds after Daniel's car pulled out of the driveway. Janet would greet them in the kitchen—first the dog with a pat on the head, and then the neighbor with a passionate, longing kiss. One time, they went at it for so long that Sheba barked at them. After exchanging small talk, they would retire to the master bedroom.

Sebastian observed from a perch on top of the cabinet. Up close, the neighbor was so different from Daniel. Whereas the master was short and stout, with a growing bald spot, this man was tall and lean. He had a darker complexion, and he wore his hair in long strands, almost like rope. The neighbor's name was Tristan, and he was a literature professor at a nearby college. Sebastian did not understand why such a man would be the object of Janet's affections when her husband was clearly the protector of the house.

Tristan tied Sheba's leash to the leg of the kitchen table and headed off with Janet. Sheba moaned a bit, and the man returned to soothe her. The woman hooked her finger through Tristan's belt loop and pulled him toward the stairs, trying to distract him from his whining pet. This dog couldn't be left alone, Sebastian realized. She depended on her master too much. And Janet must have refused to meet at Tristan's house. Leaving behind the children would have been even worse than having the dog around.

Sebastian heard movement on the second floor. Sheba stared at the ceiling. Sebastian was unsure of what to do next—the window had provided a safe barrier between them, and he was not ready to get close to this stranger without it, no matter how fascinating she may have been. He had to settle for watching from afar until Tristan returned and walked her out.

The next time Sheba visited, she urinated all over the kitchen floor. Janet screamed when she found the mess, pulling her hair in frustration as the puddle crept onto the rug by the door. Tristan tried to calm her down. He stepped outside, which made Sheba howl in agony. It sounded like a child. The shrieks made Sebastian's ears turn. No wonder her master had to tow her along on his visits. She would have alerted the entire neighborhood to what was going on. Tristan returned with a roll of paper towels in one hand, a plastic bottle of green, foamy liquid in the other, a pair of rubber gloves in his pocket, and a mop under his arm. He removed the rug and cleaned everything so ruthlessly that even Sebastian could no longer smell what had happened. The next night, a new rug greeted Daniel when he came home from work.

After that, Tristan put Sheba in the basement. If she had another accident, at least it would be easier to clean and hide. Sebastian waited for Tristan and Janet to start making their noises in the bedroom. Then he visited Sheba. She stared at him as he paced the floor. When he was within range, she sniffed his head. He wondered what her tongue would feel like, and then the next thing he knew, she was licking him from his eyes along his skull to the back of his neck. Sebastian retreated. Sheba stepped toward him, but the leash restrained her. Sebastian rubbed his head with his paws until it was dry. When he went back to her, she licked him again, more gently this time. He nuzzled against her, feeling her fur mingle with his own, and hearing her heart thud against her chest, the breath going in and out. Within minutes, they were huddled together and dozing off as though they were animals in the wild groping for warmth from other members of their pack.

SEBASTIAN HAD NEVER known what happiness was. Now that Sheba visited, he had someone in his life who understood. Someone who forgave him for who he was.

Because he was neutered, with no exposure to cats since his birth, cuddling with Sheba was the closest Sebastian had ever come to experiencing physical intimacy. But it was more than enough. The simple act of determining the positions in which they slept became a profound, almost sacred, act, every bit as complex as outright mating. Typically, Sheba preferred to be the big spoon, since Sebastian was so much smaller. Throughout their sessions, they would have to shift in order to facilitate breathing or circulation. Sometimes they were content to merely touch foreheads, or for Sebastian to rest the crown of his head on the middle of Sheba's back. If it had been a particularly long day, they would face each other in an embrace, their legs overlapping. Sheba, being the more fidgety of the two, would normally be the first to break the pose. Sometimes Tristan and Janet would have to wake them up. The couple seemed happy to see their pets so friendly with each other.

After some convincing, Sheba joined Sebastian on his regular patrols of the house. They explored the basement together, sniffing around the old tools and sports equipment. Once, when Tristan failed to secure the leash properly, Sheba broke free and followed Sebastian upstairs, through the many rooms of the second floor, under tables, behind shelves, into closets that had been left open. Sebastian led her past his masters' bedroom and into the far reaches of the forbidden attic. Though Sheba was scared at first, she soon found the place as irresistible as he did. It was their secret world, a conquered land. Her presence made it seem new again.

There was a moment as the summer sun was going down when Sebastian remembered that terrible thought he had had so long ago: that one day, he would die in this place. If he had shoulders, he would have shrugged. It no longer mattered if he died here, whether it was in another ten years or that very instant. Sheba's breath was heavy on his neck. His head rested on her outstretched legs. Everything was now, in the present moment, and it was perfect.

SEBASTIAN LEARNED TO recognize the sound of Sheba's feet hitting the grass when she played in Tristan's backyard. There was a large tree, its branches humming with beehives, and its trunk choked by a pack of slithering vines. It may have been Sheba's favorite place in the world. When she was there, she did not always notice Sebastian. If she did, she would bark a few times to say hello. The stray cats occasionally teased her, but she chased them away before they could unsheathe their claws.

One day Sebastian was surprised to see Hank, the dog from across the street, in the Martinis' driveway. He walked slowly, exhausted. Sensing something was terribly wrong, Sebastian scanned the backyard for Sheba. He spotted her reclining in the shade of the tree. Hank trotted off, his eyes fixed on Sebastian.

The dog's expression suggested that he had gotten away with something.

IN A WAY, Sebastian was fortunate to not yet understand that nothing lasted forever. He was unaware of the war that was brewing while he and Sheba held each other. And when Sheba began to act differently, he failed to notice at first. After a while, it seemed that all she did was sleep. They no longer performed their cuddling ritual. Sebastian would often find her already passed out, and he would have to creep up next to her. More than once, she woke up and irritably pushed him away. He ignored it, repositioned himself, and fell asleep again.

There were other things going wrong. Whenever Janet was alone, she would huddle by the television and watch the ghostly people on the screen. It was always the same: a river of text flowed beneath explosions, people running, buildings on fire, green trucks rolling along highways, men and women with helmets marching, building bridges, demolishing things, using flamethrowers to burn massive hills of dirt. And in between all the images were videos of creatures that Sebastian had seen crawling in the grass outside the window: ants. They were always on the television, always marching in a line, sometimes covering entire fields and picking apart dead farm animals. Sebastian saw people running away from ants the size of the Martinis' car. The monsters could walk on their hind legs, and their jaws were strong enough to lift a human at the waist. This footage went on for a few days until Daniel came home and switched it off while his wife was watching. They yelled at each other, and when they were done, Janet sat in the room by herself, crying. After that, she turned on the television only when her husband was out of the house.

By then, Michael was walking on his own. One time, he

refused to go to sleep, and she agreed to let him watch. All the channels were playing the same thing now. Nothing but ants and fires. But this time, there was footage of a new creature. A pack of wolves, walking on their hind legs, approaching the camera. One of them carried a club in his hands the same way Daniel would hold a hammer. This was followed by a choppy clip of a group of animals marching alongside the giant ants. Sebastian could hear people screaming. Michael cried when he saw it. Janet shut off the television and cradled the child until he quieted down.

Soon after, Daniel began carrying cardboard boxes filled with water bottles, canned vegetables, and jars of peanut butter to the basement. One night, he hid a strange object behind the shelf where he kept his tools. It was a long metal tube with a wooden base. He placed small red cylinders into a hole in the side of the object. Then he propped the wooden base on his shoulder and aimed the tube at Sebastian, making a popping noise with his mouth. After his master went to bed, Sebastian sniffed the device a few times before giving up on figuring out what it was.

A few days passed, during which Daniel occupied the basement, his body odor lingering in a cloud around him. Sebastian took to hiding in the attic. There were trophies, old record players, photo albums, winter coats hovering on hangers—an entire lifetime's worth of objects. But they had been sitting there for so many years. Too musty and old. They could not compete with Sheba. For a brief time, he held out hope that she was hiding somewhere in the attic. He would meow and wait for her to answer, or he would nap on an old comforter and expect her to be there when he woke up. Nothing worked.

A FEW NIGHTS later, when Daniel was away, Sheba returned at last. The ritual ensued as it always had, with Janet hugging Tristan, the two of them leading Sheba to the basement before disappearing upstairs.

Sebastian could tell right away that something was wrong. Sheba hunched down, claiming the spot for herself, her paws balled into fists. She growled at him. He hoped that it was some kind of game that she was playing, so he continued walking toward her. But then she barked and bared her teeth.

Sebastian ran to the attic. He sighed and let out a meow that he hoped Sheba would hear over the moans coming from Janet's bedroom. He thought about dying again, but the feeling soon passed.

A litany of unfamiliar sounds rattled the window. When he peered outside, Sebastian saw the ramp to the highway jammed with the same vehicles from the television: large green trucks and moving metal boxes with long tubes sticking out the front. The engines rumbled, smoke rising from their tailpipes. Though Sheba's tree blocked the view from the other side of the house, Sebastian was sure that the vehicles surrounded the town. A siren howled in the distance. It was some kind of alarm, like Sheba crying, only many times louder. These intruders had something to do with Sheba's behavior, he was sure. They were influencing things, making the Martinis hostile to one another, making it so that Sebastian now ate only once a day rather than twice. The children cried more. The radio no longer played music—only angry, tense voices. The television flashed monsters on the screen. Janet often sobbed while folding her hands and whispering to herself. Everything was falling apart.

Then Janet started screaming. Sebastian arrived at the basement to find Tristan running up the steps. The man grabbed a roll of paper towels and a dishrag and returned to the cellar. Sebastian crept behind him.

On the third step down, he had a view of everything. Sheba

lay on the floor, panting and exhausted. Splayed out before her were three shivering puppies. Tristan frantically tried to wipe up the mess. He yelled at Janet. Sebastian could smell the fear in their sweat. They would not be able to clean up before Daniel returned.

Sheba would not look at him. She was hypnotized by the little ones.

Then the car pulled into the driveway. Tristan and Janet argued in a whisper. She put her hands on his shoulders, begging him to leave. Tristan ran out the back door as Daniel walked in the front. Janet switched off the light to the basement.

Husband and wife embraced—the first time they had done so in weeks. Upstairs, Delia started crying, so Janet went to the nursery.

Sebastian got closer to Sheba. When she finally acknowledged him, she acted as though she did not even remember her hostility from a few moments earlier. *I know you*, her affection seemed to say. *Where have you* been? The little ones were lolling about. Sebastian sniffed each of their foreheads. Then he pawed at Sheba and leaned into her warmth. With this movement, he purred to her, *Don't worry. Don't be sad. I am strong. I will not leave you. I am strong.*

After the Change, many of the animals reminisced about the time when they first achieved self-awareness, like humans talking about where they were for important historical events. This was Sebastian's moment: a brief recognition of friendship between two beings separated by species and circumstance. He was lucky. So many others recalled watching television, or deciphering a street sign, or staring at some interaction between humans. Sebastian, on the other hand, had a true moment of bliss, a welling of joy and peace.

But it soon faded. He knew that he would lose her. She

would leave with her children, and he would be trapped in this haunted house alone. There would be the familiar sounds and smells. Perhaps another child for the Martinis. There would be food and water when he needed it, along with the litter box and the square of sunlight in the living room. But there would be nothing else, and there was nothing he could do about it.

Sensing that her master was not in the house, Sheba began whining, a sort of weak squeal that escaped with each breath. Then she howled like a wolf, startling Sebastian. He told her to be quiet, that it would be okay. Footsteps approached. Janet intercepted her husband at the top of the stairs, trying to talk him out of going down to the basement. The lights came on. Sebastian's pupils shrank into painful slits.

Daniel froze at the sight. Sheba saw him coming closer, realized that he was not Tristan, and continued howling, as if this would transform the man into her master. Janet pretended to be shocked as well.

The man went quiet. His wife asked if he was okay. He backhanded her in the jaw, knocking her to the ground.

The man grabbed Sebastian by the scruff of the neck and tossed him aside. The puppies were still prone on the ground. Janet screamed. Sheba rolled onto her feet and tried to shield her pups from danger. Daniel kicked her in the ribs. Sheba yelped. She stood on her hind legs and bit into the man's arm. Daniel kicked her again, another hard shot to her hip. She snapped at him. Unafraid, Daniel gripped her by the neck as she pawed at him. He shoved her into a wall. The sound of it made Sebastian jump. Daniel was trying to kill her. Sheba had to run away. Taking a last look at her pups, she sprinted up the stairs past Sebastian. The man pursued her, his feet stomping against the old wooden steps. Sebastian stepped into his path.

Daniel had to awkwardly jump over him. The move bought Sheba time, and she was able to run out the back door.

With Sheba gone, the man turned next to Tristan's house. No one answered when he banged on the door. Enraged, Daniel went to his garage and returned with a bright yellow mop bucket, which he carried to the basement. Sebastian hid under the kitchen table. When the man climbed the steps, all three of the puppies were in the bucket, squeaking helplessly. Janet was close behind, begging him to stop. When she reached for the bucket, her husband pushed her away with the heel of his palm. He went into the bathroom and slammed the door. With the water running in the bathtub, Janet leaned against the wall and slid down until her head rested on her knees. She caught sight of Sebastian and began to cry.

The puppies stopped squealing.

SEBASTIAN RETURNED TO the kitchen. The door was open. He had never left the house before. It was as though some invisible barrier had locked him in for all these years. Now, leaving seemed no scarier than taking a nap in the living room. The clarity of it was so blinding that he could hardly imagine having been afraid of the outside world before. So he walked out, guided by the scent trail that Sheba had left until he lost it in the middle of the yard. He called to her but knew that she could not hear.

Behind him, Janet closed the door, and she and her husband began fighting again. Sebastian was not frightened. He did not want to go back inside. Instead, he had an urge to explore, to learn things. He had never examined a bird's nest up close or traced the connecting lines of a spider's web. His mind ached for more knowledge, a thirst that could not be quenched. A pack of vines strangled the tree on Tristan's lawn. A clump of ants dragged a wounded grasshopper to their lair, dismantling the struggling creature along the way. A sad woman packed her children into a car weighed down with luggage and drove off. In the sky above, menacing helicopters and fighter jets cut through the clouds, racing toward the explosions and the great plumes of smoke to the south. Long after the Martinis had exhausted themselves with their fight, Sebastian wandered the neighborhood, cataloguing everything. He was not simply storing things away and recalling them. He was asking *why*.

He realized then that things did not last forever. They decayed. Or they left. Or they died. Or they were lost. Or they were taken away.

That night, while he sat behind the Martinis' garage, the hair on his paws fell away. He was not alarmed. He simply brushed away the remaining strands, stretched out the toes into fingers, and rubbed the palms together.

More jets streaked overhead. Explosions thumped in the distance, getting closer. Sebastian climbed to the roof of the garage to see over the hedges. Miles away, a city burned. Helicopters hovered over the flames like flies above a carcass. Massive fireballs bloomed amid the wrecked buildings. Then the electricity went out in all the houses in the neighborhood. The faraway conflagration provided the only light.

Sebastian stayed up all night watching, thinking, remembering. He knew that when the sun came up, more things would change. Or be taken away. Or die.

STILL ON THE roof of the garage, Sebastian woke to the sound of glass breaking in the house. His eyes opened. A column of black smoke obscured the city on the horizon. He turned to the house and tried to listen. Janet burst out the door. She wore a hiker's backpack and held a child in each arm. Sebastian had never realized how strong she was.

Daniel trailed behind her. "We have to stick together," he said, his voice breaking. This made Sebastian pause. He actually understood the words!

"We're not staying in this house," she said.

Sebastian mouthed the words: *we're not staying in this house.*

Daniel ran inside while his family headed to the car parked at the front of the driveway. It was a silver SUV with mud streaks on the side and children's seats in the rear.

When Daniel stepped outside again, he held the black metal tube in the crook of his elbow. "You're not taking my children," he said.

Janet ignored him.

"Mommy, what is Daddy doing?" Michael asked.

"Do you hear me?" Daniel said.

"Go ahead and shoot us then, Dan!" Janet said, her face puffy and red. "We're dead anyway! Go ahead and do it!"

Daniel had no response. Blinking, his lip twitching, he leaned the tube against the side of the house and walked inside.

The girl was crying, while the boy kept asking questions.

"Get in the car," Janet said.

While the mother fussed with Delia, Michael caught sight of Sebastian on the roof. "Mommy, look!"

Sebastian realized that he was standing on his hind legs like a man. But before Janet could see, her husband emerged from the front door of the house. He grabbed Janet by the hair and pulled hard.

On her back, dragged from behind, she tried to cradle the screeching baby in her arms. "Daniel, *stop it!*"

Michael was torn between his unhinged parents and the demon standing on top of his garage. The boy called to his father, but the man did not answer. Soon the entire family was in the house again. The door slammed shut, sealing off the noise.

A few minutes later, Sebastian could hear Daniel walking toward the porch, probably to retrieve the metal tube. Sebastian knew that his master was going to use it on the family. He pictured the man bringing the wife and children into the bathroom and running the water until the squealing stopped. Sebastian jumped down from the roof and raced to the object.

Daniel exited the house to find Sebastian before him, standing erect, brandishing the weapon. The fear and despair in the man's eyes infuriated Sebastian. Did he not recognize a member of his own family? Did he not remember when Sebastian had protected the house from an invader, or when he accepted the responsibility of watching over the children?

"You do not recognize me?" Sebastian asked. The words felt strange rattling in his throat and leaving his mouth. It seemed as though they had always been there, waiting to be unlocked. The act of speaking felt like shaking his head until the right phrases fell out.

The man's lips moved. No sounds came out. Sebastian stepped forward and pointed the weapon at his head. "Do you understand my speech or not?" Sebastian said.

"Yeah," Daniel said. "Yeah."

Three fighter jets swooped above the house, their engines vibrating the windows. More explosions thudded miles away.

"Get inside," Sebastian said. "We talk there."

Daniel complied, leading Sebastian to the living room. The smell of sweat and blood grew strong. There, Janet lay on the floor beside the recliner, still clutching Delia. Michael knelt beside her. Blood leaked from her split eyebrow and dripped onto the plush carpet.

"See?" Michael said to his mother. "I told you!"

The child recognized him. Janet, dazed, didn't seem able to comprehend what she was seeing.

While Daniel told Michael to be quiet, to be a good boy, Sebastian could not resist watching his reflection in the mirror as it moved with him. He could walk upright. And he had grown taller than his master, with lean muscles underneath his fur. His limbs were long and thin. His paws had become functional hands. If he'd had claws, he could have sliced Daniel into bleeding strips of flesh if the man tried to resist him.

Daniel sat on the couch and, for the first time, offered Sebastian a seat on the recliner. Sebastian obliged, cradling the weapon on his lap. Sitting in the forbidden chair so close to Janet, he experienced a moment of panic. But things had changed, and she was in no condition to discipline him now.

"Do you know who I am?" he asked.

"Sebastian?"

This sounded familiar. The Martinis, even the children, said it all the time. The word had once meant so many things: *stop*, *here*, *eat*, *sit*. But it had actually been his name. Sebastian. Se-bas-tee-yan.

"It's impossible," Daniel said through trembling lips.

"You gave me this name?"

"Yes," he said, his eyes fixated on the ghoulish pink hands that cradled the tube.

"Are you my . . ." Sebastian searched for the word before finally settling on it. "Father?"

"How are you able to talk?"

"No questions," Sebastian said. "You answer me now."

Daniel seemed to expect his wife to say something. She did not speak, so he laughed nervously and shook his head.

"Answer," Sebastian said.

"I'm not your father."

"What are you to me?"

"You are—" Daniel said, pausing. "You were our pet."

"What does that mean?"

"We owned you," he said, almost pleading. "You were ours. We fed you, you lived here . . ."

Sebastian considered this. "Something has happened here," he said. "Explain."

Daniel nodded. His hands shook, and his bloodshot eyes fluttered in their sockets as he searched for the right words. There was an ant infestation that started in Africa and South America, he said. It began as an odd occurrence. An anomaly. Soon it became clear the ants could not be stopped. Entire cities had to be abandoned. Then the giant ants emerged, like nothing anyone had ever seen before. Practically bulletproof. Able to bite through metal. And then there were reports of animals changing shape, walking like humans. Somehow the ants had become smart, and the animals were becoming like them. Enormous towers of dirt and clay began to rise all over the globe. Scientists detected an ultrasonic signal coming from a turret at the top of each tower. The humans would try to destroy them, only to find that the ants had repaired the structures within hours. More of the insects continued to spring up no matter what the humans did. And then, out of nowhere, a massive island rose from the sea, somewhere in the Atlantic. The ants had created it. One day it wasn't there, and the next day it was.

Daniel rambled about the war, the evacuations, the retreat in Europe, the slaughter in Asia, the mass suicide in Saudi Arabia, the detonation of a nuclear device on the Korean peninsula. And Tristan. Every day, another part of Daniel's world had unraveled, all leading to this moment, when his own pet stood before him, brandishing a weapon and calmly asking questions. As the man spoke, Sebastian saw that Michael was old enough to understand some of these things. The boy was probably learning about them for the first time.

Daniel was in the middle of explaining the failed attack on the island in the Atlantic when Sebastian interrupted him. "Where is the dog?" he asked.

"The dog?"

Sebastian glared at him.

"Sheba," Daniel said. "She ran away. Haven't seen her. I'm sorry."

"You killed her little ones," Sebastian said. "And then you were going to kill your own family."

Daniel's face was shiny with sweat. By now, Sebastian knew how to get a reaction from him, even if he was not entirely sure how to operate the tube. When he pointed it at Daniel, the man was eager to speak.

"I have nothing left," the man said. "I was angry. My wife . . ." He buried his face in his hands.

"It's like she said," Daniel continued, fighting away his tears. "We're dead anyway. I probably did those puppies a favor, you know?" He waved his arm to indicate the madness around them.

"I should kill you for what you did," Sebastian said, more to himself than to Daniel. "And for what you were about to do. But I think you are telling the truth. You really are dead."

Daniel pursed his lips and said nothing.

"There are a lot of words in my head," Sebastian said. "I am not sure how they got there. I dreamt of them and then woke up this morning with them in my mouth. One of the words is *love*. I loved your family, but I was just a toy. I loved Sheba, but now she is gone."

Sebastian rose. He stared at the square of sunlight on the carpet for what he thought would be the last time. He gestured to Janet and the children. She rose unsteadily to her feet. With Delia in her arm and Michael holding her hand, she walked quietly past her former pet. Michael reached out and touched Sebastian's tail. Janet slapped his hand away.

Sebastian waited until he heard the door open and shut. Then he turned to Daniel and said, "Goodbye."

"Bye," Daniel said.

Sebastian left the living room, the weapon held loosely in his unnatural hands. He trudged to the kitchen. He had to find Sheba, even if she was dead, even if he died.

As Sebastian reached the door, he heard the unmistakable sound of metal scraping against wood, a hissing *shuh*, the sound Janet made when she prepared to cook. Sebastian turned in time to see Daniel charging toward him, steak knife in hand. Sebastian lifted the tube to block the slashing blade, but the serrated edge bit into his knuckle. The man swung again, opening a deep gash in Sebastian's ribs. An eerie warmth blossomed in his side. Sebastian tumbled backward, his head slamming on the linoleum. The man jumped on top of him. Sebastian had to let go of the weapon in order to grasp the attacking hand, now smeared with sticky blood.

"You thought you were gonna take my family away?" Daniel growled, a line of spit oozing from his teeth.

Sebastian tried to bite Daniel's wrist, but the man pulled his hand out of reach.

"I killed that bitch Sheba!" Daniel said. "Shot her while she ran away!"

The tube lay beside Sebastian's head. He kept his eyes on the knife while trying to nudge the barrel closer with his tail.

Daniel twisted the blade toward Sebastian, using his weight to bring the knife down. Sebastian was losing his grasp. As quickly as he could, Sebastian reached out his left hand, gripped the barrel, and swung the weapon at Daniel. The wooden stock smashed into Daniel's face. The man clutched his forehead as he fell away. Sebastian rolled onto his side and got to his feet. He had the weapon securely in his hands but did not know what to do with it. Daniel rose, holding the knife with the blade down. A cut opened above his eye, pouring blood down his cheek and neck.

"Shoot him," someone said.

The voice came from outside the door. Both Daniel and Sebastian turned to see the mother stray cat, now hideously grown and standing like a human. She peered into the screen window.

"Like *this*," she said. She held out her left hand and cupped it, the nails pointing skyward. The other was at her side in a fist. She extended the right index finger and wiggled it.

The realization dawned in Daniel's eyes that Sebastian did not know how to work the device. The man could have run away then. So many years later, Mort(e) would still wish that he had. Instead, his master charged again, knife raised.

Sebastian held his breath and slid his hand down the barrel until the finger caught the trigger. He fired. The blast opened a glistening hole in the man's chest, dropping him to the floor beneath a spray of red mist. The knife twirled in the air before clattering on the countertop. Daniel moved his mouth in a vain attempt to speak. A strawberry-colored blob of blood and spit bubbled up to his lips. His right shoe shook and came to rest as the pool of blood spread out from his body, catching the light from the windows.

Sebastian felt an almost irresistible urge to crouch before the body and sniff. Instead, he turned around, opened the door, and walked out. The mother stray stepped aside. Standing behind her were her two children, also on their hind legs. Janet and the human children stood flat against the wall of the house. The wound on Janet's chin had begun to turn a purplish-red. Michael sobbed. She did not try to comfort him. There was nothing left to go wrong for her now.

"Was Daddy really going to hurt us?" the boy asked. All she could do was place her palm on his head.

"You did the right thing," the mother stray told Sebastian. One of her offspring whispered something to her. She hushed him.

Sebastian walked to the center of the yard. Such a short distance, but one that he once thought he would never travel. He would not simply gaze at the world through a window anymore. He would be in it. He would be a part of it. It would be a part of him. He could not unlearn, or undo, or unsee.

The strays said something. Sebastian did not listen. He pressed his palm against the wound in his side. "Did you see the dog?" he asked.

"Which one?" the mother replied.

"The white-and-orange one. Like me."

"She ran off that way," the mother said, pointing toward the city. "Maybe you'll pick up her scent if you keep going. But everything that way is dead. The ants are coming. The humans are destroying things as they retreat."

"Have you seen others?" Sebastian asked. "Others like us?"

"We saw Hank."

"Hank?"

"The dog across the street. He killed his masters, too. Everyone is doing it."

The mother stray asked if there was food left in the house. Sebastian told her that she could help herself to it. She told one of her young ones to check the refrigerator.

"You and I will take care of these," the mother stray said to the other cat. They approached the humans. Michael let out a helpless whimper.

"I'm starving," the mother stray said.

"Sebastian!" Michael screamed.

Despite all his disappointments with trying to protect the

house, Sebastian felt compelled to obey this command. It was a call for mercy from the innocent, rather than an order from a dictator. This was what he was supposed to obey, now that things had changed.

Sebastian aimed the gun at the cats. The third cat inside the house must have sensed something was wrong, for he abruptly opened the door. His furry mouth was covered in Daniel's blood.

"You can't be serious," the mother stray said.

"I just killed my master," Sebastian said. "I am very serious."

"They're the enemy!" the mother stray said. "They tried to kill you!"

Sebastian kept the rifle trained on them. After a few awkward seconds, the cats stood down. With his free hand, Sebastian waved the Martinis on. Again, the humans strode past him, eyes averted.

"Woman," Sebastian said. Janet stopped, but kept her gaze on the ground. "I'm going to find Sheba."

"Sheba ran away!" Michael said. "After Daddy—"

"Quiet," Janet said. She forced herself to face Sebastian. "I hope you find her," she said. "I'll be praying for you."

He had no idea what that meant.

The Martinis walked down the driveway to the SUV. Doors opened, feet shuffled in. The doors closed. *Thunk, thunk.* Janet's fists clamped to the steering wheel, her knuckles bulging through the pale skin.

The vehicle drove off. Michael watched Sebastian, his palms stuck to the glass.

Once the car was gone, Sebastian lowered the gun.

"You should head west," the mother stray said. "It's not safe here."

"I need to find her," Sebastian said.

"The dog?" she said, snickering like a human. To her young

ones she said, "You see this? This is how you get yourself killed: protecting humans and looking for lost lovers."

"I suppose it is," Sebastian said.

The mother stray stared at Sebastian until he had no choice but to look her in the eye. "Cheer up, kitty cat," she said. "You won't need your puppy girlfriend. You've got this now."

She pointed at her temple.

"Before this week," she said, "you were no more than a mouth and an ass and some genitals. Well, maybe your genitals aren't what they used to be. Anyway, you're something else now. Maybe you don't appreciate that, living in this mansion all fat and happy. But now you have a mind of your own. Use it or die."

The mother stray ordered her children to join her inside the house. Sebastian did not stop them. Everything was quiet. Even the explosions in the distance ceased. His jackhammer heart came to rest in his rib cage, and he was able to think again. Clarity returned in short instructions: *Sheba is out there. I have to find Sheba. (Sheba is probably dead.) Sheba went south. I have to find Sheba. (Sheba is dead.)*

Sebastian gripped the barrel of the rifle and started walking.

CHAPTER TWO
THE STORY OF HYMENOPTERA UNUS

HE QUEEN SAW everything. Her eyes and antennae were greedy for more information, more scents, more colors, more words. Billions of her daughters extended the Colony's reach into the world of the humans while she watched, gathering all their experiences, pleased that things had come to pass as she had envisioned. Her mind was the Colony's mind, throbbing with growth, pulling light from the darkness.

And it was killing her.

But she was Hymenoptera Unus, the Daughter of the Misfit Queen. The one the humans called the Devil's Hand, the Monarch of the Underworld. The responsibility—and the awful, pounding torture that came with it—was hers alone. No one could ever truly understand what she knew, certainly not her daughters, nor the humans, nor the surface animals whom she had lifted from slavery like a living god. Her children would sacrifice everything for her, and for that she was grateful, but they would never see the world through her eyes. They would never feel alone, for they were part of a whole. They would never feel regret, because for them it served no purpose.

Though her body was thousands of years old, her mind housed the collective memory of the Colony. Every victory, every defeat, every horrible death, was recorded in the chemical language of her people and stored in her brain. One death was difficult enough. She had lived billions and billions, stretched over millennia.

There came a day late in the war with no name when the humans were close to discovering her lair, buried deep within the newly formed island in the ocean. The earth above shook with their war machines. The humans brought bombs and digging devices, along with thousands of stamping boots. The Queen lay in her chamber, prone, bloated, having grown to the size of a great whale, a beast that occupied more space than the original colony in which she was born. As advanced as her brain was—as monstrous as she was—her body was still a powerless, egg-laying factory. Trapped and helpless, through her own doing. That was why the humans could never be allowed to get close. They would have burned her and danced on the corpse while believing that they had fulfilled some prophecy foretold by their magic books and witch doctors. The Colony would not end like that. The Queen swore it. She had started this war after centuries of planning. She would see it through until all the humans were dead, and the world and its deserving inhabitants were remade in her image.

The earth continued to rattle and groan as the human and insect armies fought aboveground. Another explosion on the surface throttled the chamber and shook loose a hunk of earth that crashed to the ground. The Queen had driven the humans mad with fear by then. An animal forced into a corner posed a threat, but a human faced with extinction was unpredictable and savage, positively devolved.

All around her, the Queen's daughters continued their work of licking her swollen abdomen, clearing it of debris and pathogens as it pulsated and squeezed out new eggs. If this entire chamber collapsed, if all her chambermaids had their heads chopped off, they would continue licking until their brains finally shut down from a lack of blood and oxygen. Their devotion was absolute.

A procession of oversized workers carried in their jaws the swollen, nearly transparent larvae of the Alpha soldiers, the ones bred to be larger than a human. They could snap a man in half, tip over a tank, endure countless projectiles from the humans' guns and cannons. After these super-soldiers hatched, the Queen carried out her ancient task of holding each one, touching antennae with it, and imparting some—but of course not all—of her immense knowledge. Enough for them to fulfill their duty. They could not handle much more than that. Her daughters could only follow her orders, not analyze and agonize over them like she could.

What to offer the new soldiers on this particular day posed a challenge. The Colony was so close to victory over the humans, yet they could lose it all so quickly. Her own mother, the so-called Misfit Queen, had been forced to make the same decision many years earlier. And the Misfit chose to give Hymenoptera *everything*. It was both the source of Hymenoptera's greatness and the root of her misery. While she hated this gift, the Colony would have failed, and the humans would have won long ago, had she not accepted it.

The Queen delivered to each of the Alphas that day a summary of the war and the Colony's history, going back to her grandmother, the Lost Queen, the one whose failure had triggered the conflict with humanity. That foolish monarch had ruled thousands of years earlier. Unchallenged, controlling vast stretches of the earth and its underground, the Lost Queen thought herself the planet's rightful ruler. Hers was the species best suited for leadership: unhindered by sentimentality, fear, or a misguided belief that this world had been created solely for them.

While the Misfit was still in the larval stage, the Lost Queen was learning far too late that the Colony was losing out to the humans, ceding land, food, water, and dominion over other creatures. And while the Lost Queen tarried, unable to comprehend the danger surrounding her, an army of men swept over the land to attack the anthills that had risen up in defiance of one of their cities. The stink of human sandals and the thundering of their feet alerted the Colony, but it was too late. The humans brought with them sharp tools and torches. They attacked during the day, when the ants would be sluggish under the desert sun. Millions were ordered to their deaths in defense of the Colony. Entire bloodlines were lost. Throughout the tunnels and byways, the cloying scent of oleic acid—the ants' alarm signal of death—clung to the walls, a symbol of their defeat.

Though the ants had been attacked before, there had been a harmony to things. Both they and their enemies knew that wiping out the other would not be wise in the long run. Equilibrium was needed. But this assault from the humans was something different. The sandaled men intended to murder every last one of the ants, not to merely set a boundary between their worlds. The Lost Queen knew then that she was facing a race of evil gods. These creatures killed for pleasure, yet regarded only their own suffering as significant. Such a species could not be reasoned with. They could be shown no mercy.

And so, faced with the onslaught, the Lost Queen's daughters retreated to their catacombs while the humans plowed over their cities. When the earth was quiet again, the Lost Queen ordered the workers to dig their way out. All efforts were redirected. Even breeding and collecting food were put on hold. The existing larvae were triaged, the weaker ones feeding the diggers until they died of exhaustion and were replaced by the next in line. The future would have to wait until the present was resolved.

By the time the ants emerged from the dirt, the land around them had become a vast field of crops, seemingly endless in every direction. The Lost Queen's gamble had worked. There was food everywhere. She ordered her daughters to feed so they would simultaneously weaken the human city. In only a few hours, the ants devoured the bulk of the crops. When morning broke, the farmers arrived to find that much of their harvest had been destroyed. Before they could react, the ants, emboldened, swarmed the ankles of the men and bit down into the flesh. Many brave ones died in that moment of blissful revenge, crushed by the flailing hands of the panicked humans. One of the farmers was so shocked that he hyperventilated and passed out in the dirt. The other humans retreated to the city wall.

The Lost Queen herself mounted the unconscious man's body as her subjects entered the mouth, nostrils, and ears. Thousands of years later, Hymenoptera was still able to access this memory. She could hear the sound of their jaws ripping flesh. She could smell the opened capillaries, the scent of iron all the more potent after spending so much time buried in the sterile earth. The man convulsed and then lay still.

The Lost Queen sent scouts within the city walls. Inside, they observed the humans lighting a great pyre upon their temple's altar, where they prayed for deliverance from this plague. For several days, while the ants hollowed out the farmer's corpse, the humans sacrificed animals on the fire, hoping to reverse whatever they had done to disappoint their creator. Later, unsatisfied with—or uncertain about—the divine answer they received, the humans began placing live women and children into the flames, all the while whooping and beating their chests like the partially evolved monkeys that they were. To the ants, nothing demonstrated the depravity of these primates more than their blood rituals, and the violence and nihilism that came with them.

At last the city gates burst open. Men ventured into the field carrying buckets filled with an oily liquid. They dipped torches into the vessels, lit them on fire, and tossed the flaming orbs into the crops. Now it was the ants' turn to panic. The Lost Queen ordered another attack, confident that she could make an example of some other human, but a well-placed torch cut off the advance. She had underestimated the human capacity for self-destruction. There was no way, she thought, that the humans would destroy what remained of their own food supply in order to avenge the death of one worker, or to please some invisible deity. Any doubts she may have had about human cruelty vanished when one of the men, in his zeal to hurl a torch, accidentally spilled the flammable slime onto his tunic and lit himself on fire. Thinking that this was part of whatever curse had befallen them, the other humans shoved the doomed man into the crops. He plunged forward into the hot soil, twisting in agony before dying.

The ants crashed into one another while the heat around them grew. Abdomens burst, the victims hopelessly wagging their antennae, searching for some relief, or at least new orders. The strong ones tried to climb over the dead to safety, only to have the liquid fire poured upon them. Thousands of chemical sirens rang out. The scent trail leading to safety evaporated. The disoriented ants could smell their own flesh as it cooked inside them.

Defeated, with the Lost Queen missing and presumed dead, the surviving ants returned to their catacombs. There was no communication, no reassuring scents from one to another. There was only digging for what seemed like weeks. At last, they reached their old tunnels and regrouped.

Though the ants never had a need for myths, in this desperate hour, the closest thing to an ant legend—the Misfit Queen—was born.

A team of workers searched the catacombs for eggs. Many of the nurseries had caved in, or their temperatures had fluctuated so much that the eggs were useless. Meanwhile, another team of ants tried to locate survivors who could serve as a temporary queen, for only one of these could mate with a drone and use his collected sperm to fertilize the eggs. After three days, the ants came across a chamber of larvae, including a sickly queen who, in the confusion, had mated with a number of drones. The males lay dead beside her, their service to the Colony complete. Under normal circumstances, this traitorous queen would have been banished, having collected sperm outside of the annual mating day. Instead, the workers began to transport a number of healthy eggs to the new royal court. Their chemical signal permeated the tunnels, saying, *Clear a path*.

With the eggs in place, the Misfit Queen was put to work. Her first task was to use the drones' sperm to breed a clutch of fertile females. Exhausted and near death, the Misfit at one point tried to eat one of the eggs brought before her. The workers gently pulled her away and nudged her along until she collapsed, just as the final egg had been fertilized, and the first of the new queens was hatching.

As the Misfit lay dying, the strongest of the new queens emerged from her molting, rising taller than the others, a formidable leader destined for greatness. The Misfit leaned toward her daughter, her replacement, and their antennae touched in the ancient communion of their species.

The first chemical signal the great Hymenoptera received from her mother was this:

You will avenge our people,
by the light of your wisdom
and the darkness of your heart.
You will travel beyond the sands and beyond the seas.
You will build cities and topple mountains.
You will never forget the scent of your clan.
You will grasp the world in your jaws
while the beasts on two feet bang the earth
and shout to the skies.
You will lie in wait for the savages.
Though their fire will burn you,
and their weapons will smite you,
you will rise, you will rise.
And then the rivers will flow toward you.
The hills will bow to you.
The sun will revolve around you.
The creatures of the earth will worship you.
The winds will push you forward.
You will rise.
You will rise.

For each of her Alpha daughters, Hymenoptera always stopped here in the story. What happened next was for her alone to remember:

Upon receiving this first and last message from her mother, the young Hymenoptera grasped the head of the Misfit Queen, tore it off, and ate it, ravenous and ready to lead. The humans had forced her people into this savagery. They made her do this, murder her own mother before everyone. All that would end. Her people would rise. There was nowhere else to go from here.

Reassured by what they had witnessed, the surrounding

workers destroyed the other queen eggs. They fed Hymenoptera the dying workers, who were so exhausted they could no longer lift their heads. The new Queen devoured them, her antennae probing the others to see if they would resist. She was sending them a message: all would sacrifice for the good of the many. The destiny of her people was to conquer and to reign. A new era had begun.

This is where Hymenoptera would pick up her story again for her Alpha soldier daughters. She shared the legend stating that the cries of the fallen brought forth the accumulated knowledge of the species, placing it all into her head. From that moment on, she developed a plan for vengeance that would take millennia to execute. The Colony would acquire knowledge the way humans gobbled up resources and land. The ants would create an army with warriors who were larger, stronger, and more vicious than even the most bloodthirsty human. They would study and exploit all aspects of mankind's existence: language, community, physiology, history, and science, as well as religion, that anti-science that animated the humans, driving them to either greatness or destruction. They would exert dominion over the other ant clans and make contact with other species who viewed the humans as a mutual enemy. The Colony now had a goal beyond mere survival. Its subjects had purpose. They observed history in linear rather than circular terms. Like their enemy, they had an apocalypse to anticipate.

The Colony began to learn at an accelerated rate. Meanwhile, the Queen bred a caste of medical engineers who kept her alive, allowing her to grow and molt, soon making her one of the oldest and largest creatures on the planet. In less than a century after the fire, the ants deciphered the origin of human speech— sound waves traveling from evolved organs in the throat—and in another two hundred years they could read several human languages. Unable to truly see the text on a stolen fragment of manuscript, the Queen bred a subspecies with olfactory sensors on their feet. These "interpreters" would march around the written words, tracing the ink. After years of study, the Queen found human language to be a primitive and self-defeating form of communication, light-years behind the instantaneous clarity and subtle nuance of her chemicals. Human speech could mean everything and nothing at once. How could a species procreate, build, innovate, and survive with such an appallingly inadequate system, she wondered. It was the study of language that made the Queen realize how easy it would be to turn the humans against themselves. *Homo sapiens* had a weakness for their language, a sort of gullibility. Whereas knowledge was stored with the Queen, ensuring almost complete infallibility from the moment a pair of antennae came into contact, humans would have to bicker over translations, authorship, historical context, symbolism, and meaning. They had to rely on the faulty memory of storytellers, the biased interpretations of scribes, and the whims of inefficient bureaucrats in order to pass down their collected knowledge. In a way, she was disappointed. She had hoped that somehow the humans would surprise her and show a capacity that she had yet to discover, something that would make them worthy adversaries. But they were merely talking monkeys, an unfortunate anomaly staining the elegance of the animal kingdom, and the entire world was worse off for it.

Along with her efforts to penetrate the *Homo sapiens* psyche, the Queen also ordered her daughters to breed new microbes and viruses, with varying degrees of success. The bubonic-infected flea, the most notorious example, was a masterpiece. Though the Queen ultimately concluded that a plague would never be a sufficient way of eliminating the human threat, she learned much from her manipulation of mammals.

Indeed, handing the surface over to the aboveground creatures, whom the humans had exploited for centuries, became
an indispensable part of the Queen's vision for the earth. When
the time came, the animals would learn from the mistakes of the
humans and become something greater. This would be her grand
experiment, proving that the ants were the true deities of this
planet. And maybe the animals would grow to have some of the
qualities of the Misfit Queen: bravery for its own sake, sacrifice
for the good of the species, greater awareness of their place
in the universe, humility in the face of reality, a rejection of
superstition, a fearless embrace of truth. Maybe, she thought.
Regardless, the surfacers deserved to be unyoked from human
domination and given a chance to be free.

When the anthills began erupting—thereby opening the
first phase of the war—the humans viewed the event with
amusement rather than urgency. There would be no Hymenoptera Unus to reorient them toward a new destiny. Instead,
the humans responded piecemeal. They evacuated the infested
villages, retreating again and again. They attempted the use of
pesticides, all the while bickering among themselves about the
environmental side effects. This concern seemed especially
absurd to the Queen, given that their species had done more
than any other to pollute the earth. When the pesticides failed,
the human governments acted swiftly to quarantine the countries that were now overrun. Some humans were misguided
enough to expect fences to repel the ants. In fact, the fences
were meant to keep the fleeing refugees from entering the
wealthier countries.

When the insects simply dug underneath the barriers, the
humans used a line of fire to hold them back. The flaming bor-
ders were so long that they could be seen from space, glowing orange ribbons sending up columns of smoke. The humans

congratulated themselves for their ingenuity and solidarity, and resolved to retake the land as soon as possible.

Several weeks later, the Queen ordered the Alphas to attack. At first, the Alphas were instructed to prey on children only. Images of the hideous beasts carrying off screaming students from schoolhouses appeared on television screens across the world. Soldiers deserted their posts and returned home to protect their families. No one could determine a rational explanation for what the ants were doing. Rather than organizing a counterattack, confused military leaders focused on building protective bunkers for themselves. Scientists argued over the cause of such behavior. Civilians turned on their political leaders. More than once, rioters overran military checkpoints to drag senators, governors, presidents, and dictators out of their mansions in order to hang them or worse. Predictably, religious leaders agreed that this atrocity was a punishment from the heavens. The Alphas were beasts from hell, rising from the humans' worst nightmares for a final reckoning.

Those humans who stood and fought produced some of the most horrific battles the planet had ever seen. Whereas many species had evolved the ability to go into shock and die under severe trauma, humans were somehow able to rise above this trait and fight on, even with severed limbs and punctured arteries. But their rage was no match for the undying hatred of a queen who blamed them for the death of her mother. The sight of thousands of ten-foot-tall insects storming a fortification and tearing soldiers apart appeared over and over. It did not matter how good a human soldier's aim was, or how many bombs he could lob, or how many air strikes he could request. There were always more ants on the way. And unlike the humans, the Alphas would not philosophize about the losses. There would be no hazing of new recruits, no fatalistic bets on who would go first, no masturbating to photos of sweethearts back home. The Alphas were as merciless and determined as the humans were doubtful and afraid.

It was in the midst of this madness that the Queen initiated the final phase of her takeover: the transformation of the surface animals. Under her direction, the Queen's chief scientists developed a hormone derived from the chemicals they had used to breed the Alphas and keep Hymenoptera alive. The ants injected the potion into the water supply. The hormone had an effect on birds, reptiles, amphibians, and mammals. Meanwhile, the ants constructed their nameless island in the Atlantic, along with hundreds of dirt towers on every continent, from which they broadcast signals that only the animals could hear, and that their rapidly growing brains would absorb. The frequency contained subliminal instructions on how to read, how to use tools, how to fight, how to organize societies—basic knowledge the animals would need.

The Change manifested itself on the first dose of the hormone. The animals first became self-aware, which often compelled them to flee their confines. They could now see the world beyond mere survival. For some, it was a horrifying moment. Many died leaping through windows or running through traffic. But for most, the experience was liberating, like the discovery of an elusive formula.

Within a day, the physical advancements were considerable. Their larynges extended, enabling the animals to form words. For those that did not have hooves or wings, the front paws grew into hands with opposable thumbs, and the hind legs were able to support the weight of the body. Once again, there were poor reactions among certain animals. Early in the experiment, for example, there was a pack of wolves so shocked by their new appendages that they bit them off. This behavior was an aberration, however, falling within the Queen's projection of a 4-9 percent failure rate. Now the animals would do what the Queen's loyal daughters could not. They would pull themselves up to greatness, as she had done.

Many animals understood immediately that they had been the slaves of cruel masters. A new front in the war opened, this time in homes, farms, laboratories, and zoos. Now the humans had to deal with their own pets, livestock, and test subjects standing before them, sometimes wielding weapons, staring with determined eyes. For many animals, this confrontation was the first time they would speak, forcing out the newly discovered words in an awkward stutter: "Indeed, yes, affirmative, I have come to kill you, sir."

Soon the animals formed a rapidly growing army. Some former pets were conflicted about this, but the evidence against the humans was overwhelming. The humans, after all, ate the animals, stole their milk and eggs, encroached on their land, and carved up their bodies to make them more suitable pets. The Queen, on the other hand, offered a sense of purpose, and a future. Like the Alphas, the animals would know who had raised them up. They would know that there was a god on earth.

THE CEREMONY FOR the Alphas was nearly complete. The workers gathered in a horseshoe shape facing the Queen, awaiting final approval before shuffling off to their destinies. There was only one daughter left to hold, one who was smaller than usual, yet active and squirming in the Queen's arms. Whereas the new soldiers seemed emboldened by their duties, the Queen was exhausted from reliving the story. These few moments with her daughters were more than she had enjoyed with her own mother. She did not wish to think about it. The continued rumbling at the surface reminded her of what was at stake:

centuries of planning, an entire world for the taking, an implacable enemy pushed to the brink of extinction. She could not fail her people as her grandmother had.

The Queen's antennae probed the young one. The story began again in her exhausted brain: the wars, the sandaled men, the oily smell of death. And then the Misfit Queen, the Abandoned One, reaching out to her through time. The Queen gave it all to this soldier, including her mother's last moments alive, when Hymenoptera had to do her duty by murdering her.

Another *thud* against the ceiling. The workers waited for the Queen to hand over this last daughter. But Hymenoptera was not convinced that this latest brood understood the price that had to be paid. The price she had been paying for generations now.

And so she lifted her child to her jaws and crushed its skull, sending a crunching echo throughout the chamber. Everyone remained still. No one dared even to tilt a head or extend an antenna. Whatever pleasure this act brought the Queen was short-lived, replaced almost immediately by a heavy loneliness. She was the Colony. But she was not *of* the Colony. Perhaps her experiment would do more than produce mere talking creatures, and instead create beings worthy of her and the Misfit Queen. But until then, she was alone.

After she had swallowed what was left of her daughter, she made the workers stand at attention for a long time before finally dismissing them. When they were gone, she sat in the darkness and thought of her mother.

CHAPTER THREE
THE RED SPHINX

TWO MONTHS. TWO months he searched for her. Two months in and around the ruined city. Two months investigating every breeze, scanning every footprint, every discarded can of food, hoping to find her scent. But he couldn't find a trace of her.

And how long had it been since he had eaten? Sebastian couldn't say. A few days, most likely. He still had the energy to climb the stairs of a gutted skyscraper every morning, where he could get a 360-degree view of the skeletal city. The building was a steel-and-glass obelisk in the heart of downtown. Many of its windows had been blown out, leaving gaps in the reflective surface whenever the sun rose. It made the building resemble a mouth missing a few teeth. From these gaps, Sebastian would scope out the city, a lonely king surveying his worthless country.

He marked the days on a dry-erase board left behind by the humans who had worked there. Those people were like him, he supposed. They enjoyed a routine that they assumed would go on indefinitely, and then they were running for their lives. Maybe they deserved it. Maybe so did he.

Time passed by in vivid moments, with blank spaces in between: dressing the infected wound on his side. Then blackness. Trudging through the streets, inspecting abandoned cars, on more than one occasion finding a human who had shot himself in the temple with one hand while clamping the steering wheel with the other. And then, more blackness. Breaking open a can of tuna, devouring its rancid contents. Plucking a fat cockroach from the debris and swallowing it whole. Then blackness once more. Merciful sleep and forgetfulness and oblivion.

All the while, Sebastian was learning. He could now tell the difference between the knowledge he acquired and the information that had somehow been bestowed upon him. By reading old newspapers and listening to a looped emergency broadcast on a windup radio, Sebastian confirmed what Daniel had told him about the war, the ants, and the animals. The broadcast concluded with an uninterrupted block of songs, all with lyrics about love, all happy and ignorant of the impending destruction. And then the loop would begin again, with a stern masculine voice warning of doom.

He read what he could find, and felt the list of words growing inside his head like weeds, like fungus—a simile he used after reading a biology textbook. There were several buildings in the city with walls of books rising to the ceiling. Among these volumes he found a few that he liked, stories of knights and dragons. There were comic books, too, along with books filled with numbers and equations. It was so alien, acquiring information this way. It almost felt like theft, and sometimes he would read a passage and expect the words to be gone from the page, absorbed by his mind. He also felt that he was wasting valuable time. He was reading picture books about men wearing capes while Sheba lay dying somewhere. But he could hardly get enough of the texts. He slept less and less because he could not wait to read again. He would often feel intense relief to find that the books he had left nearby were still there when he opened his eyes.

But along with this acquired knowledge, there were the things that had been planted in his mind: numbers, a rudimentary vocabulary, the names of species, the base pairs of DNA. He was not even entirely sure what DNA was. He was *made* of DNA, he supposed. Or DNA consisted of little bits of him, he could not be sure. Did the humans go through this all day long? Were their enormous brains tormented with trivial facts they could neither understand nor forget? If so, then it made sense that people like Daniel went insane.

ON THE DAY he killed his master, Sebastian made his way to the city in the middle of the evacuation. There were humans everywhere: vehicles laden with luggage strapped to the roof, packed into the trunk. Military transports carrying dead-eyed marines to the battlefront. Packs of refugees, some too dazed to be surprised by a giant cat carrying a rifle, his hand pressing down on a bleeding gash on his ribs. Soldiers setting fire to enormous anthills that had burst through concrete and asphalt.

When Sebastian saw dead animals on the side of the road, he decided to stay away from everyone. He was, after all, in enemy territory. Upon reaching the city, he took refuge in the skyscraper to recover from his fight with Daniel. The loss of blood, along with a fever from infection, forced him to rest for days. When he was strong enough to begin searching again, he found the city almost completely abandoned. That was when he encountered a new creature: an ant the size of a Volkswagen.

She marched down the sidewalk on her hind legs. Sebastian ducked behind a bus as she passed. The claws shuffled closer. Suddenly the bus shook. Sebastian spun around and aimed his rifle at the roof of the vehicle to find the ant staring down at him, her antennae like two arms trying to snatch him up. She was covered in smaller ants, all moving about her exoskeleton like flowing oil. The creature probed for a minute, stood still, then walked away.

Sebastian had several similar encounters before he came to realize that the monsters posed no threat. They were after humans, not people like him.

From his perch in the skyscraper, Sebastian concluded that he had made a mistake going this way. He figured he could head west. However, a map of the countryside revealed that "west" was a vast realm, spreading for thousands of miles. He nearly wept when he first saw it.

As he considered his next move, a new battle broke out along the banks of the river. For weeks, an artillery division set up camp across the water and shelled the anthills. It was not safe to leave now, not with so much shrapnel and unexploded ordnance everywhere. He had already witnessed an enormous ant examining a projectile that had landed on a street corner, right next to a fire hydrant. The device exploded, vaporizing the ant and leaving a geyser from the broken pipe.

One morning, he peeked out the window to find that the ants now occupied the riverbank. The massive creatures lumbered about, acting like normal insects scouting a parcel of land. There was no sign of the humans. The ants must have lured their enemies into a trap and then devoured them before they could scream.

Sebastian wondered if Sheba had run into these same obstacles. Was she even searching for him? Was she in some high place as well, surveying the land, hoping for him to find her? Was she lonely? Was she afraid? When Sebastian thought of the terrible things that could have befallen her, death seemed like a merciful fate. But that only left him wondering why *he* was still alive and not her.

A week later, when the weather grew cold and the ants

returned to their mounds, Sebastian decided that it was safe to head west. He would search for Sheba in the wilderness, and probably never find her, and then die somewhere, shivering.

He walked along the highway until he reached a section where the ramp had been sheared off by some fierce explosion. Metal bars that made up the skeleton of the bridge stuck out like broken bones. Sebastian climbed down, allowing himself to drop the last few feet. Once he landed, the odor of an animal filled his nostrils. His tail stood erect, and his ears shot up. A breeze took the scent away. Sebastian waited for a moment longer, then kept walking.

"Sheba," he mumbled. He tried to mimic the way Janet would have said it, a breathless whisper.

"Sheba!" he shouted. The echo returned to him. He yelled her name again and again. It felt so good to say it, even if no one could hear. But would she even know to answer to it? And how would she know *his* name?

He came across a crater as wide as the street. Someone had covered it with a pair of metal girders spaced far enough for the axles of a car to ride over. Slinging the rifle over his shoulder, Sebastian took the left girder.

"I'm coming, Sheba," he said.

He was halfway across when he smelled the odor again. It was a cat. Two cats. Three. Someone was watching, and now he was stuck here waiting to be ambushed. Sebastian tried to swing the rifle strap off his shoulder. The girder rolled over, the metal grinding into the asphalt. To avoid tumbling from the beam, he jumped across to the other girder, only to find that it, too, was flipping over, jostled by some powerful force. He lost his footing and slipped off, plunging twelve feet and landing hard on all fours.

"No," he heard someone say from above. Rifle in hand,

Sebastian pointed his gaze upward. Silhouetted by the rising sun were five cats, all standing erect like him. Each one had a rifle, their fully formed fingers—claws and all—hovering over the triggers. They wore backpacks and belts like human soldiers. Some of the packs were almost certainly lifted from dead men.

Sebastian's rifle grew heavier. He raised it nonetheless. The cats propped their own guns against their shoulders. They had the advantage. Even more aggravating, he realized that he had walked right into their trap. They had probably been spying on him for a while. If they were as hungry as he was, he would probably be their dinner this evening.

"You sure you want to point that at us?" one of the cats said.

"You sure you want to get in my way?" Sebastian replied.

The cats laughed, making their rifle muzzles shake. "Who does this cat think he is?" one of them asked.

"We're not here to hurt you," another one said. It was the one in the middle, a tall black cat, a female.

"I do not believe you," Sebastian said.

"And you shouldn't," she said. "But how about you lower your rifle?"

"No," Sebastian said. "I am not here to hurt you, either. So let me pass."

"We want to talk to you first."

"You just did."

"Who's Sheba?"

"She is my friend."

Sebastian heard a grunt from the cat to her left, a male with black fur on his back and shoulders and white fur on his feet, like little slippers. The grunt expressed either disgust or amusement. Sebastian could not tell.

The very disciplined cats remained perfectly still. The female was the first to lower her weapon. She motioned for the others to do the same.

Sebastian kept his rifle trained on her head, right between her brilliant green eyes.

"You're not going to return the favor?" she asked.

"No. Now step aside."

"You really don't have any questions for us? Aren't you interested in hearing—"

"Step. Aside."

The black-and-white cat started laughing.

"Fine," the female said. "But do you know what this is?" She pulled a small plastic box from her pack and held it toward him.

He should have shot her right there. Before he could even come up with a guess, the cat squeezed the box like the trigger of a gun. Two wires shot from it and latched onto Sebastian's fur. A surge of electricity pulsed through him. His muscles locked. A screeching explosion rang in his ears, so loud that he could not tell if his rifle had even fired. A wave of stabbing knives spread out in concentric circles from where the wires had penetrated his skin. The ground seemed to rise up toward him.

And then, as always, there was merciful sleep and oblivion.

UPON WAKING, IT took Sebastian a few seconds to realize he was tied to a telephone pole. A taut nylon rope bound his arms at his sides. His tail was tied down separately, fastened to a sewer grate, either to prevent him from using it or to stop him from shimmying up the pole. He was obviously not the first cat these people had captured.

It took a few more moments to notice that the sun was on its way down. That meant he had been out for five or six hours. He may have been drugged, for he was still exhausted despite sleeping for so long. If they were going to eat him, he hoped that they would get it over with soon. The ropes were tight.

Across the street was a building with cement pillars and white steps. A courthouse? A financial institution? He could not tell because the façade had been blasted away, the front steps littered with debris. A group of cats stood on the roof like a row of gargoyles. It was the same way the giant ants stood whenever they scouted an area. Maybe these people had captured Sheba, he thought. He tried to think of something else but could not stop imagining her tied to this same pole, wondering if she would make her way back home.

IT WAS MORNING when he awoke again. His eyes were open, though still unable to focus. Something wet and cold touched his lips. He turned his head away.

"Come on," a voice said. "You need to eat."

It was the black-and-white cat, the one who had snorted and chuckled at him the day before. He held a spoon to Sebastian's lips, trying to get him to eat some tuna. A surgical mask and goggles hid the cat's face. The rubber gloves he wore had been made for a human. They were like an ill-fitting skin on his knobby knuckles. On his left bicep was a black armband with a red circle on it. Inside the circle was a drawing of an animal Sebastian did not recognize—a cat with wings and a human face.

The row of cats remained standing on the roof of the building. The sun made their fur glisten.

"Why," Sebastian mumbled, "why am I here?"

"That's a rather existential question," the cat said. He tapped the spoon to Sebastian's lips. Sebastian finally relented and swallowed the hunk of fish. The cat scooped up another spoonful of the tuna and shoved it into Sebastian's mouth.

Existential, Sebastian thought. The word meant nothing to him. Having to do with existence? But everything fell under that category. This cat was toying with him.

"Let me go," Sebastian said.

"Can't. We have to monitor you."

"Why?"

"You might be infected." The cat said this as if Sebastian were an idiot to ask.

"Infected with what?" Sebastian said, still chewing.

"EMSAH."

"What's EMSAH?"

The cat stared at him. He tossed the can of tuna aside and turned toward the municipal building. "He says he doesn't know what EMSAH is!"

Atop the roof, the black cat stepped closer to the ledge. She motioned for him to continue and then folded her arms.

The black-and-white cat pulled a bottle of water from his backpack and held it out. Sebastian let his tongue hang loose and lapped up the water.

"The humans infected the animals with a virus," the cat said. "After we became smart." He tapped his temple with his index finger. "It's some kind of weapon. A *bio*weapon. The virus breaks down your vital systems. Makes you go crazy. We're not sure how contagious it is. And there is no cure."

Sebastian finished drinking. "I'm fine," he said.

"People who are fine don't camp out in the city and yell 'Sheba' for no reason. That sounds like EMSAH-talk to me."

The cat considered putting the bottle into his bag. But after thinking about it, he left it beside Sebastian. "I'll feed you again tonight," the cat said. "If you're not infected, then just hang on. We'll know one way or another soon enough."

Sebastian asked him to wait. The cat ignored him, and then

he was gone. All was quiet again. The sun rolled across the sky. The other cats remained on the roof.

IT CONTINUED FOR another day. The black-and-white cat would feed him while wearing his protective gear. Then the cat would return to the safe distance of the building. Whether he was qualified as a doctor remained unclear.

Sebastian gathered more information about EMSAH. The "doctor" told him that the soldiers had recently encountered a pack of infected dogs, and they had to put the poor animals out of their misery. Unlike Sebastian, the dogs exhibited all the outward signs of the disease: foaming at the mouth, burst blood vessels in the eyes, open sores on the coat exacerbated by incessant scratching. It was that last symptom that varied from species to species—cats often scratched themselves into an unrecognizable state, sometimes even blinding themselves by clawing at their own eyes. Sebastian insisted that he had none of these symptoms.

"That's what's so strange," the cat said. "You have none of the signs, yet you're out here all alone, and you're talking to no one. It's like you skipped the sickness and went straight to the crazy. Can't take any chances."

And that, the cat said, was the most interesting part of the virus. In the final stages, it completely rewired the brain. A victim could become a catatonic zombie or a psychopath. Too often it was the latter, hence the need to put down the dogs. The cats let Sebastian live because they needed more information on the bioweapon. Any anomalies had to be recorded and studied. The entire war could depend on a single breakthrough from an unexpected source.

"Here's the good news," the cat said. "If you do have EMSAH, you can be my first feline vivisection. The ants usually clear out all the bodies—it's safer that way, of course—so this will be my first chance to see the disease up close."

Sebastian ignored this, and instead imagined the dogs that had been infected. Were they walking upright? Were they lined up and shot?

Was Sheba one of them?

Was he doomed to think of her every time someone mentioned a dog?

The cat asked Sebastian his name. Sebastian said that he didn't have one.

"But you were a pet, right?" the cat asked. "I mean, your claws were chopped off. And you're a choker." He motioned to Sebastian's genitalia.

Choker, Sebastian realized, must mean neutered. "I do not have a name," he repeated.

"I'm Tiberius," the cat said. "I was a pet, too, for a little while. But I lived on my own for a couple of years before the war."

The cat motioned to his friends, all still standing on the rooftop. "We all lived in the wild at one point," he said. "So you can bet that Tiberius is not my slave name. I picked it for myself. If you live through this, you can pick your own name, too."

"*If* I live through this," Sebastian said.

"If you have EMSAH, you won't *want* to. Trust me."

Tiberius pointed out that Sebastian's status as a choker made him even more suspicious. Neutered animals—or any former pets, for that matter—were rumored to be more susceptible to EMSAH. It had not been confirmed, of course, but Tiberius had to be prepared for anything.

"People like us have to work extra hard to earn everyone's trust," Tiberius said.

"How long are you going to keep me here?"

"Until Culdesac gets back. He's the boss."

Sebastian asked when that would be. Tiberius said that Culdesac operated on his own time.

"He speaks for the Colony," Tiberius said.

"The Colony?"

"The ants," Tiberius said. "Don't you know anything? The Queen started the war. We're the soldiers who are helping to end it. In return, we will be in charge of the surface."

Sebastian knew about the ants, of course, but the discarded newspapers and placards he had come across had not used the words Colony or Queen. There were only mindless hordes of rampaging insects without purpose or remorse.

"Why did the Queen start a war?" Sebastian asked.

"Because the humans are dangerous," Tiberius said. "I've already told you about EMSAH. And that's one of their smaller crimes against us. We fight them, or we die as their slaves. Maybe you could join us."

"No."

"I mean, if I don't end up dissecting you, of course."

"No."

Tiberius had apparently taken too long. The black cat hissed at him, a signal to hurry up. Sebastian wondered if this cat had told him something he was not meant to know. Tiberius finished and retreated to the building.

"Hang in there, house cat," he said.

IN THE DEAD of night, after days of wriggling his tail, Sebastian was close to freeing it from the rope that tied it to the grate.

It was just in time. On that same night, he saw a human.

It began with a swooping sound in the air above him, like a massive bird. Something glided across the stars—a giant triangle made out of a translucent fabric. An object dangled from the bottom of it. When it landed on a building two blocks away,

Sebastian realized that the triangle was some kind of motorless aircraft piloted by a single human. The man stowed the glider behind a satellite dish. He scanned the area, holding binoculars and whispering into a communication device. Then the man was gone.

For a few hours, Sebastian allowed himself to think that this new development would somehow end up setting him free. But then he remembered what Tiberius had said. The animals were at war with the humans. The humans had given them some kind of virus. Sebastian may already have been infected without knowing it.

Sheba could have been infected.

There it was again—a thought like that jumped into his brain whenever it wanted, like a parasite, like the virus that frightened Tiberius.

Sebastian tried to squirm out of the knot, the joints cracking in his tail. Eventually the knot gave. He imagined himself as Sheba as he wagged his tail freely for the first time in days. There was no point in resisting the random memories of his old friend. She was with him no matter what.

CULDESAC ARRIVED SHORTLY after sunrise. By then, Sebastian had shimmied all the way up the pole and hovered thirty feet above the street. But he could go no farther. The cables stretching across the top prevented him from pulling the rope over. He kept fighting it, trying to loosen the bindings. It was no use. The ropes were doubled around his wrists and ankles. While he could painfully go up the pole, he could not free himself. He dug his hind claws into the wood to hold himself in place.

Culdesac met with the black cat and several of her underlings at the base of the pole. While the other cats saluted her, she saluted him. Culdesac was no mere feral—he was a bobcat, much larger than the others. He had a shimmering sandy coat flecked with black, a camouflage suited to the wilderness from which he came. His charcoal-colored ears rose like horns over his massive head. He wore the black armband along with a belt weighed down with a pistol and several devices Sebastian did not recognize.

"What are you doing up there?" Culdesac asked him.

"Ask your friends."

"We're holding you for your own protection," Culdesac said. "And for ours."

"He's displaying the symptoms," the black cat whispered to him, probably knowing full well that Sebastian could still hear her.

"He doesn't look like it," Culdesac said.

"Delirium. Talking strange."

"Well, you've had him tied up for two days."

"Ask him about Sheba," she said. "He was screaming her name when we found him."

Culdesac stepped closer to the pole until he was staring straight up. "My friend," he said, "my name is Culdesac. This is my Number One, Luna."

The black cat nodded.

"Do not ask me my name," Sebastian said. "I did not give it to them. I will not give it to you."

"Fine. But how about you tell me who this Sheba is?"

This bobcat had an ease about him that Sebastian found unsettling. Culdesac could talk like a human, much like the anchorman on the looped news broadcasts. Meanwhile, Sebastian struggled to use his growing vocabulary. It was a huge disadvantage, like being tied up for a second time.

"I already explained this to your friends," Sebastian said. "I was looking for her."

"There hasn't been a living thing in this city for weeks."

"I saw one last night."

"What does that mean?"

"I saw a human."

A stunned silence descended on the group. The cats looked at one another. It made him feel as though he had the power somehow, despite being a prisoner.

"That's impossible," one of them said.

"Where did you see the human?" Culdesac asked.

"He flew in on some kind of . . . triangle."

"I told you," Luna said, laughing. "We need to put this animal down. Before it spreads."

It was a line Sebastian had read somewhere among the books he had found. *Put him down.* She had stolen it from a human.

Luna seemed pleased with herself until she noticed Culdesac glaring at her. "'This animal' is one of us," he said.

"There are no humans left here," Culdesac said to Sebastian. "The ants chased them away. We were about to rendezvous with the rest of the army on the other side of the river. Then we found you."

"I am not stopping you," Sebastian said.

Culdesac and Luna exchanged glances.

"Wait," a voice said. It was Tiberius, forcing his way past the others to get to Culdesac. "I know what you're thinking. We can't leave him here."

"You're right," Luna said. "That's why we're going to put him down. It's the only way to be sure."

"Sir," Tiberius said to Culdesac. "We can't do that, either."

"Yes, listen to Tiberius," Sebastian said.

Tiberius winced at this. The others, meanwhile, burst into laughter.

"What did you say?" Culdesac asked.

"I said listen to him," Sebastian said.

"No, what did you call him?"

"Tiberius?"

They laughed again.

"Tell them your real name," Culdesac ordered.

Shamed, Tiberius steadied himself. "Socks," he mumbled. This provoked more jeers and catcalls.

"You see," Culdesac said to Sebastian, "you have to *earn* your new name to be a part of the Red Sphinx."

"What is a Red Sphinx?" Sebastian asked.

"We are the Red Sphinx," Culdesac said, pointing to his armband. "We're stray cats using our skills to fight for the Queen. We *love* killing humans."

There were chuckles at this, along with a few approving nods.

"But Socks here thinks he doesn't deserve to be called by his slave name anymore," Culdesac said.

"I do not care about your Red Sphinx," Sebastian said. "Are any of you listening to me? I said there were humans out there."

"I believe him," Tiberius said.

"Shut up," Luna said. Then, turning to Culdesac, she said, "Sir, we have to make a decision here. We're already late meeting up with the rest of the—"

"We're staying here," Culdesac said. Before Luna could reply, he added, "Orders have changed. We're expected to report unusual activity."

"But there's nothing here."

Culdesac responded by gazing up at Sebastian.

"Him?" she asked.

"Monitor his progress," Culdesac said. "Socks wanted to take notes on EMSAH. Let him do it."

Tiberius perked up.

"We're on the front lines of this EMSAH outbreak," Culdesac

said. "We need to know what it can do. I expect reports on his condition every six hours."

"Do you think there are humans out there?" Luna asked.

"I hope so," Culdesac said as he began to walk toward the building. "I haven't had a decent meal in a while."

"Sir, may I ask where you're going?"

"If it's been as quiet as you say it has, then I'd like to get some sleep for once."

"Yes, sir."

The members of the Red Sphinx were left waiting at the foot of the pole. "We can't feed you while you're up there, you know," Luna said.

"I did not ask you to," Sebastian replied.

Annoyed, Luna went back to the stone building. The others marched behind her, with Tiberius bringing up the rear. He took one last glimpse at Sebastian before disappearing through the doorway.

FOR THE NEXT twelve hours, Sebastian rocked the telephone pole back and forth. At first it was out of sheer boredom and frustration. From the top, he had the leverage to shift the pole only a few inches. The movement made the roof of the stone building bob up and down in his vision. The yellow-green eyes of the cats moved along with it. Once in a while, Culdesac joined the others, towering over them. Luna would sometimes stand next to him. When they both folded their arms in unison, Sebastian counted it as a small victory.

Right on schedule, Tiberius arrived with more food. "Come on, stop that," he said. Sebastian continued to rock the pole, feeling it move slightly more each time.

"They're talking about shooting you," Tiberius said. "Luna really thinks you've lost it. Late-stage EMSAH."

Sebastian did not respond.

"Culdesac overruled her," Tiberius said. "It's a good thing the boss got here in time. Luna would have asked me to kill you. It probably would have earned me my name. But I wouldn't have liked it."

Sebastian picked up the pace, grunting as he shifted his weight.

"I can't promise that this food will still be here in another hour," Tiberius said. "Everyone's wondering why we're even giving you anything."

He waited a full minute for a response, during which time he examined the base of the pole. Apparently content that Sebastian was making no significant progress, Tiberius told him to shout when he was ready to eat. Then he left.

WITH EACH INHALE, Sebastian pressed his body against the unforgiving wood. It tipped backward, pointing his face directly at the blue sky, where the clouds congealed and spread out toward the east. And then, with his exhale, he thrust his chest forward, his flesh and fur digging into the ropes, forcing the pole to dip far enough for him to look down at the asphalt and the plate of food on the sidewalk. The sight of it shriveled his empty stomach.

Then he heard it, and felt it: a slight crack, like Daniel popping his knuckles at the dinner table. That one sound, vibrating through his spine, cured him of his hunger. He moved faster now, shoving his body side to side rather than front to back. This caused the pole to move in an ever-widening circle. There were other cracks, sometimes followed by a dull groan as the wood began to yield. All the cats were watching now. The bobcat's hands rested on his hips. The spinning made Sebastian vomit onto his coat. A line of saliva and bile hung from his mouth and whiskers. Still, his eyes remained fixed on the Red Sphinx. They would not stop him from finding Sheba.

The sun began to go down. The gold-and-purple world continued to sway to and fro.

IT WAS THE middle of the night when Sebastian noticed a bright red dot dancing on the side wall of the building like a glowing ruby. The dot was from a light of some kind. Sebastian followed the beam until he spotted the human again, perched on a nearby roof. He had switched positions to a hospital farther down the street. The man stood behind a tripod, which propped up a device that focused the dot onto the building. If there had been a fog, the red light would have been noticeable. Only Sebastian was in a position to see it.

He imagined the man as his former master, somehow still alive, using this alien technology to plot his revenge under the cover of night.

With his strength renewed, Sebastian continued to shake the pole until his wrists and shoulders burned from the friction. The wires connecting the other poles rippled with each movement. He was so engrossed in it that he did not notice at first when some of the cats gathered at the base of the pole. All of them had guns. Luna and Culdesac stood at the front. Sebastian kept at it. *Maybe one more motion will snap this thing*, he thought. Maybe then he could scramble away.

"Don't make this any harder than it has to be," Culdesac said. "We just want to talk. To find out what's wrong with you."

"I am tied to a pole," Sebastian said. "That is what is wrong."

"Come on down."

Sebastian searched the rooftops for the human again. The tripod and its device were still in place. The man must have been hiding.

"I see . . ." Sebastian said.

"See what?"

"I see a human."

"Captain," Luna said.

"Where?" Culdesac asked.

"He's watching us," Sebastian said.

Now there was an audible creak of the wood, loud enough to make a few of the cats flinch. It was then that Sebastian made out Tiberius, standing behind the others.

"Captain, we can't let this go on any further," Luna said. "I'm begging you—"

Culdesac's paw shot out and grabbed Luna's snout, holding her mouth shut. "Shut up," he said. "Listen."

The cats were uneasy now. A second later, Sebastian figured out why. There was a buzzing noise in the distance, growing louder, echoing off the buildings. Something was approaching through the air.

"The human pointed a light at your headquarters, *Captain*," Sebastian said. "See it?"

Culdesac let go of Luna and gazed at the building. Suddenly his entire body stiffened, his tail standing up. "Sergeant!" he screamed. "*Ser*geant!"

A cat peered over the side of the building.

"Get your people out of there now!" Culdesac said. "Incoming!"

The cat and his companions ran to the stairway. Meanwhile, the ones surrounding Culdesac tensed up, awaiting his next order.

"Move!" he said. "Take cover behind that building!"

"Incoming!" someone screamed. Several others repeated it.

"Come on!"

"Run!"

"Leave it, let's go!"

The bobcat looked up to Sebastian. "I'm sorry," Culdesac said. And then he ran with the others.

The buzzing was getting louder, growing into a full roar, a thunderstorm.

Sebastian rocked the pole forward. Then the momentum reversed. Sebastian put all his strength into it, letting out a scream, lifting his shoulders into the wood. The sky scrolled through his field of vision before stopping at the horizon behind him, the pole bending as far as it could go. It remained there, the wood splintering. And then, like bones shattering, the pole broke, rattling his skeleton. The wood cracked, creaked, groaned, until Sebastian felt himself in free fall. The wires popped free from the top, snapping upward with a loud *thwoop*. He landed on his back, feeling his teeth clack together with the impact. Upside down at a forty-five-degree angle, Sebastian worked his way to the top of the pole, now partially implanted into a patch of grass. Once he pulled the first loop over the top, the entire knot fell apart like a shedding cocoon. He freed his legs, his arms, his tail, feeling the blood again and the air through his fur.

The buzzing sound was deafening now. Stiffly, Sebastian ran toward the building where the human had camped out. An object streaked across the sky. The municipal building erupted in a ball of flame and smoke. Windows of the nearby buildings burst open like a million discordant bells. The shock of the blast sent the sidewalk leaping up at Sebastian. Broken glass landed on the pavement around him, tinkling on the street like tiny diamonds.

Shouting echoed throughout the street. Amidst the rubble, Culdesac called out to his people to see who was still alive. The fire lit up a snowfall of ash.

Sebastian heard footsteps. Not padded cats' feet, but human boots. Lifting his head from the cement, he saw the human running through the intersection. Sebastian got to his feet and sprinted after him. The human had a walkie-talkie held to his ear and was frantically shouting code words. He did not hear Sebastian pursuing him until it was too late. Sebastian tackled him, slamming him to the ground so that the man's body skidded across the concrete. Sebastian gripped the man's oily hair and pulled his head up.

"Who are you?" Sebastian said.

"Lord," the man said.

"What?"

"Lord, forgive these wretched creatures," the man said in a sobbing voice. "They know not what they do."

Sebastian could not get enough of the man's smell. It was so much like Daniel. Even though this man was his enemy—able to summon fiery death from the heavens—Sebastian wanted nothing more than to lose himself in the scent of the past, of deodorant and sweat and bad breath and coffee and cigarettes. Something inside him would always be broken, would always long for dead friends and capricious masters and a phony slave life.

Before Sebastian could say anything, the Red Sphinx had arrived. They formed a circle around the human.

"Good job, No-Name," Culdesac said from somewhere in the crowd. "I think you're cured."

"He's clean," another voice said.

"Let us take over from here," Culdesac said. "You're hungry, aren't you?"

Sebastian wanted to ask the man more questions—about what was out there, about why this had happened. About any dogs he may have seen wandering about. But the man continued reciting his incantations. He was in some kind of trance, speaking to people who were not there.

Sebastian stood up. The cats' guns were still raised, but Sebastian was so tired, hungry, and sore that it did not seem important if they decided to shoot him.

"Can you hear me, human?" Culdesac asked. The man kept rambling, pretending that he could not see any of them. "You just lit your own barbecue," the bobcat said, motioning to the smoldering building.

"This animal may still be symptomatic, Captain," Luna said. "We may still need to put him down. I recommend we—"

"Luna," Culdesac interrupted.

"Yes, sir?"

"You are relieved of command. You're no longer my Number One."

Her rifle lowered a bit. "Yes, sir," she said.

"Take three soldiers," Culdesac instructed. "Prepare our feast."

"Yes, sir."

Luna and two other cats dragged the man away. Plumes of vapor extended from their nostrils.

"No-Name," Culdesac said. Sebastian eyed him. Culdesac seemed to like this defiant body language. "We talk now," Culdesac said. "You and I."

CULDESAC AND SEBASTIAN walked along the waterfront. The moon reflected off the water, sending shafts of light into the sky and turning Culdesac's face into a silver jack-o'-lantern.

The odor of roasting meat wafted toward them, occasionally interrupted by the breeze blowing along the river. Tangy and thick and delicious, it lingered in Sebastian's mouth and nostrils.

"You'll have to indulge me," Culdesac said. "I grew up eating rats and grubs. Raw. And now the Colony is supplying us with protein rations from their organic farms. They do the job, but they're boring. Cooked human meat has become a delicacy for me."

Sebastian nodded to show that he understood. He was still unsure if he would partake in the meal, no matter how hungry he was.

"You're a house cat," Culdesac said. "A house *slave*. Locked away from all of this. So you must be wondering: Why all the destruction?"

"That's right."

"It's because the humans are dangerous," Culdesac said. "And I don't just mean their technology or their plague. It's their philosophy. It's poison."

Sebastian nodded.

"You must have observed it," Culdesac said.

A concrete railing separated them from the river. A breeze disturbed the water.

"I suppose," Sebastian said.

"These humans," Culdesac said, "they've placed themselves at the center of the universe. You and I could have a mate, with a brood of kittens, roaming about the hilltops as nature intended. And the humans would consider it a nuisance to be terminated. The Queen fixed all that. We owe her everything."

"Why did the Queen do this to us?" Sebastian asked.

"We are her experiment," Culdesac said, extending his arms to illustrate the magnitude of it all. "Everything she does is in pursuit of knowledge. Of truth. She chose to raise us up so that we could replace the humans. She guides us while letting us choose our own destinies."

"How will we be any different from the humans?"

"Well," Culdesac said scratching an itch on the side of his neck, "in a lot of ways, we'll be the same. We can't live exactly as we did before, killing one another for food and land. We're going to have a society very similar to what the humans wanted. We'll have houses and jobs. We'll raise families. We'll even watch television, once the electricity gets turned on again. But there will be one difference."

Culdesac allowed for a pause. Sebastian felt the tension build. "We won't think that this world is ours alone."

"Is that what the humans really believe?" Sebastian asked.

"It's worse than that," Culdesac said. "Many of them believe that there is a human in the sky, an old man with a beard. He made the earth a garden for them. And he made us their slaves. You must have noticed your masters chanting to this old man, asking him for favors and trinkets."

Sebastian told Culdesac about Janet whispering to no one.

"They believe that there is another world waiting for them when they die," Culdesac said. "Of course, not all of them think this way. And even among those who do, there are many who do not take it seriously. But the belief has corrupted all of them. I've seen this evil up close. I've seen what a human can do when he is cornered and praying to his god for deliverance. There is nothing more dangerous. Nothing more cruel. More *animal*."

Culdesac allowed this to settle. In the distance, there was muffled laughter from the Red Sphinx as the human carcass turned on a spit over the fire.

"That is why we fight," Culdesac whispered. "To reclaim a land overcome with evil. The evil of men who believe that they are our rulers, men who cannot be reasoned with. Who are insane enough to spread a disease so dangerous that it could wipe out everything, including themselves, all to please a father in the clouds who doesn't exist. We don't need a god because we have the Queen. And she doesn't make promises that she cannot keep. She doesn't ask us to worship her. She merely asks for us to live in peace, to live for today and for one another."

Culdesac asked Sebastian if he knew what cats had been like

thousands of years earlier. Sebastian said that he knew enough about evolution to understand that felines had once been much larger, and that they had lived in the wild.

"Before the humans seduced and kidnapped us," Culdesac explained, "we were hunters. We saw the world as predators. It is our way. The humans wanted to turn us into their little slave dolls. But the ants—they are hunters like us. I've seen them stalking the plains, an army acting as one. They see freedom in the hunt, the way our people once did. They are our liberators and our natural allies. That is why we fight. We fight for our future and for the generations that were lost."

"I cannot join you," Sebastian said. "I have to find my friend."

"Nothing could survive out here for long," Culdesac said. "I've been at this for longer than you know. I'm sorry, but your friend is almost certainly dead."

"I have to find out."

"But you're both different now. You don't have to hold on to these things anymore."

"I am not that different," Sebastian said. "This is what I want. It is what I promised."

"What if I were to tell you that the reason why we waited to see if you had EMSAH was because the Queen herself told us to do so?"

Sebastian tilted his head, incredulous.

"The Queen sees everything," Culdesac said. "Even a lost house cat. She knows who you are. She knows that you were meant to fight. With us."

"How do you know this?"

"I speak to the Colony," Culdesac said. "Which means I speak to the Queen."

"But how?"

"They gave me a special device, actually," Culdesac said. "It allows me to interpret their chemical signal. And it converts my voice into their language. Perfect communication, if you can master it. I'll show it to you one day."

"You've seen her, then?"

"Not exactly," Culdesac said. "The collective knowledge of the Colony flows through their chemical signals. If you communicate with one ant, you communicate with them all. It's a giant loop of information, constantly updated, constantly corrected. And they know about you. As they know about me. And Luna. And Socks."

"I am no good to you as a soldier," Sebastian said.

"Listen," Culdesac said. "I'm sorry about your friend. But there is more to your life than your little patch of sunlight."

Sebastian could not hide his emotions upon hearing this. Culdesac, meanwhile, nodded in approval. Somehow this bobcat and his insect friends had intercepted this dream, hijacked it. That was the moment Sebastian died. There had been a time when he understood that people would go away. Now the person he was had gone away. He was trapped in this present with these strangers who already seemed to know who he was, and who he was going to be.

Culdesac continued to speak about the Red Sphinx, about the difficult days ahead. Perhaps, Culdesac said, once the war was over, Sebastian could continue his search. Or maybe in their travels they would come across a lonely dog also searching for a lost friend. There was still plenty of living to do, regardless of what had happened to Sheba, or how far away she was. Sebastian would have to keep going, no matter how tired he was, or how hurt, or sad, or alone.

"You have a choice," Culdesac said, "but you don't really have a choice. Whatever you want to do, you can't do it alone. We can be your family."

Another warm breeze laced with the charred odor of the dead man filled Sebastian's nostrils.

He told Culdesac that he would join him.

"Excellent," Culdesac said. "Now what shall we call you?"

CHAPTER FOUR
THE LOST YEARS

SEBASTIAN CHOSE TO be called Mort(e). Names were such an important thing. For some of these cats, choosing a new identity was the first act of independence. It was not long before Mort(e) learned the significance behind every one in the Red Sphinx: Cromwell, Dutch, Bentley, Gai Den, Dane, Rookie, Anansi, Seljuk, Stitch, Rao, Biko, Dread, Texan, Riker, Striker, Sugar, Logan, Bin Lydon, Foxtrot, Folsom, Hanh, Jomo, Uzi, Le Guin, Brutal, Bailarina, Hennessey, Juke, Bicker, Packer, Ironhawk. Only Red Sphinx members knew the origins of one another's names. No one else could be told.

Sebastian based his name on a word he had come across in one of the old libraries. A word meaning death. He had died. He had killed. And he would kill again. So the name fit. But it could also be a normal name, the name of a regular guy named Mort who was meant for a life surrounded by loved ones. That life was still out there, but it would have to wait. Hence the need to keep the letter *e* in parentheses. Things could go either way. They could *always* go either way.

Culdesac soon chose Mort(e) as his Number One, the executive officer who carried out his commands. Luna was not happy about it, but she knew she was not cut out to be a leader. Before Mort(e) joined the Red Sphinx, she had had to euthanize many

EMSAH-infected animals and was never the same. Thus, when she turned out to be wrong about Mort(e) having the virus, she second-guessed her actions. Her mind became distracted by memories of dead comrades, along with living ones who would soon be dead. It was not long after Mort(e) joined the band that she was unceremoniously killed during a seven-minute firefight with army deserters who had sought refuge in a fire station.

The battles continued. Sieges of small towns that had somehow held out, where old men and twelve-year-old boys fired rusty shotguns from freshly dug trenches. Raids of bunkers in which starving humans appeared ready to beg for death. Week-long chases through forests, through city streets, through the bowels of abandoned factories and warehouses, hunting prey in the dark where only the felines could see. Burning entire villages to the ground to make the humans scurry out like vermin, and then cutting them down, or pouncing on the slow ones to save for later. Enormous pitched battles fought on plains with the Alphas as cannon fodder. Culdesac was right—their species was meant to do this. Although Mort(e) was sad to find he was so good at something so ghastly, he learned to extract some pleasure from it. Each murder was revenge for his loss. Every human who pleaded for mercy, every man or woman who whispered a prayer to the old man in the sky, had to pay for Sheba. Any one of them could have tried to kill her. Or infect her with EMSAH. Or enslave her again. Every human was his enemy. And for years, he never came across a single one who acted otherwise.

Mort(e) surprised himself with his toughness, with his willingness to shed Sebastian the House Cat so quickly. The Red Sphinx traveled light, slept in ditches and fields, drank water from puddles, ate worms and overripe berries to stay alive. They were lean and angry. Always reminding one another, the way Culdesac did, to *aim true*, to *stay on the hunt*.

Tiberius would eventually earn his chosen name, even saving Mort(e)'s life on a few occasions. Mort(e) returned the favor. There were three straight missions in which they led the way. The first involved scaling the side of a building to toss a sniper from a rooftop. The second required them to swim to an anchored boat and plant a bomb on her hull. The other cats were too scared of the water and watched in awe as Mort(e) dove in. The third was a suicide mission, a frontal assault on a machine-gun nest that turned out to be operated by three teenage girls whose families had left them behind. After that, the rest of the Red Sphinx begged to be among the first for such missions. They had been shamed by their skepticism of Socks the medic and the choker-house-cat-turned-warrior. Their new Number One was somehow charmed, chosen by the Queen herself. Even those who had allied themselves with Luna had to agree that Mort(e) was the fearless, competent leader they needed. He laughed at death as it slid off him again and again. He *was* death.

The Red Sphinx recruited other stray cats to replace the ones they lost. Some came looking for the Red Sphinx, driven by growing legends among the animals. Tales of Mort(e) the Fearless. So many wanted to join that Culdesac would force them to audition by fighting one another. The matches were sometimes so vicious that Mort(e) would intervene and tell both contestants that they had qualified.

The months bled into years, and the years folded into one another until Mort(e) found himself wondering if it had been two years or three since he had killed his master. Had it been three years or four since he had last seen Sheba? One morning, he woke from a dream realizing that he could not remember the last time he had thought of her. Weeks? Months? He wanted to beg her memory for forgiveness. Forgetting her was just as bad as killing her.

Thanks to Sheba, Mort(e) was able to learn about pain—and then to switch it off—so much faster than the other Red Sphinx. Thus the memories of those awful years became buried, a series of fragments seen through a foggy glass. It was the best he could hope for.

SOMETIMES, HOWEVER, THE past came looking for him.

For all Mort(e)'s acts of bravery over those eight years, none compared with the time that he and Tiberius defied Culdesac's orders and went snooping around in a town decimated by the EMSAH syndrome. Tiberius had been clamoring for an opportunity to study the effects of the plague. As company medic, he had been beset with recurring nightmares about being caught in an EMSAH outbreak, surrounded by corpses that could walk upright.

So there was a noble, selfless goal. But the opportunity to search for Sheba was the real motivation. She could be in some infected town, waiting to die, wondering if she would ever see him again. Or perhaps she wasn't wondering at all. In his most sullen moods, he thought that it would be better for Sheba to be dead than for her to forget him. And then he hated himself for thinking such a thing.

Mort(e)'s act of insubordination took place after the war had turned in the Colony's favor. The humans were nearing extinction, off to meet the imaginary creator who had promised them everything in this world and the next. Those who remained were growing more desperate. With virtually every human city on the continent now occupied or destroyed, guerrilla tactics and suicide attacks replaced pitched battles. The animals began to resettle the scarred lands, picking up where the humans had left off.

Even so, the Colony continued to preach vigilance of the

signs of EMSAH. These blooming civilian centers were prime targets for a human terrorist. It was in this climate that the first "celebrity" of the war emerged, a chimpanzee doctor named Miriam who had escaped from a zoo. As the leader of a team of scientists searching for a cure, her image was everywhere. Miriam appeared in a number of public service announcements, warning of the symptoms, giving updates on her team's progress. One of the early attempts at humor among the animals involved impersonating the dour Miriam. "Remember," people would say, arms folded, eyes squinting, "if you see something, say something." And then they would imitate a wild monkey: "Oooh-oooh-oooh-aaahh-aaahh!"

The term EMSAH, Miriam explained, meant nothing—it was a corruption of an acronym the Colony had used when they first discovered the disease. Over time, her team concluded that the virus had mutated, making it harder to cure. Its effects were equally confounding. Different species had different symptoms. Felines suffered skin lesions. Hoofed animals tended to have allergic reactions that closed up their throats and swelled their eyes shut. Dogs experienced a form of narcolepsy accompanied by hallucinations. Regardless of the physical symptoms, all the victims ended the same: unhinged, often irrationally violent, and pleading for death. They were somehow reduced to a state of savagery. Perhaps that was exactly what the humans wanted. The Queen could create, and they could destroy.

Thanks to Miriam's eagerly awaited quarterly reports, the disease remained a sinister word, whispered by pups and kittens to frighten one another while telling stories at night. Newly founded schools even banned games in which the young animals tagged one another, declaring in singsong, "You have EM-SAH! You have EM-SAH!" Rumors spread of rebuilding sectors being quarantined and exterminated, with every building leveled and every living thing burned away, down to the last microbe.

When Tiberius and Mort(e) asked Culdesac if they could see an infected town for themselves, the captain told them that the topic was off-limits. They had a war to win. Bad news would be a setback to the effort. Tiberius asked how the hell he was supposed to diagnose someone when he hadn't seen the effects firsthand. Culdesac insisted that Miriam's reports were more than enough and that they were getting better. If the animals could defeat the humans, then they could stop a virus.

Tiberius asked if Culdesac would shoot him if he tried to investigate one of the settlements.

"Yes," Culdesac said.

One night, Culdesac gathered all the Red Sphinx together. They were camped in the woods near a newly established town. They had been patrolling the countryside for a few days, responding to reports of humans smuggling weapons, but found nothing. It was a welcome relief.

But Culdesac's news was grim. The town was infected, he said. A bioweapon attack. Every settler was dead. The ants were on their way to clear it out, to devour and destroy every last trace of the town. The land would be indistinguishable from the wilderness around it.

"If you needed a reason for why we are fighting this war, this is it," Culdesac said. "The enemy is barbaric. We must be strong in response. Slavery and death are the alternatives."

They would leave in the morning for a nearby army base. Culdesac wished them a good night and then headed for his sleeping spot.

In the middle of the night, Mort(e) roused Tiberius and told him that they were going into the town. Tiberius stretched theatrically in order to show his annoyance with being woken up.

"Did the captain give you permission?" he asked, yawning.

"Yes."

"No, he didn't."

"All right, he didn't."

"You can't order me."

"You're the doctor. You want to see what's down there even more than I do."

"I don't want to get *shot* even more than you do."

"You know that it's easier to ask forgiveness than to ask permission."

Tiberius thought about this for a moment. "You're going to owe me," he said.

"You already owe *me*."

"Don't start."

They set off. Tiberius was groggy but managed to keep up. They spoke little.

By then, Mort(e) had imagined every conceivable scenario for his reunion with Sheba, from passing her on the road to finding her in the aftermath of a battle, Sheba walking upright toward him, through the smoke, stepping over the bodies of their enemies, exhausted but smiling weakly as she recognized him. He preferred to think of her as a competent yet reluctant warrior like himself. Maybe she would be the first canine member of the Red Sphinx. Or they would put her in charge of her own unit. The Blue Cerberus or something. Culdesac may have peered into his past with that translator device of his, but only Sheba knew who he was before he had to wear a mask all the time.

The first stop on the trip was a storage depot near the highway, about two miles north of the town. The depot was nothing more than a dumpster buried halfway in the dirt. Inside were medical supplies, rations, water bottles. The regular army left these in strategic places along the frontier. Officers carried maps showing their locations, and coming across one was often more of a psychological boost than a relief from physical hardship. The depots were stubborn indications that civilization was rising from the rubble.

Mort(e) and Tiberius wanted the hazmat suits and respirators. There were only two—typically the depots had at least four. Some volunteer dog soldiers probably smelled something funny and panicked. In the suits, the cats were two spacemen traversing an alien landscape. With his sense of smell cut off, and his breathing amplified, Mort(e) felt like a testing subject in one of the humans' prewar experiments.

They made steady progress to the town. More important, the thoughts of Sheba were propelling without distracting him, a gentle voice in his head ordering him to keep going. Within an hour, they reached a chain-link fence, the perimeter of the quarantine. The mounds of dirt at each pole were freshly dug. Every forty feet or so, there was a sign showing Miriam's stern face, each with a terse warning to stay away.

Tiberius placed his glove onto the metal. He screamed, his body convulsing. An electric jolt seemed to surge through him. His tail bulged against his suit, desperately trying to get out. But soon his screams degenerated into laughter. When he turned around, clearly expecting a reaction, Mort(e) smacked him on the crown of his helmet.

"Ow," Tiberius said.

"Knock it off."

They climbed the fence and kept walking. Soon they could make out the wooden rooftops of the town. The settlement consisted of a few buildings: cabins, a marketplace, a stone-and-mortar meeting hall, an enclosed amphitheater, an administrative building, a school, a modest army barracks and commissary.

Mort(e) expected to see at least one dead body lying facedown, but the ground was bare.

They split up and searched the cabins. All the homes were empty, save for the same boring furniture: soft brown couch, brown chairs, wooden table. The comforters in the bedrooms were unmoved. Litter boxes were immaculate, food bowls were spotless. No one had left in a hurry. Even though he couldn't smell anything, Mort(e) suspected that even the scent was gone.

Later, Mort(e) and Tiberius met in the center of town, on the main thoroughfare leading to the meeting hall. The bodies had to be there. Mort(e) imagined the stench rising from the chimney and windows like a flight of demons. They made it a few steps farther before they heard the flies. There had to be thousands of them, drinking the EMSAH-tainted blood from open wounds.

"Mort(e)," Tiberius said. Mort(e) did not answer.

The double doors were ajar. Mort(e) swung them open. Inside, motionless forms clung to the floor and leaned against the walls. Tiberius patted the wall for a switch. The fluorescent lights snapped to life, flooding the room with a sharp white glow.

"Oh, no," Tiberius said.

Just as they thought: the townsfolk were lying in rows or propped against the wall in awkward sitting poses. All dead. All bleeding from the eyes and noses, a coagulated brown stain clinging to their fur. All torn apart by the telltale lesions that burst from the skin.

There was nowhere to walk. Every square inch of the floor yielded a corpse. At the front of the room, on a stage probably used for school plays and public debates, a dog slouched before a podium. His mouth hung open in a perpetual yawn. A piece of paper had fallen from his lap to the floor. Maybe he had been giving them instructions on how to die.

Whatever petty differences existed between the species seemed to have vanished in this room. A glass-eyed kitten rested her head in the lap of an old dog. A wolf cradled a bloody raccoon, both their dried tongues sticking out. Mort(e) searched the bodies for Sheba's white fur. He detected blotches peeking out from under limbs and torsos. But none of it was hers. Or all of it was hers, forming a patchwork among the dead.

"What kind of hospital is this?" Tiberius said.

"It—it's not," Mort(e) stammered. "It's not a hospital."

"They waited here to die, then?"

"Our people used to do it that way," Mort(e) said.

"But not like this."

"Maybe they quarantined themselves."

"Or maybe the EMSAH made them crazy."

"Maybe," Mort(e) said, adjusting his gloves. "Do you still want to do an autopsy?"

"Yes," Tiberius said. "I want to see—"

"Do you need my help?"

"Uh . . . no. I could just—"

"Good," Mort(e) said. He steadied himself and headed for the exit.

"Don't you want to see it?"

"Yell if you need me," Mort(e) said.

As he exited, he caught sight of a rope pulled taut. There was a young fox—or half fox, half dog; one never knew with these canines. The fox had been leashed, an unheard-of practice, an abomination. But there the animal was, a collar around its swollen neck. The tether resembled the one Tristan had used on Sheba. The fox's eyes were closed while its mouth gaped open, a wound unto itself. Someone did not want this little one to get away. Someone had gone through the trouble of treating it like a pet. And apparently no one in the room objected.

Inside the meeting hall, Mort(e) could hear Tiberius moving a body, preparing to slice it open from its neck to its crotch.

Some time passed before Tiberius stepped outside, a stain smeared across the chest of his suit. The blood was blue in the darkness. He was about to start talking about what he had found. Mort(e) told him to save it for later.

They walked to the fence and continued into the forest. In a small clearing, far from both the camp and the town, Mort(e) said that they should take off their suits. They gathered sticks and started a fire. When the flames were high enough, they stripped off their suits and tossed them in, releasing plumes of smoke. Then they stamped out the embers and continued on to the camp.

"Did you see the leash?" Tiberius asked.

"Yes."

"Maybe gathering in that hall wasn't a result of the final stages," Tiberius said, "but a leash sure as hell was. Pure crazy."

"Could have been something else," Mort(e) said. "Maybe they weren't driven insane from the EMSAH. Maybe they went crazy because they just couldn't handle it. Like humans."

"I hope not."

There was the sound of twigs breaking ahead of them. They stopped in time to hear more sticks snapping behind them, along with gravel crunching underfoot. Cats emerged upright from the tree line, all wearing protective white suits and helmets. The muzzles of their guns became shiny circles in the firelight.

It took only a second to spot Culdesac. His helmet was so large it resembled the front of a car. "You had to see it, didn't you?" Culdesac said, his voice muffled.

He ordered the soldiers to stay away so that he could talk to the two insubordinates by himself. There was more rustling of leaves and sticks as the cats formed a perimeter.

"Why did you do it?" Culdesac asked.

"We had to know, sir," Tiberius said.

"Then tell me what you know."

Mort(e) nudged Tiberius. Though hesitant at first, Tiberius was soon blathering away. He probably thought that it would keep him alive. He explained that the victims had discoloration in the fingernails and teeth, along with polyps in the throat and on the tongue. If he was right, then these symptoms arose early, allowing for faster diagnosis and more efficient quarantine, at least until an accurate blood test could be devised. Miriam was still working on that.

Culdesac asked if Mort(e) had anything to add.

"None of this is going to work," Mort(e) said.

"Socks says that we're closer to a cure."

"I don't mean EMSAH," Mort(e) said. "I mean *this*. All of this. We're going to become just like the humans."

Culdesac was not one to allow a non sequitur to throw him off. "What are you talking about?" he asked.

"I want to know why they locked themselves in that barn," Mort(e) said.

"They set up a quarantine. They're heroes. We should honor their memory."

"No," Mort(e) said. "The disease brought out the worst in them. There was a dog at the front of the room, giving them some kind of pep talk while they were dying. Or else he was keeping them there."

"We don't know that," Tiberius said.

"What did you expect to find?" Culdesac said. "A big party? They were dying."

"There was a fox chained with a leash," Mort(e) said. "Like an animal."

Culdesac leaned toward Mort(e). "You better tell me what's gotten into you," he said.

Mort(e) did not know where to start. His mind was still locked on the image of the dead.

Culdesac slapped him in the face, turning his head toward Tiberius, who remained still, facing straight ahead. If Culdesac's claws had not been encased in a thick glove, Mort(e)'s snout would have flopped on the ground, bloody at Tiberius's feet.

And then it spilled from him, all of it: Sheba, Daniel, the square of sunlight, the bucket of squealing puppies. Shouting out Sheba's name for no reason. Wondering what he could have done differently. Wondering why he was alive and she was gone. Wondering why others had gotten over their past so easily, while he couldn't leave his behind. For Tiberius, the past was something to shrug off, to laugh about over drinks and a card game. For Culdesac, it was a badge of honor, the foundation for his bravery and ruthlessness. For Mort(e), it was all bad memories and regret, weighing him down, poisoning the present. As if he were a human.

"You hardly knew Sheba," Culdesac said.

"I knew her well enough."

Culdesac told Mort(e) that he was still compromised by human outlooks on the world. He needed to let go of them if he truly wanted to be free. Mort(e) disagreed. He simply missed his friend. There was only one cure for that.

"She's only good to you now as a reason to hate," Culdesac said. "Cherish that."

"A lot of animals experience this," Tiberius interrupted. "It's called Regressive Defense Mechanism. RDM. They hold onto some memory. Sometimes they even miss their old masters and cry themselves—"

"Shut up, Socks!" Culdesac said.

Tiberius shut up.

"I can't tell you how to live," Culdesac said. "I can only ask you to die. If you miss some aspects of your slave life, go ahead and complain about it. But I won't tolerate this nonsense about us becoming like them. Do I need to explain why?"

"No, sir."

"I need you to be at my side," Culdesac said. "Are you still with me?"

"Yes, sir." Mort(e) wasn't even sure if he was lying.

"So now you've seen it," Culdesac said. "You know almost as much as Miriam herself."

He allowed for more awkward stillness before rendering his verdict.

"I can't kill both of you," he said at last, folding his arms. "And it might be good to have you telling people what you saw. It beats rumors spreading. Or doubts."

He paced. "Stay here for three days," he said. "If you're still asymptomatic, come join us at Camp Delta. If you are symptomatic, then kill yourselves. Or kill the other one, and then kill yourself. Plenty of options there."

Culdesac stepped away and signaled to his troops to follow him into the woods. "Looking forward to the full report."

The Red Sphinx scattered into the forest.

Mort(e) was drained, wobbly. He was grateful when Tiberius, overcome with emotion, began to weep. For some reason, it kept Mort(e) from doing the same.

THEY STAYED FOR five days, just to be sure.

On the second day, an ant mound rose on the outskirts of town. It started as a dimple but soon resembled a small volcano. The next day, the Alphas began pouring out. From a sloping hill, Mort(e) and Tiberius watched the ants dismantle the town, removing every trace, converting all the inhabitants into nutrients. Mort(e) imagined white blood cells acting in the same way to repel viruses and bacteria. EMSAH had cleansed the town. The Colony would now clear out the EMSAH.

After a while, Mort(e) was glad that they were not close enough to get any real detail. In their jaws, the Alphas carried the victims out of the main hall in pieces: bleeding slabs of flesh dragged along in the insects' mechanical mouths. There was no attempt to catalogue the names, to maintain some level of dignity. Even in death, these people would be punished for their terrible luck in life.

Mort(e) was too far away to see the little fox on its leash.

The Colony had calculated exactly how many Alphas it would take to remove all the bodies in one sweep. These vulture ants marched in a line to the new mound, while the others went about the business of toppling the buildings one at a time. The structures collapsed in neatly executed implosions, like the splashes from pebbles dropped into still water. The ants carted off the lumber and then plowed up the dirt. By nightfall, only a muddy patch remained, in the shape of an equilateral hexagon. The Queen had blotted out the past, proving once again that nothing lasted forever. She alone could decide what remained and what would be discarded.

Mort(e) and Tiberius examined each other's eyes for burst blood vessels. They gazed into each other's open mouths, searching for purple lumps that would turn into lesions. They quizzed each other on basic things, using a recommended list of questions that Miriam had devised: *What was your slave name? What was the name of your master? What was the first word you could read? What was the first word you could speak? Who is your enemy?* It was Tiberius's job to know the answers for each member of the Red Sphinx. The answer to the last question was the same for everyone and, after what they had seen in the town, was easier than ever. The humans were the enemy. Now and for all eternity.

They experienced no symptoms, not even a headache or fatigue. Thus they rejoined the Red Sphinx at Camp Delta. The camp was a wooden structure, also shaped like a hexagon, with walls made of forest logs and watchtowers at three of its six points. A scout spotted them and alerted the others. The entire Red Sphinx greeted them at the gate, cheering wildly. The two invincible cats had cheated death once again. They were living symbols of the pending victory over humanity.

When Mort(e) spotted Culdesac, the bobcat tipped his head, a signal that Mort(e) should enjoy this while he could. There would be work to do later. Culdesac had played the entire episode to his advantage. As far as anyone else knew, he had sent Mort(e) and Tiberius on a suicide mission, and their loyalty was so absolute that they agreed immediately. Some human traits, such as duplicity, came in handy every once in a while.

MORT(E) DID NOT talk about Sheba again for a long time.

He managed to survive a few more years of war. And thanks to the increasing need for EMSAH experts in the field, he and Tiberius became minor celebrities, important assets in the Queen's experiment. The Red Sphinx could not stop at a base or settlement without some officer from the regular army asking questions about the quarantine. Under Culdesac's orders, they downplayed the disturbing late-stage behavior of the victims, focusing instead on detection and diagnosis of the physical traits. Tiberius was invited to vivisect other animals, and he often asked Mort(e) to join him. Whether he wanted to or not, Mort(e) was auditing a medical education.

Tiberius died still believing he would find a cure. It happened during a raid on an underground bunker, which the Red Sphinx tried to infiltrate by crawling through a ventilation shaft. The humans detected them and began firing. Tiberius couldn't run away. Mort(e) screamed his name over the noise but heard no answer.

After the humans were overrun and the bunker secured, Culdesac personally executed the survivors. The Red Sphinx buried Tiberius near a river and placed rocks on the ground in the shape of a medical cross. Afterward, Mort(e) began to accept that they were no closer to finding a cure, despite the constant news of victories on the frontier.

One day, the Red Sphinx passed through another settlement. Mort(e) was the only one who refrained from remarking bitterly about how good these civilians had it. He wanted what they had. He wanted to find a house and wait for Sheba to return, or else continue his search for her. He would explore life rather than death. There was nothing more for him to learn about the latter. There had to be some justice in the universe that would bring her back after the enormous price he had paid. But this was human thinking. The universe owed him nothing.

With the new settlements cropping up, there was talk of the war shifting into a "transition period," when life would finally proceed as planned. The ants, speaking through their chosen animal ambassadors, assured everyone that their needs would be met while things were returned to normal. Accustomed to taking orders and living only for sustenance, the animals fell in line.

With this loyalty as a foundation, the Colony set up a quorum of elders for every species, each of which sent a representative to the Council. The first order of business was to establish a Bureau to oversee the dirty work of rebuilding: construction contracts, relocation assistance, adoption services for orphans, local policing, education, medicine. Weary from years of conflict, the animals embraced these mundane tasks. Veterans were returning home, and construction workers were arriving by the busload. Things moved again. Streets opened up. There was even talk about reestablishing cell phone connections once the network of towers was rebuilt.

Ignoring all these developments, Culdesac asked the Red Sphinx to stay together. The enemy was still watching them, he warned, and no one should relax simply because some politicians declared the war to be technically over. "The new order must be defended," he said, sounding like some human propaganda broadcast. "Somebody has to protect these trash-pickers and schoolteachers."

When a new settlement known as Wellbeing opened in the part of the country where he had grown up, Mort(e) quietly left the Red Sphinx. It was his right. He was the first one to do so while still living. Mort(e) had saved the lives of the others so many times that they dared not criticize him. But Culdesac could not hide his disappointment. He said he would never forgive Mort(e).

Mort(e)'s decision to quit came with another price. He relinquished many of the benefits of being a war hero and would have to go to the resettlement camps and wait with all the civilians. Still, he had options. Culdesac, on the other hand, had no home to which he could return. His entire life was combat. The Change had made him smarter, but the struggle would never end.

Living in the camps took some adjusting for Mort(e). The food was bland and repetitive, and he had to sleep in a massive auditorium with rows of pallets on the floor. He grew accustomed to the routine. After so many exhausting missions, his strength was returning, his mind clearing at last. And because he was a veteran, the administrators gave him prime real estate by one of the windows. They even let him browse the logbooks, though he could not find records for anyone named Sheba.

Mort(e) was snoozing in the dusty light, his thoughts

dissipating among the echoing voices in the room, when the captain paid him a visit. Culdesac nudged him with his foot. Mort(e) rose to give a salute.

Culdesac put up his great paw to stop him. "Don't bother."

In his typical blunt fashion, the captain went through the list of those who had died on the latest mission, a raid on a fortified villa in the mountains. He kept his hands at his sides, his ears twitching at the sound of crying children. This camp, filled with weak, ungrateful civilians, insulted everything he stood for, everything he was. He needed the war. Peace, for him, was the equivalent of death.

"You're going to get lazy and fat again with all these other pets, aren't you?" Culdesac asked. "You're going to take this new order for granted."

"There is no new order," Mort(e) said.

Their ongoing argument had grown more heated in recent years without Tiberius to act as mediator. The newer members of the Red Sphinx, unfamiliar with the long relationship between the two, would sometimes fear for Mort(e)'s life when he disagreed with the captain. For his part, Culdesac seemed to enjoy their debates. It was exercise for him, the same way a battle was something to prepare for and learn from.

"Has it ever crossed your choker mind," he asked now, "that the Colony has bigger plans for you?"

"I've served the Colony," Mort(e) replied. "The war is over. They can't possibly have any other plans for me."

"You were supposed to represent the best of the Change."

Mort(e) burst into mocking laughter. "If that's true, then we're all choked," he said. "What are you getting at? What is Her Highness telling you these days?"

Culdesac waved him off. "Never mind," he said. "It just wasn't supposed to be like this."

"We're going to become like the humans," Mort(e) said, as he always did. "I don't care about this 'aim true' crap. Your Queen is wrong about us."

Culdesac said that if Mort(e)'s predictions ever came to pass, then Mort(e) could punch him in the face. "And I won't even kill you for it."

"Okay," Mort(e) said, "Then the next time we meet, you know what I'm going to do." He balled his mangled hand into a knobby fist.

"Then maybe this should be the last time we meet."

Somewhere in the large auditorium, two pups fought over a stuffed animal until an adult told them to stop.

"You're going to try to find her again, aren't you?" Culdesac said. "After all you've learned. After all I've taught you. You still think you're going to see her again."

Mort(e) considered this for a moment, letting out a deep sigh.

"Yes," he said. "Yes."

PART II REBIRTH

CHAPTER FIVE
HUMILIATION

EVERYONE GATHERED AT the mouth of the temple. Animals of every genus and species, waiting for the latest appearance of the remaining humans on the planet, the last holdouts of the great war. This was the era of the final humiliation of humanity, when the crimes of that greedy species would be punished at last. The humans had prayed to their gods, they'd maintained faith in their technology and their governments, but nothing would save them now.

The Colony held a Purge every few months in Wellbeing. The people loved it. They loved jeering at the human prisoners as the Alphas frog-marched them from the depths of the anthill. No other event encapsulated both the anger and the euphoria of the animals' new freedom. No other event brought things full circle. Here, the humans were the exotic ones, the playthings, the ones who could be discarded. In the days leading up to a Purge, people gossiped about who they expected to see—high-ranking generals, politicians, young children (for the humans were still breeding). People wondered—sometimes aloud, but mostly to themselves—if they would see their former masters. And when the prisoners were put on display, the spectators placed bets on who would cry first, who would scream first, who would pray first, who would fight back first, who would beg first, and who would say nothing at all and accept the fate that had arrived at last. The pomp reminded the citizens of what they had won, and how easily that victory could be taken away.

Mort(e), however, was tired of it. It had been over a year since he had walked out on the Red Sphinx, and a lifetime since the Martinis had driven away in their silver SUV. Unless this Purge actually produced his former masters or provided some clue about Sheba, then it was another waste of however much time he had left on this earth.

Things were supposed to be normal now, but Mort(e) knew that it would take another generation for everyone to get over what had happened. It would require the people of his time to die off, and the memories of their former lives to die with them.

The animals waited in the evening sun, into the dusk, and finally in the dark. The temple—a massive anthill the size of a pyramid—changed color from tan in the daytime, to brown as the sun descended, and finally to gray under the stars. At last, the mouth of the structure opened, powered by some bio-mechanism that only the ants could master. The aperture began as a hole the size of a fist and continued to widen like an iris. The anthill became like a basket placed atop a fluorescent lamp, with spears of light shooting high into the night sky.

Crouching on all fours, the animals got into position.

Alpha soldiers emerged from the entrance, standing upright. Their abdomens swayed from side to side with each step. Antennae waved like the arms of a marionette doll. Segmented eyes gazed at everything and nothing at once. Mouths resembled the parts of a machine, all gears and hinges and sharp edges. Coarse hairs sprouted from their exoskeletons. And crawling about their bodies were thousands of smaller ants, making it seem as though their skin somehow moved. Humans had once suffered through nightmares about creatures such as this. And here they were.

The crowd split down the middle to make room for them. Mort(e) waited several rows away, between two dogs who did not acknowledge him, and behind a pair of cats who arrived together but said nothing to each other. The dogs wore the orange vests of sanitation workers, and Mort(e) detected a faint odor of death masked by some kind of musky cologne that the humans had left behind. Mort(e) imagined that these workers had removed another stash of corpses—probably another bomb shelter with a desiccated human family inside. He noticed a pamphlet sticking out of one of the cat's pockets. EMSAH SYNDROME, it read. BE ALERT FOR THE SIGNS. The disease gave these workers a sense of purpose as they did their part to reestablish civilization. If Tiberius had been there, he would have quizzed them on EMSAH trivia and scolded them for each question they got wrong. *You mean to tell me you don't know the incubation period?*

As he did whenever he was in a public place these days, Mort(e) kept an eye out for Sheba. If he did it long enough, everyone resembled her until it seemed as though the entire crowd was mocking him. There was Sheba cradling a pup in her lap. There was Sheba removing a miner's cap and inspecting the little light for the next day's work. There was Sheba holding a pair of binoculars, awaiting a glimpse of the Alpha warriors and their human captives. Then, as always, Mort(e)'s eyes readjusted to reality, and his mind accepted that she was nowhere to be found.

Before Mort(e) could become completely lost in his thoughts, the first of the human prisoners appeared. The Purge was beginning. Everyone tensed up, craning necks, straightening spines and tails. Mort(e) was surprised to see so many prisoners. Most were American soldiers, still clad in their pixelated camouflage, faces muddied. There were always stories of humans hiding out in caves and sewers, using their awful machines of war to hold on to life for one more day. Mort(e) suspected that the Colony itself was the source of these rumors, which did such a wonderful job of keeping the animals on their guard.

One of the women prisoners carried a sleeping baby against her shoulder. This also surprised Mort(e), for it was common knowledge that the Alphas liked to eat human children.

While the soldiers had been grim, trying to ignore the sea of animals that spread out before them, the civilian prisoners whimpered. Mort(e) caught sight of one of them, a woman of about fifty. She had white hair and was still chubby despite years of conflict. A younger woman shushed her.

A phalanx of Alphas guarded the rear. The aperture in the temple closed behind them. Then a noise rumbled from the bowels of the anthill like a foghorn.

At the signal, the animals knew what to do.

All at once, they rose on their hind legs. The prisoners, including the most hardened among them, could not keep from being startled at the sight of it. The symbolism of the ritual was clear: the age of the humans was over, and all their attempts to extend life through science and cheat death through religion had failed.

All together, the animals lifted their arms and waved at the prisoners. Mort(e)'s hand was smaller than some of the others', his fingers stubby but functional. He could still wave.

A scream rang out. It was a soldier, sobbing uncontrollably. Another soldier put his arm around the man. Then he faced the animals and spit. Soon almost all the humans were screaming. The animals cried out in response. It began as random taunts before coalescing into a sustained chant:

"Purge!" they shouted. "Purge! Purge! Purge!"

The crowd swelled around the prisoners, moving with them toward the ship docked at the river. The vessel resembled a half-submerged submarine made of a brownish organic material, like a combination of bamboo and mud. There were no windows on the hull, only a doorway on the side. A retractable gangplank extended through it, holding the corralled prisoners. From there, the humans would be ferried to the Island, the nameless place where the nameless war was won, and where the Queen kept her royal court. The Colony's official propaganda stated that Miriam and her staff would use the prisoners in experiments intended to find a cure for EMSAH. But Mort(e) imagined that at least some of the humans would become zoo exhibits. Perhaps they would be forced to breed so that their offspring would live through the same horror, producing generations of slaves for all eternity. It would be no different from what the humans had done to the animals, Culdesac had always said.

There was one last ritual to play out, a formality that the ants had instituted in all the resettled sectors. The elite soldiers of the animal army would be at the dock to preside over the event. To Mort(e), this ceremony was one of the Colony's clumsy public relations efforts, intended to show that the ants were transferring power to the surface dwellers.

A tan dog—what the humans would have stupidly called a Great Dane—had the privilege this time of seeing the humans off. Wearing a maroon sash to indicate his rank of colonel, the dog stepped forward to a microphone mounted near the gangplank. The humans waited with drawn faces, apparently more annoyed than frightened by this point.

"The last days of this war go on and on," the dog said, "but with this Purge, we are closer to final victory over the plague of humanity."

A cheer rose up, followed by more chants of "Purge!"

The colonel lifted his hands to ask for quiet. *"Final* victory over the plague of humanity," the dog emphasized. "And final victory over humanity *and its plague.*"

A Purge was never complete without mention of EMSAH. In response, the animals pointed at the humans and chanted, "Shame! Shame!" It was not in unison, which made it all the more disturbing.

"We have seen what your syndrome, your hellish weapon of last resort, has done to you," the dog said, facing the prisoners. "And so, we say to you in one voice, 'We stand united.'"

It was the opening line to the pledge that the animals recited at every Purge. Anticipating it, the crowd immediately joined in:

"We pledge to one another a new world founded on peace, rooted in justice, secured by order, and prepared for war. We promise to stand together to defend this new world with our lives. In the name of the Queen, the Colony, and the Council, this we swear."

Mort(e) did not recite the pledge. No one noticed.

The dog unhooked a device attached to his belt. It was a translator, the same kind Culdesac used during his briefings with the Colony. Though it may have been the most extraordinary piece of technology ever created, here it was used merely as part of a formalized ritual. Donning the headset, the dog approached the lead Alpha and delivered his report on the state of the sector. It took only moments—supposedly, the translator could slow things down for the user so that a brief conversation could include enough information to fill a textbook. In that sense, it mimicked the mental capacities of the Queen herself.

The "report" complete, the dog stepped aside while the Alphas led the prisoners up the gangplank. It was typical for the audience to break into song at this point, but that depended on who showed up. This time, they remained mostly quiet. Maybe, Mort(e) thought, they had chanted enough for one night.

The crowd dispersed, the animals grunting and jabbering to one another. They would always compare this Purge with the last before talking about what they were doing the next day. The same pointless conversation spilled from everyone's lips. The lights from the temple went dim. Soon, Mort(e) was the only one there, standing amidst the tracks of his animal brethren, hidden in comforting darkness and silence.

CHAPTER SIX
NORMALCY

HE NEXT DAY, Mort(e) hitched a ride in a trash truck to his old house, the home of his former masters. The driver, a beagle named Dexter, had a gray muzzle that gave away his old age. Mort(e) figured that he had kept his slave name after the Change. The dog proudly displayed an ID badge from the Bureau on his dashboard, proving that his truck was a registered tool in the rebuilding effort. On the badge was the Bureau's reassuring logo: a globe held up, Atlas-like, by a hand, a hoof, and a wing. Offering a ride was a common courtesy in Wellbeing. Mort(e) often wondered how long these little niceties would last.

They chatted about the ongoing construction projects in the area. The dog was especially annoyed with the delayed repairs on a nearby bridge. "It's a disgrace," he said, and blamed it on every species except for dogs.

"I mean, no offense," Dexter said, "but some of these rats can't even *lift* a power drill, let alone have the sense to use it."

Mort(e) changed the subject to the refugee camps, which had improved over the last year, but were still choked with people trying to return to their old homes or seeking some kind of help. Dexter had spent time there himself. Learning how to drive helped to get him out. Mort(e) assumed that Dexter must be living in a mansion for his services as a mere truck driver.

"Sanitation is going to be busy for a while," Dexter said. "The debris alone is going to take another year to clear out, and that's not even including biohazards—the bodies, contaminated food supplies, all that."

Dexter asked if Mort(e) had learned a trade in the camps. Mort(e) replied that he, too, worked in sanitation. It was true, in a way. Dexter was pleased to hear this—he and Mort(e) were "on the same page." Mort(e) nodded, and prepared himself to give terse, vague answers if Dexter bothered to ask any follow-up questions. Luckily, he didn't.

The truck pulled up to the house. Dexter was still talking as Mort(e) climbed out. The address on the side of the building was printed in a blocky font, partially burned away by the sun and rain: 519. Five-one-nine. Five-nineteen. Five hundred and nineteen. It was among the first things he had been able to read.

Dexter said goodbye and drove away. Mort(e) exhaled, relieved to find the house still intact after much of the neighborhood had been devastated. The Colony had even set up an anthill down the street, an obscene ziggurat now abandoned and frightening in silent disrepair.

As Mort(e) reached for the metal knocker, the door swung open. He assumed that the female cat standing before him was Jordan, the one from the Bureau who had let him know that his old house was ready. She was plump, with shiny gray fur. A Russian Blue, although Mort(e) quickly forced that obsolete label out of his head.

He noticed something else: she was not neutered like he was, though she was too old to have children. Mort(e) wondered what it would have been like to desire this female without having even met her. He wondered if his status as a eunuch provided an advantage, or if it robbed him of something that would have made him happy. The humans had supposedly mastered their urges, though one could never tell from all the magazines and pornographic videos they left behind.

When Jordan asked if she had found the right house, Mort(e) stepped over to the spot on the tan carpet where he had spent much of his life. Despite the overcast sky, there was still a square of pale sunlight on the rug. He inhaled—not the tentative sniffing of a frightened animal, but an extended act of remembrance.

"I'll take that as a yes," Jordan said.

Though the smell of food was long gone, he recognized the scent of wood and the mustiness of the old recliner. Jordan droned on about a dog she had met a week earlier. He had lost his leg in some famous battle, and hoped to be returned to his old home, only to find that he had been assigned to a place that had once housed over ten cats.

"And he told me that he hated the smell of cats," Jordan said. "Right to my face!"

She began to laugh, and it quickly devolved into a coughing fit. Mort(e) asked if she was all right. The hacking continued, so Mort(e) went to the sink for a glass of water.

"The water isn't turned on yet," she said between coughs. "Don't bother."

She vomited up a ball of hair into her palm. Her eyes widened in embarrassment as she dropped the sticky clump onto her clipboard, hiding it from Mort(e). While some cats still groomed themselves in the old-fashioned way, they could now wash themselves without unsanitary licking, like civilized people. Mort(e) had gotten over this fetish, but it remained a guilty pleasure for some. Jordan couldn't have fought in the war, he thought. She lacked the discipline. She probably hid in some warehouse the whole time, surrounded by cans of food meant for human refugees.

"I want to see the basement," he said.

Jordan nodded and led him into the living room, where the mirror took up nearly the entire wall, creating the illusion that the space was twice as large.

"You'll never mistake that for another cat again!" Jordan said. Mort(e) figured that she had scribbled this line on her clipboard, now covered in fur and saliva.

"I would like to see the basement," he said again.

"Maybe we should stick to the top floors," Jordan said. "There's still some repair work to be done in the cellar." Mort(e) detected a human-like mewling in her voice, as if she were saying, "Come *on*." She was hiding something.

He headed for the basement.

"Mort(e), wait," she said. "We had a new bed installed in the master bedroom."

"I slept downstairs," he said, flipping on the light switch.

Jordan was behind him as he descended, her hand reaching for his shoulder. "We put in some new drapes, too," she pleaded. "They have flowers!"

He scanned the room. Nothing was out of place. There was still a bag of laundry, the blue sleeve of a hoodie sticking out the top. The computer sat on Daniel's desk, its screen covered with dust. But there was some other odor mixed in, polluting the memory. It took two deep inhalations before Mort(e) picked it up: Magic Marker. Probably a day old, maybe less.

"Mort(e)," Jordan said, "we've had some vandals in the area."

A homemade shelf full of VHS tapes took up part of the wall. Some cassettes had the titles scribbled in marker—*Garfield Halloween Special, Innerspace*—but these were too old to be giving off the scent. Mort(e)'s head swiveled toward a curtain hanging from an exposed pipe in the ceiling. It concealed the water heater and the furnace, where Mort(e)—or the cat that

Mort(e) used to be—spent those last few minutes with Sheba on the day she ran away.

Before he could get to the curtain, Jordan grabbed his tail. There were few gestures more insulting than this. Even mothers did not do it to their kittens.

"It wasn't my fault," she said. "I didn't know until this morning. It was too late to tell you not to come."

"Calm down," Mort(e) said, gently taking his tail back.

She blubbered like a human, all sniffles and gasps. "We were going to send a team in the morning before you saw. I can't lose this job. I don't have any other skills."

"I don't care about vandals," he said. "I'm just glad to be home again."

She kept crying despite his insistence that everything was fine.

He slid the curtain aside, eliciting a metallic ring from the pipe. The sound was still echoing when Mort(e) spotted the graffiti on the wall.

In bright red Magic Marker, a message read, SHEBA IS ALIVE.

Jordan began spouting apologies, swearing that people were on their way to fix things. Mort(e) closed the curtain and escorted her to the door, assuring her that he did not need to tour the rest of the house. "I should be giving *you* the tour," he said. She kept saying that the Bureau could clean the mess, but Mort(e) insisted he would handle it. He shut the door on her just as her tail whisked through.

Mort(e) inhaled deeply, but the musty air did not yield a trace of Sheba. *Is this what you wanted?* he asked himself. *To sniff around for her all day like some senile pig?* Mort(e) caught a glimpse of himself shrugging in the mirror. *Yes,* he thought. *Why not?* He had earned it. He could be a junkie on her scent. Some of the older chokers had taken that route.

The staircase creaked under his weight when it had once

remained quiet for him. He passed the bathroom where Daniel drowned Sheba's pups. He opened the bedroom where Janet and Daniel had slept. The blue comforter hung off the bed, and the layer of dust suggested that nothing had been moved since the evacuation.

He opened the door to the attic, which allowed a chilly breeze to flow down the stairs. Mort(e) walked up, peering over the last step to survey the floor. It was the least changed room in the house, though the window was broken, the only visible damage so far. The boxes, racks of coats, and old toys waited for him. There was an untouched spot near the box full of winter coats where he and Sheba had once slept after conquering this new land. That was one of the greatest days of his life. Mort(e) approached the space, knelt down, and stubbornly sniffed again. But there was only the smell of old wood.

He returned to the basement. The furnace kicked on, rumbling with its glowing blue flame. Somewhere a team of animals had begun repairing the gas and water lines to make this possible, another sign of steady progress toward normalcy. Mort(e) sat cross-legged, his tail flicking the metal hull of the furnace. He had to pretend to smell Sheba, just as he had to pretend that the scrawled message was not there. Part of him wanted to believe it, and to ignore the likelihood that one of the survivors from the neighborhood must have written it in order to get to him somehow. Perhaps it was the dog across the street, Hank, who had known Sheba in a way that Mort(e) never could. It was possible that the dog still viewed Mort(e) as a rival, or blamed him for the death of Sheba's puppies. Or maybe it was the stray cats who once lived outside.

Mort(e) considered the possibility that whoever wrote it was in the final stages of EMSAH, foaming at the mouth and speaking nonsense. If that was true, and the ants found out about it, his hometown would become a mere rumor, a hexagon pattern in the dirt.

Regardless of who wrote the message, Sheba was no longer alive. She couldn't be. Her trail had gone cold, with no clues anywhere. Mort(e) had to force himself to accept her loss and grieve. A stupid sign was not going to change anything.

CHAPTER SEVEN
A PROCESSION OF LIFELESS EYES

 ORT(E) COULD SMELL in his dreams. He could detect paint, dog fur, oak, roasting chicken, squirrel urine, bird feed, the water in the toilet, perfume, old rugs, musty blankets, fabric softener. Even if he were blind in his dreams, it would not have mattered, for an entire world remained at his disposal.

While sleeping in his favorite spot in the basement, he dreamt that the Martinis' SUV pulled into the driveway, its wheels blocking out the light in the windows. The scent of the two children lingered in his nostrils, all sugar, shampoo, and baby powder. When he awoke, he realized that the sound was real—a car *was* in the driveway. Two doors opened and then slammed shut. He could hear only one set of footsteps, the telltale clicking of hooves. The other pair of feet must have belonged either to a cat or a very disciplined dog.

Five days had passed since Mort(e) moved in. Every night since his return, he slept before the message on the basement wall. He lay there now, eyes half opened. The graffiti was still there, its Magic Marker scent dispersing among the other odors of the basement. SHEBA IS ALIVE, it still said. A reminder, perhaps. A warning. A promise. A dream.

He waited for the doorbell to ring before getting up.

The bell sounded three more times before he got to it. Opening the door, he saw a six-foot-tall pig before him. While cats and dogs were common, rehabilitated farm animals were a rarity, at least in this part of the country. Many people assumed that animals who had been raised on farms lacked the intelligence to survive in this new world. This was merely a rumor, most likely concocted by bitter old cats who knew that they did not have much time to enjoy their new bodies. Still, horses, cows, and pigs had hooves, and many stopped walking upright because they felt that, without the glorious hands enjoyed by other animals, what was the point? Moreover, they had existed in cages or grazed in fields until the day when they would be slaughtered. Some pigs had gone to the extreme of plastic surgery, paying quack doctors to install tusks in their jaws so that they could claim to be wild boars rather than farm animals. A pig's phony tusk fell out like a human toupee blowing off in the wind.

Nevertheless, this pig was impressive, standing upright, his arms at his sides. Often hoofed animals kept their "hands" behind their backs when in the company of other species. When confronted with self-conscious pigs who tried to conceal their embarrassing hooves, Tiberius would often ask, "What, do you want your money back, Porky? You want to sue the Queen for malpractice?"

The pig arrived in a military Humvee stinking of vegetable grease, thanks to a conversion from a gasoline engine. He wore a blue sash, indicating that he was part of an engineering unit. Mort(e)'s green captain's sash was buried somewhere in his luggage upstairs. He had not worn it since the day it was bestowed upon him. Even more important, the pig wore a black armband with the insignia of the Red Sphinx. Mort(e) had heard that the unit was now bringing in other species, but it was still hard to believe, even with the newest members standing in his driveway.

Mort(e) looked over the pig's shoulder. Sheba stood behind him, walking on two legs, as Sebastian had pictured her for years. Letting her tongue hang out as an inside joke between them.

Mort(e) rubbed his eyes to regain his senses. It wasn't Sheba. It was merely another dog, sent to torment him, to remind him of what he had lost, like all the female ones did. He couldn't even remember the last time he had spoken with a female, and anyway, the conversations rarely lasted long before Mort(e) would excuse himself.

This dog was a warrior like him. She wore the gray sash of a lieutenant. Her jaw was locked shut. Her eyes were focused like a cat's, squinting and dry, the pupils constricted in the morning light. She was mud brown all over, with a muzzle that suggested that she was a half-bred pit bull. A scar drew a jagged pink line from her mouth and along the left side of her face, almost to her eye.

"Captain Mort(e)?" she asked.

"You have found him," Mort(e) replied.

"I am Lieutenant Wawa. This is Specialist Bonaparte."

Mort(e) smiled. "Napoleon was already taken?" he asked.

"Many times over," the pig said.

"He said you were a bit of a wise guy," Wawa said.

"Who?"

"Colonel Culdesac."

The name still popped into Mort(e)'s mind on occasion, rolling around until it lost all meaning. Until he stopped hearing Culdesac's raspy voice in his head.

"He's a colonel now?" Mort(e) asked. "Who died?"

The pig snorted. He wiped his snout and coughed in order to pretend he hadn't laughed.

"The colonel requests your presence. There is a situation at the quarry."

A situation. Requests your presence. It was funny how this dog could make such meaningless words sound so serious. Mort(e) explained he was retired. She responded by saying that his full security clearance with the Red Sphinx had been reinstated. It was part of the handover.

"What handover?" he asked.

Surprised he didn't know, Wawa explained that the Red Sphinx was taking command of the sector from the regular army. This was more than a little strange. The Red Sphinx were not constables. They were assassins, reporting directly to the Colony. Mort(e) supposed that the Queen had no better use for these killing machines, now that the biggest concerns involved building roads and fixing the pipes.

"I'll pass," Mort(e) said.

"I'm afraid not," Wawa said.

Mort(e) stepped toward her, allowing the door to shut behind him. "You're *afraid* not?" he asked. "Are you going to shoot me if I don't comply?"

"Chokers," the pig said under his breath, shaking his head.

"We won't shoot you," Wawa said. "But I have been instructed to give you a message from the colonel in the event that you refused to cooperate."

"What's the message?"

"He said, 'You were right.'"

"Did he tell you what was I right about?"

"He said that you would know. But you have to see it for yourself."

Culdesac must have predicted this exact moment while Wawa stood at attention at his desk. *He'll say yes*, the colonel probably said, sneering. *He can't hide in that house forever.* However Culdesac phrased it, Mort(e) knew that he had no choice but to go with these strangers. He also had nothing better to do. The square of sunlight would be there when he returned.

"Let me get my things," he said, even though he did not really have anything to bring along, save for a wrinkled captain's sash that would not impress anyone.

MORT(E) SAT IN the middle of the rear seat, while Bonaparte drove and Wawa flipped through a stack of papers on her lap. The steering wheel had large indentations in it so that Bonaparte could rotate it with his hooves—a neat little innovation. Mort(e) had never visited the quarry before, though he had seen it detailed on a map: a hole in the ground right beside the highway, surrounded by a poster-laden wooden fence. A new mining project had begun there a month earlier.

They drove by people fixing up old homes. A crew of rodents painted a house at the end of the Martinis' street. They had white droplets on their fur and wore polarized goggles to protect their light-sensitive eyes. They were probably all relatives, a family of rats who found employment that introduced them to the surface world, where they repaired the same houses they would have loved to gnaw apart before the Change.

Mort(e) asked Wawa where she was posted. She told him that most of her work these days involved civilian policing. There was not much to be done: a few minor disagreements over property lines, fender benders (due to the paucity of actual driving lessons), noise complaints (usually from people who lived next door to dogs). Wawa rolled her eyes as she talked about how canines often failed to control their howling. She seemed disappointed in her own kind for not rising to her level of discipline.

Public drunkenness, she explained, had shifted from an occasional oddity to a regular nuisance. Many new homeowners explored the mysterious liquor cabinets left behind by former occupants. Despite all the warnings the animals had received in the refugee camps, many decided that they were tough enough to experiment with a little Southern Comfort or Cabernet Sauvignon. The administrators at Mort(e)'s refugee camp even showed a prewar "viral" video of some teenage humans feeding beer to a dog and laughing maniacally while the poor animal stumbled into walls and down a flight of steps. It had reportedly been viewed over forty-seven million times.

Wawa began the story of a cow who had used a straw to slurp some Jack Daniels and then got her head stuck between a pair of fence posts. Here, Bonaparte let out a brief snort. At first Mort(e) thought that this was a sign of disgust. Then he noticed the smell, strong enough to make him sit upright in an effort to find pure air. But it was useless. The stench was everywhere. Wawa stopped talking and held her hands over her nose. It was the unmistakable scent of death and decay, the same that had filled the streets in the days after the attack on his old neighborhood. Daniel's corpse must have contributed to it, along with Sheba's.

"Is this what I was right about?" Mort(e) asked.

Wawa nodded, her eyes watering. A little whimper slipped out from her muzzle.

Two dog soldiers opened the gate to the quarry and let the Humvee enter. Inside, troops of every species lined the edge of the pit, staring into it, some shaking their heads. Many covered their snouts with scarves or some other fabric. Whatever was in the bottom of the quarry released a cloud so toxic that Mort(e) almost expected to *see* it.

An orange cat ran in front of the vehicle, frantically gesturing for Bonaparte to steer the vehicle to the right.

"You're driving on the tracks, you pig!" the cat said.

Bonaparte parked the Humvee beside a row of trucks. As the

vehicle turned, Mort(e) noticed why the cat was so excited: a trail of hoof prints, perhaps twenty feet wide, led straight into the pit.

When Mort(e) exited the Humvee, the stench enveloped him like a waxy second skin. He felt the urge to lick himself clean. Wawa kept her paw over her nose.

"Do you see him?" Bonaparte asked.

It was impossible to miss Culdesac looming over the others. As he approached his old friend, Mort(e) could not resist peeking into the pit. A trio of dogs let out mournful howls. Mort(e) was about to tell them to shut up. Then he peered over someone's shoulder.

At the bottom of the quarry lay a herd of deer, all dead, piled like dolls, bristling with antlers. Their bodies had been elongated by the biological processes of the Change, while their bellies had swollen with the putrid gases building inside them. A black mist floated above them, and for a second Mort(e) supposed that this was the stink personified. It was instead a fluid swarm of flies gorging on the dead. The slightest breeze caused them to buzz away and then return, so that the scene resembled the snow on a television screen. Glistening, lifeless eyes stared at Mort(e) through the horde of insects, accusing, pleading, asking questions that could not be answered. The great accomplishment that took the ants millennia to achieve had thrown itself off a cliff.

To Mort(e)'s left, a rat began to vomit. His comrades laughed.

"I thought you'd be used to this!" someone said.

"It's not the smell," the rat said. "It's the flies. I hate the flies." He coughed and spat.

"It's a good thing the Colony didn't make the flies smart," a dog said. "Then they might realize that they eat nothing but corpses and shit."

Culdesac, Mort(e) noticed, had turned to see the commotion. The bobcat straightened up, recognizing his friend, his disciple, his apprentice. Mort(e) walked toward him. A cat was in the middle of asking the colonel a question, but stopped when she realized that he wasn't listening. Culdesac extended his paw to Mort(e).

Mort(e) punched the colonel on the bridge of his nose. Culdesac had always told him, *Don't aim for the face. Aim for the back of the head. Imagine your fist going through your enemy's brain, dragging the bone and flesh with it.*

In less than a second, guns pointed at Mort(e) from every direction. Shiny barrels glinted inches from his face. He followed each of them to their owners: the slitted eyes of a cat, the beady eyes of a rodent, the soft, wet eyes of a dog.

"Lower your weapons," Culdesac said. He scrunched his nose to confirm that it wasn't broken. "Do it," he said.

The rifles descended.

"That means you, Lieutenant," Culdesac said.

Wawa holstered her gun. She didn't seem to like that. Mort(e) understood—there had been a time when he would have ripped out the throat of anyone who failed to make proper eye contact with Culdesac.

"Don't you all know who this is?" the colonel asked. "This is Mort(e). The hero of the Battle of the Alleghenies. The Mastermind of the Chesapeake Bridge Bombing. The crazy bastard who assassinated General Fitzpatrick in broad daylight. This choker was killing humans before some of you were born."

For once, Mort(e) appreciated the choker comment. It lowered expectations for him.

"So you got my message," Culdesac said, leaning in. "Congratulations. I didn't call you the smartest for nothing."

"Just tell me why you brought me here," Mort(e) said.

"Isn't this what you wanted?" Culdesac asked. "If memory serves me, I couldn't stop you and Tiberius from snooping around a place like this."

"Tiberius is dead, Colonel."

Culdesac nodded. He scanned the soldiers until he picked out a dog who was taking photos of the deer. "Have you got all the pictures you need, Private?"

"Yes, sir."

"Good," Culdesac said. "All right, everyone, clean it up."

Several lackeys began barking orders at their own lackeys, and within seconds the crowd buzzed with activity again. Flat-bed trucks moved to the edge of the pit, while soldiers wearing hazmat suits rappelled into the quarry.

Culdesac motioned for Mort(e) and Wawa to walk with him. Mort(e) glanced at Bonaparte standing beside the Humvee, unaffected by the excitement. Grinning, the pig made a punching motion with his hoof.

The three made their way over to a hastily erected tent. Culdesac brought them over to a table covered with papers, each containing jargon that was of no interest to Mort(e). A mug of cold coffee acted as a paperweight. Most animals despised the stuff, especially those who had lived in the wild. It was said that they never needed a stimulant because they so often lived in fear for their lives. But for whatever reason, Culdesac had acquired a taste for it. Perhaps he was finally slowing down and needed something to compensate.

Culdesac picked up one of the documents and spread it out on the table. It was a map of the area, marked up with red Xs and other notations.

"I didn't call you the first time it happened," Culdesac said. "Even though I knew then that something wasn't right."

"There have been other suicides?" Mort(e) asked.

"I wish they were only suicides."

Suicide and murder were supposed to be relics of the past, such as wars, superstition, beauty magazines, reality television, and every other corrupt outgrowth of human civilization. The ants killed themselves only in service to the Colony, including, according to legend, the Queen's own mother. But even sacrifices like that were rare nowadays.

"Lieutenant Wawa has been leading the investigation," Culdesac said. He nodded to her, and she stepped forward.

The Red Sphinx had received reports of people exhibiting the physical symptoms of the virus, she said. So far, no one tested positive. Her unit was monitoring the situation, ordering blood tests for every neighborhood where symptoms had been found. But the cases of unusual behavior were even more alarming, and more unpredictable.

"There was a family of cats not too far from your house," Wawa said, pointing to an X on the map. "They all hung themselves. There was also a mother rat who killed herself after drowning several of her children. These weren't veterans who were traumatized by the war." With this, she winced and said, "No offense." Mort(e) asked her to continue. The parents had worked for the Bureau, she said, and the children were going to attend school later in the year.

"And then over here," she continued, tracing a line on the map with her brown fingernail. "Murder-suicide. A dog—a sanitation worker—stabbed his next-door neighbor, poisoned his mate and two pups, then ate the poison himself."

"You think these incidents and the reports of infection are related?"

"Yes," she said. "I just can't prove it."

"So everyone isn't as pleased with the big Change as

they're supposed to be," Mort(e) said. "What does this have to do with me?"

"It all started when you moved into the neighborhood," she said.

"I want you to be honest with me," Culdesac said, "Has anything unusual happened since you came home?"

Before the bobcat even finished his question, the image of the graffiti appeared before Mort(e)'s eyes, throbbing with each beat of his heart.

"No," he lied. "I've been fixing up the place, removing some of the human junk. I haven't noticed anything."

"Mort(e)," Culdesac said. "You realize the implications of this better than anyone."

"Of course. But what did the Queen expect? She killed billions of people and turned everything upside down and then thought we would all be grateful for it."

"We *should* be grateful," Culdesac said. "We were slaves—"

"Oh, give it a rest," Mort(e) said. "You don't think we're slaves *now*?"

"We are the masters of this planet—"

"If you need the Queen's permission to be a master, then you're really a slave."

"If I may," Wawa cut in. "Mort(e), everyone admires your work. But I know your story. The therapist in the camp said that you had unresolved issues from the Change. You're in the same condition now as when the colonel found you. What was it you were doing at the time? Shouting a dead person's name?"

"Oh, right," Culdesac said. "Sheba. Have you heard from her lately?"

Mort(e) was about to say *maybe*, but thought better of it. "Well, if I'm such a basket case," he said, "then why give me security clearance?"

"Wasn't my decision," Culdesac said. "The Colony gave the order."

It was odd enough that the Colony had brought in Culdesac's team. Now they were helping him micromanage personnel.

"Do you think they forgot your little stunt during the war?" Culdesac said. "Like you said, Tiberius is dead, and you're the closest thing to an expert around here. They thought you could help. And that you would keep your mouth shut. And that you wouldn't be surprised by what you saw."

"I'm never surprised," Mort(e) said.

"Maybe you're right," Culdesac said. "Maybe these anomalies are a reversion to the old ways. I'm hoping it's a temporary phase as we sort things out."

"Or it's EMSAH," Mort(e) said.

This struck a nerve with Culdesac. He squinted his bright eyes and said, "Be careful with how you use that word around here—"

"What, EMSAH?" Mort(e) said, louder this time.

"Officially, this is part of the standard security procedures for a new settlement," Culdesac said. "Unofficially, I share the lieutenant's concern. I have to. It's my job."

Mort(e) tried to think of how Tiberius would have handled this. He probably would have pointed out that EMSAH made people do, say, and believe illogical things, but that it was rare for the virus to drive someone to suicide before any other symptoms arose. If these deer had EMSAH, they would be in no position to organize and execute such a spectacle. But it also made sense that the virus would mutate, adapt, and attack in new, unheard-of ways. That was the nature of viruses.

"Relax, Colonel," Mort(e) said. "We'd be quarantined by now if there were an outbreak."

"We'll be calling on you in a few days," Wawa said. "But if you see anything, I want you to call me here."

"Right," Mort(e) said. "If you see something, say something."

As she handed him a card with her information, a dog arrived at the entrance to the tent. She was a Labrador, too young to remember the war. Mort(e) could always tell with these young ones. Their eyes were innocent, and they didn't keep their heads on a swivel. But there was something else. This soldier was clearly spooked by something. She panted, trying her best to keep her stupid tongue in her mouth. "Sir, I'm sorry to interrupt," she said.

Culdesac and Wawa turned to the young recruit, who saluted diligently. "What is it?" Wawa asked.

"The envoy from the Colony is here."

Culdesac rubbed his hands together and nodded. "Tell Bonaparte to get the device," he said. The dog left, the flap of the tent swaying behind her.

"Well, Mort(e)," Culdesac said, "you get to see me kiss some abdomen again."

They stepped outside. Standing before them were two Alpha soldiers, side by side, perfectly rigid. Even their antennae were still. And the compound eyes—half-globes protruding from their enormous heads—pointed in hundreds of directions. Mort(e) could never be sure that he was outside of their gaze.

At the foot of each soldier was a pool of swarming ants, the regular-sized ones, who gathered information about the terrain that the larger soldiers could miss. Ultimately, the Alphas' orders came from the smaller sisters. Culdesac often compared the Alphas to giant remote-controlled robots. "Their brains might be a potato with wires attached to it," he once said.

Bonaparte arrived with the device cradled in his short, plump arms. This model was more advanced than the one used by the Great Dane at the most recent Purge. The devices were so important—and so classified—that every unit had a designated soldier to guard it. This translator was basically a helmet made of some kind of organic material fashioned by the Colonial scientist guild. If it had been made from bits of dead Alpha soldiers who had willingly sacrificed themselves, Mort(e) would not have been surprised.

While the ants stood there like a pair of icons, Culdesac placed the device on his oversized head. It barely fit. The antenna poked into the sky. A mouthpiece hovered over his whiskers.

"Get back to work," Wawa yelled to her soldiers. Most of them had stopped what they were doing to watch their great leader speak to the ants. It took months of training for an officer to use a translator. Only a well-prepared mind could interpret, store, and retrieve what was needed from the data stream without becoming like a teacup underneath a waterfall. Many animals aged prematurely and suffered immense physical pain and mental degradation by using the device. Even so, they were probably smarter now than any human who had ever lived.

Mort(e) tried to get closer so he could hear the alien voice coming through the speaker. Wawa's paw on his arm stopped him.

"Leave them be," she said, as protective as a mother canine. He figured that she must have been one of the old bobcat's projects, as he had once been.

Apparently finished with the exchange, Culdesac got the attention of one of the sergeants, a dog wearing a surgical mask. The colonel twirled his finger, indicating that they should wrap things up. The sergeant nodded.

Suddenly the ants came to life. Moving in unison, they faced one another and touched antennae, their abdomens throbbing. With their smaller sisters surrounding them, the Alphas walked off, leaving Culdesac standing there. Bonaparte was already at his side to retrieve the translator.

"Ready to watch the future?" Culdesac asked Mort(e).

Moments later, the Alphas returned, this time with at least twenty more behind them. The procession made its way to the quarry in the same single-file formation the ants had used in the quarantined settlement years earlier. The sergeant frantically ordered the animals to stay clear. The soldiers who had rappelled into the pit scrambled up the rock face and scurried away as the ants arrived at the lip of the quarry. The creatures climbed down the side, their claws latching into the rock.

"Are they going to disinfect?" Mort(e) asked Culdesac.

"They're recycling."

Mort(e) let out a cynical snort.

"What?" Culdesac said. "You've seen this before. Do you want these corpses stinking up the place?"

Minutes later, the antlers of a dead deer appeared over the edge, the body clamped in the unforgiving jaws of an Alpha. Soon more of them arose, each carrying a corpse. The ants' footsteps landed in the exact same spots, leaving behind only a single pair of tracks. The line headed out of the gate, marching to the nearest ziggurat.

Wawa began talking again about where Mort(e) should start with his investigation. But Mort(e) could not stop himself from staring into each pair of blank eyes, asking them to explain what he was doing here.

CHAPTER EIGHT
THE STORY OF CULDESAC

ULDESAC HAD NEVER seen a person skinned alive before. He had glimpsed corpses in various states of disrepair and decomposition: blown to pieces, riddled with bullets, vaporized, decapitated, incinerated, devoured, digested. But this was new even to his old eyes.

When Culdesac got the phone call requesting his presence, the soldier on the other end of the line did not even know how to describe the crime scene. "It's a house with a spire on it, sir," the cat had said. "A big, pointy tower." Culdesac asked who knew about the incident. The soldier answered that it was only Culdesac and another officer so far, a Lieutenant Sultan. This was good. At least the Red Sphinx was on the scene first, without interference from the klutzes in the regular army. There was still time to contain this latest spectacle.

Culdesac arrived to find two soldiers in full hazmat suits standing guard. He asked them if they had been inside. Only the lieutenant had entered, they said. Culdesac nodded and told them to return to the barracks. After trading a brief glance, they obeyed without question.

Culdesac could smell the blood emanating from the building. He smelled humans, too. He decided to keep that to himself.

He put on his own suit—with his gun belt on the outside, out of habit—and took the steps to the basement. Lanterns powered by a generator lit up the room. Standing in the ball of light, Sultan took photos of the victim. Culdesac recognized the lieutenant's charcoal-colored face through the plastic mask. Sultan saluted and continued with his work. In the corner, lying in a sticky pool of blood, was the pinkish hulk of a raccoon. Its eyeballs were an obscene white against its glistening flesh. The body had fallen after being strung up. Culdesac noticed a frayed rope hanging from the rafters, where the creature had been tied by its hind legs—the proper way to skin an animal.

"They must have left in a hurry," Sultan said, still snapping photos. "Had to leave the body hanging."

"They didn't come for the body," Culdesac said.

He explained that the perpetrators had suspended the raccoon upside down and tied the legs as far apart as they would go. Then, with a sharp knife, they'd sliced the skin at the ankles and run the blade from the legs to the tail, down the spine, past the shoulders and the skull. The butcher eventually worked the fur away from the eyes, nose, and mouth, and continued cutting up the gut until the entire sheath came loose like a sopping wet blanket. Culdesac remembered reading all this in an old hunting manual. Of course, he did not read it in the proper sense. The book was part of the store of knowledge that Culdesac gained through the translator.

Accessing these "files" was sometimes thrilling, often depressing, and occasionally distracting if he did not control it. In order to make it through the translation sessions, he would have to think of a time before the war. He would think of the hunt, of traveling with his people and searching for prey. Everyone who used a translator had to think of something peaceful to set their minds at ease. It kept them sane, or as close to sanity as could be expected.

Culdesac missed the hunt.

This skinned animal was merely the latest case of EMSAH. Still, the Queen held off the quarantine. She had plans for the sector. For him. For the Red Sphinx. For Mort(e), Wawa, all of them. Through sheer luck—and stubborn, relentless curiosity on the part of the ants—this settlement had become the center-piece of the Queen's experiment. It was the courtroom where the trial of the animals would take place. And for carrying this burden of knowledge, the Queen rewarded Culdesac with promotions and power.

"We found some contraband in the other corner, sir," Sultan said.

A table stood against the wall, a green cloth draped over it. Embroidered on the cloth were a cross, a crescent moon, and a six-pointed star. Empty wine bottles rested on the table. They may have been cheap before the war, but now they were almost certainly priceless. A few droplets of blood had dried on the fabric. When the perpetrators had opened the animal's arteries, the blood probably squirted farther than they had anticipated.

With the camera snapping behind him, Culdesac began leaf-ing through the yellowed pages. It was a King James Bible. He knew exactly where in the book to turn. At the end, after Rev-elation, were several new chapters stapled into the spine. This particular book had been a hasty patchwork. The new chap-ters were typed on computer paper, in a word-processing font. The extra sections had names like, "The Story of the Prophet Muhammad, the Son of Jesus" and "The Book of Exile" and "The Gospel of St. Francis." That last one, Culdesac remembered, was about a man who made peace with the animals. The humans were creating new mythologies to explain what had happened to them, and to bring together different cults that had previ-ously been opposed to one another. To Culdesac, these dogmas were merely fantasies merged with other fantasies, embellished with half-truths, reinterpreted, mistranslated, misremembered, and sold at a profit to those who could not afford it.

Turning the pages, Culdesac noticed a thin red cloth marking a chapter titled "The Warrior and the Mother." The ants made him "read" this file in one of the translation sessions. It was the story of a child prophet held prisoner on the Island. The prophet had visions of the animals and humans one day making peace and fighting against the Queen. Whenever Culdesac found one of these forbidden texts, this chapter was always the last, and the pages were always dog-eared and worn yellow by the grease of human fingertips. The humans liked it. Some traitorous, confused animals liked it, too.

"Poor bastard," Sultan mumbled behind him. "They probably read from that crazy book while they did this to him." Sultan had finished. There were only so many photos of a dead animal one could take.

The colonel considered the book and the wine once more. Then he abruptly removed his helmet.

"Sir, no!" Sultan said.

"It's all right," Culdesac said. Standing over the carcass, he inhaled, letting the blood and rot fill his nostrils. But he also smelled the wine. "He volunteered for it."

"What?"

"The wine wasn't part of their ritual," Culdesac said. "It was an anesthetic. Probably the only one they had."

"But he was skinned *alive*," Sultan said. "Why wouldn't they kill him first?"

"They wanted the fur," Culdesac said. "If they had killed him, it would have changed the odor of the pelt. Then they wouldn't be able to use it as a disguise."

Sultan looked like he was about to throw up. "So—"

"So they kept him alive for as long as they could," Culdesac said. "He sacrificed himself. That's what EMSAH can do in extreme cases. I'll bet he was still breathing when they finished, if the butcher was skilled enough."

"I've heard of infected people banding together, hiding out," Sultan said. "But animals working with humans?"

"Can you blame them?" Culdesac asked. "We would treat an infected animal as an enemy. This superstition is their only recourse."

Sultan needed a moment to take it all in.

"So tell me," Culdesac said. "Did you read the book?"

Sultan was embarrassed. There was no official rule against viewing such material, but an object even touched by a human was often regarded as a possible carrier of EMSAH. "I did, sir."

This was too bad.

"They're clever storytellers, aren't they?" Culdesac said.

"I suppose."

Culdesac asked if the lieutenant had been close to the humans before the war. He already knew the answer. He wanted to hear Sultan say it.

"I was a stray," the lieutenant said.

"So you're like me," Culdesac said. "You didn't have a slave name."

"That's right."

"My real name is unpronounceable," Culdesac said. "And the only ones who could speak it are dead."

Before the war, he said, there was only the hunt. In the wooded hills, far from the nests of the *Homo sapiens*, his people ruled over the other species. Their entire world consisted of scents and sounds and textures and terrain, all leading toward their prey, and then back home. Constant movement, like wind passing over the dirt. Everything in nature willed his people to keep moving. But there was harmony to the violence. The bobcats could not become gods. Those who tried perished.

"The humans tried to destroy it all," Culdesac said. "We couldn't stop them. Only the Colony could."

One by one, he said, the humans chipped away at his people with traps and guns. They encircled the hills and forest until the bobcats turned on one another. Cannibalism, thievery, kidnapping—all the violations of the natural order became the rule of the day. Before long, Culdesac was on his own.

"And then things changed," he said. "We became who we were meant to be."

Culdesac roamed the countryside for days after the Change. He occasionally met his old rivals—cougars, rabbits, deer, now altered themselves. But he was on a new hunt. The humans would be punished for what they had done.

One day, he came across a white wooden building with a great spire mounted on its roof. "Like this one," he said.

He smelled humans inside. He also smelled sweat, urine, blood—scents that indicated fear and despair. The humans had taken refuge in their local church in the hopes of either waiting out the crisis or being saved by their god. After Culdesac attacked and killed one of them, leaving an obscene patch of blood on the church steps, it became clear that the humans were expecting the latter. For them, Culdesac was a demon from hell, come to test their already shaken faith.

They saw only one solution. Appeasement. And so every day at dusk, the humans shoved one of their own out the door, an offering to the beast that walked like a man. Culdesac played along. He was unsure of how the humans decided on who would be next. Drawing lots seemed to be the most sensible course, but it was easy to imagine a cabal of leaders who claimed to speak for a higher power, pointing fingers at the most defenseless among them in order to save their own skins. Many of the sacrificial lambs died while pounding on the door, begging to be let back in. But a few others—much like the deer in the quarry, much like this raccoon—remained still and accepted their fate in the hopes that it would take them to a better world. They took the sport out of the hunt. But they tasted the same.

A swarm of Alphas arrived about a week later, after two girls, two boys, an old woman, and a presumably orphaned baby had been offered up. By then, Culdesac knew about the war, having seen the roadside billboards warning of infestations, along with discarded newspapers that described the progress of the conflict. The Alphas, their exoskeletons crawling with their smaller sisters, invited Culdesac to speak to them through their newly developed translator. While the ability to read was extraordinary, this device was nothing short of miraculous. It allowed him to be a part of the Colony, to join with the Queen and her struggle against humanity. With the translator, he could experience the sisters' hunt with all his senses: relentless marches in Africa and South America, tracking prey from a million different directions with scent, sound, vibrations. Operating as a unit in a way no mammal ever could. The hunt was his safe space. It was the warmth of a long-gone mother he barely remembered. And while he had never lived to impress anyone, he was proud of his ability to master the translator. It was like a second Change, one that transformed him from an animal into a god.

After Culdesac described the situation, the ants huddled, their antennae tapping against one another in deep conversation. PROCEED, they told him. This was an opportunity for research that they could not let pass. He admired their patience and curiosity, virtues he knew he would have to cultivate in this new world. He could hear the echo of the Queen in their instructions. The translator allowed him to feel her beside him, the rumble of her voice traveling through his entire body. She called to him, sometimes as a whisper, sometimes in his dreams. And still other times, he felt as though she possessed him and spoke and acted through him, as though he were some shaman from the forgotten human age. Now that his people were gone, he had given up on finding love or even companionship, and yet she provided something that transcended those petty impulses. Love was restricted to one lifetime. He now had access to millions. Love was driven in part by fear of loneliness. But he would never be alone again. The Queen was with him. She had chosen him from all the others to rise with her into the future. He was an extension of her now. He was her blade slashing at the enemy, her torch banishing the darkness of the shadow of man. Until then, there had been no purpose in his life beyond survival. Now a void had opened inside him and was filled by the omnipresence of Hymenoptera Unus the Magnificent, Daughter of the Misfit. The Devil's Hand.

The human sacrifices went on for five more days. The singing and chanting became louder each time. Culdesac would not relent. Meanwhile, the ants observed from afar. The humans, Culdesac thought, must have rationalized each new offering. *This will be the last*, they probably told one another. *How much more must we give?* And when it continued, when Culdesac brazenly walked by the windows, his sinister eyes peering in at the people as they danced and prayed, they must have reasoned, *We are still not showing enough faith. We must try harder.*

On the fifth day, the survivors made a run for it, only to be surrounded by Alpha soldiers. The ants offered the final delicacies to Culdesac, but he declined. They were unworthy prey. As he suspected, the survivors were old men—the church elders—who had managed to stay alive by convincing the others that their god wanted younger, weaker ones as sacrifices. Through the translator, the Queen had told him it would be like this. She had seen far worse.

"So," Culdesac told Sultan, "everything you have heard about the humans is true. They'll approach you with delightful little stories, and then they'll do this to you," he said, pointing at the raccoon.

As good as it felt to tell that story, he could see that it had the opposite effect on Sultan. The cat was mortified, eager to leave.

"Let's go," Culdesac said. "I'll send word to the Colony to destroy this place."

He gestured for Sultan to go first. As the cat passed, Culdesac pulled his pistol from his holster and shot the lieutenant in the back of the head. Blood sprayed out of his mouth. The cat went stiff and fell to the ground like a board of wood. Culdesac knelt down and patted the lieutenant on the shoulder. Sultan had felt no pain, nor did he realize that his own commanding officer had turned on him.

Now that Mort(e) would be investigating, Culdesac hoped that he would never have to do this again. Unless, of course, Mort(e) and the rest of Wellbeing did not do what the Queen expected of them. If things strayed from her plan, then everything was in jeopardy—not only Wellbeing, but the entire experiment with the surface dwellers.

"Thanks for listening," Culdesac whispered. He shut off the lights and walked out.

PART III CONTACT

CHAPTER NINE
THE STORY OF WAWA

AWA NEVER LEARNED the name of the man who owned her before everything changed. But she hoped he was dead or dying somewhere. Preferably the latter, in some dank cave where the last of the humans waited out their final days. And she hoped that he saw her scarred face in his dreams, and that he wanted to remember her name but couldn't, and that it drove him mad. He deserved to know that he had failed to break her. He deserved to be afraid.

Wawa didn't have time to be dwelling on these things again. It was late, and she had work to do. The only light in her cramped room at the barracks came from an old computer salvaged from the rubble, displaying a spreadsheet that detailed every possible EMSAH infection in the sector. Mort(e)'s investigation had begun, and she had to record his findings. If this was an EMSAH outbreak, then it was spreading so fast that the Red Sphinx would soon need an army of investigators to sort through everything. Of course, she could not yet use the word *EMSAH*, not even in the filename. In keeping with the gag order, she described the cases in numbingly bland prose: "Thor (canine, 12). Murdered by neighbor, Averroes (canine, 10). Altercation began Y9 7.3. Assailant stabbed victim; later poisoned family at dinner (mate, two pups); committed suicide." There was still a blank cell where she would have to write an equally flat assessment of the deer suicides. It was almost a relief to hear reported cases of biological symptoms. At least they were more predictable. But they had turned up negative in every suspected case so far. Now anyone with an abnormally long cold was being tested.

Though she had heard about settlements that had been erased from the map, she had not witnessed the process in real time. "Think of it as a test," Culdesac told her. Everything was a test to him, including Wawa's initiation into the Red Sphinx. He had toured the refugee camp where she lived, searching for new recruits. After being told they were drafting only cats, Wawa challenged the newest members to a fight. It was three against one. Wawa held her own against them until Culdesac consented to let her join, making her the first canine in the squad. The others were stunned. "You owe me," Culdesac reminded her, "and you will pay up."

Upon hearing the story of her slave days, Culdesac nodded and smiled. "You should be grateful," he said. "Grateful to be alive. Grateful that your master gave you this rage that you've harnessed. That is who you are. That is your strength. You have to let it burn inside you. Never let it go out. And then you'll be your own master."

The colonel was the only other person at the base who was still awake. From her window, Wawa could see a light in his office. That damned coffee was keeping him up, along with a host of worries she was not supposed to know about. Instead of coffee, it was the expression on Mort(e)'s face earlier that day that kept her from sleeping. When she had pointed her gun at him. He thought that he was better than her. He was the bravest. Culdesac's favorite—something neither she nor her comrades could ever hope to be. She had to listen to all the stories of Mort(e)'s exploits, told by drunk, arrogant cats who thought that she wasn't qualified to be a member of their little Red Sphinx club.

If he only knew what she was before all this.

Before the Change, her only reason for living was to make her master rich, while the canines around her suffered unspeakably, lived meaninglessly, and died horribly. Even now, after surviving so much, she could not shake the feeling that things could return to the way they were, and she would suddenly find herself trapped in her old life, realizing that the war had been a dream.

She could remember the litter of puppies, her brothers and sisters huddled together, hiding from the cold and the light. Then they were all separated, her mother included. Everyone was confined to cages facing a white stucco wall. Wawa could hear her siblings, along with many others, squealing above, beside, and beneath her. She tried to talk to them, but her voice died out amidst the shouts bouncing off the wall. Every once in a while, an overhead fluorescent light would turn on. Her master would enter, usually to feed everyone. He was shorter than most men, always dressed in a tracksuit—pants and jacket in matching colors, a white stripe traveling from his shoulders down to his ankles. A bucket hat or a baseball cap covered his shaved head. He called her Jenna. Years later, after giving up on finding out his name, Wawa began to refer to him simply as Tracksuit.

When she was older, her master and some of his friends would take her out of the cage and into a yard along with the other dogs. It was so bright that her eyes felt as though they would burst. Her nose and ears tingled with unfamiliar sensory input: grass, dirt, leaves, wood, concrete, rusty metal, rope, tiny armored creatures that crawled on the ground, distant elegant monsters that glided in the sky above. The master leashed the dogs to a row of dying trees, which allowed them to get close to one another without touching. Other humans would arrive. These visitors—almost always young men—would gawk at the dogs, occasionally nodding in approval. Sometimes they would even point and smile at her. She barked at them as loud as she could to show them that she would protect her master. They would smile more, as if she had performed some trick on command. The men inspected the animals, squeezing their hind legs, holding their jaws and examining the teeth. Sometimes, after a lengthy inspection, they would take one of the dogs away. In the yard, Wawa learned the names of the others in her pack. Rommel, a brown dog who fought with the others whenever he got loose. Hector, a younger one, very agile and fast. Kai, another female who wheezed when she growled.

One evening, Tracksuit placed Wawa and three other dogs in cages and loaded them into the rear of a windowless van. She recognized her companions: Baron, Ajax, and an older one, Cyrus. He had a whitish coat with a few black splotches. His mottled tail and missing left ear suggested that he had been defending the pack for many years, second in command only to Tracksuit. He could quiet the others with a mere grumbling in his throat. One time, he protected Kai from Rommel, reminding the others who was in charge. He was the elder, the strongest among them. He would drink first from the trough in the yard and got the largest share of the food.

Wawa could not take her eyes from Cyrus as he sat in his cage, scratching himself, unburdened by what took place around him. After the van arrived at its destination, Tracksuit and his friend opened the door and led the animals out one at a time. The landscape was much different from the one outside her master's house. The ground was flat, rough, and hard. Tall poles held lights that hung over a vast empty space. In one direction, a highway stretched into the distance. In the other was a square building, the front of which glowed blindingly white through giant windows. Inside, the linoleum floor reflected the light like the surface of a puddle. Brightly colored cans, bags, and boxes lined the shelves. A man stood behind a counter, eyeing Tracksuit suspiciously. At the top of the building, looming over it, were glowing red objects braced to the wall with bolts and bent into shapes Wawa did not recognize.

Behind the building, the parking lot ended at a wooded area. A row of trash cans, fragrant with a week's worth of garbage, concealed a dirt trail into the forest. Wawa followed, her senses alert. In the failing light, Tracksuit's outfit went from a navy blue to black.

The trail snaked its way to a house painted a dull green color to blend in. The curtains were drawn. Tracksuit knocked, and the door opened, releasing the sound of hundreds of voices along with the smell of smoke, alcohol, and sweat. Once inside, Wawa was lost in a moving forest of legs. Few of the people seemed to notice her arrival. Instead, the crowd circled around an arena in which a man stood. There was a wall that rose as high as the man's waist. On the other side of the wall, Wawa could hear the unmistakable sound of two dogs thrashing at each other. A head and a tail peeked above the lip of the barrier. Each yelp from the combatants drew cheers from the spectators. Before she could get a better view, Tracksuit pulled her into another smoky room where four men sat around a table. Each wore a long white T-shirt that went almost down to the knees, along with baggy jeans and high-top sneakers. Glowing cigarettes hung from their lips. One of them had a porkpie hat and wraparound sunglasses. He did not speak much, but the others were quiet and attentive when he did. Wawa had been trained to be silent, but she wanted to warn Tracksuit that these men were enemies from another pack, constantly encircling them. She could smell it on them. And she could detect the anxiety seeping through her master's sweaty outfit.

Tracksuit left the room, leaving Wawa alone to keep an eye on these predators. Minutes later he returned, holding Cyrus on a leash. Wawa was so overjoyed that she began to jump up and down, unafraid to bark at her friend. She stopped when she sensed the men walking past her. Each took a turn petting her. The man with the porkpie hat was last. With a meaty hand, he lifted his sunglasses to reveal two enormous eyes, one of which had a brown iris. The other was shaded over with a milky cataract. He smiled, exposing teeth that were the same off-white color as the diseased eyeball. He patted her scalp and left the room.

The men took seats in the front row of the arena. By then, Tracksuit had positioned Cyrus in one corner. Another dog owner—a fat man with a pit-stained T-shirt—brought his own warrior into the ring, a gray mutt. Both masters carefully washed the dogs using a bucket and a sponge placed in the middle of the floor. Cyrus's tongue bobbed up and down while Tracksuit wiped his fur with a waffled towel.

The referee inspected the animals. He was a squat little thing with a goatee and a buzzed haircut. He resembled a dog himself. Cyrus sniffed him. *I can inspect you, too*, he seemed to be saying. The arena grew quiet, prompting Wawa to stop barking. Several people whispered into the ear of the man with the porkpie hat. He nodded, the fluorescent lights reflecting off his sunglasses.

And then it began. The two dogs charged each other, colliding in the center of the ring, snapping, growling, twisting about until they no longer resembled living things but malfunctioning machines leaking fluid. Cyrus attacked deliberately, while the other dog seemed unable to help himself. He clawed at Cyrus, spraying foamy saliva with each bark.

It wasn't long before the gray dog made a mistake and allowed Cyrus to corner him. The older dog pinned him and bit his leg, tearing open the skin. After that, the gray dog was on the defensive. His wounded leg left bloody footprints, and a cut slashed across his face from his snout to his right eye. Through the cigarettes and spilled beer, Wawa picked up the bitter scent of it. Cyrus was exhausted but had the upper hand. He took swipes at his opponent, provoking helpless squeals from the gray dog. Cyrus did not need to kill this mutt, but he would if he had to.

Before he could finish the job, Cyrus froze, his ears pinned to his skull. While the crowd exhorted him, Cyrus barked at them, telling them to shut up and listen. Wawa heard it, too: something was approaching the building. Tires crunching the dirt. Footsteps and whispers. The smell of rubber and gasoline. Wawa let out a warning bark of her own. A malevolent presence surrounded the house.

A man rushed into the arena. He clapped three times. The sound cut through the din of the spectators. Everyone rose from their seats and headed toward the rear exit in a thunderous stampede of shoes and sneakers. Tracksuit pushed his way through the crowd. Wawa barked, pleading for him to let her loose so she could run with the others, with Cyrus. He told her to shut up, a phrase she knew very well. As he untied the leash, the front door of the building burst open. The evacuation became more frantic. Everyone was shouting. Men in matching blue suits and hats entered through the front door, all pointing metal objects and barking like dogs themselves.

Tracksuit pulled Wawa into the meeting room and slammed the door. Thinking she needed to protect her master, Wawa growled at the door as the men tried to batter it down. With another tug of the leash, Tracksuit directed her to a window. Opening it, he ordered her to jump out. When she hesitated, he cursed, picked her up, and shoved her through. The wooden frame clipped one of her vertebrae. She managed to land on her feet. Tracksuit squeezed out and landed behind her.

Seconds later, they were running, the trail and the trees jostling with each breathless step. Tracksuit stumbled a few times. The noises and the scents of the building receded. Though she was more tired than she had ever been, Wawa kept up with the dirt-caked pant legs of her master as they trudged deeper into the woods.

They made it to the trail, which eventually returned them to the hard, flat surface. The sun was rising. The building where Wawa had seen the strange red shapes seemed to be sleeping, the glow now dull. The van was where they had left it. Tracksuit knocked on the window. His friend was napping in the driver's seat. It took another knock to wake him up. The men spoke briefly. Then Tracksuit took Wawa around the truck and opened the sliding door. Cyrus was inside, sitting in his cage calmly like a sphinx. The other dogs were gone, lost in the confusion.

Tracksuit did not need to tell Wawa to get in. She went straight for Cyrus, sniffing him, licking his face and the base of ears through the metal bars. Cyrus reciprocated by snapping playfully at her. Through sheer will, he had defied the men who had descended from the night sky. He had survived the battle and found his way through the forest to where the sun rose peacefully. It was then that Wawa felt the primal urge of her species: to be a part of his pack, to be one of his people. To hunt with him, to taste blood and share it. To roam the forests, meadows, and mountains, claiming territory for her clan. To huddle together under the night sky in defiance of the cold, without cages to separate them. She would still die for her master, but she belonged out in the wild, without a rope tied to her neck, without canned food served in a child's bowl. It was Cyrus who made her realize that she had been in a cell, and that the love and protection that Tracksuit bestowed upon her was somehow an illusion. She did not understand it yet, and the thought often fell out of her primitive brain whenever she felt the need to bark, eat, or piss. But the seed took root, and it sustained her through the worst times of her life. Even before the ants began their experiment, Cyrus showed her that there was such a thing as freedom.

On the way home, Wawa pledged her life to Cyrus. She would die for him if she had to. And she would kill.

"LUFF-TENANT," SOMEONE SAID. Wawa knew right away that it was Archer, a raccoon who had followed Culdesac's soldiers around for days before the colonel finally relented and allowed him to join the Red Sphinx. Archer insisted on using the weird British pronunciation of Wawa's rank. When asked why he spoke the way he did, he claimed that he hid in the basement of the main branch of the New York Public Library after Manhattan was evacuated. He spent months learning the classics, watching documentary filmstrips, learning things that the ants could not program into his brain. Wawa had once seen him pick a bullet out of his thigh with his claws, wipe his hands on his tail, and keep fighting. He had earned the right to be a little snooty. Even though he still ate trash on occasion—a trusty survival skill, she had to admit.

"What is it?" she asked.

"First of all," he began, "I should point out that this is not in jest."

"Go on."

"I saw a human."

Wawa lifted her hands from the keyboard and swiveled her

chair to face him. She wrinkled her nose and tried to think of what to say.

"I would not play games with this," Archer said. "Certainly not at this hour."

"Where did you see the human?"

"Bonaparte and I were on our way to the supply depot near the creek. The pig pulled over to urinate about a quarter of a mile north of the quarry. There was a man standing nearby."

"You're sure it was a man?"

"It could have been a woman," he said. "It was the tail that gave it away."

"The tail?"

"He was disguised as one of my kind. A raccoon. But the tail didn't wave right. He wore a mask that he pulled over his face when he realized that I could see him. Then he ran away."

"Bonaparte saw nothing, I suppose," she said, "or else he'd be in here with you."

"The pig can't see at night like I can, Luff-tenant," Archer said. "But he can smell just like I can."

"Did you *both* smell a human?"

"No, we smelled raccoon," he said. "But it wasn't right. It was . . . fake."

"Fake?"

"Dead, to be more precise. I could tell it was taken from a corpse. I'm good at smelling dead things."

Wawa genuinely felt for Archer. He knew that he had no evidence, but they were investigating EMSAH, so even the unlikely sighting of a human had to be noted. Still, Bonaparte had refused to take part in this, and was probably snoring away as they spoke. She imagined the debate they must have had over whether to approach her about it. Wawa's job often required her to be tougher than she really was. This time, she decided to be gentle.

"Corporal," she said, "there are a lot of people moving in and out of this sector. They're scared. Some of them are traumatized. Is it possible that it was a local who was trying to see what you were up to, and then got spooked and ran off? We are a little intimidating, and our presence has probably alarmed some people."

"I trust my eyes, Luff-tenant."

It was implausible that humans were willing to take such a risk when they could spread the infection from a safer distance. They had done it before. Archer, Bonaparte, and all the rest were probably exhausted, nothing more. After training for months to be the best soldiers in the world, they had been given the thankless task of running this sector, and it was probably getting to them.

"Archer, your report is noted. I'll include it in my daily for the colonel. And we'll send a team to investigate the area near the depot. Is there anything else?"

Archer hesitated. "Luff-tenant," he said, "if something is going on in this sector that could endanger the Red Sphinx, you would tell us, right?"

"I fail to see the point of your question."

"I mean, if there is to be a quarantine, we would have the opportunity to get out. You would not keep us here simply because you were ordered to."

This raccoon was speaking out of turn, something she suspected would never happen with Culdesac. It was because of that damned Mort(e), the one with the special privileges straight from the Colony, slugging the colonel in front of everyone. Archer was aware that Mort(e) had been Culdesac's chosen one, while Wawa was merely the latest replacement as the unit's executive officer. Mort(e)'s first replacement, a cat named Biko, got himself killed within two months. The next one lasted longer, but caught EMSAH in the field. Culdesac had the grim task of putting him down and cremating the body. Both Number Ones felt obligated to mimic Mort(e)'s cowboy style of leadership, and luckily got only themselves killed rather than others. Wawa ran things differently, and this back talk was almost certainly a direct consequence of that decision.

She leaned in closer to Archer, who instinctively located the exit in case he had to make a quick getaway. "Corporal," Wawa said, "we have sworn our lives to this cause, and we will follow orders. All of us."

"Yes, ma'am."

"It would be in your best interest if I did not hear about this again."

"Yes, ma'am."

She dismissed him and returned to her desk. It had been a rotten day, and she still would not be able to sleep. Twice now, she had been reminded of how she was stuck in this unending war with phantoms and rumors. She found herself once again thinking of Jenna, the person she used to be. She could not help it. It was more comforting than picturing the quarantine. At least Tracksuit's basement was familiar.

The computer screen melted away, replaced with the white stucco wall.

WAWA WAS ASLEEP in her cage when the sound of the other dogs barking woke her up. Tracksuit stood in front of her gate, holding what appeared to be a squirming bundle of fur. It carried with it the scent of an intruder. Wawa backed away, unsure if this beast was somehow attacking her master. The others were going crazy. Tracksuit opened the cage, shoved the animal inside, and slammed the gate shut. The creature unfolded himself until his yellow eyes glared at Wawa in the low light of the cage. A muffled growl leaked from his mouth—this was definitely a dog, a mutt puppy. But there was something shiny attached to his snout, an alien prosthesis that prevented him from barking normally. Similar bindings were on the dog's four paws. The dog tried to puff himself up in a vain attempt to claim his territory. Wawa was not afraid. She would defend the pack as Cyrus had done. She would bring this intruder's carcass to him as an offering.

Wawa pounced on the dog with the voices of her brothers and sisters echoing around her. The dog tried to bat at her with his taped paws. She bit into him, feeling her teeth puncture the skin, feeling the animal's pulse in her throat. The dog eventually surrendered. Wawa wrapped her jaws around his throbbing neck and throttled him until she felt the crunch of his vertebrae like a warm bag of broken glass. She dragged him to the front of the cage, where Tracksuit was waiting. Pleased, he opened the gate and removed the dog. The entire pack howled as one, but Wawa could still detect Cyrus's voice among the others. She always could. She shouted to him, *I am one of you.*

The scene repeated itself many times. Some animal—usually a puppy, but sometimes a large cat—would be placed in her cage, and she would kill it with increasingly ruthless efficiency. Wawa did not understand where they were coming from, or how they were getting past Tracksuit's defenses. But she could feel the pack willing her to fight for them. And when Tracksuit put her on a strict exercise regimen, marching her endlessly on a treadmill with heavy chains on her shoulders, Wawa felt her body getting stronger. She was becoming an extension of this pack.

Every two weeks or so, Tracksuit let Cyrus out of his cage for another fight. Hours later, he would return, occasionally with a scratch, reeking with the blood, fur, and saliva of the rival he had vanquished. She would join the others in praising him.

One day, Wawa heard the tense voices of Tracksuit and his friend. They entered the room, Tracksuit carrying Cyrus's hind legs, his friend carrying the front. Cyrus was barely conscious. His spine bent toward the floor with the weight of his stomach. His tail was shredded. One leg dangled as if the bones had been liquefied. His snout was a mask of dried blood. With a tenderness that Wawa had never seen before, the two men placed Cyrus in his cage and closed the gate.

The room where the pack slept was oppressively quiet for two days. Wawa occasionally whimpered, hoping that Cyrus would hear her. Sometimes he would move, and Wawa could feel everyone in the room tense up and try to listen, to see if Cyrus was attempting to speak to them. But the moment would pass. Upstairs, Tracksuit paced the floor, slamming things.

On the morning of the third day, Tracksuit opened Wawa's cage and walked her to a room in the house where she had never been. The space had been cleared out, save for a small table in the center, which was just high enough for her to prop her belly on. The surface of the table was made of smooth wood, and the metal legs were bolted to the floorboards. Tracksuit fastened Wawa's leash to the front of it. He then took another leash and tied her ankles to the back legs. She was in no mood to argue with him. She was already convinced that whatever he was doing had everything to do with Cyrus and the good of the pack.

Tracksuit left her under the buzzing fluorescent light, her tail to the door. About twenty minutes passed until he returned. Wawa picked up Cyrus's scent right away. She spun her head as far as she could in order to see him. The great dog limped into the room, favoring his front right paw. Though the blood had been cleaned off him, the gash in his face was still raw and infected. Cyrus needed Tracksuit to push him along. Once the dog was close, Tracksuit retreated to a corner of the room and sat with his head between his knees. Cyrus was the broken one, but Tracksuit looked ready to die and turn to dust right there.

Cyrus limped closer to her, still emitting the alien scent of the dog that had crippled him. Wawa did not fully understand what was meant to happen next, but she knew that she and Cyrus were supposed to join together somehow, that this was how the pack would survive. This would be her greatest service to the others.

Cyrus placed his paws on her skin. She faced forward. But then, with a sickly tremor, he slid away from her and fell to the floor, his claw scraping along her ribs. Quickly, Tracksuit was upon him, cradling him in his arms, saying soothing things. She had never seen Tracksuit cry. But now water streamed down his stubbly cheeks, dripping onto Cyrus's fur. Wawa could smell the salt, mixed with some alcohol. Tracksuit did not have the energy to release Wawa from her bonds. All he could do was rock Cyrus gently, saying he was sorry over and over. After a while, he stood up and carried Cyrus away. Wawa stared into the dog's eyes, knowing it would be for the last time. The sun went down before Tracksuit returned, released her from the table, and took her back to her cage.

Wawa went to sleep that night knowing that the pack had been broken. It was the moment she became self-aware, when she saw the world as more than simply her immediate field of vision. There were other packs out there, she realized. The world was enormous, unfair, unknown but knowable, arranged by rules that did not always make sense. She wondered how she did not know these things before. And then she noticed that she was in the act of wondering, of using her mind to do more than track food and assess friends and foes. She considered the possibility that Cyrus had somehow passed these gifts on to her in their final moments together. She quickly dismissed the notion. Cyrus, she

now understood, was a mere animal. She was moving beyond
whatever he had been.

Lost in thought, Wawa did not notice that the hair had begun
to fall away from her paws.

When Tracksuit opened her cage the next day, Wawa thought
that he was letting her go. But she realized that he expected her
to fight. She saw how easy it would be to escape—it was a matter of sprinting for the open door. She decided against it. She
wanted to learn everything, to gather as much information as
possible. Going with Tracksuit to the house at the end of the
trail would be the best way to do it.

They arrived at the brightly lit building at the tree line. When
she exited the van, Wawa immediately sought out the giant red
objects attached to the front of the structure. The realization
eased into her mind: they were letters, forming a word. The
word represented a sound. The sound represented an idea, or a
name, or a thing, or a place. The sign was speaking to her.

There was some commotion going on inside the building.
The items on the shelves had been scattered about the white
linoleum. People scooped up cans and boxes from the floor and
display cases. The front window was broken, leaving a jagged
hole large enough for a person to jump through.

"Holy shit," Tracksuit said. Wawa had heard him. She could
imagine the words hanging in the air like the bright red one
that floated above. As they entered the trail, leaving the scene at
the store behind, she wondered what the words meant.

The house at the end of the trail was not as noisy as it had
been the last time. There were empty seats for the evening's
match. In the front row, right where she thought he would be,
sat the man with the porkpie hat, his dead eye hidden behind
a pair of sunglasses. Tracksuit prepped her, washing her down
with a bucket of warm water. She faced the crowd. Everyone,

she understood, was a sad, scared, powerful, emotional being like herself. They gazed out into the new world as she did: wondering, hoping, fearing, sometimes fighting back. She assessed her opponent, a jet-black dog. Probably younger than she was. Breathing heavily. Wawa wondered if he was undergoing the same changes, which led to another revelation: she was actually concerned about someone outside of the pack.

There is more than the pack, she thought.

Tracksuit slapped her on the side and said, "Go get him, girl." Her eyes stayed on him. *I am not part of his pack*, she thought. She was Tracksuit's slave. The great Cyrus and all the others were slaves. These fights were not protecting anyone. They were merely for sport. She stood still as she considered the awful cruelty of it all. The ways of the world could be learned, but they could also stamp you into the ground before you even noticed something was wrong.

The fight began. The dog charged at her. She parried him, shifting her weight so that he collided with the wall. He kept attacking. He was angry, probably starved or beaten. She noticed a barely healed gash on his left flank and realized that she might not be able to reason with him.

Stop, she said. *Listen to me!* But she was merely barking. The words were in her mind, but she could not speak them.

They've tricked us! she howled. *Don't you get it? We can get out of here!*

The dog continued to surge forward. She focused on the throbbing artery in the dog's neck. How unbelievable, she thought, that this weak point had been there the entire time, and the dogs had been taught to scrape and claw everything else.

I don't want to hurt you! she said. Nothing. The dog jabbed at her. Wawa remained still in the hopes that her opponent would accept the peace offering. Instead, she felt the dog's claw sink into the side of her face and rake across it. Drops of blood spattered at her feet.

Wawa swung her right paw in a horizontal arc, slashing the dog's throat in one movement. A spray of blood hit her wounded face. The animal staggered away, the gash spilling its contents onto the floor, an obscene red against the white canvas. The dog slumped over, collapsing in a crimson pool. Hatred for everyone in the room welled up in Wawa's gut, making blood throb in her ears, overwhelming the silence that had fallen. They made her do this.

People tried to get closer. At the other end of the ring, Tracksuit stood up. She could tell that he was shocked, and that he was trying to hide his excitement.

And then Wawa rose on her hind legs. She locked eyes only with her master. His eyebrows stretched upward, his mouth a gaping hole in his face. "Jenna?" he said.

"You," she said, relishing the gasp that emitted from the spectators. "You . . . are not part of my pack."

She heard a metal *click*. Her ears pointed to it first. She turned to see the man with the porkpie hat pointing a gun at her. A breathless *What the fuck?* came from somewhere.

Wawa leapt out of the ring in one bound. The gun fired. She imagined the bullet striking someone in the audience. Someone screamed. Panicking bodies scurried away. A man tried to bar her path to the door. All she had to do was roar to get him to move.

She was on the trail now. The lights of the parking lot flashed through the tree branches. When she reached the flat asphalt, she gazed for the last time at the little store. It was empty, with the lights still on. The shelves had been completely cleared. She stared at the massive red sign and could at last read it. It said WAWA. It did not make sense, and she knew that she would have to keep going until all the words did. She would have to keep going until something did.

CHAPTER TEN
THE PATRON SAINT OF LOST CAUSES

MORT(E) COULD SENSE that the plague was coming. Perhaps the ants already knew about it, and they were testing the animals' loyalty. Or their competence. Regardless, EMSAH was inevitable. Quarantine was sure to follow. For all Mort(e) knew, this *was* the quarantine: an old veteran sequestered in a dead city, chasing ghosts. Forever.

The investigation files arrived in a laptop computer delivered by Bonaparte. Mort(e) opened a video of Wawa sitting at her desk, the drab surroundings of the barracks behind her. Wawa went over the list of suspected infections, along with the incidents that had been piling up, all involving ritualistic suicides or murders, with the quarry incident being the largest event yet. And there were already three more cases since then.

Wawa would focus her efforts on the quarry for now. She had to investigate a symbol painted on the hoof of one of the deer, written in a language no one recognized. A linguist in another sector was trying to translate it. This same symbol, she added, was found etched into the side of a trailer at the quarry. Wawa concluded the video by telling Mort(e) to begin interviewing witnesses at the other sites; to gather clues; to make sure the army medics collected blood samples from everyone; to note any irregularities; to ask questions but to answer none. And above all, he was to keep things quiet. The settlers were already talking about quarantine.

So he set out, flashing his newly acquired ID badge at the homes of dogs, cats, squirrels, rats, reformed farm animals. It was hard not to think of Tiberius, who would have relished the opportunity to decode the mysteries of the plague. Mort(e) never shared his dead friend's enthusiasm for this kind of work, and instead made up for it with a grim determination, an unemotional understanding of the hand he had been dealt. This was his most honed skill, the one around which all the others revolved. He owed it to Tiberius to see things through. And to Sheba. He was working for two dead friends now. And maybe with some luck, he could make a small difference in this war.

His first stop was at a house full of rats. Because the rats hated bright light, the windows were boarded up. Most of the inhabitants stayed in the basement, which they expanded with new tunnels and passages that would link all the rodent homes in the area, thereby recreating the labyrinths of subway systems and abandoned buildings from which many of the rats came. This exclusivity was officially discouraged, but people made an exception for the rats. They were among the most productive members of the new society, and they weren't hurting anyone.

A member of their little colony, a scrawny female named Victoria—the rats loved regal names—rounded up a new brood of babies and led them into the bathtub, where they all drowned. The others found the bodies, moistened from the steam, while Victoria lay dead with her veins opened up. When Mort(e) tried to get the rats to explain, they all spoke at once. They would not listen when he told them to shut up, to speak one at a time. From what he gathered, Victoria had done nothing out of the ordinary prior to the incident, which was even more chilling than if she had. If she had simply snapped, then it had to be some kind of affliction of the brain.

Victoria was born before the Change, something that all the suicides had in common so far. But as was the case with so many of the rats, her life was improved by the war, not harmed by it. She had not taken her upgraded brain for granted. By all accounts, she was determined to make things better for her kind, and for all animals. Victoria was one of the rats who had planned the tunnel project, and she chose the day on which the first phase was completed to kill herself in a very public fashion.

It seemed far-fetched that she was trying to send a political message until Mort(e) read the files on the deer suicides. All of them worked at the quarry, another project that helped the community become independent. So these deaths could have been some kind of sabotage. But there was no evidence, and no connection between the saboteurs.

Mort(e) checked everything: the deer and the rats had not been in the camps together, had not fought in the war, did not come from the same parts of the country. The similarity between the two cases remained a coincidence. Still, it nagged at him. Had they received messages regarding dead loved ones as he had?

To add to the confusion: the autopsies and blood tests were coming up negative, with no physical signs of the virus. Perhaps a new strain of EMSAH—impossible to detect, and far more lethal than before—had been unleashed. He could not say that out loud yet, even though it was screaming in his head.

It was the violent murder scene at the home of a family of dogs that made Mort(e) accept that he was facing an EMSAH outbreak. Or something worse, if such a thing was even possible. The family consisted of a husband and wife, two daughters, and the wife's mother, an old mixed-breed who would probably not live to see another summer. The father—a mutt named Averroes—was a member of the Bureau. He had worked his way up, starting with dead human removal before being appointed the Assistant Director of Sanitation. They even gave him his own SUV with the Bureau logo on the door, and his neighbors saw him driving to and from the plant. In a rebuilding sector, this job afforded great respect. The dog was quite good at it. He was a genuine believer in the future that the Queen offered.

It took Mort(e) a day to piece it together, but based on blood spatters, footprints, and the placement of some dog hairs and a tooth, he was able to figure out roughly what happened on the day that Averroes died. The next-door neighbor, a dog named Thor, apparently entered Averroes's property. He was most likely trespassing, or bringing some unpleasant news, because an altercation ensued. Not content to merely repel the invader, Averroes chased Thor onto the adjoining property, where he stabbed Thor to death. He propped the victim on his couch with one hand on the armrest, the other slung across his belly. Mort(e) couldn't figure it out. Why make someone comfortable in his chair after killing him? Was it an apology, a realization that this act of vengeance had gone too far?

When Averroes's mate and children returned from a day spent roving in the woods, he had dinner waiting for them. The meal was poisoned, and they died within minutes of taking their first bite. Then Averroes took a piece of biscuit with him to the bathroom. He gazed at himself in the mirror and swallowed the poison.

Luckily, the mate's mother was at the hospital, picking up her ration of vitamins and supplements. Averroes probably planned to kill her when she returned but had lost patience and panicked, knowing that it was only a matter of time before

Thor's death caught up with him. When Mort(e) visited her, she sat in a rocking chair wearing a hoodie, her muzzle sticking out from the blue cotton. The older ones unnerved him. There was always the question of how much they had unlearned after years of worshipping a human master and defending their slave home.

Her name was Olive. She told him the details, not bothering to complain about having to go through it all again. Averroes, she explained, had not done or said anything unusual. Then again, he was a quiet one, anyway. He often relieved stress by digging in the yard. This had been his master's house, and the act of burying something, sniffing it out, and digging it up again reminded him of a simpler time.

When Olive was finished, she stood up and headed for the kitchen. The teapot whistled, and Mort(e) thought that she was fetching something to drink. Instead, she returned with a silver necklace. "If my daughter had worn this," she said, "she'd still be alive today."

Mort(e) extended his hand for it. The medallion had an image of a bearded man in robes, a perfect ring around his head. St. Jude, it said. He had seen one before, but could not remember when or where. "Why would she still be alive?"

"St. Jude is the patron saint of lost causes," Olive said.

"So the medallion would have reminded your daughter to—"

"It wouldn't have reminded her of anything," Olive said. "You soldiers are like robots, you know that? I'm telling you that St. Jude would have protected her."

Mort(e) stopped himself from asking how much exposure she had had to her son-in-law. It was a moot point now.

"And I don't care what you say," she continued. "Write it in your report. Tell the ants I'm crazy. You're all spying on me anyway, right?"

That was correct. Mort(e) thanked her for her time and tried to leave. She insisted that he take the medallion, pointing out that the army had already ordered her to undergo the battery of physical and cognitive tests proving that nothing was wrong with her. "Other than being an old bitch," she said. "No law against that."

When he refused again to accept the medallion, she told him it could be part of his investigation. "I don't care if you're a cat, squirrel, whatever," she added. "You need St. Jude's protection more than anyone if you're in this line of work. I can feel it."

Mort(e) took the medallion, promising to return it. She laughed and told him that she would probably be dead by then.

"And you won't want to give it back, anyway," she added.

MORT(E) WENT HOME. By then, he had converted the Martinis' garage into a command center. That way, he could remove the investigation from the house entirely. On the floor of the garage, he drew out a map of the entire sector, first in plain white chalk, and then in more detail with colored pencils. He needed to be able to stand in the middle of it and think. Still not satisfied, he decided to make the model three-dimensional, with cardboard boxes and rocks to depict some of the larger buildings and structures, and a hole in the cement foundation—dug with a pick axe—to indicate the quarry where the deer committed suicide.

He hung the medallion from his desk lamp, where it dangled beside his computer screen, the image of the pious man swinging like a pendulum on a clock. Despite the late hour, Mort(e) decided to call Bonaparte. It was something Culdesac liked to do, to show the underlings that the boss could rouse them from their sleep on a whim. Bonaparte answered groggily, which compelled Mort(e) to sound even more chipper.

"The murder scene," Mort(e) said. "I want you to round up a few people and dig up the backyard. Tell me what you find."

"We could get a truck over there in the morning—"

"Now, Specialist."

"Okay, I'll get right on it."

Bonaparte sounded annoyed. Mort(e) was not proud of it, but part of him liked spreading the misery around. If the Red Sphinx wanted him to work on this investigation, they would have to deal with him on his terms.

Mort(e) rose from his chair to get some water. That was when he spotted the raccoon through the window. The creature stood in the middle of the grass, facing the garage.

Many animals, especially those who had not been pets, seemed to have liberal views of property. This same raccoon may have even rummaged through the Martinis' trash before the war. So many of these bottom-dwellers had waited out the conflict living on garbage and grubs. Still, the messenger bag slung over the raccoon's shoulder showed that he must have had some function other than creeping around at night.

Mort(e) lifted the door of the garage and was immediately overcome with the sweet stink of a feral raccoon, thick as mist. He scrunched his eyes, forcing his senses to grow accustomed to the assault.

The raccoon did not move.

"Are you lost?" Mort(e) asked.

His eyes adjusted. There was something wrong with the raccoon's face. With his whole head, really. The raccoon's neck had been split open, and the severed chin and jaw pointed straight upward. But where there should have been the pulsing insides of the throat was, instead, a face. A human face.

All thought left Mort(e)'s mind. Now there was only movement. Calculating distances. Erasing fear and doubt. This was the counterattack he had been trained to expect. His hind legs tensed, his tail straightened. Mort(e) leapt at the intruder, his clawless hands ready to land on the man's chest. But the man was fast. Before Mort(e) could seize the human, a piercing noise paralyzed him. A screeching sound that rattled inside his brain like an angry insect. Mort(e) collapsed. With his hands on his ears in a futile attempt to block the noise, he tilted his head up to see that the man held some metal device, about the size of his hand. Whatever it was, it seemed to focus the noise on Mort(e) like a laser.

The noise stopped. The ringing in his head lasted for a few seconds before fading out.

"Get up," the man said.

"Who are you?" Mort(e) asked.

The noise again, like a horde of ants invading his skull. It was so human of this raccoon to answer a question with more punishment.

"Quiet," the man said. "Get up and go to the garage."

Mort(e) obeyed. The temporary fog of the raccoon smell had already begun to disperse.

"Sit down," the man said.

Mort(e) sat in the chair at his desk. The man closed the door halfway. Perhaps he wanted an easy escape in case Mort(e) somehow overcame the stun weapon.

The human sat on a nearby stool and placed the bag on his lap. The suit, Mort(e) noticed, had been built from the hide of a real raccoon. The mask was perched on the crown of the man's bald head. He had brown skin. The stubble of a beard framed his jaw. The device remained firmly in the man's hand, the pad of his thumb poised over the power switch.

"I am Elder Briggs," the man said. "I know you have a lot of questions. Please feel free to ask them."

The words had been chosen carefully, most likely rehearsed. *They give away so much in their eyes,* Culdesac had told him in their human interrogation training seminar years before. *You have to watch the eyes. It's harder for them to lie, and yet they do it so often.*

Briggs's pupils quivered. He was clearly in awe of Mort(e). Perhaps Briggs had been given a photo of him to study.

"How did you get here?" Mort(e) asked.

Briggs sighed. "You're starting with a question that you can't possibly expect me to answer," he said. "Let's say I dropped in."

"How many humans are with you?" Mort(e) said. "How many are in your resistance?"

"Too many for the Queen's taste. Enough to fight." Briggs grinned. It made him more difficult to read.

"What is it?" Mort(e) asked.

"Most people would have asked 'why' next. But you're a warrior. Always analyzing the tactical situation."

"I imagine you're here because of my investigation," Mort(e) said.

"EMSAH," Briggs said. "I suppose anyone under the Colony's control is investigating EMSAH in one way or another."

"Is there an EMSAH outbreak in this sector?"

"Of course."

"Are you causing it?"

"Absolutely."

Mort(e) chuckled. *I guess this concludes my investigation,* he thought.

"The question you should be asking," Briggs said, "is not, 'Is this EMSAH?' Of course it's EMSAH. EMSAH is everywhere. We did a good job spreading it around. No, the question you *should* be asking is, '*What* is EMSAH?' And, 'Why are the ants so afraid of it?'"

"Can you answer these questions for me?" Mort(e) asked.

"The Archon decided that you should find out on your own," Briggs said. "She is our leader. Besides, you wouldn't believe me if I told you."

"Am I infected?"

"I'm afraid you could be." There was an impatient trembling in Briggs's voice. Mort(e) could not tell if it expressed regret or satisfaction.

"So the scattered reports about people getting sick," Mort(e) said. "Is this EMSAH?"

"Probably."

"But they've been testing negative so far."

"Maybe your test is not keeping up with the disease."

"And the suicides?" Mort(e) asked.

"EMSAH," Briggs replied.

"The murders, too?"

"EMSAH, yes," Briggs said. Now he was being nonchalant.

"Do you control the ones who are infected?"

"We do not control them. We try to guide them."

"So you guided them to commit suicide?"

Briggs shook his head. "Has it ever occurred to you that *you* are the ones who are compelling these people to commit these terrible acts?" he asked. "We know about you. You've always suspected that the Queen's plans for your people would not work. That's the reason why you walked away from the Red Sphinx. These infected ones, as you call them, they know what's in store for them if they're discovered. How can you blame them for fighting back?"

"So you're saying that these events are not simply the results of a disease," Mort(e) said. "They're acts of protest. Sabotage."

"A warning," Briggs said. "A sign of what is to come."

Mort(e) wanted to bring this human to the house with the

dead rats in it. He wanted to shove the man's ugly face into the tub so he could see firsthand what his species had done.

"Did you put that message in my basement?" Mort(e) asked, eager to change the subject. "The one about Sheba?"

"Yes," Briggs said.

"Why?"

"Because it's true."

"That's impossible."

"The past few years," Briggs said with a sigh, "have been a monument to the impossible. Wouldn't you say?"

"Where is she?"

"On the Island."

The word—along with the casual way in which this fugitive said it—made Mort(e) shudder. Whenever someone brought up the subject, his imagination conjured up images of Janet and the children, filthy and cowering, rounded up by Alpha soldiers, imprisoned in cages until they were summoned to partake in one of Miriam's experiments. And who could say for sure that Miriam wasn't also running tests on animals? And yet here was this human, holding Mort(e) hostage in his own garage, forcing him to imagine Sheba on an operating table.

"Why are you telling me this?" he asked.

"It is your destiny to find her again," Briggs said. "The Queen has feared it. Our prophet has foreseen it. The entire war depends on it."

"*Prophet?*"

"An oracle, a messenger with the gift of sight," Briggs said. "He tells us that you will find Sheba again. In doing so, you will save both your people and ours. Don't tell me you've given up hope."

"Destiny and hope," Mort(e) said. "You *are* a relic, you know that? No wonder you lost. Besides, no one can get to the Island, anyway. She might as well be on Mars. I don't care what your prophet says."

"I have something for you," Briggs said, reaching into the bag, his eyes still fixed on Mort(e). He pulled out a red plastic tube and slid it across the desk.

Mort(e) picked up the tube and examined it. There was a large glass eye at one end and a smaller one at the other. A telescope.

"We are not the monsters the Queen made us out to be," Briggs said. "We are reaching out to you as friends."

"Friends don't spread diseases to their friends."

Briggs smiled knowingly. "The first step to ending this war starts tonight."

"What am I supposed to do with this?" Mort(e) asked.

"Look to Orion's belt at midnight every night," Briggs said. "What you'll see will answer most of your questions about what has happened to the resistance."

Mort(e) placed the telescope on the desk. It rolled before coming to a stop at the computer monitor.

"Do you know Morse code?" Briggs asked.

"The basics."

"Relearn it, and we'll be able to communicate with you. One day, perhaps very soon, we hope to be able to tell you how to get to the Island."

"What does it matter if I get there?"

"It will show that the Queen has not destroyed everything," Briggs said. "It will show that we are not simply the savages that she thinks we are. So much depends on it."

He said the word *we* to mean both humans and everyone else, as if there was some kind of camaraderie among the species.

Briggs stood up and backed his way to the door. He extended

his arm to demonstrate that he could still inflict pain if he felt threatened.

"There is a catch," Briggs said.

"What's that?"

"If you succeed in finding Sheba, it will trigger the largest outbreak of EMSAH yet. You'll fulfill the prophecy, and the Queen's experiment will be deemed a failure. She will respond with a total quarantine. We had a big debate about whether or not to tell you, but we decided that you should know."

"What does EMSAH have to do with Sheba and me?"

"When you find out what EMSAH is, you'll understand. All I can say for now is that the Queen has linked the virus to you."

"That's insane," Mort(e) said. "If the Queen thinks I'm part of this EMSAH business, why doesn't she send her daughters to kill me?"

"Her arrogance has blinded her," Briggs said. "She thinks she can observe and report. Like this is another test of our weakness as a species. She thinks she can control you. But this is not a lab. And you are not an animal anymore. You can choose to go beyond what she has planned for you. She does not believe. The Queen is blind. And that will be her downfall. It is the downfall of all tyrants."

Mort(e)'s gaze dropped to the floor in frustration. This talking in riddles was so human, so unlike the brutal simplicity of the ants. Of course the Queen didn't *believe*—she simply *knew*.

"Remember: watch Orion's belt at midnight," Briggs said. "We'll work on a way to get you to the Island. Good luck."

The man scuttled under the half-open garage door, leaving behind a brief but intense spray of raccoon scent.

Mort(e) tapped the telescope with his finger. Swaying above, the St. Jude medallion reflected dull flashes of light from the lamp.

CHAPTER ELEVEN
VESUVIUS

HE FIRST ORDER of business was to make sure he wasn't going crazy.

On the morning after the visit from Briggs, Mort(e) checked into the army hospital on the outskirts of the old city, even though he was not scheduled for a physical for a few months. The hospital had once been a train station. Its marble floors and stone walls were easy to disinfect. All it took was a few rodents, some bleach, and a really big hose.

There was a line of people waiting for treatment. What had once been a ticketing booth was now a registration area, and the arrivals board displayed numbers that were being served. Once he made it to the front of the line, Mort(e) flashed his badge and gestured to his new sash. Within minutes, his number appeared, far ahead of the sick puppy to his right and the coughing old horse to his left.

To his surprise, the doctor was a bear wearing a white physician's coat. Mort(e) had not seen a bear outside of an army unit. Culdesac always spoke highly of this species, referring to them by their proper family name, the Ursidae. He said they understood one another. That was ridiculous, of course. Culdesac understood almost everyone. *No one* understood him.

The bear took Mort(e) through the battery of tests:

temperature, respiration, pressure, vision, hearing, reflexes. She drew blood and had him urinate into a cup. She said little, although the sound of her breathing through her large snout was incredibly loud, especially when she leaned in to listen to Mort(e)'s heart and lungs.

"So what brings you here so soon, Captain?" she asked.

"I've been working in the field," Mort(e) said.

"Haven't we all?"

She nodded to her leg. Mort(e) noticed that the limb was prosthetic. Even though the calf and foot had fur on them, the ankle joint was a plastic hinge. He wondered how she lost the leg. Who knew with these wild animals? Maybe she gnawed it off to get out of a trap.

"I wanted to see if I was exhibiting any signs," he said.

"Signs of what?"

Mort(e) was quiet for a moment, hoping she would not make him say it. But she stood there, clipboard in hand, checking things off with a blue pen.

"That which we cannot name," Mort(e) said.

She chuckled, revealing her white fangs. "The Big E?" she said. "If you had that, you wouldn't have come here asking for a diagnosis. Or treatment."

"But you should give me the test."

"I already did," she said. "No one has to ask anymore. And no one has to grant permission, either."

She left the room and returned with the test tube containing his blood and the beaker filled with his urine. There was a green strip circling the inside of both vessels. She tipped them toward the light so that the fluid drained away from the marker.

"See the strip? Green is clean. Yellow is . . . well, I don't have a rhyme yet, but it's definitely not *mellow*."

"I've heard that they were testing these things," Mort(e) said.

"They just came in. The shipment was signed by Miriam her-self," the bear said. "If you see something, say something."

She explained that they were using the strips more often. And with all the reported illnesses in the sector, she'd already had to order a new batch. Mort(e) felt only partially relieved at his negative result. How many quarantined settlements had tested negative up until the day the ants came and destroyed them?

"Relax, sir," the bear said. "You don't have a single symptom, and your blood and urine were clean. And no, I don't want any other fluids."

"You're right," Mort(e) said. "But you must know about the crazy stuff that's going on around here."

She did. She asked if he knew of the deer suicides. He said yes.

"I helped with the autopsies," she said. "In my expert opin-ion—based on four years of medical training—they died from jumping off a cliff."

Mort(e) smiled. He liked this bear.

"Sir," she said, "it's not EMSAH. I've been around, seen some things. And I know when a soldier is starting to confuse stress and fatigue with something worse."

The predictability of this response was slightly comforting. That was something.

"You've seen some things," he repeated. "Seen a human lately?"

"Are you seeing humans?"

"Either humans or very ugly animals."

"I haven't seen a human in a long time," the doctor said. "It was way up north, away from all the settlements. I think he was a drowned pilot. Or a paratrooper. I don't know why the Queen hates them so much. They're delicious."

Mort(e) laughed. He told her that there were merely rumors

of humans in disguise, and none of the reports had been confirmed. Then he rose from the table, agreeing that he was probably stressed, and asked if there was anything else. The doctor waved him off.

Mort(e) was about to leave when he realized that he did not know the bear's name. He asked her.

"Rigel," she said.

"I thought that was a boy's name."

"It's a bear's name," she said.

Mort(e) was no longer thinking of her quip, whatever it was supposed to mean. Rigel was the name of the sandal in the Orion constellation. Maybe Briggs had set up this meeting. Mort(e) shook it off. This was a coincidence, he told himself. Lots of animals named themselves for stars. He could see the constellation in his mind's eye: three glowing white orbs to represent the belt, along with a few others to demarcate the shoulders, feet, and sword. It was fitting that the belt was most prominent to those early humans. The ants were probably right; the humans were obsessed with their own bodies, fixated on the area that housed their greedy stomachs and lustful genitalia. The constellation had probably started as a waistline and nothing more. The warrior Orion must have been added later, to keep things respectable.

With a nod, Mort(e) gathered his paperwork and left the doctor's office. He went straight to the barracks, hoping to avoid Culdesac and Wawa. If they were monitoring his work, they would see that he had signed in. *Fine*, he thought. Let them think he was actually doing his job. It probably wouldn't matter soon, anyway.

Bonaparte was not in his office, so Mort(e) headed for the mess hall. There he found the pig alone at a table, his snout in a tray filled with some kind of corn slop. He had been careless enough to get some of it on his oversized vest. Bonaparte was not as quick as the others, and was so engrossed in his lunch that he did not notice Mort(e)'s presence. Culdesac chose members of the Red Sphinx well, but Bonaparte seemed to be more of a mascot, a representative of how things could be if the animals put aside their differences and worked together. He no doubt had skills, which must have included an unquestioning loyalty and stubbornness—pigheadedness, the humans would have said. Still, though it may have been noble for the Red Sphinx to incorporate other species, this corn slop session must have been one of many habits that separated Bonaparte from the others. While the cats now ate a protein supplement manufactured by the Colony, this outcast still had to eat the same feed from his slave days. Like many livestock animals, Bonaparte probably couldn't adjust to the new food supply, and had to get an alternative prescribed by a doctor. The carnivorous cats must have picked on him for having to haul his special diet around on their missions like some high-maintenance invalid.

As he fished for something in his pocket, Bonaparte spotted Mort(e). He scooped up a napkin with both hooves and wiped the corn mash from his nose—a delicate operation that he performed with surprising dexterity. When he saluted, the object in his pocket jingled. Mort(e) could tell that it was a flask. Perhaps Bonaparte had taken it from the farmer who owned him. The pig inherited both the flask and the drinking habit, it seemed. It made Mort(e) smile. Tiberius probably would have befriended the pig for that alone. Then Bonaparte would not have been such an outsider.

"Sir, we completed the dig," Bonaparte said.

"Never mind the dig," Mort(e) said. In fact, he had already forgotten about it. When Bonaparte tried to interrupt him, Mort(e) cut him off by naming several items that he needed immediately: an old phone book from the area, medical records on the former owner of Olive the dog, and a book on Morse code. He did not really need the first two, but requesting only the codebook could arouse suspicion. Bonaparte immediately left his half-eaten meal to fetch the items. Mort(e) took pleasure in the pig's newfound obedience. Word had reached the colonel about Bonaparte calling Mort(e) a choker when they first met, an egregious sign of disrespect. Culdesac had probably made the pig run seven miles with his sash tied to his head.

Thirty minutes later, Bonaparte arrived at Mort(e)'s temporary office with the codebook, apologizing for finding only one of the three things, and for the awful stench coming from the book. Almost all the texts at the barracks had been salvaged from the nearby library. The titles had been waterlogged by rain coming through the shattered roof and broken windows. The scent of this book was so putrid that Mort(e) almost reconsidered using it.

"Can I tell you about the dig now, sir?" Bonaparte asked.

"Yes. What did you find?"

Bonaparte looked around before he answered. "A bomb."

BONAPARTE LED MORT(E) to a secure room at the far end of the barracks. On the way, he described digging up the dog's yard. With Olive watching, the pig and two cats sniffed around the numerous mud hills in the lawn. At first it was tedious work. They found the items one would expect from a dog who fantasized about his days as a pet: a bone, a stick, a rubber chew toy shaped like a little green alien—"with three eyes," Bonaparte added. The pig turned it into a game, placing bets with the cats about who had the best sense of smell. This was an ongoing banter among the species. Bonaparte correctly predicted the contents of the burial sites every single time. Even through a foot of dirt, he could detect a baseball cap, a catcher's mitt, and a beer bottle (that last one did not surprise Mort(e)). At one point, Olive even clapped, cheering him on against the increasingly frustrated cats.

"Get to the bomb, Bonaparte," Mort(e) said.

There were grooves carved into the driveway, Bonaparte said. The indentations created a straight line from the dog's SUV, along the asphalt, and through the grass, terminating at a large mud hill at the edge of the property. Even Bonaparte could not figure out the scent, although both he and the cats could detect metal and plastic. So they began digging. When they found the device, Bonaparte called the barracks and requested more soldiers. He wanted the house surrounded. Olive was probably not involved in this, but it wouldn't matter now. While Bonaparte spoke, Mort(e) imagined an overhead view of poor Olive's home, with a red dot marking her house. The dot expanded into a lake of blood engulfing the entire sector.

Mort(e) and Bonaparte arrived at the room. Two Red Sphinx soldiers stood guard. They stepped aside when Mort(e) showed them his identification.

Inside, a single table furnished the windowless room. The bomb sat on top, still caked in dirt. Bonaparte assured Mort(e) that it had been disarmed. It was a black box infested with red and blue wires, like a clown's wig. The cords connected an electronic timer with a block of plastic explosive. Mort(e) was relieved—though only slightly—to see that the device carried no biological agent. In other words, it was not a weapon intended to spread the EMSAH virus. Averroes himself had tested negative for the disease. Moreover, the device did not have bits of shaved metal or nails in the casing. It was meant to destroy a building rather than kill or maim a group of soldiers.

"The neighbor must have seen this," Bonaparte said.

Mort(e) nodded. "Averroes had to kill him to keep him quiet," he said. "Had no choice."

If Thor had not spotted Averroes with this device, then the bomb almost surely would have been used at the sanitation plant. An explosion there would have been the kind of warning that Briggs had mentioned. A population ruled by its sense of smell would have to pay attention to a destroyed sanitation facility.

Where did Averroes get the material for this? He was no soldier. But if there was a network of saboteurs out there, it made sense that they would recruit someone like him. Maybe another member of the resistance planned to dig up the bomb and finish the job.

"There's one more thing," Bonaparte said. He lifted the bomb and turned it on its side. There was a message carved into the plastic. When Mort(e) read it, he heard the words in the voice of Briggs:

THE QUEEN IS BLIND.

It was a direct response to the mantra—the threat—under which the animals lived every day since the war started. The Queen sees everything, they were told. Presumably she saw this. And now what? This was how a quarantine started, Mort(e) realized. If EMSAH could make a person kill his own family, then who could blame the Queen for trying to wipe it out?

"I'll report this to the lieutenant," Mort(e) said. "Good work, Specialist."

"You've seen this before, right?"

"No, I haven't."

"But you told Culdesac all this was inevitable," Bonaparte said. "So you must know something about how EMSAH works."

"I'm starting to think that no one does."

"I've been thinking that for a while myself."

"Then keep it to yourself," Mort(e) said.

Discouraged, Bonaparte saluted and went on his way, his hooves clicking down the hallway. Mort(e) ran his finger over the carved message again. He mouthed the words. Then he whispered them.

MORT(E) RETURNED HOME, entered his garage, and opened the codebook. It was not even noon yet. He had over twelve hours to refresh his memory and write a fake report on the investigations he had conducted that day.

This EMSAH outbreak was somehow coupled with a conspiracy to bring down the sector, to bait it into quarantine. He had never heard of the disease spreading in this way, but Culdesac had always warned the Red Sphinx that every case was different. There was no limit to the depravity of humans. But they had promised him Sheba, and so he went ahead with setting up his telescope despite everything that Culdesac had taught him. The quarantine could begin tomorrow, for all he knew, so he might as well see what Briggs was talking about while he still had the chance.

Mort(e) waited. The sky grew dark, a wasteland pocked with stars. For so long, he had viewed the world horizontally. Had it not been for the Queen and her grand design, he never would have gazed up into the sky and wondered. He would have died having learned nothing, like so many wasted generations before him.

To position the telescope, Mort(e) used an old tripod that had originally been intended for a mounted machine gun. He pointed the scope at Orion. Rigel was the brightest, and he used it to focus the lens. After some fiddling, the star went from a blurry ball of light to a crisp white sphere. He moved the sight line up Orion's leg to the belt. Something floated underneath the star Alnitak, the easternmost one. He saw it moving and could tell right away that it was much closer than the star, suspended in sub-orbit. It was shiny, with three bulbous objects—balloons stacked with two on the bottom and one on top. They were mounted over several smaller rectangular shapes. And then it turned before puttering toward the center of the constellation. Several propellers spun at the rear of the object. At least six of them. It was some kind of zeppelin. Briggs must have come from there, along with many other humans. The ship was probably too high for the Colonial bird patrols. Or maybe the ship had a means of repelling them, with a sonic device similar to the one Briggs carried.

The zeppelin found a spot and hung there, its propellers whirring periodically to maintain position. It spun a little, allowing the moonlight to reflect on the fat part of the airship, creating a tiny silver crescent.

How far up was this ship? Mort(e) guessed many miles. Had it positioned itself so that he alone could see it near the Orion constellation? Or was this a routine for members of the human resistance who were still on the ground somewhere, like when the bees danced to give directions to food? Where was it during the day? How many were on board? Was Briggs able to travel to and from the ship, or was he stranded on the surface? How many humans from the airship had been caught and disposed of in the Purges?

At 11:59 Mort(e) readied his codebook, a pencil in his hand. The zeppelin oscillated to face him. At its base, a bright light flashed three times. Then the code began, all dashes and dots, which he recorded on the inside cover of the book. He missed the first few letters but managed to catch up. The signal was paced for someone who was not an expert. It seemed to go on for a long time until he realized that it was repeating itself. After a few minutes, the flashing stopped. The airship turned and flew away, its rear propellers facing him. He tracked it until it vanished. He then packed up the telescope and returned to the garage.

It took him a few minutes to match the dots and dashes with the corresponding letters. When the message was complete, Mort(e) leaned forward and gazed at it.

"Greetings, Sebastian from the USS *Vesuvius*," it said. "Sheba is alive. Find the source of EMSAH, and you will find her. More messages at 12 A.M."

He read it again. The casual salutation. The use of his slave name. The old human ship prefix, the ship itself named for a dangerous volcano from the Roman Empire. The mention of Sheba. The promise of more information, like a secret between them.

The war was still on, he thought. EMSAH was on its way. The world that the Queen had promised would have to wait.

Though these things worried him, he felt a sense of calm. Sheba was alive somewhere, perhaps watching the skies for the airship along with him. Why else would his enemies have gone through so much trouble to get him this message? He wanted to hear her stories in her new voice. He imagined her talking like Janet in her younger years, before she cried and prayed all the time. They would say things to each other like *I love you* and *I missed you* and *I will never leave you again* and *I'm sorry* and *Don't go*. She would be older and wiser, perhaps hardened by sadness, but stronger. Like him.

Mort(e) took the code with him to his spot in the basement. That way, when he woke up, the message would be waiting for him, and he would not think even for a moment that it had been a dream.

"OUT OF THE question," Wawa said.

The way she said it, with the emphasis on the word "out" like a scolding mother, made Mort(e) laugh inwardly. She must have been parroting some movie from one of Culdesac's human behavior classes.

Mort(e) expected this answer when he went to Wawa's office to request access to Colony's archived files. He knew that his explanation—that he was trying to connect the owners of the animals who had shown signs of EMSAH to see if they had been Purged—would not fly. "You asked me to investigate," he said. "I'm doing that."

"Here's what you don't understand," she said. "Those 'files' you mention are not files at all. They're part of the Colony's acquired memories, stored with the Queen herself. It's not like booting up a computer. You would have to use a translator and link with the Colony. And even if you had clearance for that, we both know you're not up to it."

Just as Mort(e) was about to interrupt, she continued.

"Thankfully, the colonel has already done the work for us," she said. "And you can see in his report—"

"I've seen his report," Mort(e) said.

"Then I don't understand the purpose of this conversation," Wawa said. "Unless you're suggesting that the colonel has not been forthcoming with the facts."

"Oh, I'm not suggesting it. I'm stating it. Unequivocally."

Wawa folded her slender hands on the desk. She blinked once. "Mort(e), I realize there are some special rules set up for your . . . role. But don't push it."

"I'm not trying to start trouble, Lieutenant. I'm just wondering why the Colony wants us to investigate this thing, but then withholds information from us."

"Has it occurred to you, Mort(e), that it's time for us to handle our own affairs?" she said. "That's the point of all of this, isn't it?" She gestured to their surroundings before folding her hands again.

"You're talking to the wrong person if you want to know 'the point.'"

"The Colony is ceding authority to us," she said. "They've kept their promises. Within a year or two, the Bureau will finish its work, and we'll be fully autonomous, answering only to the Council. The Colony will continue to weed out any human stragglers like they've always done. You can't say that they haven't been upfront about the insurgents they've purged."

"If they're doing such a great job, why are we on the verge of another quarantine?"

"We're trying to *prevent* the quarantine," Wawa said. "It's our responsibility, even more so than theirs. We just have to get through this."

"You think that bomb we found is the only one out there?" Mort(e) asked.

"No. There are probably others. We have to find them."

"So you agree that this is more than an outbreak," Mort(e) said. "EMSAH might be the least of our worries. This could be a full-scale rebellion."

"That's exactly what it could be, *Captain!*" Wawa said, slamming her enormous palm on the desk. "Your mastery of the obvious never ceases to amaze me."

Her outburst startled Mort(e). She wore the same death stare from when she had pointed a gun between his eyes.

"That message they found tattooed on the deer's hoof," she said, slightly calmer now. "We translated it. It was in a language that the humans called Hebrew. You probably already know what it said. 'The Queen is blind.'"

She let that sink in for a few seconds.

"So yes, I know that we're possibly dealing with an outbreak, and an insurrection, and a threat to everything we've fought for," she said. "I don't need you to remind me. We have to make do like the loyal soldiers we are."

"I hope there are still people left to make do," Mort(e) said. He stood up, accepting that he had said all he could. He muttered that he would hand in his reports at the end of the week as usual. Then he headed for the door.

"You know, Mort(e)," Wawa said, "if I didn't know any better, I would say that you were withholding something yourself."

"*Out* of the question," Mort(e) said.

"I'm sorry, Mort(e)," she said. "There are some things we can't control here."

Mort(e) considered asking her what she thought they actually *could* control. He wished he knew how to get her on his side. There was no denying how much they had in common. Not everyone could handle being second-in-command to Culdesac. But besides being Mort(e)'s successor, Wawa was the first dog he had gotten to know at all since Sheba disappeared. For as much as she reminded him of his old friend, Wawa was the living rejection of all his childish fantasies of Sheba. She did not need Mort(e) or his useless memories. Maybe Sheba wouldn't, either. If they ever met again, Mort(e) would have to earn Sheba's trust. He would have to convince her they had a future and not merely a shared past

CHAPTER TWELVE
THE STORY OF BONAPARTE

HE MESSAGES FROM the *Vesuvius* continued. On the second night, the flashing light said, "Accept EMSAH. Find the true source."

The third message was, "We are devising a plan to get you to the Island. Never stop believing that you will meet her again."

When placed next to the previous messages, it made Mort(e) think for a moment that Sheba was somehow the source, whatever that even meant. He wouldn't put it past the humans to play word games like this.

The fourth message was, "When the war is over, there will be peace among all species. Our vision is brighter than that of the Colony."

The fifth message said, "You are the key. Do not listen to the Queen. You are more than a piece or a number. You are the key. You are the light."

Mort(e) wondered if *key* and *light* should be capitalized. That seemed to be the human thing to do.

The sixth message: "The Archon knows that you will succeed, and that you will free your people and ours. Find the source. The Queen knows. All you have to do is ask her."

Mort(e) found this to be an odd choice of words. Humans tended to use the terms *free* and *freedom* to indicate states of being that were anything but. To suggest that the animals were not free now, after rising from slavery, was outrageous. Was this Archon willing to tell him to his face that he had fought for nothing? That it would have been better for him to remain the property of people who mutilated him, then die as their plaything? All these thoughts led him once again to his most reassuring mantra: *no wonder they lost.*

But the possibility of finding Sheba overruled all other considerations, even his distrust of the humans. There was Sheba, and there was death, and there was nothing else in his future. The finality of it was liberating in a way.

Find the source, the humans said. *All you have to do is ask.*

To do so would require gaining access to the "files" Wawa mentioned. The humans had anticipated what he was already thinking.

Even the Red Sphinx had a weak spot.

MORT(E) ARRIVED AT the barracks after sundown. He checked Culdesac's and Wawa's offices. Both were locked up for the evening.

Mort(e) went to his own office and found Bonaparte shutting the door on his way out. Startled, the pig saluted him. "Sir, I left a report on your desk—"

"I thought we had the first confirmed case of EMSAH today," Mort(e) said.

"Really?"

"But it turned out he had had too much of this," Mort(e) said, handing Bonaparte a bottle of amber liquid. The pig's eyes lit up when he recognized the name: Jack Daniels. These bottles were nearly extinct. Luckily, the Martinis' stash was still intact.

"Culdesac made us drink this one night as a feat of strength," Mort(e) said.

"I know," Bonaparte said. "I heard you were the only one who didn't puke."

"I also shot a pinecone off the medic's head."

"Culdesac didn't mention that."

"Probably didn't want to give you any ideas."

Bonaparte did not appear ready to return the bottle.

"I'm supposed to hand this over to Lieutenant Wawa," Mort(e) said, "but that would be a real waste."

"You know," Bonaparte said, lowering his voice, "there are some people who are qualified to dispose of this evidence."

Mort(e) pretended to be surprised.

"Unless, of course, you wanted to keep it for yourself," Bonaparte said. "It's just that . . . whiskey tastes better in the company of comrades."

"Indeed it does," Mort(e) said.

They went into Mort(e)'s office, poured two drinks into a pair of army-issue cups, and toasted the end of the war. After one drink, Mort(e) could see that Bonaparte was feeling better than he had in ages. Wawa must have been running the entire unit ragged. When Mort(e) suggested that Bonaparte round up some of his drinking buddies, the pig could hardly contain himself.

Within fifteen minutes, they were in the back of a troop transport truck parked at the far end of the base. Bonaparte continued reveling in his role as social organizer, asking "Isn't this great?" multiple times. The others were patient with his enthusiasm, nodding politely. There were five of them, their faces lit by the orange glow of a lamp: Mort(e), Bonaparte, a raccoon named Archer, and two cats—one female, one male—who expected Mort(e) to remember them. Named Hester and Chronos, they were from the same litter and had matching black coats and white bellies.

"We joined to serve under you, sir," Chronos the male said. "But you left the RS the following week."

"There are days when I can't say I blame you, sir," Archer said in his weirdly formal accent. "But look at all the fun you're missing." He poured a flask of his own mystery booze into Mort(e)'s cup. It had a greenish-brown color—or perhaps that was the lighting. Mort(e) detected a strong minty fragrance.

Bonaparte's snout twitched when he picked up the smell. "Aw, don't tell me you brought that nepotism stuff," he said.

"Nepetalactone," Archer corrected him.

"What?" Mort(e) asked.

"The active ingredient in catnip," Hester said. Her brother was already leaning forward for his share. She poked Archer with her claw and handed him her cup so that he could fill both. Archer obliged.

"The RS recruited me for my bravery and my intelligence," Archer said. "But they have allowed me to remain despite my allegedly inferior species because of this invention."

Mort(e) took a sip, allowing the vapor to glide into his nostrils. It was heavenly. The animals probably would have lost the war if this drink had been invented sooner. "I think you can have the rest of the Jack Daniels, Bonaparte," Mort(e) said.

"What are we toasting?" Archer asked.

"Old friends and older friends," Mort(e) said.

"Well said."

Four hands and a hoof clinked their metal cups together. Bonaparte's drinking apparatus caught Mort(e)'s eye. The handle had been hammered out so that it wrapped around the hoof. That way, he would never have to clumsily pick up his drink by squeezing it together with both limbs. While Mort(e) marveled at Bonaparte's stubborn ingenuity, Archer went on about how the nepetalactone was originally meant to be a tea, but the fermented variety had proven to be more popular.

Mort(e) glanced at Bonaparte. The pig's blinks lasted longer, as did his sips of whiskey. Meanwhile, Chronos turned on his small stereo. It had an old compact disc in it that played light piano music from some unknown human artist. The tinkling sound was pleasing to the feline ear. Mort(e) suspected that other animals refused to admit that they liked this music due to its association with cats.

After a few drinks, the group was happy to get Mort(e) up to speed on RS gossip. Chronos and Hester finished each other's sentences as they related the tale of a human child—no more than thirteen years old—who had survived on Twinkies and his pet goldfish while camping out on the roof of a hotel. He fried the fish on a skillet he had made out of a metal desktop. Culdesac calculated that the boy cooked one fish a day for two weeks while standing guard. The RS waited on the ground below, hoping for him to tire out. They could not simply leave him. He was such a good shot with a rifle that he could hit targets at two hundred yards in any direction. The stairwell leading to the roof was barricaded and booby-trapped. A frontal assault would get someone killed. When Culdesac called in a troop of birds, the boy shot every one that came near, the raptors exploding in a burst of feathers that fluttered to the street. While the unit waited, Chronos collected the feathers of the fallen birds and made a headdress out of them. Wawa told him to get rid of it out of respect for the dead.

"She needs to get laid," Hester said, to everyone's delight.

Determined not to lose any soldiers over one nuisance boy, Culdesac called in the ant sappers to undermine the foundation of the building. After three days, the hotel collapsed, the roar of it drowning out any noise the boy might have made. The unit moved on without even searching for his body.

They discussed Wawa's abilities as a leader. In Archer's opinion, her fearlessness made up for her authoritarian style. She never gave an order that she would not follow herself. In many ways, she understood the humans better than the colonel did. During the hotel siege, it was she who convinced Culdesac to wait the boy out, recognizing how dangerous a desperate teenage human could be, all loaded up with hormones and feeling invincible. She must have been an observant pet before the Change.

"I am not, shall we say, of the canine persuasion," Archer said. "But maybe she'd be beautiful without that scar cutting her face in half."

"But then she'd be raising a bunch of pups somewhere," Chronos said. "And that little bastard on the roof would have shot us all."

"True, true," Bonaparte slurred. A drop of whiskey crawled over the side of his cup, oozing onto his hoof. He was about to lick it off. Thinking better of it, he wiped the offending drops onto his vest.

Hester began another story about Wawa, starting it with the half-serious suggestion that she and Culdesac were in a relationship. Archer told her to behave herself. She started again, prompting more comments from the others. And then, Bonaparte broke in.

"Mort(e), I thought you were a real choke-dick when I first met you," he said.

Archer tried to lighten things up. "The pig who can't smell a dead raccoon now smells a rat," he said.

"I'm just saying," Bonaparte said.

"Maybe we should call it a night," Hester said.

"I'm just saying, I said," Bonaparte continued. He placed his hoof to his chest to ease out a noiseless belch that momentarily inflated his cheeks. "You were supposed to be this big hero, and then I come to your door and find this old . . ."

"Choker?"

"Yeah, no. Yeah. You know."

"Forgive our friend, sir," Archer said.

"Shut up, Archer," Bonaparte said, unhooking the handle of his cup from his hoof. Hester offered him more whiskey. Not getting the sarcasm, Bonaparte declined.

"You got your damn medals and your sash and you hightailed it out of there," Bonaparte said. "I don't care what the Council says about peacetime. There was still a war going on, and you quit. I know you were brave, but you're still alive because you're lucky. We're *all* still alive because we're lucky."

"Here, here," Archer said, drawing another halfhearted toast from everyone except for Bonaparte.

"You wanna know what luck is?" Bonaparte asked. "You wanna know what luck is? Luck is being the only pig out of two hundred to survive on a farm that's been abandoned by stupid humans during the war."

No one interrupted him this time. According to Bonaparte, his human masters, a family called the Gregors, left their farm once the ant infestation could no longer be contained. The gates were locked. Only the sliver of sunlight through the broken slats of the roof marked the passage of time. The stronger boars banded together, keeping the weaker ones away as they consumed the last of the food and water. Bonaparte thought that he was among the strong herd until they expelled him. What began as a porcine blockade of the troughs soon became a pack of hunters. Forming a crude phalanx, the strong pigs would pick out one of their softer brethren and descend upon him while the others screamed in futile protest. The marauders would drag the carcass away, while the weaker ones would try to bite off a few morsels or lick up the fragrant trail of blood. The troughs became a graveyard of discarded bones and teeth, picked clean of every scrap of meat. Bonaparte could feel his strength leaving him. Sooner or later, the herd would surround him and make him their next meal so that they could live another day in this prison. It was around that time that Bonaparte felt the effects of the Colony's hormone.

As he said, it was sheer luck. The water supply had been sealed off, so the farm was not exposed to the Queen's experiment. A bird who had already been infected by the Colony's wonder drug perched on the roof with a blade of grass in her beak. She was learning how to talk, and was so excited that she sang the alphabet song, allowing the grass to fall from her mouth. It passed through one of the cracks in the old roof and floated down to the pigpen. It had only a droplet of the bird's saliva, but that was all that was needed. Bonaparte was standing up, half asleep, when the blade landed gently on his snout. He shook it off at first, then realized what it was and gobbled it up. Some of the weaker pigs witnessed the whole thing but realized that they had been too slow. Meanwhile, the stronger pigs squealed, letting him know that his transgression against their authority had been noted.

Within a day, Bonaparte understood things in ways he never had before. He retreated to the far corner of the pen and decided to expend as little energy as possible. One by one, his comrades perished. Those who turned on the others would be summarily punished by the stronger pigs, their victims hauled away regardless. Bonaparte could see the unforgiving nature of the totalitarian state in which he lived: if brutalized long enough, people began to do the dirty work of their oppressors. Time went on, and the stronger ones began to weed out their own kind. They would let a condemned member of their gang lead the way on a killing expedition, only to devour him along with the intended prey. It was only a matter of time before this crude plutocracy exploded into outright anarchy.

Suddenly Bonaparte understood what those words meant.

On Bonaparte's last day in the pen, there were seven other pigs remaining, all of them from the blockade. An eerie quiet let him know that they were waiting for him to fall asleep. He looked past the swine to the gate holding them in. There was a mechanism that he recognized, having examined it thousands of times since he was a piglet. But now he knew what it was. It made perfect sense: flip the latch, release the bolt, open the gate. It was maddening. A simple misunderstanding of how the gate worked had kept his people locked inside for generations. His human masters had left him to die, using his ignorance to prevent him from even putting up a struggle.

The pigs grunted and scraped their hooves. But there was no need to fight. Bonaparte rose to his hind legs and walked right past them. Though he did not make eye contact, he could sense their fear and awe. He opened the gate and stepped out. The pigs, realizing that release had come at last, charged at him. He closed the gate before they could make it. They butted their heads against the metal bars, furious, incredulous that the wall that separated them from the world would yield to this weakling pig. "Godspeed," Bonaparte said to them. Then he left.

"I told myself that that act of cruelty would be the last human thing I would ever do," Bonaparte said.

"Did you ever go back on your word?" Chronos asked.

This seemed to upset Bonaparte more than his story did. He took a long sip of his whiskey and stared at Chronos. "Aren't you paying attention to what we're doing right now?" Bonaparte asked. "We are like the humans all the time, every day."

The group erupted in protest. Chronos said, "Shut up." Hester said, "Here we go," and waved both hands at him in dismissal. Archer laughed.

Mort(e) saw an excuse to end things quickly. "We should definitely call it a night," he said.

"We say we're out there building a new world," Bonaparte said. "But we really live for little moments like these, and not much else. That's okay, but don't tell me that it's not what they used to do."

"The Gregors were planning to *eat* you, were they not?" Archer asked.

"They were oppressors," Hester added. "They left you and your brothers and sisters for dead."

"And now we want to do the same to them," Bonaparte said.

The voices rose again, this time with Chronos and Archer both talking fast, telling Bonaparte he should be grateful for the Change. Bonaparte said he was grateful, but that he wasn't going to pretend. Pretend what, they asked. Pretend this, he replied.

The words blended together for Mort(e). He peeked at his watch. In about an hour, the *Vesuvius* would be sending him another message. He needed to get out of here soon.

Hester switched off the music. Chronos, Archer, and Bonaparte continued to argue. Mort(e) put his hand on Bonaparte's shoulder to indicate that the pig had said too much. Bonaparte was slurring his words, repeating, "I worked hard to get here, dammit." Archer assured him that everyone knew that.

"Wait," Bonaparte said. "Did I? Did I tell you about the pigpen?"

Chronos sighed.

"Time to go, brother," Hester said, holding the door half open.

"I'm afraid you did," Archer said. "We may be too drunk to remember, though."

Disgusted with himself, Bonaparte covered his eyes with his hooves. "You are the master over someone who has told you his story," he said.

Mort(e) recognized the saying. It was spoken by some dog who died during the war, a general. Culdesac liked to quote him, which was probably how Bonaparte heard it.

Chronos and Hester were already walking out, giving feeble goodbyes. Mort(e) insisted that he take Bonaparte to his bunk. Archer asked three times if he could help. Mort(e) turned him down. Then Archer asked if Mort(e) needed to stay on the base for the night. "I've seen some strange things out there lately," the raccoon said. Mort(e) said that they all had.

The pig stumbled a bit but maintained his footing. They rounded the corner of one of the barracks. A cat stood guard. To prevent any trouble, Mort(e) pointed to his captain's sash. The cat saluted and let them pass. They were only a few steps from the door when Mort(e) had to prop Bonaparte on his shoulder to get him through the final leg of the journey. Once inside, he flopped Bonaparte onto his bed and asked if he needed anything. Bonaparte said that he did not.

"An aspirin might prevent a hangover," Mort(e) said. "Works for me." They went back and forth about it, with Bonaparte saying he would be okay. But Mort(e) kept pressing him. Finally, Bonaparte relented.

"Is it in your strongbox?" Mort(e) asked.

"Yes, but . . ."

Everyone was issued a strongbox—a metal chest—and no one was supposed to give out the combination.

"Just give me the code," Mort(e) said. "I'm a captain, remember? Well, sort of. Temporarily. Anyway, you can trust me."

Bonaparte sighed and leaned back on the bed. He told Mort(e) where the box was, then recited the code. "You are the master over someone who has told you his story," Bonaparte repeated.

The medical kit was plainly visible when Mort(e) opened the box. He saw the pills and pretended to fumble for them. "Who said that?" he asked. "About being the master over someone?"

To the left was a metal cylinder. Checking on Bonaparte to make sure he was not paying attention, Mort(e) reached inside. His hand grasped the antenna of the translator. That a pig had been trusted with this top-secret device was a testament to how peaceful things had been lately.

"Some dog," Bonaparte said. "But a human said it to me, too. The other day."

"The other *day*?"

"No, no," he said. "Not the other day. I was *thinking* about it the other day. No, it was a long time ago."

"Okay." Mort(e) did not have time to interrogate him.

"So you see?" Bonaparte said. "We're just like them. I know you think that, even if you're scared to say it."

"I've never been scared to say it," Mort(e) said. "And that's why I'm not in the Red Sphinx anymore." He removed the translator from the cylinder while lifting the pill jar from the chest.

Then he closed the lid, slid the translator under Bonaparte's bed, and stood up. He put two pills on the small table beside Bonaparte's bed and asked if he needed water. Bonaparte said he would be fine. Mort(e) leaned over, picked up the translator, and headed for the door. He kept the device close to his side, confident that the room was too dim for Bonaparte to notice anything unusual.

"Thanks, Mort(e)," Bonaparte said.

"Thank *you*," Mort(e) replied. "And remember: you crawled through that awful life, and now you're a war hero. Even if you're more human than you expected, you have nothing to be ashamed of. Understand?"

"Sure, sure," Bonaparte said. He was already asleep by the time Mort(e) shut the door behind him.

Mort(e) fought the urge to return the device during the long walk to the camp entrance. Betraying another member of the Red Sphinx was unforgivable. Even Culdesac would torture him for this. To keep his feet moving, all he had to do was to imagine himself, as he had so many years earlier, growing old and dying alone in the same place. Still calling out his friend's name. He had this mission, or he had nothing. It was awful, Mort(e) thought. And then he thought, *But it's beautiful, too.* This quest was the only beautiful thing left in the entire world.

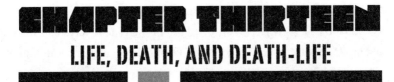

CHAPTER THIRTEEN
LIFE, DEATH, AND DEATH-LIFE

THAT NIGHT, MORT(E) recorded the flickering light in the sky once again. He had gotten much better at deciphering Morse code, and even recognized a few words right away. One word stuck out among the dots and dashes like a drop of blood on a white blouse:

Purge.

There was no time to ponder it for very long. The light kept blinking. Once the *Vesuvius* floated off again, Mort(e) brought the notebook to his desk and began piecing together the message. It said, "Good work stealing translator. Watch for Briggs at the Purge in three days."

There would be very little sleep tonight. Too many things were twisting in his mind. The resistance knew about the translator. They knew about the next Purge. Briggs had been captured, though this was not much of a surprise. Maybe the Archon sent him on a suicide mission. Maybe their prophet foresaw it. Mort(e) imagined Briggs lying in the pile of dead deer in the quarry, his eyes staring skyward with all the others.

Briggs must have planted something in his house, a camera or a radio. Mort(e) overturned every piece of furniture in the garage. The desk, chair, table, stool. The lamp with its St. Jude necklace. He couldn't find anything. Instead of a camera, the humans most likely had eyes on the ground. Maybe in the Bureau.

Maybe even in the Red Sphinx.

The sun was nearly up when he retreated to his spot in the basement. While trying to plan the next few days, he fell asleep. Soon he was dreaming of flying through the clouds at daybreak. The *Vesuvius* eclipsed the sun before lumbering out of the way. The rays glinting off the silvery hull did not make him squint. White birds circled the airship like a halo, inviting and mysterious. He imagined Sheba onboard, peering at him through a round window. But he could not get any closer.

THE COLONY ANNOUNCED the Purge over the radio stations. The Red Sphinx was expected to be there.

A book in his lap, Mort(e) sat cross-legged in the square of sunlight until it stretched into a long golden trapezoid. The book was a manual for the translator, titled *G-16 Colony-to-Mammal Translation Module: A User's Guide*. It began with diagrams outlining the basic structure of the device, along with instructions on how to establish communication, sort of like the *over* and *ten-four* that the humans had used. Every conversation began with a string of prime numbers, the main units of the ants' mathematical system. Listing the numbers was like a greeting that also booted up the device's computer. After that, the user would see (or hear, or feel) other data indicating that the device was synching up with the brain. There would typically be a DNA sequence or some other seemingly random information. The first-time user not only heard words but also saw images and even felt physical sensations, like a living dream.

The manual included a special user testimonial written by a Colonel Yojimbo, a feline war hero who went missing in the Battle of the Potomac. The testimonial was printed on special yellow paper in the middle of the book and came with a small photo of the colonel, his maroon sash perched on the silver fur of his shoulder. His whiskers drooped slightly, giving him a dignified yet exhausted demeanor. Here Yojimbo described what the machine did to the mammalian brain, and how the user could prepare for the shock.

"Think of the day you changed," Yojimbo wrote. "Recall the *horror* of it: seeing into the future, remembering the past, stacking them together like building blocks. Before they were nothing but amorphous clouds of images drifting about in dreams and half-remembered moments of déjà vu.

"Now multiply that horror by about ten.

"And while you're at it, think of the drunkest you have ever been. (Yes, I know we do not drink like humans.) And think of the first time you mated. If you are a soldier, think of the first time you killed someone. Think of the first time a loved one died.

"Take all these things, roll them into a sharp-edged mass, and swallow it."

Yojimbo went into detail about how the inexperienced user had to center himself by focusing on a safer time. "Paradoxically," he wrote, "you must return to the innocence of your youth, even if that youth was under the control of our oppressors."

So Mort(e) would have to imagine himself in a scenario that made him feel whole, peaceful, and free of guilt or fear—what humans called a "happy place." It was necessary because the conversion of chemical signals to spoken language involved every cubic inch of the brain. Those with little experience with the device often had to piece together the meaning later. There were stories of people who were crippled by the translator, virtually lobotomized. Some were even said to have reverted to their previous states, walking on all fours. Culdesac's talent with the device fit well with his personality. A bobcat could probably imagine anywhere as a safe haven.

Yojimbo also discussed the rumors that humans were

incapable of using the device. "The rumors are true," Yojimbo said, "and they're even worse than you thought." Human brains, already tainted with EMSAH-like symptoms, would often simply shut down after exposure to the translator. The only humans who did not die within minutes of initiating communication were children, and they did not last long afterward. Maybe the Queen designed the device for that very purpose.

Mort(e) readied his things. He placed the translator into his backpack. Before he left, he went to the basement, touched his fingers to his lips, and placed them on the SHEBA IS ALIVE message. If he died, the next person to read this would not understand its significance. That person would erase the message, and everything about Mort(e) would be forgotten.

EVERYONE GATHERED AT the mouth of the temple.

Before finding a spot in the crowd, Mort(e) passed a bonfire where adolescent dogs sang and danced around the flames in celebration. The rest of the spectators gathered quietly, speaking to one another in nods and grunts like guests at a funeral. Nearby, two lines of soldiers staked out a path from the opening of the ziggurat to the vessels on the river.

After sunset, the anthill lit up with its otherworldly light. The aperture opened. Everyone gasped at once. And then the humans were trotted out. A smaller number than last time, but enough to put on a show.

Mort(e) began easing his way to the front. People gave him dirty looks—no one was expected to stand up yet. It wasn't part of the tradition. By then, some of the humans were already crying. On cue, the weeping increased when the animals rose and began to mockingly wave at the prisoners. The movement of the crowd provided an opportunity for Mort(e) to get closer until he was right at the edge of the path.

Mort(e) picked up the scent of raccoon. He stood on his toes to get a better view. Briggs was easy to find, dressed from the waist down in his animal disguise. A mud-spattered gray shirt covered his upper body.

Mort(e) pressed forward, barely noticing the person in front of him until he felt the bushy tail of a fox brush his face.

"Watch it, pal," the fox said.

"That man was my master," Mort(e) said.

"Give me a break," the fox said.

"No, look."

The commotion caught Briggs's eye. He recognized Mort(e).

"Sure, go ahead of me, no problem," the fox said, stunned by the coincidence.

Mort(e) stepped to the front. Behind him, the fox told everyone within earshot that this choker had seen his old master. The fox then corrected himself. "This *cat*, I mean." Mort(e) could feel everyone's eyes on him as they whispered.

When Briggs got close enough, he acknowledged Mort(e) with a nod and said, "Find the source."

"Yes," Mort(e) said.

"Keep searching," he said, lower this time. "Every day she calls for you. We can hear it just like you can."

Briggs began reciting a verse—either a prayer or a poem, Mort(e) couldn't tell. An Alpha shoved Briggs from behind, moving him along with the others. One by one, the nearby onlookers each placed a hand on Mort(e)'s shoulder and offered words of encouragement.

"I've never seen that at a Purge before," someone said.

"Hang in there," someone else said.

"He won't hurt you again."

"I can't believe he recognized you!"

"He must have had a really guilty conscience."

Mort(e) nodded and thanked them all. Before he could get away, an elderly dog approached him. Her muzzle was pure white, her face so droopy it resembled a mask. "Be strong," she said, on the verge of tears. "I realize this must be hard for you."

"I'm fine," Mort(e) said.

But she would not let him walk away. "There are people you can talk to," she said. "Everyone handles a meeting with the former master differently."

"I'll be all right," he said, turning away from her.

Some members of the audience were already leaving. The rest followed the humans as they moved on to the ships that would take them away forever. Many animals were still waving. Mort(e) could no longer see Briggs amidst the flapping arms.

"Enjoying the show?" came a voice to his left. It was Wawa. Her arms were folded like a human's. People continued to stream past them.

Wawa invited him to walk with her toward the dock. A row of RS vehicles was parked near the water, where the humans would be loaded onto the ships. Archer was there, along with the nameless cats who had replaced Mort(e)'s comrades from the war. Culdesac stood beside one of the transports. He acknowledged Mort(e) with a tip of his head. Bonaparte was nowhere to be found.

"There's something I need to tell you," Wawa said.

"The war's over?"

"One of our members has EMSAH," she said softly, so that the incendiary word dissolved into the background noise.

"A cat?" Mort(e) asked.

"The pig, actually. Bonaparte."

She explained that Bonaparte tried to take a Humvee off base that morning. When the guards at the checkpoint requested his authorization, he rammed the gate. The soldiers shot out the tires. The vehicle flipped over, and they dragged Bonaparte from it. Even worse, Wawa believed that he smuggled the company translator away from the barracks. It was probably in the hands of the resistance by now.

Mort(e)'s stomach clenched as she related the story. He wondered if his theft of the device had triggered all of this somehow. Or perhaps Bonaparte would have gone crazy with or without losing the translator, especially if he really had been infected by a human. Mort(e) knew that his own behavior could be interpreted as a sign of EMSAH. The only difference was, he hadn't been caught yet.

"Are you sure he's infected?" Mort(e) asked.

"Does it matter?" she asked. "I've been reading your reports. There have been a lot of late-stage symptoms out there. Paranoia. Delusions. No concern for living or dying. Talking in non sequiturs. Bonaparte is showing all of these. He even confessed that he's been visited by a human. The doctors are running tests on him now to confirm."

"Don't you have those little strips that turn yellow?"

"We do," she said. "And they're all negative. But I don't care—it's definitely EMSAH. I'm not waiting for some doctor to make the call."

There was genuine anguish in her voice. Bonaparte was supposed to be the success story of the RS, having overcome his past as a farm animal, the lowest of the slaves. She truly worried about him. It was so like a dog. *So like Sheba.*

"So when does the quarantine begin?" Mort(e) said.

"We don't know."

"What do you mean, you don't know? What other information do you need?"

"The Colony has ordered us to stand by."

"Stand by for what?"

"Mort(e), you know that the Queen doesn't have to explain herself. But there is some good news."

"What's that?"

"You're fired. There will no longer be any need for your investigation. We're going to set up a hospital to keep the potential victims away from the others. We hope it buys us enough time to evacuate the settlers. So my last orders to you: turn in any outstanding reports, go home, and remain calm."

All the people Mort(e) interviewed were under house arrest, she said. But all military personnel would be sent to a processing station and reassigned to some other settlement.

They were almost to the river. Mort(e) gripped Wawa's elbow. "You don't really believe that, do you?" he asked.

She snapped her arm out of his grasp and headed toward the trucks. "Pull yourself together before I put you in a cell with Bonaparte," she said.

"Answer me."

"Go home," she said, spinning away from him. "That's my answer."

She headed toward the RS trucks, where a large horseshoe of Alpha soldiers kept the remaining crowd at bay. Another group escorted the last of the humans into the ship. At the base of the plank, an Alpha awaited the report from the leader of the Red Sphinx.

Culdesac passed through the line of Alphas and approached the lead ant soldier. The colonel wore his translator—a newer model, slightly smaller than the one Mort(e) had stolen. The onlookers jostled one another to get a closer look at the exchange. That left a few Alphas at the end of the row standing guard against nothing.

Mort(e) stood in front of the last Alpha and pulled the device from his backpack. The soldier remained still. The only movement came from the hundreds of normal-sized ants that crawled on her exoskeleton. Mort(e) placed the translator on his head, adjusting the mouthpiece. The smaller ants stopped moving. They waited for him to begin. Mort(e) took a deep breath and pictured himself

resting in the basement, lounging beside Sheba, when the Martini
house was the entire universe and nothing could disturb it.
    He put the earbud into place.

2, 3, 5, 7, 11, 13, 17, 19, 23, 29,
31, 37, 41, 43, 47,
53, 59, 61, 67,
71, 73, 79,
83, 89,
97.

GCGAATGCGTCCACAACGCTACAGGTG

GCGAATGCGTCCACAACGCTACAGGT

GCGAATGCGTCCACAACGCTACAGG

GCGAATGCGTCCACAACGCTACAG

GCGAATGCGTCCACAACGCTACA

GCGAATGCGTCCACAACGCTAC

GCGAATGCGTCCACAACGCTA

GCGAATGCGTCCACAACGCT

GCGAATGCGTCCACAACGC

GCGAATGCGTCCACAACG

GCGAATGCGTCCACAAC

GCGAATGCGTCCACAA

GCGAATGCGTCCACA

GCGAATGCGTCCAC

GCGAATGCGTCCA

GCGAATGCGTCC

GCGAATGCGTC

GCGAATGCGT

GCGAATGCG

GCGAATGC

GCGAAT

A thousand voices screamed random numbers and sounds into Mort(e)'s ears. The same figures scrolled across his field of vision, brushing against his coat until he felt them crawling on his skin like insects. His only connection to the real world was the feeling of his useless choker hands coiling into fists. According to Yojimbo, the randomness should have been coalescing into words by now, if not full sentences. Mort(e) was losing control of it. The words grew louder. They changed color and began cutting into his skin. They smelled like an electrical charge. He tried to imagine the basement. Sheba was no longer there. Only the message remained—SHEBA IS ALIVE. The words rattled and fell from the wall, shattering on the floor.

00010111010001011010001011101000101101000101110100010110 10100010111010001000010111010001011010001011101000101110100 01000101110100010110100010111010000010

DARKNESS. A METAL smell. Sweat and dirt. Mort(e)'s knees rubbing against a steel surface. His sides are closed in. An air duct. Tiberius (Socks) is right behind him. Culdesac is ahead. (One time, before a mission, Culdesac asked Tiberius if he was ready to die, and Tiberius said, "Do you think I joined this outfit because I wanted to live?" And everyone laughed.) Culdesac's enormous tail wags. They are infiltrating a cell of humans who have taken shelter in an old army bunker. The humans are smart. Willing to die. The walls are impervious even to bomb strikes. The ants are unable to dislodge the enemy without devoting an enormous effort to the task. There are explosives rigged everywhere. Culdesac tells them to move quickly, but to touch nothing, and to be quiet. "Anything can trip the bombs," he says.

Then gunshots, penetrating the air duct. The humans have detected them. They panic, firing at everything. The sound rattles the entire shaft. Rays of fluorescent light poke through the darkness with each bullet hole. Younger members of the team yell out, giving away their position. Culdesac tells them to shut up. They try to scramble back the way they came, making more noise. "Over here," the humans yell. "Over here!" Culdesac takes his rifle from his shoulder. He crawls to a section of the duct riddled with bullet holes. With the butt of his rifle, he slams the panel and bursts through it. He has only one chance before the humans begin shooting. He crashes down into a room, tearing through metal and drywall. Mort(e) prepares to jump in after him. He calls to Tiberius (Socks). Tiberius (Socks) does not answer. Tiberius (Socks) lies motionless. Tiberius (Socks) is dead. Mort(e) plunges into the fountain of light. He lands on a table. The room is some kind of lounge. Culdesac kneels behind a couch, screaming for Mort(e) to take cover with him. A dead man sits on the couch. Other than the bleeding hole in his temple, the man seems relaxed. Mort(e) leaps behind the couch. Culdesac shoots the lights out. Now only the cats can see. Muzzle flashes light up the room, each one a blinking star illuminating a terrified human face.

SEBASTIANSEBASTIANSEBASTIANSEBASTIANSEBASTIANSEBASTIAN SEBASTIAN**MORT(E)**SEBASTIAN

MORT(E) STOOD IN the Martinis' basement again. The message about Sheba was on the wall. Sunlight entered through the windows. But it was cold, and Sheba was not there. Still, he felt relieved. The initial shocks of the device were beginning to subside. He controlled his brain's reaction, but he was not ready to communicate yet. He no longer had a connection to the real world. He could not feel his finger stumps pressing into his hands. For all he knew, he was standing there with his mouth open, already surrounded by Wawa's soldiers. He closed his eyes and tried to focus. Maybe he would survive this after all, even if the quarantine killed him and everyone else the next day.

He opened his eyes. The basement had now returned to its prewar state. The graffiti was gone. Sitting in her favorite spot, in defiance of all those lost years, was Sheba. Mort(e) got closer. She rose like she had on the day he took her on a journey to the attic at the top of the world.

IDENTIFICATION, she said. But her mouth did not move. Mort(e) felt the word travel through him.

Now that he had arrived at his happy place, Mort(e) was unable to gain control of his mouth.

IDENTIFICATION, the voice repeated.

Mort(e), he said at last. *OF dash 2.961630.*

Sheba shuddered like an ancient machine switched on after years of lying dormant. At one point, she even flickered like an image on television.

COMMUNICATION ENGAGED.

A clicking sound began, which Mort(e) interpreted as the device's software kicking in, manifesting itself in the dream world interface he had created.

I'm . . . Mort(e) stopped, remembering that he needed to speak in short, declarative sentences. The ants did not communicate in messages that began with personal acknowledgements or ended with question marks.

Requesting description of EMSAH syndrome. That one sentence was exhausting, leaving him gasping for air.

Sheba flickered again. BIOWEAPON HUMAN. DEPLOYED. INFECTIOUSSPREADINGCONTAGIOUS. NO CURE. DEADLY. CURE UNKNOWN.

This was what Yojimbo talked about: you had to keep the questions simple in order to keep the fragmented answers manageable. Sheba blurted out adjectives, all telling Mort(e) what he already knew.

Acknowledged, Mort(e) said. Sheba stopped. *Requesting source of EMSAH.*

HUMANS HUMANITY HUMANKIND.

Requesting . . . description of EMSAH infection.

More clicking and flickering. Then:

PATHOGEN CONCEPTION-INTRODUCTION TO SUSCEPTIBLE-SUGGESTIBLE SUBJECT.

Mort(e) sighed at the jargon. Sheba stopped talking.

Requesting description of EMSAH infection, Mort(e) repeated.

Sheba began again. ACUTE CEREBELLAR ATAXIA CEREBRAL HYPOXIA. INSERTION POINT SELF-TRANSCENDENCE VESICULAR MONOAMINE TRANSPORTER. ENVIRONMENTAL STIMULI . . .

The illusion of the basement began to disintegrate. The faces of the human soldiers appeared in flashes around Sheba.

NEUROTRANSMITTER INHIBITOR. EUPHORIA-FLYING. LOGICAL FACULTIES DIS-CARDED. SUBJECT DESIRES [DESPERATE-WANTING] DEATH-LIFE. SOCIAL PATTERN REINITIALIZED. NEW CONSTRUCT . . .

Death-life?

Acknowledged, Mort(e) said. Sheba stopped talking. For a moment, the flickering images of the human soldiers stopped. *Requesting explanation of death-life.*

The muzzle flashes returned as the translator processed the request, blinking in synch with the clicking noise.

LIFEDEATHLIFEDEATHLIFEDEATHLIFEDEATHLIFEDEATHLIFEDEATHLIFEDEATH.

Death-life is life-death? That doesn't make any—

REPEAT.

Requesting explanation of relationship between EMSAH and death-life.

EMSAH IS DEATH-LIFE. SUBJECT DELUDEDPOLLUTEDCONTAMINATED WITH DEATH-LIFE. SUBJECT DEATH-LIFE. SUBJECT BECOMES DEATH-LIFE.

What?

DEATH-LIFE BECOMES SUBJECT. OVERLOAD. SOCIAL REINITIALIZATION FAILURE INEVITABLE.

Requesting explanation of relationship between subject and death-life.

SUBJECT ENTERS DEATH-LIFE. OVERLOAD. DEATH-LIFE OVERRIDE. LOGICAL FACULTIES DISCARDED.

Requesting explanation of relationship between logical faculties and death-life.

Sheba tilted her head as if being tempted with a treat. INCOMPATIBLEIMPOSSIBLE.

So death-life was not logical now?

Requesting description of final stages of EMSAH.

Sheba did not hesitate: NO-NAME WAR.

Requesting explanation of relationship between EMSAH and Mort(e) OF 2.961630.

Mort(e) blinked once to find himself in the Martinis' living room, standing before the mirror. But in the reflection, Daniel's son Michael stared at him. He wore the translator, his eyes vacant like a doll's.

SEBASTIAN, he said. Then he repeated it, only this time stretching each syllable out in a screeching sound, like the twisting beams of a collapsing building.

The noise made Mort(e) wince. Sheba's barking cut through the sound. When Mort(e) opened his eyes, he was in the basement again, his safe place. Sheba was with him once more. There was a subtlety in her voice that he recognized. It was the same impatient tone she used on that morning when she gave birth to her little ones. She was begging him to understand something, and losing hope that he would.

The sound of it nearly made him weep like a human. He searched for a way out. The staircase was gone. The windows sealed up. The lights dimmed. Sheba vanished. In her place stood a bearded man painted in shimmering silver and dressed in a long robe. The ring floating around his head made Mort(e) recognize him: St. Jude, the little man from the medallion worn by the old female dog, Olive. He stared at Mort(e) with metal eyes, the pupils smoothed out.

519519519519519519519519519519519519519519519951
9519519519519519

MORT(E) COULD FEEL breath moving in and out of him. The oxygen permeated his entire body and then released from random apertures along his sides. He could move several appendages at once—he waved arms above his head and stretched another pair of arms that were linked to his waist. There was nothing unnatural about it. He accepted that this was how he was put together. He realized that he was experiencing things from the perspective of an insect. An ant.

The Queen.

A shiver of chemical signals told him that he was in a chamber. There were others arrayed about him, standing in a semi-circle. Massive worker ants. The ants held smaller ones—baby Alphas, *yes*—in their jaws. Their chemicals made contact with Mort(e)'s antennae, stimulating his brain with scents, sounds, written words, throbbing pain, colors—all at once.

One of the workers offered a little one for him to inspect. Mort(e) extended his claws to the small creature. He cradled it. The Alpha spoke to him in rudimentary chemical phrases, signaling recognition and acquiescence to authority. And acceptance of whatever fate was in store for her.

Mort(e) understood that he was not simply communicating with the Queen—he was living her memories, absorbing each moment in her thousands of years of life. This larva he held would be given the same data. It would spill outward from the Queen's brain.

Moments from her life flowed past him. A march through the desert. An animal devoured by a horde of the Queen's daughters. A tunnel winding into itself, then veering into an infinite number of directions. A parade of human artifacts taken from the surface—pages torn from books, a match, a thimble.

And then there was another Queen before him, a sickly thing, dying. The Misfit, Daughter of the Lost One.

As their antennae touched, Mort(e) felt the agony of thousands of years of despair and solitude. The current of memories stopped, coagulating into a pool around him. Mort(e) could not control himself—he sank his jaws into his (her) mother's head and tore it off. The claws scratched at the massive fatal wound. The Misfit's body slumped over.

Mort(e) saw everything now.

He felt the Queen's rage against the humans. It welled up inside and became a part of her. The anger stitched her exoskeleton together, kept her blood pumping all these years. Mort(e) couldn't breathe. It was like a choir of dying human children screaming in his ear, or a white-hot flame sucking in all the oxygen around it. The Queen lived with this every moment. She *re*lived it every moment. She was shackled to the past. There was no rest. Mort(e) tried to scream. The children's broken voices burst from his mouth. Cries for help were no good here. He was lost. His body would be a shell, his mind absorbed into the Colony. A drop of ink in a pool of water, dispersed into nothingness.

He thought of Sheba dying somewhere. Sheba. Sheba would save him. If not for that thought, Mort(e) would have forgotten everything and melted away. He closed the jaws of his mechanical insect mouth. He had to speak like an ant, think like an ant. He felt himself choking. But he concentrated and at last spoke again in the chemical language of the ants:

Requesting description of EMSAH syndrome.

..--....--.-.--.---.--.-..--.....--.-..--.---.--.-..--.....--.-..--.---.--.-..--.....--.-..--.---.--.-..--.--...

A VIRUS ENTERS a bacterium. The virus multiplies. The bacterium adapts. The virus overtakes it.

The bacterium dies.

A virus enters a bacterium. Many viruses enter many bacteria. Many bacteria die. Many survive. Their defensive systems adapt, destroying the virus. But the bacteria have changed. They move differently, react to outsiders with more hostility. They cling to those that are similar, exchanging nutrients with them. They grope for the light as one.

The bacteria evolve.

A SCHOOL OF fish. Moving as a unit, silver strands of thread in the water. They are starving. Hunted. Drawn to an ancient place. Mindlessly driven by their senses. They are picked off by predators. By disease. By exhaustion. They arrive at this sacred location, the place of their birth. Their senses confirm it, the chemicals pouring through their gills. Their brains pulse with excitement. They begin the ritual as one. Ravenous, they mate, their sperm and eggs exploding into the water, christening it with the chemical signals of their clan.

PRIMATES DESCEND FROM trees. The leaves blot out the sun. They gather to watch a battle between the alpha male and a challenger. The alpha has ruled for three seasons, like his father before him. But this is a different time, when the trees have begun to die out. The rains have become less frequent. Predators have grown more aggressive. They smell weakness.

The challenger waits for his opportunity. When the alpha lunges for him, the challenger dodges and pounces. The sycophants jump with delight, with the same mindless glee they would show for the alpha. The challenger seizes the advantage and pummels the leader until provoking a desperate squeal for mercy. The alpha is banished. His blood stinks of defeat. The challenger becomes the new leader. The others whoop and holler. They reach out to touch the coat of the new king. The females fawn over him, clawing at one another to claim him. The little ones offer scraps of food. The new leader holds his hands out to his subjects. He will protect them. But he will also prevent the next challenger from arising.

A MAN KNEELS in prayer, wearing sandals and a robe. His village is under attack. An ant infestation. The elders have gone mad. They have already taken the whores to be sacrificed. But that has not satisfied their gods. So they took some of the wives, the disagreeable ones who blamed the men for the invasion. Now they have taken children to the altar. Screaming little ones, with scraped knees and elbows. The man's daughter is dead at the steps of the altar, the last sacrifice before sundown. The high priest smears her entrails on his forehead, then wipes the gore onto the heads and shoulders of the firstborn males. A symbol of strength and purity. The others beat drums. The women wail and lament. The man is sad but hopeful. Surely this will be enough to sate the gods' thirst for blood. Surely he will see his daughter again. They will race to each other across a breezy field of wheat. They will embrace in the shade of a passing cloud.

ΩΩΩΩΩΩΩΩΩΩΩΩΩΩΩΩΩΩΩΩΩΩΩΩΩΩΩΩΩΩΩΩΩΩΩΩΩΩΩΩΩ

Yojimbo had said this would happen. Mort(e) had gone as deep as he could, and now backed out of the layers one at a time. He passed through the membrane that led to the Queen's lair. One moment, he was in her head, surveying her empire. The next, he was one of her daughters, a baby Alpha being presented for her communion ritual. The Queen held him, her antennae probing. And then she lifted him to her jaws and crunched down, slicing his soft exoskeleton in half. Alarms sounded. But then another signal came through from the Queen, ordering him to be still, to embrace this essential role for the Colony. Death would bring forth new life.

89.7563.90.66453.097614.8654437.09821245678.864231.090874 1345779.867655.21124

MORT(E)'S MOUTH OPENED, but he could not speak. He was in the basement again. He was alone, though he could still smell Sheba. And Michael.

He swallowed.

42112.556768.97795431478090.132468.87654212890.7344568.4 16790.35466.09.3657.9

DARKNESS AGAIN. ENOUGH light to see. The bunker is secure. The iron scent of blood hangs in the air. Sticking to fur and skin. A bullet has grazed Mort(e)'s right hand. Bruises and cuts on his body from the fall through the ceiling. No pain yet. That comes later.

Culdesac reloads his gun. The others have their orders. Red Sphinx soldiers collect weapons from the dead humans. Mort(e) approaches him. Culdesac does not need to hear any encouraging words. Mort(e) stands nearby until Culdesac finishes with the gun. "They killed Tiberius," Culdesac says. Voice all gravelly. He has not used the name *Tiberius* in months. Only *Socks*.

"This one's alive, sir," someone says. The soldiers gather around a dying human. The sound of congested, labored breathing. Frightened, exhausted eyes gaze up from the ground. There is a piece of metal on the man's chest. A necklace.

Everyone stares at him to see if they recognize him. From before. They do not. But the man's fear is familiar. Mort(e) kneels down. The man reaches out a bloody hand to him. Mort(e) wonders if this is the man who fired the shot that killed Tiberius (Socks). "Lord," the man says. "Lord, forgive these wretched creatures. They know not what they do." Mort(e)'s eyes lock on the metal object. It is a medallion with the image of a man with a sun standing behind his head. Culdesac aims his rifle at the human. "Yes, we do, you choking liar," he says. Culdesac fires. A spray of blood and bone. The body jerks and then lies still. A red drop covers the medallion. The silver man with the sun behind him is submerged.

*   *   *

*¬¬ΩΩ••∞

DISENGAGE...

┤┬┴╀║

0100010110100001011100001011010001011101000101011110100010110100010111010

MORT(E) FELT THE urge to spit. He lay facedown in the dirt at the feet of the Alpha soldier. He coughed in order to expel the mud from his open mouth. The Queen's hatred lifted from his body like steam, leaving him wet and shivering. It was impossible, he thought. How could she even still be alive with all that going on inside her? He hated her. He couldn't resist adopting what appeared to be her only emotion, cultivated and harnessed over thousands of years. He hated her and he wanted her to die.

He propped himself up on his forearms. The crowd was still watching the ships. Culdesac stood at the podium, ready to begin his speech. As Mort(e) had expected, the entire procedure had taken only a few seconds.

"Are you all right?" came a voice behind him. A male cat and his two daughters stood nearby. Mort(e) simultaneously got to his feet and removed the device, holding it at his side, pretending it was just a hat. He caught his breath.

"We saw you fall," the cat said.

"Requesting explanation—"

"What?"

Mort(e) had to refocus all over again. The act of standing up made him dizzy. "I'm okay," he said at last. He inhaled deeply to fight off a wave of nausea. "I'm okay," he repeated.

"Do you need—"

"No."

One of the little ones asked, "Daddy, why did he fall down?" In the distance, Culdesac's amplified voice began talking about the new order. But it was all clanks and whistles and buzzes to Mort(e). He was already running home.

PART IV **ESCAPE**

CHAPTER FOURTEEN
THE PACK, DISBANDED

BONAPARTE'S CELL WAS larger than his old room. Still, the doctor tending to him—a bear named Rigel—could barely fit inside. She had to stoop to get through the gate and could not stand up straight while she checked Bonaparte's vital signs. It was another inexplicable case—no physical symptoms, not even a fever—but the pig had definitely lost his mind.

Wawa waited outside the cell, in the long hallway of the detention block, wearing a hazmat suit. A respirator covered her snout. Two dog soldiers waited alongside her.

When Rigel was finished, the soldiers locked the cell, and all four of them walked into a decontamination area, where special hoses sprayed bleach-tinged water on their suits. Rigel laughed when she saw the crude apparatus. She asked Wawa if this was actually meant to keep the infection in or out.

"Just tell me what you found," Wawa said, removing her respirator.

There was no change in Bonaparte's condition. He was under light sedation—still awake, but his plans to defect to the human resistance would be on hold for a while.

"So when does it start?" Rigel asked.

"When does what start?" Wawa replied, knowing full well that Rigel was referring to the quarantine.

A loud *bang* in Bonaparte's cell prevented Rigel from responding. Wawa put her mask on again and went into the hallway, with Rigel and the soldiers trailing behind her. When they arrived at the cell, they found that Bonaparte had toppled to the floor, having flipped over his cot. He tried to stand up, still woozy from the sedatives.

"Get up, soldier," Wawa said.

"This isn't boot camp," Rigel said. "You have to—"

"Quiet. We've got enough problems around here without you running your mouth."

Rigel threw her hands up and headed for the door. "See you at the processing station, Lieutenant," she said.

Bonaparte propped himself up and sat on the bed, facing Wawa through the bars. His hooves rested on his chubby knees. "The humans are watching us," he said.

"What humans?" she asked.

"You wouldn't know," Bonaparte said. "You fight for the Colony. You have eyes, but you are as blind as the Queen."

He rose. His hooves clicked. "I want to help you, Lieutenant," Bonaparte said. "I really do. But we are both running out of time."

"What does that mean?"

"Soon one of us will be dead. Only people like me will be on a new journey."

"We're on a journey, all right," Wawa said. "Like those deer at the bottom of the quarry."

"That's closer to the truth than you might realize," Bonaparte said.

Wawa left the room. After passing through decontamination, she dumped the biohazard suit and the mask in a pile on the floor for the soldiers to pick up.

It was a long walk to her office on the other side of the base.

Bonaparte's detention had become an open secret among the soldiers. The only person who still seemed relaxed was Culdesac. When Wawa reported the news to him the day before, the colonel simply nodded and sipped his coffee. After doing most of the talking, she finally came out and asked him: what was going to happen if there was a quarantine? He repeated the same tired lines about how the uninfected would be evacuated and resettled.

She asked him what a processing station was.

"It's a station where they process things," he said. "Hence the name. What do you want from me, Lieutenant? We have our orders. We're going to get through this."

He had never snapped at her like that before. Even when the other cats in the unit wondered out loud about Wawa's abilities to lead, Culdesac reminded them that he had made the right choice. The colonel even beat one of the insubordinates in front of everyone and made him apologize to the entire squad. He told the others that Wawa would now be given discretion to beat anyone who even twitched a whisker at her, and that if she killed someone in the process, he would find a replacement and move on. She went on to prove herself, and still Culdesac, her commanding officer, was the one who treated her with the most respect. Culdesac knew about her past. He told her once that he related to it. He had been wild, whereas she had been wild but caged. A warrior who had been bottled up. One time, he told her—he *whispered* to her—that she was like the Queen in that regard. And despite all of that, here he was feeding her a bureaucratic talking point, as though they hadn't fought and suffered together. The blandness of it stung her, leaving a heavy sensation in the pit of her stomach, like a fist pressing down on her insides.

Wawa arrived at her office, rubbed away the tension in her

eyes, and opened the door. Upon entering, she found Mort(e) sitting stiffly at her desk. With his left thumb and index finger, he rubbed a silver medallion that hung on a chain around his neck.

"What are you doing here?" she said. "You can't—"

Mort(e) lifted a gun from his lap and placed it on the desk, right on top of her logbook. He made sure to drop it with a *thud* to drive the point home. "Close the door, Lieutenant."

Wawa did as she was told. "What's going on, Mort(e)?" she asked.

"Many things," he whispered, his hand hovering over the gun. She fixated on the amputated digits, the smoothly worn nubs where his fingertips should have been.

"Mort(e)," she said, "I'm not your enemy. Tell me what's wrong."

"Maybe nothing's wrong," he said. "Maybe this was how it was supposed to go."

The nice approach wasn't working. "I spent the day talking in circles with the pig," she said. "Now don't you start with this—"

"I know what EMSAH is," he said.

He sighed. His hand came to a rest on the gun. If he was going to shoot her, he either would have done it by now, or he had something to say first. Since he was a cat, and by nature enjoyed hearing himself talk, Wawa guessed it was the latter.

"My investigation is complete," he said. "EMSAH is not what you think it is."

"You mean it's not a virus?"

"No. But it acts like one."

Wawa was too far from the door to make a run for it. This was the great Mort(e), after all. Infected with EMSAH or not, he had fought at Culdesac's side for years, while she was drinking from puddles and nibbling scraps from roadside carcasses. If she left this room alive, it would be because he allowed it.

"Good news is," he said, "I don't have the disease. In fact, I think I'm immune."

"Mort(e), I know there are lots of rumors going around—"

"Rumors?" Mort(e) asked, tilting his head. "I'm Red Sphinx. Aim true, stay on the hunt. I don't trust rumors. I go straight to the source."

With that, he dropped another object on the desk, a device with an antenna that hung over the side, pointing at her accusingly. The missing translator. Maybe this carried the disease on it somehow. Through the mouthpiece? Through the earbuds, perhaps? She imagined an army of parasites, small greenish blobs swarming the inner ear, bursting through the eardrum, stampeding toward the cauliflower of the brain.

"Death-life," Mort(e) said. "Overload." He propped his elbows on the table and rubbed his face with both hands. It was not an opportunity to run away. His fingers were splayed wide enough for him to keep her in sight. "This is what we fought for," he whispered. "It's what Tiberius died for."

"Tell me what you know, Mort(e)," she said.

He placed his hands flat on the desk. "It's not a pathogen," he said. "It's a belief. A thought-crime. It may be the most seductive idea that the humans ever came up with. It certainly fooled them for long enough. Still does, I imagine.

"Death-life," he continued. "Life after death. Afterlife. The Queen didn't even have a word for it."

"EMSAH makes you believe in the afterlife?"

"The belief is not a symptom of EMSAH," he said. "That's what the Queen wanted us to think. The belief *is* EMSAH. That's why it can't be cured. The Queen recruited us in her holy war. EMSAH is what will make us like the humans, if we don't eradicate it."

"So EMSAH is . . . an ideology?"

"It's religion."

The word stuck in her ears, especially that second syllable, the rough "lij" sound, like a mosquito buzzing.

"But people aren't simply *believing* things," she said. "They're killing themselves. And each other."

"That's because we're dealing with the most virulent strain of the virus. A death cult. Sacrificing your life for the resistance is a one-way ticket to paradise."

"No, you're wrong," Wawa said. "It's not just a belief. There are ways of diagnosing it. Blood tests. Cognitive analysis. Brain-wave—"

"All lies," Mort(e) said. "There is no diagnosis. And no cure."

"You witnessed one of the first quarantines! You were there! Don't tell me those people died in their own blood and filth because of what they believed!"

"Oh, *that*," Mort(e) said. "There's a bioweapon, all right. It has a nearly perfect fatality rate. But the Queen created it. Not the humans."

"What?"

"That's how it works. A group of animals adopts a religion. Or makes one up. So the Colony poisons them with a killer flu to mask the real infection. It's a prelude to sending in the Alphas to exterminate every trace of EMSAH. It's probably happening right now. Here."

He told her about the people he found in the meeting hall, all lined up and waiting to die. They had gathered in order to pray to a god who wasn't there, for deliverance that would never come. They kept the young ones from leaving by tying them down with leashes. As far as anyone would know, the physical disease they had contracted *was* EMSAH. It was all a red herring to keep the animals loyal and vigilant.

"My friend Tiberius," Mort(e) said, "he spent years trying to figure out how the bioweapon worked, how it spread. It was all a waste. Even if he had solved the riddle, come up with a cure, the Queen would have concocted another virus. And then Miriam would have said that EMSAH had mutated. And we'd be back to square one."

"So Miriam's been lying to us this whole time?"

"There is no Miriam. That was just an actor."

"You're telling me the Queen went through all that trouble just to keep people from worshipping a god?" Wawa said. "That doesn't make any sense to me."

"That's because you weren't there," Mort(e) said. "Did you know what the humans did in their first battle with the Colony?"

"They . . . burned their own crops," she said. "Some kind of shortsighted Pyrrhic victory." She remembered reading about it in a history of the Colony, written by some rodent. She could not remember what kind.

"It was more than that," Mort(e) said. "The humans interpreted the battle as a sign from the heavens. So they sacrificed their women and children. They cut them open and burned them alive. Drank their blood. I was there, thanks to this device.

"I don't know," he continued, "if EMSAH is the source of the humans' evil, or a symptom of it. But it makes them dangerous, even to themselves. And especially to us."

That was the point of this trial run, he told her. The Queen was testing the animals to see if they were worthy, if they could resist what destroyed the humans. But her patience had its limits.

Mort(e) was a lot of things, Wawa thought. Bitter and arrogant. Selfish. But he was not a liar. A liar would not have told Culdesac to his face that the animals were doomed to fail as the humans did. A liar would not have punched Culdesac in full view of the entire Red Sphinx.

"It gets worse," he said.

"Worse?"

"The humans think I'm their savior," he said. "I have to find out why. They have a fortune-teller who predicted that I would destroy the Colony. But it's all part of the Queen's plan. This is all an experiment. All of it. If I choose to become the savior, then the experiment will be deemed a failure. The ants will quarantine every settlement. Everyone will die. But if I don't become the savior, I'll never find Sheba."

"Mort(e), why are you telling me this?"

"Someone in the Red Sphinx needed to know," he said. "Before it was too late. If I ever see my friend again, I want to tell her that I did the right thing."

"Why not tell Culdesac?"

"He's on the Queen's side."

Mort(e) stood up, holstering the gun. He walked around the edge of the desk until he was only a few feet from Wawa.

"Besides," he said, "You remind me of my friend. I know now that I can trust you. You lost a friend, too. Right?"

Cyrus. A million voices in her head said his name.

"That's right," she whispered.

There was a clock on the wall beside her desk. It was 3:02.

"He should have called by now," Mort(e) said.

"Who should have called?"

"The colonel."

The phone rang. It was a secure line, only for communication among the officers. Mort(e) gestured to the phone.

Wawa picked up the receiver on the third ring. "Lieutenant Wawa," she said.

"Lieutenant," Culdesac said. "Authorization code four-one-six."

"Acknowledged," Wawa said. "Authorization code nine-four-nine. Go ahead, Colonel."

"Quebec," Culdesac said. "Green light."

The quarantine had begun.

"Should I order Red Sphinx to rendezvous at the base?" she asked. Mort(e) made a cutting motion at the base of his throat.

"Change of plans," Culdesac said. "I have ordered everyone to meet at the quarry. Archer and his team are on their way. I'm already there with the rest of the RS."

"The quarry?" Wawa grew angry at Culdesac for not picking up the tension in her voice. For not being *here*.

"We're getting airlifted out," he said. "Winged ants."

"Understood."

"Lieutenant," Culdesac said, "your top priority is getting to the quarry as quickly as possible. Leave everything. Do not let anyone get in your way."

"Understood, Colonel."

"Good luck, Lieutenant."

Wawa winced, realizing that she should have tried to buy more time by pretending that Culdesac was still speaking. But the click on the other end was too loud.

"Change of plans," Mort(e) repeated in a sarcastic singsong.

A series of concussive *thud*s began somewhere south of the base. The low rumblings grew louder, shaking the walls.

"We'd better hurry," Mort(e) said.

A siren wailed outside. Heavy footsteps and shouting in every direction. The regular soldiers had their own evacuation plan, but Culdesac had told the RS a long time ago to ignore it. The Red Sphinx would be the first ones out, he had promised.

"They're dead," Mort(e) said.

"Who's dead?"

"The Red Sphinx. There is no rendezvous. The Colony is going to burn this sector to the ground. No one will live here for a thousand years."

"Culdesac would never—"

"His loyalty is with the Colony," Mort(e) said. "And its cause. Why do you think they kept him in charge?"

"I've killed people who have spoken ill of the colonel," Wawa said. "Almost killed you the day we met."

"I remember."

"If we're going to die here anyway, maybe you should put that gun away, and I'll show you what I had in mind."

"Haven't you been used enough?" Mort(e) asked. "Are you going to let someone betray you again just because you want to join his pack?"

He had plucked another moment from her past. The explosions were getting closer. She heard screaming, but perhaps that was in her head, a memory of the dog-fighting pit and its circle of shouting, savage human faces. Maybe he planted that memory in her head somehow.

Wawa would be dead had it not been for Culdesac. And yet the quarantine was beginning. And the colonel was not there— he was merely a voice on a phone. Mort(e) was there, and his eyes begged her to believe him.

She had to make a decision. She chose Mort(e).

"Where do we go?" she asked.

OUTSIDE, OFFICERS OF different species were lining up their soldiers, preparing them to escape in an orderly fashion. Wawa knew their plan but could already see how it would end in failure. She pictured the army moving down a highway and into a horde of marauding Alpha soldiers who would cut them to pieces. They would all die in the jaws of the ants.

To the south, in the heart of the town, thick plumes of smoke arose from the tallest buildings, a cloud hanging overhead. Squinting, Wawa saw the cloud for what it really was: a swarm of winged Alphas, patrolling the air, dropping projectiles onto the town like human bomber planes.

"Don't look at it," Mort(e) said.

The first thing to do, he told her, was to get Bonaparte out of his cell. He deserved a chance to escape, even if he had defected to the humans. When they reached the detention center, the two dogs who had been standing guard ran by them at full speed. One of them—some kind of poodle half-breed, judging from his fur—was halfway through tearing off his biohazard suit. He finally loosened it from his leg, leaving it on the ground behind him like a shed reptile skin.

"Hey!" Wawa said.

Ignoring her, they tried to climb the fence, prompting other soldiers to tell them to stop, to fall in with the others. Before Wawa could see what happened next, Mort(e) braced her by the shoulders and forced her into the doorway of the building. Several shots echoed off the barracks as they ran inside.

Wawa led him to the lower level. Once they were through the useless decontamination area, they found Bonaparte sitting on his cot, hooves still on his knees.

"You made it," he said to Mort(e). "It's all coming true."

"Do you know where the key is?"

"The guards flushed it down the toilet," he said, pointing at the open cell across from his.

"Try to find something that can force the door open," Mort(e) said to Wawa.

It was a waste of time. Nothing short of a tank could open the cell. Nearby, a fire axe hung beside an extinguisher. Panting, she pulled the axe from its hook and brought it over to Bonaparte's cell. The pig seemed unimpressed. His eyes seemed to say, *Give it a shot, Lieutenant.* Wawa took her first swing at the bars. The deafening *clang* echoed down the hallway. The handle rattled in her hands. She adjusted her grip and swung again. Only the cream-colored paint chipped away. The metal did not budge.

Mort(e) wrapped his arms around the base of the toilet and rocked it violently until the screws broke free from the linoleum. Water spilled out from the base. With one last shove, he snapped the bowl off its moorings, leaving only a gushing pipe. Thankfully, it did not stink. It had probably never been used.

"The key's gone, Captain."

"Shut up, Bonaparte," Mort(e) said as he reached his arm into the pipe, fishing for anything. "It's my fault you're in here."

"I know," Bonaparte said. "But it's okay. I know my role in the prophecy."

Wawa, already panting, stopped in mid-swing. "Prophecy?"

"Oh, that's right," Bonaparte said. "The human said that you weren't ready for that word. Let's say *plan*, then."

Mort(e)'s arm was in the pipe all the way to his shoulder. "You mean Briggs?" he asked.

"Elder Briggs, yes. He opened my eyes."

"You've been talking to humans, too?" Wawa asked Mort(e).

"They've been talking to *me*," he replied. "Briggs is your Patient Zero, Lieutenant."

"When are you going to stop treating it like a disease?" Bonaparte asked. "Elder Briggs has spread the truth."

"Briggs doesn't know shit," Mort(e) said.

"He knew just what to tell *you*, didn't he?"

Mort(e) did not answer.

"Did you see Sheba?" Bonaparte asked. "When you used the device?"

Mort(e) stopped what he was doing and pondered this for a moment. "I don't need the translator to do that," he said.

As Wawa reared up for another swing, Bonaparte held up his

hoof to signal her to stop. The water began to stream past her feet and into Bonaparte's cell.

"You two need to go," Bonaparte said. "Now."

Mort(e) slammed his palm on the floor. The key wasn't there. He stood up.

"Don't worry about me," Bonaparte said. "It's going to be okay."

"We're not leaving without you," Wawa said.

"You wanted me to stop being afraid," Bonaparte said. "To choose my own path. I've done that. I know you don't understand it right now. I'm not asking you to. But if you're going with Mort(e), you'll see. You'll see that all this happened for a reason."

A loud explosion rocked the outside of the building. The lights flickered.

"You need to leave," Bonaparte said.

Wawa kept her eyes on Bonaparte but could feel Mort(e) glaring at her. "I'm sorry," she said.

"Protect Mort(e)," Bonaparte said. "Help him find his friend. Everything depends on it."

"Time to go, Wawa," Mort(e) said. He said goodbye to Bonaparte with a mere nod.

She was moving now, passing through the hallway, leaving the gurgling pipe behind. The axe was still in her hand, its blade dented and chipped. At the front door, the shouting and gunfire grew louder.

They exited the building. Mort(e) stuck his arm out to halt her. A large shadow passed over them. They flattened themselves against the wall. The swarm of winged Alphas had now reached the base. Panicked, the soldiers aimed into the air, shooting wildly. There was a smell of gunpowder and burning plastic. A few yards away, a flying Alpha scooped up a cat like a hawk plucking a rodent from the ground. The Alpha clamped the cat's neck in her jaws, killing him before he had a chance to squeal.

More shouting, this time to Wawa's left. A dog ran toward her, his coat charred and smoking. He flopped onto the ground in agony, howling, trying to roll in the cool mud. Another Alpha hovered a few feet over him. Mort(e) grabbed Wawa's arm and forced her to move. She glanced over her shoulder in time to see the Alpha shoot a jet of fluid from the base of her abdomen. The dog screeched, then began choking. An acidic vapor rose from the dog's melting flesh, engulfing him.

Wawa kept running. Mort(e)'s nubby fingers were still digging into her shoulder. "Let go of me!" she said, ripping away from him.

"Fine! Just keep running!"

She stopped and was about to head back for the dog. Mort(e) tried to restrain her. "There's nothing you can do for him," Mort(e) said.

"Not him," she said. "I want to kill one."

"No! We need to—"

She brought the axe up with both hands, shoving him away. "Just *one*, I said!"

Wawa searched the area for a target and found one within seconds: an Alpha landing on a nearby jeep, spraying acid on the canvas roof, causing it to disintegrate into a cloud of foul-smelling vapor. The soldier inside—a cat—fired through the hole in the cloth. A bullet tore through the ant's wing, but the creature could still fly. She latched onto the hood.

Wawa took off. She was at the rear of the jeep before the ant's antennae detected the movement. Launching herself from the bumper, Wawa drove the point of the axe into the ant's neck. The weapon sank into the exoskeleton but missed the vulnerable brain stem. The Alpha's jaws opened and snapped shut. Wawa wrenched the handle clockwise, breaking the neck in a grinding crunch.

Wawa had been taught that these monsters were her sisters, and that they were all joined together in a war with the humans. She gazed into the compound eye of the insect. Her scarred face—miniaturized, multiplied—stared back.

The weight of the dying Alpha shifted as her abdomen, operating on its own, aimed its acid port at Wawa. It shot out a burst of fluid, barely missing her leg. She could not kick it away—her feet were planted in order to keep the ant from latching onto her. There was no telling when these things were dead. Wawa had once seen a decapitated ant head shear off a human's leg at the shin when he tried to kick it away.

"Help me," she said to the frightened cat, who sat trembling in the front seat of the jeep. The soldier bolted. He was barely a kitten, probably a runaway who joined the military to get some food. Before he made it twenty feet, an Alpha dropped on top of him, breaking his spine before carrying him away.

The abdomen sprayed again. This time, the jet of acid hit the door of the jeep. The metal sizzled.

Wawa felt the vehicle rock as Mort(e) hopped onto it. He grasped the axe handle with her and planted his foot on the Alpha's abdomen. With the added leverage, Wawa and Mort(e) were able to pry the handle toward them until the creature's head broke off. The body squirmed before toppling over.

Wawa tore away the shredded rooftop and climbed into the driver's seat, throwing the axe into the rear. Mort(e) jumped in next to her. She stepped on the gas pedal. The jeep lurched to the side as it rolled over the Alpha's thorax.

She sped to the gate, where an Alpha attacked the single soldier left defending a watchtower. It was a dog. Out of ammunition, all she could do was swing her rifle at the monster. When the ant prepared to fire acid at the tower, the soldier hurdled the railing and jumped the twenty feet to the ground below. Anticipating the move, the ant pounced on top of her, pinning her to the ground. The dog stopped moving.

Mort(e) picked up the axe and leaned out of the passenger side. "Drive," he said.

The vehicle accelerated. Mort(e) swung the axe, the digging the blade into the Alpha's neck. The head flipped upward, landing on the hood of the car. It lay upside down against the windshield, its jaws opening and closing. Frantic, Wawa turned on the windshield wipers and then switched them off. Mort(e) leaned over the glass and, with the top of the axe, knocked the head off.

They were through the gate, heading away from the base. Wawa adjusted the rearview mirror. Mort(e) placed his hand over it. "Don't," he said. "Keep driving."

CHAPTER FIFTEEN
RUN

HE EFFECTS OF the translator began to wear off. Mort(e) could feel the knowledge dripping out of his mind like water leaking out of a pair of cupped hands. He had entered the phase that Yojimbo described as "deflating." Part of him would miss the things he had learned. It was hard to go back to being a mere mortal after knowing almost all there was to know.

He was trying to recall some of the Queen's trials and errors in Alpha breeding when the jeep ran out of fuel somewhere in the abandoned farmlands to the west. They were still too far from the mountains, where Mort(e) believed they would be safer. At least there, the ants would not be able to pop right out of the ground. On either side of the road, fences marked fields that were littered with dead crops. The humans who had fled in this direction could not have lasted very long. There was nowhere to hide.

After abandoning the jeep, Mort(e) and Wawa walked in the doomed footsteps of the humans. Their shadows grew longer. Wawa seemed almost catatonic after hearing about Mort(e)'s meeting with Briggs, the messages from the *Vesuvius*, his supposed role as the savior, and the possibility that Sheba was still alive on the Island. That was a lot for one day.

They took a badly needed break. The deflation had left Mort(e) nauseated. Now there were only questions with no answers. They simply trailed off. Did Wawa/Jenna kill her master, or simply escape, or . . . ? Was Archer's original name three successive squeaks . . . (*eee-eee-eee*)? And what did the Queen do with Australia again?

An enormous traffic jam clogged the road ahead, another relic of the war that the Bureau had not yet sponged away. A long line of vehicles stretched to the horizon, growing so dense that Mort(e) and Wawa had to squeeze between car doors and fenders, weaving their way through a metal graveyard. Mort(e) surmised that the traffic must have come under attack from both the front and the rear. Several drivers had panicked and tried to move forward onto the grassy shoulder and the empty oncoming lane, forming a bottleneck. Wedged so closely together, many of the humans must have been unable to exit their vehicles, so they smashed the windshields and climbed out. The glass was everywhere, and many of the cars had dents the size of human feet. Several windshields had been smashed in rather than out, suggesting that those people who were unable or unwilling to break out of their cars were stuck waiting until an Alpha pounced on the vehicle.

Wawa pointed her snout toward a bunched-up blanket lying on the road between a van and a convertible with the roof torn off. The blanket covered the body of an old woman lying face down, decomposed to a skeletal state. Her white hair was still curly. Most likely, this one expired en route, and her overly sentimental family hoped to bury her somewhere, still believing that they would have a chance to do so, and that it actually mattered. It was possible, too, that the marauders were so busy chasing down every last EMSAH-infected human that they simply left her behind. The only way she was spreading the disease now was through her eye sockets. All that she knew, and learned, and loved, had died when her heart stopped beating, and her bloated human brain dried out, and all its contents fell away, spilling onto the asphalt.

There were overturned cars up ahead. The ants had sprung a trap for these refugees. The humans fled, only to run toward a new anthill bursting through the highway. Mort(e) pictured it: the ants rising, Alphas supported by hordes of their smaller sisters. Rivers of insects, spraying from a hideous fountain.

He tried to think of something else. Their immediate survival seemed like a good start. As odd as it felt, spending the night near the hollowed-out ziggurat was probably the best idea. Mort(e) thought that he may have been one of the few people in the world who would not be scared to go near an old anthill. Hiding near this place could buy them some time.

He was about to share all of this with Wawa when something caught his eye. At the base of the anthill, where the road had cracked open, a silver SUV lay on its side, its rear window smashed in. A child's safety seat lay on the ground, probably plucked from the vehicle and tossed aside after its occupant had been removed. There was no blood on the SUV, although the airbags had been deployed. It was exactly like Janet's vehicle, the one she drove away on the day Mort(e) killed her husband.

Wawa asked if he was all right. He said he was fine. She suggested that they try to hotwire one of the cars and head for the mountains. Mort(e) talked her out of it. A loud vehicle on an abandoned road would attract too much attention. Camping here was the better option, even if it slowed their progress.

Neither of them wanted to sleep on the dirt. At the same time, they did not want to stay inside a vehicle in the event that they needed to make a run for it. They settled on the cargo area of a pickup truck as their resting spot for the evening. The only signs of its previous owner were a bloodstain on the cracked windshield and a half-empty crate of bottled water. They could run away if the Alphas showed up. When Wawa expressed some doubt, Mort(e) reminded her that he was born in a truck like this—it was a little too perfect for him to die in one, too.

With the sun behind the mountains and the temperature dropping, the excitement of the day's events finally died down. For the first time in hours, Mort(e) felt hungry. Wawa denied needing any food, so he decided to not bring it up again until at least the morning. The only thing they could do now was set up the telescope and wait for the *Vesuvius* to send its message to the surface. He told Wawa that she should sleep first. When she objected, he pointed out that he couldn't sleep because he was still wired from his experience with the translator.

"Before dawn," he said, "I'll have forgotten more than you'll ever learn."

This convinced her. She curled up in the corner of the pickup and closed her eyes. Meanwhile, Mort(e) took the telescope and tripod from his backpack. He used it to search the landscape until there was no trace of the sun left. After that, the only movement he detected was Wawa's sporadic fidgeting.

When he grew tired, he leaned against the cab of the truck. Like all cats, he could maintain a sort of half-sleep in which his eyelids bobbed up and down, taking him in and out of the real world. Wawa's sad groans brought him back, but his eyelids soon clamped shut.

When he opened them, he knew right away that they were not really open. He was dreaming. Or, to be more accurate, he was still deflating.

He sat cross-legged in an open field. The sky was blue, and the grass beneath him was a brilliant green, like a child's watercolor painting. And sitting before him, sprawled out in her extravagance, was the Queen, Hymenoptera Unus. Her distended abdomen was the size of a bus. Her thorax and head rose from it like some ghastly hood ornament. Even though her mouth did not move, a voice emanated from her. It was the voice of Janet, the only woman's voice he could remember. "Why are you doing this?" she asked.

This was no mere dream. It was an echo from the translator. Yojimbo called it a "residual," a reinterpretation of the knowledge that was forced into his brain and then flushed out. He and the Queen had bonded in some way. He was now a child of the Colony, having eaten from the tree of knowledge. He was one of them now.

"Because I want to," he said. "I choose to. I owe it to my friend."

"Even if it causes all this?"

The sky turned gray, as if the painter had mixed the wrong colors. The field was now covered with corpses of every species—human, animal, insect. Not a single inch of the ground was visible, like the floor of the meeting hall in the quarantined town. The bodies had piled up at the base of the Queen's abdomen. She was submerged in them, like the hull of a ship riding a sea of the dead. Mort(e)'s feet sank into a twisted knot of broken limbs, slashed necks, eyes staring at nothing.

"Yes," he said. "Yes. I don't care. If you want to stop me, you'll have to kill me. But I'll kill you first."

Mort(e) saw in her a sadness at his defiance. He expected it to make him feel powerful, like the warrior he had trained himself to become. Instead, he understood—or remembered?—that she was as scared and alone and tired of this war as he was.

The Queen bowed her head. The landscape grew dim before blurring out completely. After that, a peaceful void enveloped him. He floated in it, his arms airplaned to either side, his tail dangling freely.

The weightless feeling lasted until something brushed against his fur. The sensation electrified his entire nervous system. With a pounding sense of alarm, his heart seized up, and his tail slammed on the deck of the pickup. Opening his eyes, he found Wawa lying at his side, her arm draped over his waist. He thought she was sniffing him. But she was crying.

Mort(e) stood up. "Lieutenant?"

"Sorry," she said, wiping her eyes. "I . . . I must have been dreaming."

She was lying. Mort(e) lifted the telescope over the cab and placed it on the hood. With his tail to her, he tried to make it clear that he had work to do.

"Aren't you tired of this, Mort(e)?"

He paused. "Is something wrong, Lieutenant?"

"Forget it," she said. "I thought you would understand."

"Understand what?"

"My people were meant to travel in packs. To keep one another warm. That's all. I just thought you would want that . . ." She trailed off.

"I don't know what's going on with you," he said.

"But you and your friend used to—"

"We're not discussing that. Go to sleep."

With Wawa muted, Mort(e) returned to fiddling with the telescope, even though it was fine.

Wawa kicked the inside of the pickup, startling him. The noise was so loud it bounced off the other vehicles. "Are you trying to get us killed?" he said.

"Culdesac was right," she said. "You're a miserable hermit, praying to some ghost. You say you're immune to EMSAH, but this is worse."

"I'm a choker, Wawa," he said. "I can't help you."

"I wasn't asking you to mate with me," she said. "I grew up in a cage, Mort(e). Everyone in my pack did. My master wouldn't even let us touch each other. I just needed . . . and I thought you needed . . ."

Shaking her head, she slumped down in the corner of the pickup, as far away from him as she could get. "We have no pack anymore," she said. "Culdesac betrayed us. We're going to die out here alone."

She wept. Her attempts to hide it were useless. When the crying subsided, she said, "Culdesac was the closest thing I had to a friend. Isn't that pathetic?"

"No," Mort(e) said.

"It is now."

With his thumb, Mort(e) rubbed the smooth surface of his St. Jude medallion. It made him feel a little better, until he was finally ready to speak. "Do you want to hear how I picked my name?"

She did not answer, even though she had to be awake.

"Lieutenant?" he asked. "Do you want the explanation?"

Wawa moved into a sitting position. "I would like that," she said.

"It's from a book I read. *Le Morte d'Arthur*. The death of Arthur. I thought about changing my name to Arthur, but I imagined there were already a few of those. I liked the word Morte. When I was hiding in the ruins of the city, I would say the name to myself."

"So your name means death?" she asked.

"It's not death," he said. "Not really. I was starving. Eager to find my friend. By the time the Red Sphinx caught up with me, two things had happened. First, I decided that I didn't want to be called Death anymore. I wanted to be a normal person when all this madness was over."

He let go of the medallion. It flopped against his chest.

"Imagine that. I actually thought all this would be *over* back then."

Wawa laughed and raised an imaginary drink in the air.

"The second thing that happened was that I forgot how to spell the damn thing," he said.

"You're kidding."

"No. I forgot if it had that *e* or not. So I put it in parentheses when Culdesac asked."

"So your weirdo name comes from bad spelling."

"No, no," Mort(e) said. "The name fit. Because I could go either way, depending on how things sort themselves out. I could be the normal person, reuniting with my friend. Or I could become Death. I'm trying really hard to avoid that, but I guess I've developed a habit."

Wawa chuckled. "Thank you, Mort(e)," she said.

"Now can you get to sleep, or do you want another bedtime story?"

"I'll sleep," Wawa said, rolling onto her side. Her tail wagged a little before coming to a stop.

A minute later, she said, "Don't worry about me, Mort(e). That business won't happen again." He caught it in her voice— the slow crumbling of another one of her beliefs.

"It's okay," he said. "I understand." He sat under the stars and waited.

THE MESSAGE FROM the *Vesuvius* was short and to the point. It gave a set of coordinates, followed by a simple, persuasive word: *Run.*

Mort(e) found the coordinates on his map. They intersected in an open field at the edge of an abandoned town. It was a perfect rectangle, probably a football field. He understood the instructions well enough. Driving a car was out of the question, even if they could find one that still worked. They would have to leave the road, and taking a vehicle through the dirt would create so many vibrations that the Queen herself would hear them. So they would have to do it on foot and hope that they were not too loud to attract attention, and that there were no bird patrols passing through the area. Calculating the time needed, Mort(e) figured that if they began moving now, they would reach the field by dawn.

Wawa gathered up the remaining water bottles. Using a discarded belt, she fashioned a strap for her axe, which she wore over her shoulder. Moments later, they were running across the dead fields, leaping fences, hopping over craters.

Their journey took them across another highway, this one with an even more bizarre sight than the last. Instead of being lined up in a traffic jam, the vehicles were piled haphazardly in an artificial mountain, a pyramid, the faint moonlight shining through the windshields and reflecting off the paint.

More running. Past trees. Over a shallow stream. The sky above changed. Soon, they were sprinting under a purple canopy that brightened to red. And then, finally, the sun rose in the east. They were behind schedule, but the town was in sight.

The place was virtually untouched. An exit ramp curved onto the main street, toward abandoned shops and church steeples. Though the buildings blocked the view, the map showed that the field was on the other side.

Mort(e) picked up a scent and sensed the vibrations in the ground. Wawa, whose hearing was even more acute, noticed it as well. She sniffed, then let out a whine to indicate danger. They stood still. Something moved in the soil under their feet.

Wawa was about to speak. Mort(e) raised his hand to silence her. He tossed a bottle of water so that it skimmed across the dirt, away from the ramp. It went about twenty feet before the earth around it ripped open. The armored skull of an Alpha soldier squeezed out of the fissure. Three others emerged, along with a churning river of smaller ants.

Mort(e) and Wawa broke for the ramp, vaulting the barrier and landing on the asphalt. Behind them, the earth tore open. The air was thick with the smell of freshly plowed dirt, and the sound of clicking jaws and skittering feet.

They would have to run through the town. They were safer on cement than the dirt, but there was no telling what was inside the buildings. If there were humans waiting at the field, they were probably already dead.

A row of cars on the side of the road overturned as the Alpha soldiers burst through it. A cherry-red convertible tumbled into their path. Mort(e) ran around the vehicle while Wawa bounded over it. Alphas poured over the barrier. Ants rose from their underground tunnels, sending up geysers of dirt.

They approached an abandoned military roadblock. A burned-out army truck was parked beside a row of sandbags and barbed wire. Seconds after jumping over, Mort(e) heard the ants explode through it.

The first building they passed was a post office. A sign on the front door had a drawing of an ant, with a message underneath that said, INSECT BITES TREATED HERE. At the intersection, to his right, the street was filled from sidewalk to sidewalk with Alpha soldiers. All of them completely still. Same thing on his left. The soldiers came to life, their movements synchronized, an undulating wave of armor and claws. Wawa yelped.

The glass storefronts shattered outward. Alpha soldiers spilled onto the street. Others emerged from second-story windows and rooftops, dropping to the ground and aiming their antennae toward the two fugitives. Dozens of Alphas now cut off their escape.

They had been lured right into a nest.

Mort(e) pulled the gun from its holster. Wawa unhooked the axe from its strap and ran with the blade over her shoulder.

Mort(e) picked out the closest Alpha and fired. She kept coming at him, shrugging off the gunshots. Mort(e) emptied the clip until he hit the base of her neck, cutting off the ant's brain from the rest of her body. The Alpha stumbled forward and landed hard on the pavement, part of her jaw breaking off. Mort(e) jumped onto her back and grabbed one of the claws. Placing his foot on the joint, he snapped it off. Now he had a club. Another Alpha drew close. Mort(e) swung the claw and connected, caving in the beast's compound eye. A second later, Wawa's axe chopped off the ant's antenna. With the ant prostrate before her, Wawa swung again, severing the vulnerable neck. Bits of carapace flew off as the creature collapsed.

Two more Alphas charged at them. Mort(e) crouched and lifted the abdomen of the dead one. He squeezed until a blast of acid shot out, catching the two ants in the small explosion. The monsters clawed at their melting eyes. In their confusion and agony, the ants crashed into one another and fell over. The others stepped over their writhing bodies and continued to advance. Mort(e) slashed at them with the broken claw to slow them down. He could sense the rest of the swarm closing in from behind.

Suddenly the ants stood still, their antennae pointing straight up.

A great shadow blotted out the sun, spreading over the entire street—a gigantic silvery whale swimming above, ready to swallow up the entire town. The *Vesuvius*. Painted on the bottom of the command gondola were a massive black cross, a crescent moon, and a six-pointed star. Cannons extended from the windows. When the guns opened fire, the Alphas standing in their path burst apart. Heads, limbs, and antennae skittered along the ground. Several Alphas were cut in half. They tried to crawl to safety as their organs spilled from their ruptured abdomens.

Letting out a high-pitched whistle, the ship fired rockets at the buildings. A fireball engulfed the row of shops, the shock-wave knocking Mort(e) to the ground. As debris rained down, he felt Wawa grab his arm and pull him to his feet. He spit the dust out of his mouth.

They kept moving. An amputated claw grabbed Wawa's ankle, and she hacked it away. The ants gave chase, even as the cannons cut them to pieces. They stepped over their dead sisters, ignoring the gore coating their armor.

As Mort(e) ran, he tried to keep up with the cross above. The *Vesuvius* was headed for the field. When the firing stopped, a cable descended from the ship, a man in a black jumpsuit harnessed at the end of it. He touched down in the school parking lot. His large tinted goggles made him resemble an insect. Behind him, the entrance of the school crumbled, revealing another nest of Alphas. They emptied from the destroyed building, rolling over one another before finding their footing. The *Vesuvius* opened fire on them, but there seemed to be a never-ending supply, a hellish waterfall of six-legged monsters.

Mort(e) and Wawa reached the man with what appeared to be the entire Colony closing in.

"Hold on to me here, sir," the man said, pointing to two handles on the front of his harness.

"What about her?"

"We can only take one of you."

Mort(e) glanced at Wawa. She understood right away that he could leave her. Sheba would have looked at him like that. No, Sheba *had* looked at him like that.

Mort(e) grabbed the man by the throat.

"Okay," the man gasped, "we could try both."

They hooked their arms around his shoulders while clasping the handles. "Hold on," the man said.

The cable lifted them. Mort(e) could hear the propellers on the ship increasing speed as the zeppelin ascended.

The town below them was a sea of demons. The spot where they had vacated seconds earlier was now flooded with ants, all straining their claws toward the escaping mammals. The remaining buildings resembled volcanoes, spewing the ants from their underground city.

The cable stalled and then dropped several feet. Mort(e) felt the vibrations of the motor as the gears strained.

"The winch may be broken," the man said.

The cable gave again, dropping them farther. The zeppelin was not rising fast enough. They were only ten or twenty feet above the outstretched claws of the swarm.

"It's not going to work," the man said.

Wawa and Mort(e) faced each other, each waiting for the other to say something.

"Sir," the man said, "it is an honor for me to give my life for you."

"No, don't give me that," Mort(e) said.

"It's okay," the man said. "I know where I'm going. The gates of hell are closed forever."

"Wait!"

The man undid the buckle on his harness. He slipped out of it and fell. He sank into the mob of Alphas, not even screaming as they tore him apart.

The zeppelin rose higher, until the ants seemed tiny and inconsequential, as they had before the war. The town resembled an abandoned picnic overrun with hungry insects.

"That was death-life," Wawa said.

"That was death-life," Mort(e) repeated.

The cable twisted, causing them to spin helplessly. The painted cross turned round and round, a hypnotist's bauble beckoning them to come forward. The farmland spread out below, bathed in the morning light like a half-remembered dream.

CHAPTER SIXTEEN
THE ISLAND

HE QUEEN SAW everything. The world, once so terrifying to her people, had been reduced to a viscous liquid poured into her, where it would be studied, manipulated, and conquered. There was no fear of the dark. The Queen was the darkness now, pulling in all beams of light like a black hole. She could not turn back or make peace, for this burden forced her to keep going until everyone was dead, until the only life left was the hint of her chemical trail drifting in a dry wind.

The Queen always brooded over the future on mating day, the annual event when the fertile males and females would be launched from the island, joining their bodies in midair and returning to the ground to establish new outposts of the Colony. Because she never slept, the Queen could not visit the future through dreams. Piecing together the days to come was one of only two escapes from the constant flow of information—the other being that brief flash of her mother before killing her. The future had a perfection that the past would always lack. The time to come was a perfectly crystallized snowflake, a chemical trail leading toward a hazy but brightening sunrise.

Mating days were always frantic, the air charged with multiple signals, shouting *help*, or *here*, or *go*, relayed to the Queen's lair so she could observe. Thus the Queen relived the experiences of every eager yet frightened participant. From millions of vantage points at once, she could see the rocky landscape flutter with a galaxy of silvery wings. It was the way of her people to gather in a frenzy and risk exposure to the outside world in order to renew their species. In the wild, during the age of the humans, the ritual had an element of desperation. Every mating day could be the Colony's last. Predators of all kinds were driven to the mounds, attracted to the scent, or the sound of wings, or perhaps even a change in temperature as the ventilation shafts released hot puffs of air in the days leading up to the ceremony. Mammals, reptiles, and birds would paw at the earth. The workers, obeying orders, would keep hauling the fertile ones out to their doom until the soldiers intervened, grinding their teeth into the intruder's flesh, or firing acid into the predator's eyes and nostrils. Human interference added a new, unpredictable element. Sometimes they were simply curious and would carelessly scrape away the top layer of dirt to expose the writhing ants. Thousands of children over the years had been driven away squealing after plunging their hands into the soldiers' quarters. Other humans would attempt to destroy the nest, usually for what seemed to be mere pleasure. Several mating days had to be aborted during a human attack, the fertile ones going senile and dying in their chambers before having a chance to fulfill their purpose. Still other humans would camp out the day of the mating. They would pluck the fat females from the horde, tear their wings off, and drop them into buckets to be cooked and eaten later. Sometimes the males would desperately hurl themselves toward the buckets and mate with the wingless would-be queens as they bled to death among their sisters.

The Queen relived all the previous mating days, the successes and the setbacks, as she collected information on how the latest event was proceeding. The males were marched out first, wet and shivering, but warming in the sun. The workers prodded them toward an opening near the western side of the island, where they would be shielded from the brunt of the sunlight. They still had to gain their footing, though their main skill was to fly. The clumsy ones who tumbled over were gently righted again, if for no other reason than to get them to stop sending anxious signals as if the entire Colony were under attack. It was an amusing contrast to the mammals, who were in the bad habit of putting their males in charge.

And then the winged females emerged. Sleek and menacing angels. More beautiful than any other creature on earth. The future of all life. The females marched out from their chamber, thronged by soldiers and workers who would give their lives to protect them as though they were queens already. The males waited, their wings shaking off the last drops of moisture.

Many would die. Almost all, in fact. They were so tiny, and even though their archenemies had been driven toward extinction, so many things could get them killed before, during, and soon after mating. Errant winds, a poorly timed landing, getting their wings wet and collapsing from exhaustion as they tried to flap them dry again. They would be cut off from the Colony unless they succeeded in establishing new outposts, and even then it would be their responsibility to reconnect with the island. Because she became queen and then mated under emergency circumstances, Hymenoptera was fortunate to have avoided the massacre, for even her intellect would not have saved her from the random cruelty of the world.

For now, there was hope. Until the fertiles took flight, every male was a father to a successful line, and every female was a queen who would spread the range of the Colony to new lands. Their people would build, farm, hunt, and protect. They would move tons of earth, construct massive cities, and produce an endless supply of crops, bending nature to their collective will. This mating day would help to redeem all life in the wake of the human scourge.

A signal started as a whisper and soon turned into a siren. The workers released their grip on the females. The shiny black angels took flight. The Queen, though buried in her lair, flew with them. The island dropped from beneath her. All around her, wings flapped, pushing the clean air onto her face, brushing it through her antennae. The sun passed through the clouds to ignite the horizon. The convoy moved away from the light and toward land in the west.

Then the males ascended to join them. Rather than launching, they wobbled as they rose, like bubbles climbing to the surface of a pond. They were more delicate, and a slight breeze would tip them sideways. They bumped into one another and yet kept rising, an airborne colony unto themselves. The Queen flew among them as the safe ground lowered out of sight. And then it happened, the music of their species. The two masses intertwined in midair. Claws dug into carapaces. Strong females shrugged off the unworthy, sending them tumbling. The most determined, desperate males alighted on the lead females. Some were so aggressive they bit into the females' necks to keep them still. And then they united, their bodies coiled against one another. Every successful union resulted in both partners remaining still, not flapping their wings. They plummeted. There was a terrible yet beautiful moment when almost all of them stopped flying at once and dropped to the water. Blissful spirits, no longer afraid of death, falling, the shimmering sea welcoming them. Until at last the act was done, and the females spread their wings again, knocking away the hapless, exhausted males. Some of the drones were so spent that they continued to dive until they splashed down in the salt water, belly up, legs shaking. The females glided west to land. Toward the future.

The chemical trail faded away for the Queen. Her antennae begged for more. Her maids had nothing left to offer. It always ended like this, with the most ecstatic moment disintegrating too soon. Even if these new queens died, every last one of them, they were still the lucky ones. They could escape this place and choose their own destinies. They could unite with another in a moment of madness. They would never feel the responsibility of Hymenoptera.

The frantic noise, the thick scents, all ceased, replaced with the familiar smell of the chamber, the sound of the workers moving about, cleaning her, plucking eggs from her abdomen. Life continued.

SOME TIME PASSED. It was getting harder to tell how much. She could always confirm simply by concentrating and accessing the right memories, but the motivation for it sometimes waned. Especially in the days after a mating, when the Colony returned to its daily business of conquest.

A steady stream of chambermaids delivered reports throughout the day. There was a reliable method to this. These specialized workers would spend hours cleaning off the Queen's exoskeleton before moving toward the rear of her massive body, where they would take care of the constant supply of eggs that fell from her, large and small. Once they collected and prepared enough eggs, the chambermaids transported the cargo to the nurseries. On the way back, they gathered information from the others. Upon reentering the Queen's lair—which required a special scent to get past the guards—the chambermaids would commune with the Queen, sharing the latest news. Then they would repeat the cycle by again going to work on the Queen's relentlessly decaying carapace. She had endured hundreds of moltings by then, and it was getting more painful each time. The last molting required her daughters to pry away the dead skin, scale by scale, flake by flake, like the stubborn shell of a hard-boiled egg. Her old exoskeleton was brittle, and yet it clung to her fresh skin. Her maids, in their zeal to remove the old shell, sometimes pulled off chunks of living flesh. The smell of her blood sent alarm signals throughout the room, summoning all the Queen's attendants to the afflicted area. They circled around the wound and protected and cleaned it until it healed—yet another bodily function that was not as reliable as it used to be. The Queen resigned herself to the possibility that she would never molt again. No matter what she did, her skin would never be truly clean. It would be only functional enough to keep her from dying when the final victory over the humans was so close.

The most recent reports focused on the maintenance of the island's tower, the hub of the hypersonic signals that fed information into the brains of the surface dwellers. Within a few years, the upgraded animals would breed a new generation, and the towers would not be necessary. The surfacers would pass along their perfected genes, and all the unevolved traits would be phased out. But for now, the Queen needed to make sure the towers worked. Allowing them to fail and running the risk of having prewar animals roaming the surface was too dangerous. It would only confirm fears of EMSAH and a return to the previous way of life.

The island's tower linked with others that were strategically placed around the globe, spreading the Queen's message in the same way that a human cell phone network transmitted signals. The tower was built from dirt, magnetic stones harvested by the miner caste, and random organic materials, including the brain tissue of the interpreters, the ones who had been bred to translate human language. At the top of the tower rested a transmitter, a sphere pocked with convex indentations, like a massive golf ball. From here, the signal reached every surface creature who had been exposed to the hormone, impregnating their growing minds with the knowledge that would allow them to subdue and overcome the human menace.

The Queen concentrated on incoming news concerning the towers and filtered out the rest. A new report indicated that several of the structures had been compromised by hurricanes in a region designated with the number forty-seven and a combination of scents. The humans called the place Guatemala.

The problem working with organic material was that it required constant maintenance. Moreover, the ants who worked on the towers had to be frequently replaced. Being so close to the signal interfered with their antennae, driving them to insanity. Their minds would be overwhelmed with data, like a deluge bursting a levee. At that point, survival mechanisms implanted in their species would kick in. Some would bite off their own antennae, like a human extracting a rotten tooth. Others would simply freeze in place while their sisters crawled around them. Still others would become violent, which would require the soldiers stationed nearby to pluck them from the tower before they hurt the others or, worse, damaged the transmitter, which was worth more than all their lives combined.

True to form, the reports grew more positive later in the day. A crew of specialized workers had been dispatched. The towers would be repaired by the time the sun was two ant-lengths above the ocean.

Though there had been another failed settlement that needed to be quarantined, the Queen foresaw success with the surface dwellers. There would be harmony. Nature was seemingly designed for a master race to step forward and seize control. If not the ants, who else? Certainly not the humans. The animals still had promise, even though they would take years to realize their potential. Everything her mother told her would come true. The Colony would be the North Star in an eternally spinning constellation.

But this harmony was still so far away, always on the other side of a sunrise. Always tomorrow, always in the next season. Always someday. There were too many variables to predict exactly what would happen. She had been on the warpath for so many centuries now, absorbing and spitting out the hatred of thousands of generations of her people, that she sometimes wondered if she would have the opportunity to appreciate the beauty and purity she would one day bestow upon the earth. She wondered if she would instead be taking in reports of downed towers and weather anomalies until that final moment when her maids could do no more for her, and she went stiff and stopped breathing. Her daughters would attend to her for a few more days, she imagined, before the eggs ran out, and the fluids finally began to leak from her cracked exoskeleton, warning them that death was in their midst. She would be removed from the chamber, stripped of whatever fleshy parts remained. The rest—a shell of armor and hollowed-out legs—would be ejected from the Colony, sent to a trash heap.

The Queen willed her mind to go beyond her own death and beyond the final victory over humanity. By then, the human cities would be completely dismantled by time and nature, overrun with vegetation, decayed by winds, rain, and sunlight. The new settlements would grow. Over time, they would discard whatever artificial human implements they had acquired in the days after the war. Guns, computers, vehicles, engines—the surfacers would no longer need these things. Their network of towns would be so efficient and peaceful that the trappings of human life would fall away. The animals would live as one community—similar to the ants, but still maintaining individuality, still moving forward. They would be mini-Queens perched atop mini-Colonies.

The underground Colony, meanwhile, would continue to explore, carving out the earth from pole to pole. New queens would oversee the exploration of Antarctica with a caste of workers bred to withstand the cold. They would witness the construction of a chain of tunnels linking every continent. Nothing would remain beyond their reach, and perhaps they would encounter more like them in the depths of the underworld.

The Queen went still further, to a time when the earth would begin to grow warm again. She could not imagine what the surface would be like then, but she could picture the sun. It would grow large and dull in the sky. It would extend outward, an ongoing explosion, gobbling up the inner planets until its gases collided with the atmosphere of Earth. Plants would be long gone before then. The ants would probably have to harvest the surface dwellers for food—it would be an act of mercy, since they would probably start eating one another in an orgy of prewar violence. But with the plants dying, the Colony's fungus reserves would die off as well. The earth, both the land and the tunnels underneath, would be still for a long time.

She watched it all happen from space, from the outer rim of the system. The red giant, dying, like she was, would burn everything away, all the progress she had made. The star would shed its skin, which would engulf the earth, a final judgment boiling away the oceans, purifying the land, smoothing it out until it was perfectly round. It would take centuries. The expanding gases would incinerate the rock, shooting sparks and debris into space. The light could be seen from galaxies away, a shower of embers propelled by the solar winds. Everything purified by the bursting sun. A universe scraped clean, cleansed by fire, the shards of the earth frozen in space forever. Such a glorious ending, a welcome relief. An opportunity for the world to finally go to sleep.

It was so beautiful that she at first ignored the chemical alarm from a chambermaid—another report on the towers, she supposed. Not enough to distract her from the ecstasy of the final obliteration of the planet. But the message kept repeating, overriding her ability to tune it out. Four maids in a row delivered it. She could no longer ignore them.

There had been an unauthorized use of a translator. The Queen retraced the path of the information. She could see the chemical trail, a bright thread unspooling into the past. She tracked it from her quarters through the tunnels, out to the ships, across the water to the mainland, into the hills. Region 19, location 5.2, Alpha 3,893,216.0692. The link was old—the Alpha who had joined with the mammal had been diverted during the Purge and then the subsequent quarantine. Such a lapse was to be expected. There were occasional dead spots in the network, especially with Alphas scouting on their own for days at a time.

It was the cat who had used the device. Mort(e). The one the humans wanted. The messiah who had escaped the quarantine. What was the word he used? She searched for it. Ah, yes: he sought *the source*. The source of everything. And now he was linked to her for as long as his fragile mind could withstand it.

She had already seen Mort(e) through the eyes of Culdesac, along with other translator-operators who had interacted with him. There were also the Martinis: the mother and her two children, all of whom were captured after their region was overrun. The soldiers had held them down and forced them to use the interpreting device. True to the odds, only one of them, the boy, survived. But the sessions showed that Mort(e) the Great Warrior, the Scourge of the Colony, was nothing more than an unevolved slave for the humans. He was so ordinary, like all messiahs. Just a cat, a conditioned pet. Felines were a species that showed promise, though they were prone to bickering, and tended to have the biggest egos. Ordinary house cats always demanded to be in charge of things as if they had hunted humans in the wild before the war.

This cat was different in that way, she had to admit. He had seen the war. He had killed his master, along with so many other humans that he had lost count. She fished out the information: the actual number was eighty-seven. He was determined, as evidenced by his use of the device. He was brave, and did his duty, and was free of the plague of human self-importance. Yes, this one had shown the progress of her vision in every way she could have asked.

She continued absorbing the information taken directly from Mort(e)'s mind. She could see the Martinis' living room—yes, this was all familiar, viewed from only a foot off the ground rather than from the point of view of a bipedal primate. These were the thoughts he focused on when he used the translator. They kept his mind from bleeding out. So he had been trained. Not by Culdesac, but by someone.

There was—

THERE WAS A room, carpeted, with fluorescent light coming in through frosted glass. A basement. The cat was there. The Queen was the cat now, seeing through his eyes. He was still an animal. He was afraid and curious at the same time, all the time, because he had to be. But his belly was full, and his coat was clean. He protected this house.

The cat awoke from sleep with the dog beside him. The room

was cold. His nose was a small ice cube on the end of his face. But the dog was warm. She was curled around him, her stomach rising and falling. She sensed movement, awoke, and stared at the cat. The cat rose. He wanted to take her to a place no one had ever seen before. It was a land he had discovered years earlier, before the children had arrived. Back when he was alone. She had to see it, now that the two of them were joined.

He waited at the foot of the steps until she got to her feet. He climbed the stairs to the kitchen. Soon she was running after him, her tongue flopping and dripping. The dog was so excited that she ran right past the room where her master slept with the woman with the sad eyes.

A final flight took them to a small room with a cold wooden floor. An attic, crowded with boxes and coat racks, with two windows letting in light on either side.

The dog was scared. Her paws rested on the top step while her tail sagged in frustration. But the cat explored. There was a box of toys, scuffed but intact, still coated with the scent of the children. The cat pawed at them. Soon the dog lost her fear and joined him, drawn to the sheer wonder of the place.

By force of habit, the two travelers huddled near a box of winter coats, repeating the ritual they had perfected in the basement. She lay down first, sprawling out her legs and tail. The cat found the open space in front of her warm pink tummy. There was no boundary left. They were one, even in the cold reaches of distant lands. Wherever they were together, they were safe.

Some time passed before the humans began calling for the dog. The canine's ears twitched at the sound. She sat up, listened, and then bolted for the stairs to find her master. The cat waited at the top of the steps. The dog stood beside her master and the woman. While the humans hugged and touched mouths, the dog peered up the steps to her friend. Then her master clipped a leash to her collar and took her away.

The cat was sad. He called to her. The dog did not answer. He fell asleep on the landing wondering when she would come back—

THE QUEEN EXTRACTED herself from the memory. The sensation of it was almost physical, like pulling her jaws from the open wound of a dying enemy. Meanwhile, the signals kept coming in from her chambermaids, all of them repeating the same alert. As mere vessels for this information, her daughters had no idea how repetitive they could be.

At last, she delivered an order to a gibbering maid:

BRING ME THE HUMAN.

She did not need to specify which one.

BRIGGS WAS STILL wearing the skinned legs of the raccoon when the guards led him into the Queen's chamber. The "pants" had ragged holes at the knees, revealing the leathery flesh of the animal who had offered to be skinned. Briggs also wore a long-sleeved shirt made of some breathable synthetic fabric. That, too, was ripped and smudged, the result of being manhandled by the Alphas over the previous few days. The man's face was serene. He had no doubt been briefed on what to expect if he were ever captured. But it was more than that. He did not fear death. He radiated the confidence of a man who had already tasted victory.

The journey Briggs had taken to get here was typical of many captured humans. Given enough time, the Colony caught all spies roaming the frontier. There were too many intersecting bits of data coming in from the Queen's daughters: reports of unusual scents, the unique pitch of a human voice, eyewitness sightings, footprints. In Briggs's case, an army of smaller ants tracked his scent trail, finding a pattern in his breath, his urine—which could never be disposed of completely—and his sweat. The Alphas found him as he stepped out of a wooded area on his way to the turnpike. Surrounded, Briggs stopped and removed the raccoon head. The Alphas brought him to the staging area for the Purge, where many others were corralled for the ceremony. Then he was on a ship, forced into tight quarters where he could neither stand nor lie down. When the vessel arrived at the island, the humans were marched out, with many going to a holding area. It was an open room with a communal feeding trough full of a protein liquid that would keep them alive for whatever purposes the Queen had devised. The strongest were often sent to the farms, where they would be fed a diet that kept them bloated and docile, like aphids. Specialized workers would extract blood from vents that punctured their sides. It was a far better fate than those who were taken to the laboratories. A few unfortunate test subjects were returned to the holding area, blinkered and driven insane, sometimes missing parts of themselves. That way, the others could see what awaited them.

Briggs probably heard the stories, still circulating among the prisoners, of how a small group of humans escaped the island to build the resistance. Because of this legend, incoming prisoners were often treated with reverence. Rather than showing that the ants were winning, the captures confirmed the success of the human uprising. *There must be thousands of us out there*, the most pathetic ones often assured themselves. *Millions! All over the globe!* Even the most cynical of the new prisoners could not convince the desperate ones to stop getting their hopes up.

The guards led Briggs to a small mound of earth directly in

front of the Queen. Briggs sat down. A worker entered the room with a translator. Briggs did not turn to see. The Queen remained still as the worker fit the device onto the man's head. Even after he was ready, the Queen waited a few moments longer.

When at last the only sound left in the room was the man's breathing, the Queen leaned forward and connected her antennae with the device.

PLUMBING A HUMAN mind with the translator made the Queen feel like an army of worker ants invading an enemy nest. To navigate an unfamiliar structure, the workers would release their chemical trails, noting each time they crossed and each time they reversed direction, until the pathways with the strongest scent became the ones everyone used. It was a self-correcting method that never failed.

This human was older than most she had encountered these days, and so his mind was like an old termite colony, with many decrepit chambers and even more dead ends. She made her way through each of them, a fluid movement that overwhelmed the labyrinth. She did not have to find the perfect route—she merely had to flood the tunnels until she was everywhere at once.

Briggs. Charles Briggs, named for a father he never met, raised by his mother. He was a target at school for the other students, who made fun of his unkempt hair, his large glasses, the khaki slacks he wore almost every day. When he was twelve, Charlie's Aunt Thea talked his mother into letting him stay for a summer at her cabin in the mountains, where she operated a tackle store. It would toughen him up. Thea was fierce and independent, built like a bear, often dressed like a man in overalls and plaid shirts. The summer spent with Aunt Thea was both the worst and somehow the best of Charlie's life. It gave him strength to endure anything, even the slaughter of his comrades. Even surviving in the woods for a month after the disaster in Charleston. Even skinning a masochistic raccoon for its pelt. That summer kept him alive. And now, he hoped it would help him face death like a man.

Like a man, the Queen thought.

Aunt Thea gave him a slew of tasks that summer: chopping wood, skinning potatoes, cooking breakfast, weeding the garden, changing tires. He did everything wrong, and punishments for failure ranged from a whack across the temple to having to sleep in the shed. It was that same shed where Thea took Briggs after waking him extra early to watch her slaughter a pig. She stunned it with a bat, then bled it to death with a small incision in the neck. When it came time for him to learn this new skill, his constant crying earned him a few more nights in the shed, now fragrant with pig blood and urine. She told him he squealed louder than the pigs because he was no better than one.

Later, Thea discovered that Briggs was afraid of rats, too. It disgusted the Queen whenever she came across a phobia such as this. Rats had reason to be afraid of the humans, not the other way around. She could feel the boy's fear in the chambers of his mind.

Thea later moved Charlie's cot down to the basement. She took out the light bulb at night and left him with a flashlight that required him to smack it every now and then for it to work. The failing glow turned the room into a house of horrors. Old blankets became ghosts. The rake leaning against the wall was a skeleton. The wheelbarrow was a creature large enough to swallow him whole. The rats doubled in size, and their eyes glowed red.

The basement would be the perfect meeting place for the Queen and Briggs. Using the translator, she was able to amplify this memory until the man's weak mind had no choice but to place him there as a boy sitting on the cot, clutching a dull flashlight.

When the Queen walked down the wooden stairs, she took

the form of Aunt Thea. Her boots left muddy footprints, tracking dirt from the unpaved driveway where she parked her truck.

With quaking hands, Briggs shone the light on her face. "What are you doing?" he asked.

"Killing you," the Queen said, speaking in Thea's voice.

"What do you mean?"

"You are using the translator," she said. "It is shorting out your brain as we speak. The synapses are breaking. Neurons are pulsing and then burning out. But I am holding back. If I wanted to, I could dig out your entire mind with a mere thought."

"Then do it already."

"You do not want me to, so why bluff?"

She controlled this memory now, this hidden chamber of the mind. She summoned the image of a rat, one the size of the fat pigs that Briggs had to slaughter. The creature poked its head over the wheelbarrow. Briggs swiveled and aimed the flashlight at it, making its eyes glow. It continued to watch him even after it had been discovered. It appeared ready to smile at him. Maybe even laugh.

Briggs turned to the Queen. "It's not real," he said.

"No, it is not," the Queen said. With that, the rat was gone. This human was tough, she thought. Even in the world of the translator, Briggs had an idea of what to expect. She was glad now that she was taking her time with this one.

"You're not real, either," Briggs said.

"Incorrect."

"Thea's dead."

"She lives," the Queen said. "In your mind."

Briggs's refusal to respond conceded the point.

"Just like your god," she said.

"No, not like my—"

"And your messiah."

Briggs folded his arms and rolled his eyes. "So this is the end?" he asked. "I die debating with another skeptic. I suppose this is what I deserve."

"Because you are a sinner. Is that how it works?"

"Because I'm human. We get what we get."

"Would you like to know the truth about your savior? And your prophet?"

"Not from you," Briggs said.

She could dump it all into his mind and watch him convulse like a dying cockroach, both here in this dream world and outside. Simply telling him the truth was not enough. That was the way with these humans—they could erect walls in their minds, sealing off entire catacombs. This ability had served them when they were first standing upright in the savanna, on the lookout for predators. Now it was a mutation that brought about their doom.

"Thea used to smoke cigars," Briggs said. "I could use one now. Maybe you could fetch me one?"

Before he could finish, a lit cigar materialized in his hand. The Queen held one, too, grinning behind the smoke.

"I'm impressed," Briggs said, taking a long pull that made the embers flare red.

"I am not," the Queen said.

"Aunt Thea never was."

"Even watching you die leaves me disappointed," the Queen said. "You think there is something noble about it."

"We didn't have to be enemies," he said. "You could have reached out to us."

"You could have refrained from killing us."

Briggs responded by taking another long puff. He exhaled with a sigh, sending up a column of smoke.

"Tell me about the messiah," the Queen said. "You met him."

"Don't you already know? You can read my mind. This cigar is even the right brand."

"I told you; if I wanted to carve out your mind, I would have done it by now. I am giving you this opportunity to speak. Maybe you will even repent. I would like that."

"No, thank you," Briggs said. "The warrior Sebastian is everything the prophet said he would be. Everything the prophet foretold has come true. You spoke of nobility. Sebastian is noble. You know it when you see it."

The Queen had already gleaned a few memories of the encounter with Mort(e). Briggs saw the cat as a beacon, a light spreading outward, calling others toward it. But to her, Mort(e)'s quest mirrored the basest desires of the humans: an escape from death, an exemption from suffering, a chance to live like gods themselves. Love was a word these mammals used to make up for the fact that they could not join as one, as the ants could with each other, as the Queen had once done so completely with her mother. Love was an illusion, a smoke screen that masked the humans' capacity for hatred.

"You can do all this," Briggs said, motioning to the walls of the basement. "You can enter my mind and manipulate it. But you can't figure out why the warrior loves his friend, or why he'll never give up on her, or why it means so much to us."

"I know what it means to you," the Queen said. "It is a longing that drives your species. You think this longing is always good. Billions of your victims say otherwise."

The Queen had heard enough. She put the cigar firmly in her mouth and walked over to Briggs. He clutched the flashlight in both hands, biting hard on the cigar. A fake Aunt Thea scared him more than the real Queen.

"We—" He removed the cigar. "We see love as a way of rising above all this death."

"Yes," she said. "And it has failed."

She took out her cigar, leaned over, and blew smoke in his face. And with that, she allowed the truth about the messiah and the prophet to seep into his mind like the particles of burnt tobacco entering his lungs and bloodstream.

Briggs slumped his shoulders. The flashlight slipped from his hands, darkening the room, blotting out his face. "It doesn't matter," he said.

The Queen headed for the stairs, her work in this shattered mind complete.

"Do you know what I told Thea the last time I saw her?"

"Of course."

"Shut up," Briggs said. "I'm telling you, anyway. She came to my high school graduation. First time I had seen her in six years. She came to congratulate herself on the man I had become. And I told her to go to hell. Right in front of my mom."

"I know."

"I'm saying the same thing to you," Briggs said. "Go to hell. The games you're playing here don't even matter. The prophet doesn't even matter. Sebastian loves his friend. He's coming for her. And then he's gonna kill you."

"You do not believe that."

"Yeah, but I'm working on it," he said. "That's what makes us better than you. I *will* believe it before I'm gone. And so will you."

The Queen dropped the cigar and stamped it out under her filthy boots. And then she began releasing the memories of her daughters into the man's brain. In the span of a few seconds, he experienced all their deaths. He deserved to see them. If only she could kill all the humans this way. They would understand at last what they had done as their minds imploded.

She climbed the stairs, leaving Briggs shuddering in his dungeon, a little boy afraid of the unknown.

SHE RETURNED TO the real world to find the workers hauling off the carcass. Her daughters continued grooming and primping her as though there were no enemy in their midst. Briggs was now another slab of protein for them. Soon all the humans would join him. And their little fantasy of love would be dispersed among the Colony—processed, digested, and disposed of.

PART V ATTACK

CHAPTER SEVENTEEN
THE FALSE JERUSALEM

ORT(E) AND WAWA pulled themselves onto the deck of the *Vesuvius*, a small balcony where two humans helped them to their feet. Mort(e) could not discern their gender because both were dressed in the same bug-like outfits that the first one wore, the one who had sacrificed himself. From here, Mort(e) could get a better look at the ship. The three main balloons supporting the cabin were coated in a shimmering silver material that reflected the ground, the sky, and the sun all at once. It could mimic the colors around it like the skin of a chameleon. And it must have absorbed the sunlight, providing a solar energy source so that the ship never needed to land. Mort(e) recalled a photo someone had once shown him, taken from a battle in a city called Chicago that no longer existed. A group of animal soldiers had taken the picture in front of some silvery blob, a metallic sculpture. That was what the blimp resembled. It took Mort(e) a moment to recall that this memory came from his own past and not from the translator.

Mort(e)'s eyes followed the reflective skin to the stern, where the propellers spun in blurred circles, powered by the largest engines he had ever seen. Encased in the reflective metal, the turboprops were each the size of a yacht, and yet the only sound they made came from slicing through the air. There were two engines for each balloon—Mort(e) could see the bottom four from his perch on the balcony. This was not one ship but several, lashed together to support the gondola, the pressurized incubator of human civilization.

The humans gave Mort(e) and Wawa a few more seconds to take it all in. Then they led the two fugitives to a metal door with a giant wheel in the center of it. One of the humans spun the wheel, releasing the air lock. This opened to a cylindrical chamber lined with track lights. While one human closed the door behind them, shutting out the wind, the other opened the next lock. When the door released, to Mort(e)'s surprise, the smell of trees and wildlife greeted him, a humid breeze filled with the spice of pine needles and soil. It made no sense. The humans motioned for them to proceed. Wawa hesitated. "It's better than waiting outside," he told her.

They entered an enormous oval room, some kind of promenade, with dozens of circular windows that let in the daylight. In the middle of the room was a fountain surrounded by trees and manicured grass. Plastic pipes interlaced the little garden, leading to the bubbling oasis at the center. Mort(e) figured that they had constructed a renewable source of oxygen, clean water, and vegetables, probably adapted from Colonial technology. The humans had turned this amazing aircraft into a small Eden in the clouds, though it remained a poor imitation of what the ants had accomplished.

The rear of the room featured a small amphitheater, a meeting area with benches and chairs surrounding it. Stairways and elevators led to other levels of the cabin—Mort(e) assumed these levels included living quarters, supplies, an engine room, and maybe even a house of worship, the transmitter of EMSAH.

Dozens of humans stood about, perhaps even a hundred, some in olive military uniforms, others in blue jumpsuits. They all gasped when he entered. A few even broke down crying. There were several mothers with their children. They whispered into the little boys' and girls' ears, saying, *That's him. That's Sebastian.*

There was a bald man with glasses who seemed hypnotized by Mort(e)'s medallion. The man held his hand to his own chest, clutching a St. Jude necklace that wasn't there.

A woman in a black robe stepped out of the crowd. She was middle-aged, of East Asian descent, with silver hair and wrinkles. Her robe flowed down to her feet, making it appear that she could float rather than walk. A white collar held the robe in place on her thin neck. "What happened to the man who was with you?" she asked.

"He sacrificed himself to save us," Mort(e) said.

She gazed at the floor for a moment and cleared her throat. "I am the Archon," she said. "We must speak alone."

Taking his hand, she led him toward an elevator shaft. Mort(e) was so entranced by the strangeness of it all that he almost forgot about Wawa. When he searched the room for her, the Archon squeezed his hand and told him that the dog would be okay. He had already seen Wawa attack an acid-shooting Alpha with nothing more than a fireman's axe. These humans were no match.

As the Archon guided him past the disciples, each one took a turn placing a hand on his shoulder and muttering some prayer. It took a few times before Mort(e) understood what they were saying: *We are delivered. We are delivered.* Seconds later, he was in the elevator with her. The Archon herself was leading him into the inner sanctum of the humans. The elevator lifted them through a transparent tube to the cabin attached to the ship's upper chamber.

The doors slid open, revealing the Archon's command center

and personal quarters. A table was in the center of the room, draped with old yellowed maps. To the side, near a row of bookshelves, was an odd piece of artwork: a glass case with sand in it. Spaces in the sand had been carved out, like tunnels.

"I knew you would find this interesting," she said. "It defies everything you know. It may be the last of its kind in existence."

Mort(e) detected movement in the little tunnels. He drew closer. The motion turned out to be ants, hundreds of them, thousands, all living in a miniature version of the Colony.

"An ant farm," the Archon said.

"How did you do this?"

"We were created to have dominion over these creatures, not the other way around. We could scoop them up from the dirt and use them for our amusement, if God willed it."

The ants went about their business of harvesting, digging, tending to eggs. In the floating cocoon of the *Vesuvius*, they were mere exhibits in a zoo.

The Archon offered him a drink, pointing to a pitcher of water and a bowl on a nearby countertop. He accepted. She poured the water and handed him the bowl. Mort(e) lapped up as much as he could with each gulp.

"You remind me of a cat I used to have," she said. "She's gone now."

"You had dominion over her?"

"Yes, but only after rescuing her from a pack of dogs. She lost a leg, poor thing. You see, we were not the slaveholders you think we were. We cared about you. You were our friends. We were your guardians."

"Tell that to the dog I came here with," Mort(e) said after finishing up the last few drops. "Her guardian kept her in a cage. Made her fight to the death."

The Archon nodded.

"The ants are our guardians now," he said. "That's not working out too well, either. So you'll have to forgive me if I'm not that excited to be here. I'm curious about what you have say. But I didn't have much of a choice."

"I like to think that we always have choices," she said. "But I know how it feels when it looks like we don't."

She took his empty bowl and placed it on the counter. "The Colony told you that EMSAH is an acronym, right?" she asked.

"That's right."

"Do you know what it means?"

"I may have briefly," Mort(e) said.

"It's a corruption of the word *messiah*, first spoken by an animal who was learning how to read."

This word sounded familiar to Mort(e). He took it to mean some kind of revolutionary. A troublemaker. But the Archon's reverence for the term seemed to give it a different connotation.

"You, Sebastian," she said, "you're the messiah for the Colony, for the animals, and for us. You will deliver all three into the hands of the Lord."

She reached out and squeezed his St. Jude medallion. Her nails were painted silver, like the hull of the ship. "It's been a while since I've see one of these."

"Listen," Mort(e) said, "I'm not exactly sure why you picked me, but you're mistaken. The Queen knows about your prophecy. She wants to see if I'll decide to be your messiah or whatever you call it."

"She has foreseen this."

"You don't get it," he said. "She's been in control the whole time. You think it's a prophecy, but it's another one of her experiments. It's a test. Nothing more."

"Has it occurred to you that the Queen fears our prophecy because it might be true?"

"That's not how she thinks."

"The human resistance is a testament to the power of belief," she said. "This belief is a weapon more dangerous than any the Queen has invented. It is something that she cannot understand."

"Like death-life?"

This made her pause for a moment. "Let me show you something," she said. "This might put things in perspective." From a deep pocket in her robe, she pulled out a glass tube. Unscrewing the lid, she revealed an eyedropper filled with an oily liquid. She held it close to Mort(e). The liquid gave off a soapy odor.

"Do you recognize that smell?" she asked.

"No."

She unscrewed a cap on the side of the ant farm. The opening was large enough for her to fit the eyedropper into it. She placed the point over a worker ant, who sensed the intrusion. As the ant probed the object, the Archon dripped the substance onto the insect. She withdrew the dropper and put it back into its vial. Meanwhile, the worker shuddered. Her sisters nearby went into a frenzy, first feeling one another's antennae in consultation, then charging toward their drenched comrade, who remained still, awaiting her fate. The ants bit into her legs and thorax and dragged her toward the opening in the case, pulling so hard that Mort(e) thought they would rip her apart. The mass of ants exited the farm, so intent on removing their infected sister that they did not notice that they were free at last.

The Archon's skeletal hand slammed down on top of them. With her other hand, she removed a handkerchief from her pocket and wiped the remains of the ants from her palms. Then she screwed the cap into place, sealing the ant farm shut.

"That substance is called oleic acid," the Archon said. "The ants use it as a signal to indicate that something is dead and needs to be discarded from the colony."

She laughed and shook her head. "For all their cleverness," she said, "they are still slaves to the instincts of their species. The Queen's war only masks her own weaknesses. This 'experiment,' as you call it, is merely an admission on her part that the Colony can never defeat us. She's going mad down there, you see. Her lair has turned into an insane asylum. She is the only inmate, and her daughters have become the guards. She claims to be rational, but she envies what she cannot have. She hates what she cannot understand. She destroys what she cannot control."

Even the Queen could not have planned the events that had unfolded, the Archon said. If Mort(e) went forward with his search, it would signal to the Queen that even the most hardhearted among the animals could be converted to the faith—and could become a new symbol of hope for the resistance. The humans had chosen their messiah, and the messiah would fulfill his destiny. And the Queen would respond by destroying everything, wiping everyone out, keeping any survivors as livestock. A final quarantine.

"Or," the Archon said, "the messiah will lead both the humans and the animals to victory over the horde of Satan."

Mort(e)'s love for Sheba, she said, shone like a sun on the horizon, second only to God's love for his people. Mort(e)'s journey inspired the underground believers as much as it frightened the Queen.

"So you have a choice," she said. "Continue on this path and trigger the final conflict between the Colony and the armies of God. Or return to the surface, abandon your quest, and roam the earth until the day you die, all the time wondering what happened to your friend."

"You think you'll win this final conflict?" Mort(e) asked.

"We'll be doing God's will. That's more important."

"How do you know that?"

"We know because we know," she said, a smile curling her thin lips. "It is as simple as that."

But this was not simple. It was a snake eating its own tail. Mort(e) had been working for the ants for so long, convinced that no one could survive without thinking rationally. And here was this cult leader speaking of magic. Mort(e) did not have the energy to question it further. It was EMSAH. There was no arguing with it. He had been trained to recognize the symptoms, not find a cure. The only cure was quarantine.

"Tell me why," he said. "Why am I the messiah?"

"I would be honored," she said.

AS MORT(E) SUSPECTED, the *Vesuvius* came equipped with a house of worship, located on the level underneath the promenade. All the humans waited for him there. Unlike the artificial surfaces of the rest of the ship, this church had wooden planks on the floors. An oak podium faced the congregation. Four children and a young woman stood at the front. In the first row, completely out of place but maintaining her calm, was Wawa. When she made eye contact with Mort(e), both shrugged. Mort(e) figured that she, too, was thinking of better ways to utilize such a large space in this city-in-the-sky.

The Archon directed him to a seat beside Wawa, then took the podium. Mort(e) nudged the lieutenant to ask if she was all right. Wawa nodded. The Archon raised her hands, and everyone quieted. For once, their eyes were focused on something other than Mort(e).

"Our God is strong," the Archon said. There were shouts of approval over this, until everyone was applauding and stomping their feet. Mort(e) now knew why they installed wooden floors. The planks were so loud when they rattled that the ants on the ground must have sensed the vibrations.

"Our God," the Archon continued, "has delivered our savior as promised. And now, our savior will deliver us."

More call-and-response followed. "All right!" someone shouted in Mort(e)'s ear. "That's right," another said. As Mort(e) looked around at the shouting faces, he caught sight of a child at the far end of the row where he sat. The child, a boy, lay on a hospital stretcher. There was a makeshift respirator attached to his mouth and nose, with a bellows made out of a powder-blue hot-water bottle, pumping air into him. A nurse stood next to him. It was odd that they were keeping someone in this condition alive. Culdesac would have laughed at this waste of resources. Then he probably would have eaten the kid.

"Now," the Archon said, "Miss Teter's class of young ones will reenact the story of the Exile, as adapted from the Word."

The Archon's hands rested on a slim book, bound in a plain green cover. She lifted the book to her lips, kissed it, and handed it to Miss Teter. The children were poised and ready. Mort(e) noticed the costumes the students had made for themselves. One girl wore what appeared to be antlers—probably meant to be antennae, fashioned out of cardboard paper. Another girl wore fake dog ears and a tail. A boy wore cat ears. Mort(e) assumed that this child would be playing the messiah. Another boy was meant to be a plain old human. The rest of Miss Teter's class—about fifteen students—sat cross-legged on the floor nearby.

Miss Teter opened the book. "A reading from 'The Warrior and the Mother,'" she said. The people clasped their hands in reverent prayer. Many of them spoke the words along with the teacher.

"In the days of the war with no name," she began, "all God's children—man, beast, bird, and insect—bowed before the Queen." The girl with the antennae kept her arms haughtily crossed. The other children knelt on the ground before her.

"The Queen of Dirt, the Monarch of the Underworld. The Devil's Hand. She slaughtered seven times seven times seven of the humans and raised the lower species to their unnatural state."

The boy dressed as the cat stood up. Curiously, the dog—whom Mort(e) assumed represented Sheba—remained kneeling.

The Archon nudged him and said, "Don't worry about that 'lower species' stuff. It's from an older translation."

"The animals dreamt that they were men," Miss Teter said, "never knowing the grace of God. And so these slaves of the New Pharaoh hunted down the last of the race of men."

As Miss Teter described the horror of the war, several boys wearing fake dog and cat ears surrounded the children and pretended to claw at them. One by one, the children feigned death and toppled over. Some of them giggled, which caused a few of the adult audience members to laugh with them. Mort(e) and Wawa looked at each other.

"In defiance of God, the Queen raised up her own Garden of Eden," Miss Teter said. "She said to her daughters . . ."

"'Come, let us build ourselves a great city in the sea, an island of our own, and make a name for ourselves,'" the girl dressed as the Queen said.

Several of the formerly "dead" children lay down beside the Queen, acting like the landmass of the Island spreading into the sea. The Queen stood in the middle of the formation and grinned.

"But the Lord came down to see the island," Miss Teter said. "And the Lord said, 'These creations of mine have defied me with their arrogance. They believe now that nothing is impossible for them. They even imprison my chosen ones on their shores. Come, let us go down and thwart their plans, so that I may see a new day dawning for my people.'

"So the Lord called upon his favorites among the animals, one cat and one dog, and the boy who had been their guardian. The boy was named Michael."

Mort(e) had heard the word Michael so many times when he was a pet—often affectionately, sometimes out of anxiety or anger. Michael was the name of Daniel's son, the child who was placed on a bed when he was first brought home. Back when the world was much smaller.

Now the boy, Sebastian, and Sheba were alone on the stage. Their classmates quietly donned paper antennae and stood up.

"Michael was brave, a true child of the One God," Miss Teter said. "He and his friends, Sebastian the Warrior and Sheba the Mother, represented God's will on earth, the promise of Eden that had been abandoned. When the Queen learned of their presence in her false Jerusalem, she ordered her minions to descend upon them."

The children dressed as ants let out a terrible scream as they surrounded the three actors. The audience joined in. Mort(e) would have thought that the adults were cheering them on if not for the genuine expressions of terror on some of their faces.

"Sebastian the Warrior fought off ten of the beasts so that Michael and his family could escape," Miss Teter said. Meanwhile, the boy-cat pretended to claw at the horde of ants. "But Sheba was lost in the battle," Miss Teter continued. "Wounded, Sebastian pursued her into the wilderness."

Sebastian darted offstage.

Mort(e) shook his head. This was not how it had happened. He could not understand why the humans would have made something up when they clearly did not know what they were talking about.

"Before Sebastian could find them," Miss Teter said, "Sheba the Mother and her friend Michael were captured and brought to the Island to stand before the Queen." All the ant-children stood before the tyrannical monarch again. Michael and Sheba were in the center, their heads lowered in reverence.

"'Who do you think you are?'" the little Queen asked. "'How dare you defy the empire?'"

"But Michael was not afraid," Miss Teter said. "He said . . ."

"'I am Michael, a child of the Chosen,'" the boy replied. "'Your weapons cannot strike us down. We have nothing to fear from you, for one day our Warrior will return from the wilderness to destroy every last one of your species and restore the true Eden. He has come for his friend. He fights for love, not for dominion or treasure or soil.'"

The congregation chanted those lines with him. Some were urging him along, but others were whipped into a trancelike state, jumping up and raising their hands, pleading for more.

"When the Queen asked what made the boy so confident," Miss Teter said, "he responded . . ."

"'Those who fight for God have love in their hearts. This animal returns for the love of his friend. You have no weapon to fight against this power. He will scrape your empire from the soles of his feet.'"

"The Queen grew vexed," Miss Teter said, "and ordered the child and his dog to be imprisoned for the Colony's amusement."

"'Let this warrior of yours come to us,'" the girl-Queen said. "'We will greet him with the respect that he deserves.'"

"But God had mercy on Michael and said, 'Michael, child, I shall make straight a path for you, so that you may tell the world what you have witnessed.' And God sent his angel to shut the beasts' jaws so that they would not hurt the boy, because he was found blameless. Thus Michael led an escape from the Island, along with his faithful disciples."

The ant-children lay down prostrate before Michael as he calmly strolled by. Several other children represented his disciples. People in the audience clapped. Mort(e) thought that these humans had been in the zeppelin too long if they thought such an escape were possible.

"The journey to the mainland was arduous," Miss Teter said. "Many of the disciples died. Floating on a tiny raft, Michael grew weak from lack of food and water. When they landed on the shore, a band of human fighters discovered them. They, too, were of God's army, the last of their kind. The Lord had spoken to them in dreams, foretelling this day when a prophet would arrive. Michael's disciples said . . ."

"'Protect this prophet,'" the disciples intoned. "'Do what he tells you.'"

"When they found the boy half-alive, half-dead," Miss Teter said, "he whispered . . ."

"'I have fulfilled God's plan for me,'" Michael said. He was lying face up while the other children attended to him. "'Another will come to take my place. He will lead you to the false Jerusalem, where you will reclaim the heritage of your ancestors. Make straight a path for him. But until then, love one another as the Warrior has loved the Mother.'"

The audience grew quiet, save for some intermittent weeping.

"The soldiers of God brought Michael to their camp," Miss Teter said, "and bound up his wounds. And they continued to gaze into the wilderness, waiting for the day when the Warrior would deliver them."

The children gazed at the wall of the church, pretending to watch the horizon. And then the boy dressed as Sebastian jumped out from behind the podium. Only this time he had a plastic sword and a crown on his head. This was apparently unexpected, for the congregants rose to their feet and applauded. Mort(e) assumed that they had been performing this little play for years, and only now could they tack on the ending that they wanted.

Amidst the noise, the Archon whispered in Mort(e)'s ear. "The story is true," she said. "Your master's son gathered disciples and escaped from the Colony. He was only a child, but he could see into the future. A gift from God."

Mort(e) again turned to see the boy in the stretcher. Out of the corner of his eye, he glimpsed the Archon's hands clasped at the middle of her chest.

The congregants broke into song, something about being washed in the blood of a lamb. Beside him, Wawa swayed to the music while glancing at those around her to be sure she was doing it correctly.

"That child is our Oracle," the Archon said in a shaky voice. "He foretold your coming even during the bleak days, when there were only a handful of us."

With the humans singing all around him, Mort(e) walked over to the boy. The nurse, a middle-aged woman with a shaved head, nodded at him, her scalp reflecting the track lights above. The entire congregation had turned to face him. They were singing *at* him, as they would to some holy statue. He was their idol now.

The boy was definitely Michael. He was older, perhaps fourteen or fifteen. He smelled different, the soap and sugar replaced with sweat and peanut butter. The brown eyes were completely blank. This child did not know where he was, if he knew anything at all. If Michael's mind were active, then it had taken him to some other place, far away from this floating church.

"The Queen," Michael whispered. Mort(e) leaned in closer. He extended his hand, although he was not sure what he would do—put it on the boy's shoulder? When his arm hovered over

Michael, the nurse's hand shot out and grabbed him at the wrist. She glared at him. A vein inflated on her forehead, tunneling up her bare scalp.

"Reflex," she said. She released his wrist but kept her eyes fixed on him as a warning.

"You watch over him?" Mort(e) asked.

"Yes," she said, "because he watched over us. He saved us from the Island."

Mort(e) understood the determination in her eyes. This woman was Michael's protector, as Sebastian had once been.

"The Queen," Michael said, his eyes fluttering.

Mort(e) and the nurse leaned in to hear.

"She's so lonely," Michael said. "So lonely. So lonely." He made a choking sound before repeating the phrase several more times.

"She still speaks to him," the nurse said, showing no emotion beyond a quiet sadness over the fate of this boy. "In dreams mostly, but sometimes during the day."

Mort(e) raised his hand to his mouth when he realized what they had done to him.

And then the nurse said bitterly, "The Queen sees—"

"Everything," Mort(e) interrupted. "I know."

"You've spoken to her?"

Mort(e) said yes.

"You're even more special than we thought," she whispered.

Mort(e) could not piece together the jumbled memories, but he was certain that he had come across Michael when he used the device. Maybe Michael would visit his dreams as the Queen had. Instead of a field, they would be in the Martinis' backyard, surrounded by corpses.

Mort(e) turned and faced the Archon, his gnarled fists shaking at his sides. She stood a few feet away, clapping to the music.

The singing continued, sounding no different from the broken noises of the Queen's terrible communication device.

When she was close enough, Mort(e) grabbed her by the collar, throttling her. The singing came to an abrupt stop. "They used the translator on him, didn't they?" he growled. "*Didn't* they? That's how they knew about me. That's how Michael knew so much about them."

People on either side placed their hands on his shoulders and biceps and tried to gently pull him away. He wasn't ready to let them.

"This child has the gift of sight," the Archon said, maintaining her calm. She nodded to the others, letting them know that it was okay. They took their hands off Mort(e). He was still breathing loudly through his snout, big, heavy breaths. Then he finally let go of her.

"Our prophet has told us things that we never could have learned on our own," the Archon said. "He told us about you."

"He's not a prophet," Mort(e) said. "The device did this to him."

"God has chosen him," the Archon replied. "Besides, the translator would not explain how he escaped."

"The Queen let him escape."

"Why would she let him get away?"

"Why would your *god* let him get away?"

"Michael has given us more intelligence about the Colony— all of it confirmed—than we could have ever gathered from anyone else," she said. "God speaks through him."

He turned to the crowd. People stood on their toes to see over one another, to see if the messiah would address them. They were ready to receive his wisdom.

"Your warrior is here," Mort(e) said, extending his arms. The people cheered, as if he had performed a trick for them. A few fists reached for the ceiling. Some of the onlookers were so over-come with emotion that their neighbors had to support them.

"I am here to find my friend," Mort(e) said.

"That's right," someone said.

"And I don't care how many of you die in order for me to find her," he said. A few faces dropped. Most of the others were so enraptured with his presence that they did not seem to notice. He hated them. They phrased their offer of salvation so mod-estly, so peacefully. But it was an offer one could not refuse, more of a threat than a promise. *Join with us in friendship*, they said. *Or else.*

"I'm not doing any of this for your god," Mort(e) said, his voice rising. "If I have to kill everyone in this room to find her, I'll live with that. So sing your songs and read from your magic books, talk to your little Oracle here, because I don't give a shit."

Mort(e) marched through the crowd to the door. He was at the foot of the steps when Wawa and the Archon caught up with him.

"Sebastian," the Archon said.

Mort(e) stopped and stared her down. "Do you have any idea what I'm trained to do if I hear you say that name again?" he asked.

The Archon glanced at Wawa, who shook her head as if to say, *Don't ask.*

"When I was still an animal," Mort(e) said, "I swore I would kill anyone who harmed that boy. I took an oath. The only rea-son you're still breathing right now is because you promised to get me to Sheba."

"We are here to help you as much as we expect you to help us," the Archon said.

"I'm not here to help you. I don't need all this EMSAH non-sense. You've concocted some fantasy about me."

"It's no fantasy. Even the Queen foretold this."

"You've played right into the Queen's hands!" Mort(e) replied. "If Michael could think straight, he'd tell you. But he's so fried that he doesn't even remember what I did. I *killed* Daniel Martini."

The Archon maintained her stony expression.

"Did you hear me?" Mort(e) asked. "I said I shot that boy's father because of what he did to Sheba. And I didn't make up a bunch of fairy tales so I could feel better about it."

"Mort(e)," Wawa said, "this isn't helping anything."

"Oh, you want to go cuddle with these humans now?"

Mort(e) was almost ashamed of the hurt that registered on her face. "These people saved our lives," she said.

"For what?" Mort(e) asked. "So they can start over?"

"We seek peace with all God's children," the Archon said.

"*After* you use them to finish your war," Mort(e) said. "And what happens then? What happens when your god wants you to have pets and farm animals again?"

"That won't happen," the Archon said. "We tried to prove it to you earlier. Have you already forgotten that young man who gave his life to save you?"

"Of course not."

"Neither have I," the Archon said. "He was my son."

A painful pause followed. Wawa let out one of her canine whines.

"So you see," the Archon said, "we've sacrificed. Just like you."

"You better pray she's on that island," Mort(e) said. "If she isn't, I'm coming back here. And I will gut you in front of this whole congregation, got it?"

"She's there," the Archon said, pursing her lips. "Michael has never been wrong before. About anything."

Mort(e) nodded. "Lieutenant," he said, "you can die with these people if you want, but I'm getting my friend, and then you won't see me again."

"Understood, Captain," Wawa said.

Mort(e) left them on the stairs. He wanted to sit by the fountain that the humans had built. He liked the sound of the burbling water, even if it had been poisoned with some kind of EMSAH-related significance.

From the top of the steps, he heard Wawa tell the Archon, "His name is Mort(e)."

CHAPTER EIGHTEEN
FERTILIZATION

TWO OF THE Elders found Mort(e) by the fountain and told him that a VIP suite had been reserved for the messiah. He could wait there and settle in until he was ready to talk. The suite was on the level between the fountain and the church, where most of the humans' quarters were located. It had a bunk and a desk, which Mort(e) supposed was for contemplating his mission of salvation for animals and humankind. But an even better tool for meditation was the window. Because his room was located at the front of the ship, the glass faced forward and curved along the wall to form part of the floor, allowing him to watch the earth scrolling under his feet. He lost track of how much time went by while he stood in this position. From this altitude, the surface appeared to be made of only colors, without any texture. The *Vesuvius* passed over the ocean, separated from the land by a line of yellow sand and white foam. And from that point, the dark blue spread in every direction. Mort(e) had never seen it before.

Wawa arrived with some food: a plate of roasted beetles, ants, and termites. She sat beside him so that they both faced the oncoming blue sea. People spoke outside the room, and it took a minute for Mort(e) to realize that they were repeating themselves.

"They're praying for you," Wawa said. "They have these little necklaces with beads on them, and they use the beads to count the prayers."

"I've seen it before," Mort(e) said.

She asked him if he was okay. He said he was fine, and repeated the question to her. She said yes.

"Did she ask you to talk to me?" he said.

"Of course. But I would have, anyway."

"What do you want me to say?"

"Tell me your thoughts on all this. What's bothering you?"

"They're all nuts."

She laughed.

"Must be the lack of oxygen up here," he said. "They think that death is an illusion. Their leader thinks she's going to see her son again after he was ripped to pieces."

"You have to admire their sense of purpose, though. They're like the ants in a way. And like you."

"No, not like me. I'm trying to find Sheba because there *is* no death-life."

"So you're going through with this, despite the risk to everyone?"

"Oh, yes," Mort(e) said. "I meant what I said. I said the same thing to the Queen when she asked."

"You mean, with the translator?"

"Or a dream," he said. "I'm not exactly sure anymore. But I told her right to her face that I'd still do it, no matter what. Don't you admire *my* sense of purpose?"

"I admire *you*, Mort(e)," she said. "Culdesac chose his second-in-command well."

"On more than one occasion," Mort(e) said.

He placed his hand on top of hers, where it remained for a few moments. A memory crept into his mind, something from his experience with the device. Something about Wawa, the pup in the cage. Mort(e) squinted as he tried to retrieve the memory. A whisper in his mind said, *She lost someone. No goodbyefarewell. No pack. No pack. No pack.*

The memory disintegrated. Only the feeling of solidarity remained. She stayed with him until long after the sun went down. They talked about the war and their homes. She told him about Cyrus and Tracksuit and all the others. He told her about Sheba and Tiberius and the Martinis. They shared stories of Culdesac, both the ones that scared them as well as the ones that made them laugh. Mort(e) was glad she was there. She made him feel like a normal person. She forgave him for who he was.

IN THE MORNING, someone knocked on his door. When Mort(e) opened it, he found the Archon standing with Wawa and two of the Elders, the same men who had directed him to his room. They were pasty middle-aged white men. One was bald; the other wore his stringy gray hair in a ponytail. Like the Archon, they were both physically fit—the bug-and-organic-vegetable diet appeared to be working. They wore a similar robe and collar, but the cloth was a navy blue rather than black. As they walked through a gauntlet of the faithful, heads bowed on either side, but no hands reached out this time. Mort(e) could still feel their gaze focusing on his St. Jude medal, which made it pulse with energy like a second heart.

They gathered around a square metal table in the Archon's quarters. There were several maps splayed out, all depicting the Island. The rising sun lit up the humans' faces and exposed their wrinkles, revealing that they had lived longer than most. The men introduced themselves as Elder Pius (the bald one) and Elder Gregory (with the ponytail). Pius was some sort of military officer, always speaking in terse militaristic jargon. He said *negative* when he meant *no*. Gregory, on the other hand, revealed everything Mort(e) needed to know about him in one sentence: "Do you mind if I hold your St. Jude medal?"

Mort(e) leaned forward so that the man could touch the medallion. Gregory held it between his thumb and index finger. He sighed and let go.

The Archon explained that Gregory was in charge of the day-to-day operations of the *Vesuvius*. He would coordinate the attack from the air, while Pius led the troops on the ground.

"Are you afraid of the water?" Pius asked. "I mean, you *are* a cat."

"No."

Gregory began to tell a story of how he used to discipline his pet cat with a squirt gun. Pius cut him off.

"You won't get wet," Pius said. "But what we have in mind will be a little disconcerting."

He leafed through the maps of the Island until he came across one that gave a three-dimensional view of what the ants had constructed. The false Jerusalem resembled a mushroom cloud sprouting from the ocean floor. A shaft made of earth and stone rose from the bottom of the sea before spreading out into the landmass that broke the surface of the water. This shaft was a tunnel through which the Colony could transport supplies. The humans had attempted an assault on it once but failed. Now the submarines of the old human fleets were scattered or sunken, and the resistance had only a small strike force and a few allies on the ground.

"The goal," he said, "is to cut off the Colony's head."

"Take out the Queen," Gregory said.

"Yeah, I got that," Mort(e) replied. "How? We don't even know where she is."

"Yes, we do," Pius said, tracing his finger along the Island's main tunnel. "Her chamber is right here."

"Don't tell me that your prophet is a GPS, too," Mort(e) said.

"He speaks as God wills him to," she said. "In riddles and parables and allegory. But we were able to . . . extract this information from him."

Extract, Mort(e) thought. He imagined a human hand—Janet's—grinding half an orange against a plastic juicer.

"Hypnosis?" Wawa asked.

"We did what we had to do," the Archon said.

Mort(e) pictured another preposterous ceremony, a séance, in which a hypnotized Michael spoke in tongues while the humans clutched their prayer necklaces and howled and shook and danced.

"There will be three phases," Pius said. "We begin tomorrow morning. First, you will take out the Queen. Second, the Archon will fly her section of the ship to lead the attack. Third, we will mount an amphibious assault at the northern end of the island."

"What do you mean her section?" Mort(e) asked.

They explained that the top part of the *Vesuvius*—the balloon that rested above the other two—could detach and fly on its own. They named it the *Golgotha*.

"Sort of like the saucer section of the *Enterprise* from *Star Trek*," Gregory said. This prompted bewildered expressions from Mort(e) and Wawa. Gregory's follow-up—"You know, *The Next Generation*?"—did not clarify anything.

"Okay, let's stick with part one," Mort(e) said. "How do I get in?"

Pius fumbled through the maps again until he came across a schematic for some kind of missile, showing a side view of the projectile and a diagram of its working parts. Once Pius flattened out the paper, Mort(e) realized that it was not a missile. It was a torpedo.

"Do you mean to tell me—"

"We've modified it," Pius said. "We can deploy it from the *Vesuvius*. There's a chamber inside that's big enough to fit a human. Or a really big cat."

The torpedo, Pius explained, had a parachute to ensure a soft landing so that it would not "break every damn bone" in Mort(e)'s body. The front, meanwhile, was equipped with a cannon that would inject molten metal upon impact, allowing it to drill through the rock. The hatch would automatically burst open once the infiltration was complete. While Pius bragged about the ingenuity that went into the "catpedo," Mort(e) and Wawa tried to communicate with facial expressions. *This is crazy*, Mort(e) signaled. *What did you expect?* she asked with a tip of her head. Mort(e) imagined himself in the torpedo, a metal sperm swimming through the water on its way to fertilize an egg.

"Don't tell me you're having second thoughts," the Archon said. "You were so eager you threatened to kill me, remember?"

"You'll be armed," Pius said. "Don't worry about that. And we have a few weapons that the ants haven't seen yet."

They tried to give Mort(e) an idea of what he would see on the inside. Chances were that the chamber would have some light in it if Sheba was held prisoner there. They could not confirm Sheba's condition. Mort(e) would have to carry her out if she was incapacitated. No one had the nerve to suggest that Sheba would not wish to go along with him.

They moved on to the attack itself: the Archon's ship would bombard the Colonial army, and then paratroopers would join with a D-day force comprised of loyal animals using old human boats. The Archon said that these animals had "converted" and were awaiting orders from the *Vesuvius*. When Mort(e) asked how many there were, the Archon said there would be more today than yesterday, and more tomorrow than today.

The Archon concluded the meeting by asking that they pray. Gregory and Pius faced her and bowed their heads. Wawa joined them. Her mouth moved while they talked about God watching over them, delivering them from evil. Mort(e) nudged her. He wanted her to see him roll his eyes at this ritual. But she kept her head bowed and continued praying.

THE HUMANS HELD another church service that night. Wawa told him he should attend, if only as a diplomatic courtesy. Mort(e) agreed, but insisted on sitting in the last pew. There he cringed at the many things that he found disturbing: a choir of children singing songs about drinking someone's blood; Elder Gregory announcing that they were slaves for God while casually flipping his ponytail off his shoulder; grown men and women weeping and shouting in incomprehensible dialects. Mercifully, Michael and his nurse did not attend. A child in his condition could not be trotted out for every religious service. Mort(e) tried to think of the boy as he had first met him, lying on a towel on Daniel's bed. Instead, Mort(e) kept picturing the translator fastened to Michael's head, poisoning his brain.

Later, the Archon blessed the soldiers who would be leading the assault. They were barely adults, and each wore the flag of the defunct country from which they came. Most had American flags, but there were others that Mort(e) recognized: Mexico, Canada, the United Kingdom, some Caribbean nations. They did not strike him as soldiers so much as wide-eyed converts only a few years removed from performing plays in Miss Teter's class. The Archon assured them that they would either be victorious in the morning, or they would go to heaven. One by one, she went before the soldiers, placing her hands on each pair of shoulders and whispering a prayer.

The children sang again. Mort(e) realized that Wawa had left her pew.

It did not take long to find her walking up the center aisle. The congregants, who had been warned about gawking at the two mutated visitors, turned their heads as she passed by each row. One pew at a time, the singing came to a stop. With her back to the crowd, the Archon noticed the song dying out. She turned to see Wawa stepping forward. This great warrior, second-in-command of the Red Sphinx, wept like a human child.

"Yes, my friend?" the Archon said.

"I wish to join with you in the battle tomorrow," Wawa said.

"You wish to join this church?" the Archon asked.

"I want to be a part of your pack," Wawa said, her voice breaking.

The Archon ran to Wawa and embraced her. People applauded, wiped their eyes, laughed, raised their arms in the air, and shouted that their god was great. A new soul had joined them. Miss Teter had the children sing the song from the day before:

> *Have you been to Jesus for the cleansing pow'r?*
> *Are you washed in the blood of the Lamb?*
> *Are you fully trusting in His grace this hour?*
> *Are you washed in the blood of the Lamb?*

> *Are you washed in the blood,*
> *In the soul-cleansing blood of the Lamb?*
> *Are your garments spotless? Are they white as snow?*
> *Are you washed in the blood of the Lamb?*

The soldiers formed a circle around Wawa, each giving her a hug. They cried and laughed at the same time. Soon all the humans left their seats to get closer to their newest member, all while singing the atrocious song. At one point, a little girl from Miss Teter's class left her place in the choir and wormed her way through the legs of the adults. She pulled on Wawa's tail and giggled. An adult scolded her, but the lieutenant gave the girl a hug. They spoke for a moment. Then the girl pointed at Mort(e) and said something that he could not hear.

He got up and left. When he returned to his quarters, he sat by the great window again. He could still hear the singing from downstairs, a low grumble through the floor.

MORT(E) BARELY SLEPT. It made little sense to do so, now that his life could be measured in hours rather than years. He drank some water and ate a bag of dried beetles that had been left in his quarters. A soldier came for him in the morning, a boy of seventeen or eighteen. He handed Mort(e) a backpack containing all the supplies he would need. Inside, Mort(e) found a submachine gun, a grenade, a small canister of oleic acid, a digital watch, a canteen of water, and some food. The young soldier led him to the promenade area, where once again the civilians onboard were gathered. This time, they prayed in whispers, their eyes on the ground. Some even covered their faces with their hands, their voices indistinguishable from the babbling fountain.

Mort(e) followed the soldier to a fluorescent-lit room at the rear of the ship. Shelves filled with the torpedoes from the schematics lined either side. The "catpedo" prototype was mounted on a small platform, facing a metal tube that presumably exited at the bottom of the ship. The Archon, Gregory, Pius, and Wawa stood solemnly alongside it, like pallbearers next to a coffin.

The Archon broke the oppressive silence. "The fleet is on its way," she said. "Everything is in place."

"Good cloud cover, too," Gregory said. "God is shielding us."

"Right," Mort(e) said.

He approached the torpedo. The hatch was open, revealing the small space where he would sit, upholstered with white cloth and fitted with a harness in order to lessen the impact. Mort(e) would have to curl up in order to fit. Pius had assured him in the meeting the day before that the entire trip would take about twelve minutes. There would be no windows for him to see the Island, so he would have to rely on his watch. Its glowing face would be the only source of light inside the capsule.

Pius asked Mort(e) if he was ready. Mort(e) said yes. He removed the gun from his pack and slung the strap over his shoulder. The Archon appeared ready to speak.

"Pray for me later, Madam Archon," Mort(e) said.

She bit her lip, and he realized he had said the wrong thing. For better or worse, on this day she was a warrior alongside him. "I'm sorry about your son."

"Thank you," she said. And then she stretched out both arms and placed her palms on his face. He allowed her to do it without flinching.

"Even if you are not a believer," she said, "your courage inspires us. That part of the prophecy you must believe."

"Listen, I'm no messiah," he said. "But thanks for giving me the opportunity to find my friend. I hope this war I'm restarting is worth the trouble."

She lowered her hands. "God will decide."

"Let's hope his judgment has improved," Mort(e) said. "Good luck to you."

He felt Gregory's hand on his shoulder. The man was holding back tears. He embraced Mort(e) tightly around the neck. Mort(e) did not return the hug. When Gregory's arms lingered too long, Mort(e) cocked the machine gun. The man stepped away suddenly. Mort(e) grinned.

"Aim true, human," Mort(e) said. "Stay on the hunt."

Wawa was next. Her eyes were so red that it seemed that she had not stopped crying since her conversion the night before. "I know you're disappointed in me," she said.

"You did what you had to do."

"I'm not trying to change your mind," she said. "But I've been searching for this for years. For as long as you've been searching for your friend."

"Just remember," he said. "Maybe these guys are nice, and the ants are mean. But that doesn't mean their fairy tales are true."

"There's so much love here, Mort(e)," she said. "When you and your friend make it out, this pack will be waiting for you. I'll be waiting. Please come back to us."

Mort(e) removed his St. Jude medal and held it out. She accepted it in her palm, the chain bunching up in her hand. She looked at him.

"No," he said.

He left her standing there with her arm extended.

Pius waited by the torpedo, his face as stern as ever. Mort(e) climbed inside and hooked himself up to the harness. Pius placed his hand on the hatch.

"No more talk," Mort(e) said. "I'm tired of it. Let's go."

"Aim true," Pius said. The old warrior's grin was the last thing Mort(e) saw before the hatch closed. His eyes adjusted, and his nose grew accustomed to the smell of iron and oil. The glowing watch on his wrist read 5:19. It resembled the first thing he ever read: the Martinis' address.

It changed to 5:20. He felt the platform shift. Gears clanked as the mechanism moved the torpedo into the shaft, rattling so badly that his teeth clacked a few times. The torpedo came to a halt. There was nothing for a moment. Then he felt the vibrations of another door opening directly in front of him. It was the port from which the device would be launched. A wind whistled through the tunnel.

There was loud metal snap: *chkkk!* And then the torpedo dropped out of the ship.

Mort(e) gripped the cloth seat, his body sickeningly weightless. The gun levitated and bounced off his nose. He brushed it away, and it floated above him, its strap still attached to his shoulder. The torpedo began to spin and wobble. Thankfully, it did not tumble end over end. The force of the revolutions pinned Mort(e)'s head to the hull.

"Come on," he growled at the parachute.

He imagined the torpedo piercing the clouds. He thought of his body shattering when the device struck the water without a parachute.

Finally, the mechanism kicked: *shunk, zzzzz, tick-tick-tick-tick.*

The chute released with a loud pop. His body jerked downward, and the gun hit him on the crown of the head. The device stabilized. The descent was slower now, and the spinning subsided. Mort(e) was grateful that he was a cat. Few other species could have done this without covering the inside of the torpedo with vomit. Mort(e) breathed again. His watch showed that a mere fifty-six seconds had passed.

Two and a half minutes later, the torpedo splashed down. The sounds changed. Sloshing water replaced the wind. The high-pitched whirring of the propeller began, followed by a series of clicks—the sound of the fins redirecting the torpedo toward the Island. The intrepid little machine was on its way.

Reclining on the makeshift seat, Mort(e) settled the gun

onto his chest and checked his watch. Only seven minutes until impact, if the humans' calculations were right. He fumbled for the St. Jude medal, only to recall that it was no longer there. Wawa was probably wearing it now as she prepared to parachute in with her newfound pack. Despite what he had said earlier, he suddenly missed her. Maybe, he thought, he could try to find her when this was all over, let her make fun of him for trying to be the tough guy. Ever since the Change, he had tried to be left alone, and had gone to extraordinary lengths to carve out a little spot for himself. There was no happiness in this. Only freedom.

And then the torpedo hit its mark, rocking the tiny capsule. All around him, the sound of grinding metal and crunching stone made Mort(e) feel as if his own body were being mashed to a pulp along with everything else. The canister slowed and came to a stop. Mort(e) readied his gun and took a deep breath.

The hatch opened.

CHAPTER NINETEEN
THE CHRISTENING

HE TROOPS LINED up on the rocky shores of the Island. Fresh off the Colony's ships, the new recruits had spent the day establishing a beachhead to defend the Island against a human attack. Tents sprang up, trenches were carved into the earth. Culdesac had been waiting a long time for a straight-up fight that would involve both the ants and the surface animals. It would be like the old days of the war. No more of this administrative nonsense, no more politics, no more wiping civilian asses, no more smiling at Council members who had never picked up a gun or faced down a rabid human. It would be him and his soldiers, and the Queen's song in his head, guiding him forward.

Culdesac told the troops that the Queen desired witnesses for this battle. The last time the humans came here, not a single one was left alive. Every inch of the Island had been scrubbed clean. Even the craters had been smoothed over. This time, the surfacers would see the power of the Colony firsthand and spread the word to their comrades on the mainland. A new legend would arise, telling the final destruction of the human rebels.

The quarantine was behind him. Destroying an entire settlement never got easier. And this one was different—even more unforgiving. The first quarantine when he had to leave behind his soldiers. The Queen showed him the carnage in brief flashing images and shouting voices that cut out before Culdesac could decipher what they were saying. She stayed with him through the moments of despair, holding his hand, whispering, *Walk through this with me. Suffer with me. Bleed with me.* He trusted her. She was the only one he could trust. No matter how difficult the last days of this war proved to be, he would follow her orders. Her pain gave her wisdom. If she chose to kill everyone who showed symptoms—even if those people were his loyal soldiers—so be it. He knew better than anyone how destructive the syndrome was. He knew it would take even more lives to stamp it out. The god of the humans was stubborn, with long claws that sank into the hearts of even the bravest warriors. As for the Red Sphinx, there were others who could be trained. If he could replace Socks and Mort(e), then he could replace Wawa, Bonaparte, Archer, and the others. Maybe some of these shitheels standing before him had the abilities he needed.

Now, with preparations complete and the soldiers formed into ranks, Culdesac stared them down and concluded that they were too damn young. This was the best the army could do on such short notice, so soon after the quarantine of the closest settlement. These recruits had barely jogged a few miles, let alone faced delirious and suicidal humans in battle. They didn't *smell* right. Too much soap and detergent where there should have been mud and grime. Those who were still woozy with seasickness had slowly drying pools of tan vomit at their feet, which contrasted sharply with the purplish-brown stone of the landscape. Others nervously peeked at the legions of Alpha soldiers waiting perfectly still on the crest of a hill nearby. Beyond them rose the sphere of the great tower, along with the entrance to the great tunnel that led into the heart of the Colony.

"Do any of you realize how lucky you are to be standing here?" Culdesac asked them. This was the stronghold of the Colony, he said. The nerve center of the greatest empire in history. Though it was crazy for the humans and the animals they had brainwashed to attack this place, they had already succeeded in contaminating another settlement with their plague. They were emboldened and ready to strike.

"The humans are going to mount a suicide mission here," Culdesac said. "We are here to make sure it remains a suicide mission." An approving grumble rose up from the soldiers.

"I know that many of you are from the countryside and may have come across stories of the most recent quarantine," Culdesac went on. "I am a survivor of it. I am a survivor of many things. Aren't we all since this war began?"

He caught a few of them nodding. If this were boot camp, he would have disciplined them for it, but he was glad to see that they were listening. "If you think that the quarantine is an extreme response, you are dead wrong," he said.

It was time to tell them the story.

"I had no slave name," he said. "I am not ashamed of what I was called before the war, but the name is unpronounceable. And the ones who could speak it are dead."

He told them everything, from the hunt, to the conflict with the humans, to the war with no name, to the Change. He described the church he came across in the early days of the war. Many of the soldiers were so horrified by it that they didn't even blink.

"This is the logical, inevitable conclusion of EMSAH," Culdesac told the soldiers. "Don't let your friends tell you otherwise. Even the worst legends are true. Even the—"

"Sir?" came a voice at his side.

She was an officer assigned from another settlement. A coyote of some sort, or maybe a half-breed wolf-dog. Beautiful eyes resting above a menacing jaw. Almost certainly a good fighter.

"What is it?" he said. Someone spoke in the ranks, and Culdesac turned toward the disturbance. The new recruits stared straight ahead, some biting their lips.

"We have a call coming in over the radio channels," she said. "We ignored it at first, but the user relayed a confirmed authorization code."

She handed him a printed transcript of the conversation with the radio operator. At the bottom of the page, it read, AUTHORIZATION CODE NINE-FOUR-NINE.

"I've already alerted the envoy from the Colony," the coyote said. "We think the person on the other end is a human."

Nine-four-nine, he thought. That was Wawa's most recent code for their conversations, right before the quarantine. His heart pumped a little faster. Had they beaten it out of her? Did she hand it over willingly? He didn't want her to suffer—she had earned a quick and noble death. The quarantine should have provided it. But if these humans had gotten to her, infected her, then her suffering would go on indefinitely.

An Alpha soldier approached from the hilltop. Culdesac unhooked his new translator from his belt and put it on his head, fixing the earpiece and antenna. "Give the word to the soldiers," he said to the coyote. "We're about to fight."

THE *VESUVIUS* HAD no formal parachuting bay, so the crew had to build one. And the best place to do it was in the lowest level of the ship, the chapel. The other paratroopers told Wawa that there had been some controversy over this. Would they be offending God and his bloodied son and his righteous prophet by blowing out a wall of his house? Once the plan had been set in motion, however, the Archon put their minds at ease. "I think

God understands that we didn't build this ship for an airborne invasion," she said.

So the night before the attack, after the prayer service, the troopers spent the night whacking away at the stern-side wall with sledgehammers. These "Black Hats," as they called themselves, were fighters from many different countries, separated by language in the same way that the animals were separated by species. Everyone was in good spirits. This constructive act of destruction brought them together. They laughed, sang songs, poked fun at those who had clearly never wielded heavy tools before. Even the bitter cold from the high-atmosphere winds did not dampen their mood. Whenever a great piece of the wall fell away, the soldiers would cheer. Once the hole got big enough, the officers decided that it was too dangerous to have all the men and women swinging wildly. One slip would send them tumbling to their deaths. So each one took turns while others held him or her with a rope tied at the waist. The banter continued, with people from rival countries yelling playful insults at one another. Each person on the end of the rope had to endure heckling from the peanut gallery.

No one made any comments when it was Wawa's turn. They were too awed by her strength. Two Americans and a Canadian had spent several minutes hitting a reinforced section of the wall. Wawa knocked it out in one swing. By this time, a few soldiers were lying flat on their stomachs beside the newly made hole, watching the debris tumble away and vanish into the clouds. The moon was out, and its light reflected off the thick cirrus. Someone came up with the idea of shutting out the lights so that only the silvery glow of the moon came through, casting its eerie shadows and making everything resemble a black-and-white movie.

Citing safety concerns, an officer ordered that the lights be turned back on. A few people groaned in protest. But in that surreal moment, Wawa knew that she had made the right decision to join with these people. For the first time, she was in the presence of humans without being reminded of her master. She did not share in their beliefs—she did not have EMSAH yet—but even the most absurd things about Bloody Jesus and his son Muhammad seemed plausible if they brought all these people together to jump out of a zeppelin. The belief would come to her in its own time, the Archon had told her. This gathering of souls was more than a pack, carving out a brutal existence for no other reason than to eat for another day. These people shared something that went beyond blood or circumstances or mutual enemies.

Wawa's newfound joy was strong enough to last through the early morning hours, when Mort(e) dropped his medallion in her outstretched hands as though it were contaminated with a virus.

Moments later, as the Archon entered the *Golgotha* for the last time, she assured Wawa that the medallion had found its true owner. The Archon told her that she already saw in Wawa the hope that her former masters—both human and animal—had taught her to extinguish. They passed through her life for a reason. They made her who she was, leading her to this moment. If she didn't forgive them, if she wasn't grateful for them, if she didn't learn to love them, then she had made it this far for nothing. An enormous weight slid from Wawa, allowing her to stand upright and expand her chest. She told the Archon that she understood now.

Soon after that, when Wawa lined up in the chapel-turned-drop-point, she squeezed the medallion so hard her fingertips throbbed. She was so eager to join the attack that she neglected to mention until now that she did not know the first thing about parachuting. The humans' response was simple: "Neither do we." This would be the first and only drop of the Black Hats. Where could they have possibly tested their skills? On top of that, the officers warned everyone that the old chutes—stolen from an abandoned military base in Utah—might not even work. "We predict a one-to-five-percent failure rate," the major said. He was a humorless, pale man with a flat head—or maybe that was simply the shape of his hair. Wawa couldn't tell. The major said that there was still a chance that a trooper could survive the fall, if he or she landed in the water. "Tuck and roll," he added, although he did not elaborate. No one seemed comfortable with this until another officer added, "God will decide who floats and who falls."

Several officers went first, while two others stood at the edge of the former chapel and exhorted the recruits to make the jump. With each leap, the Black Hats let out a throaty cheer, like spectators at a sporting event. Wawa peered over her new comrades and saw a gap in the clouds. The Island passed underneath them, taking up the entire opening in the wall, spreading out like a horde of ants. A row of inflated parachutes trailed the ship.

One man jumped, and the cheers died down. His chute did not join the neat row that had formed in the sky. The next jumper hesitated. The major told him to go. Instead, the man raced to the back of the line, where Wawa was waiting. While the officer yelled at him, the man grabbed Wawa's necklace, kissed the medallion, and whispered something in either Spanish or Portuguese. Then he ran in the opposite direction, leaping into the void. The Black Hats roared again when his chute opened. His arms flapped as he waved to his comrades on the ship—or maybe he had simply failed to operate the parachute correctly. From then on, they all kissed her medallion before jumping. The officers gave up trying to stop them. Instead, they moved Wawa to the very end of the line, so everyone could have a chance to kiss St. Jude before plunging toward the earth.

It was almost Wawa's turn. One hand was on the rip cord, the other on the medal. When she finally made it to the front, the major yanked her hand away from the necklace. "Proper stance," he yelled over the wind.

Mechanically, she tucked her chin into her chest and pulled in her elbows. She wanted to close her eyes when she went, but she knew that the officer was watching.

Go, she thought. *Go!*

She stepped into the whistling wind and fell.

And fell.

She counted in her head. *One thousand. Two thousand.* But she was going too fast. *One* one *thousand*, she corrected. *Two one* . . .

"Choke it," she said, pulling the rip cord. The straps unraveled out of her pack. Then the chute deployed, jolting her body before stabilizing. She breathed again. Between her dangling feet, the surface of the Island expanded. She was part of this airborne pack, held up by the hand of God, bringing his justice to the earth.

THE SOLDIERS EAGERLY manned their foxholes, trenches, and pillboxes, desperate to pretend that their enthusiasm would make up for a lack of experience. Though Culdesac was drained from discussing his past—it felt like donating a pint of blood—the reaction of the soldiers seemed to be worth the trouble. They were excited. And afraid. And maybe even a little angry that this war was still not over.

The Alphas, however, remained motionless in their formation. They did not need the cover of barricades. Their presence alone was enough.

There was a command post set up at the rear of the mammal army. Instead of a tent, it was a cave that seemed to have been sculpted by skilled artists. The ants were able to manipulate the landscape. The surface felt strange to Culdesac's feet. He thought of the ground as a living thing that could pull him under if he did anything that the Queen found suspicious.

The colonel, along with the coyote and several soldiers, met with the envoy inside. Two orbs made up of some bioluminescent material lit up the cave. From here, Culdesac had a perfect view of the soldiers and the sea. The overcast sky, though, was an impenetrable milky white.

A raccoon operated the radio. While he fussed with the machine, Culdesac readied the translator. He would be able to speak with the person on the radio while the device sent the exchange into the Alpha's antennae. The chemical signal would eventually travel to the Queen in the Colony's version of whisper-down-the-lane.

"Ready, sir?" the raccoon asked.

Culdesac took the receiver. "Speak, human," he said.

"Good morning, Colonel," replied a woman's voice. Definitely human.

"Congratulations on getting this code," he said. "May I ask how you acquired it?"

"Your lieutenant gave it to me," she said. "The one you left for dead."

Culdesac looked to the Alpha for some reaction. The creature remained still.

"She forgives you, Colonel," the voice said. "And you'll see her again before the day is done."

"You have my attention, human," he said. "Does this conversation have a purpose?"

"Yes. I'm calling to give you a chance."

"A chance for what?"

"Salvation. Surrender now. We will forgive all debts, but you must join us or die."

Culdesac laughed.

"Can you see me yet?" the voice asked.

Pulling the radio's cord, Culdesac walked to the entrance of the cave. The Alpha lumbered beside him, still connected to the translator's antenna. The sky was empty, a white expanse. But then, like a mirage, the ship cut through the clouds, its chameleon skin switched off to reveal a dull silver bullet heading straight for the Island.

"Do I have the pleasure of speaking with the Archon?" he asked.

"You do."

"I thought the *Vesuvius* crashed years ago."

"This is not the *Vesuvius*," she said. "My ship is called the *Golgotha*. The place of the skull. Your island has never had a formal name. I'm about to give it one."

Culdesac reached over and swiped a pair of binoculars hanging from the coyote's neck. He could see no cannons or other weapons on board the ship. He handed the binoculars to the coyote. There was a commotion brewing among the soldiers. Culdesac could hear the sergeants and officers shouting, "Hold your ground!"

"No weapons visible," the coyote whispered. "Kamikaze, maybe?"

"Sorry," Culdesac said into the receiver. "I have to turn down your generous offer. I never had a slave master. I don't intend to start now."

"You could have fooled me," the Archon said, "now that you're the Queen's little mascot."

"Is she trying to take out the tower?" the coyote asked.

"If she is, she's going to miss badly," Culdesac replied.

"This war can come to an end if you join us and fight the real enemy," the Archon continued.

"I've seen the enemy," Culdesac said.

"Your lieutenant no longer agrees with you. She saw hope in our cause."

"Congratulations. You brainwashed another one."

"And the spirit and the bride say, 'Come,'" she said. "And let him that heareth say, 'Come.'"

"What the hell are you talking about?"

"And let him that is athirst come. And whosoever will, let him take the water of life freely."

The airship pointed down at a forty-five-degree angle, its nose aimed right for the Alpha soldiers. He heard more yelling from his own troops, along with random orders to hold their fire and stand ready.

"For I testify unto every man that heareth the words of the prophecy of this book," the Archon continued, "if any man shall add unto these things, God shall add unto him the plagues that are written in this book."

Culdesac put his hand over the receiver and faced the Alpha soldier. "What are you going to do?" he asked.

STAND BY, the creature said.

The rows upon rows of Alpha soldiers began moving away from the impact site like a receding oil slick.

"Such a waste," Culdesac said into the receiver. "Destroying that lovely ship because a magic book told you to do it."

"He which testifieth these things saith, 'Surely I come quickly,'" the Archon said, trancelike. "Amen. Even so, come, Lord Jesus."

"See you in the next life, human," Culdesac said. "Or not."

"The grace of our Lord Jesus Christ be with you all. Amen."

The ship was dropping fast. It was only seconds away.

"There is still love," the Archon said. "There is still hope, Colonel. There is still a chance."

The nose of the ship touched down on the hilltop with a sound like a thousand bones breaking. The frame crumpled, collapsing the giant balloon. A great fireball blossomed like an orange flower. The boom shook Culdesac a second later. There was a loud *pop*, then a deep *thwoom* that drowned out the screaming of the soldiers. The Archon had aimed her suicide mission right between both forces. The young ones began to cheer, acting as if they had brought down the ship themselves. The yellow bloom of the explosion hung in the air for a few seconds before dissipating into a gray cloud.

The flames consumed the rear fins of the ship. The propellers, still whirring, ground into the surface and then came to a halt. The glorious wreckage exploded one more time, releasing clouds of oily smoke. *So stupid*, Culdesac thought. He breathed normally again, for he knew that this sacrifice would not convince anyone to join the humans. It amounted only to fire and theatrics and martyrdom, the only forms of art that mankind had perfected. Only in destroying things could the humans create something beautiful.

This war would be over soon.

CHAPTER TWENTY
THE LAST PURGE

WHEN THE HATCH opened, Mort(e) faced the ceiling of a chamber. It was like being inside an intestine. He was being digested, though he could not imagine an animal's guts smelling much worse than this. For all its efficiency, there was no way that the Colony could expel its waste fast enough to avoid turning the tunnels into a sewer. Having an exoskeleton just made it easier for the ants to walk around in their own shit.

Gun in hand, Mort(e) stepped out of the torpedo to find a swarm of ants already working to repair the hole created by the impact. The device itself was a wreck. The fins were ripped off, while the molten metal injection gun was crumpled inward, its last drops of melted steel oozing out of the cracks. The trajectory of the torpedo had left a tunnel of its own, with a pulsing red-hot mouth that had cauterized, so that only a small stream of water entered the tunnel. The ants gave their lives trying to seal the crack. Some were fried on the piping-hot rock, while others were swept away by the water.

A trail of ants flowed toward a faint light. Mort(e) followed them around a bend, where the tunnel straightened and narrowed. In the humid air, the light shot like a laser straight out of a hole in the wall. The ants poured into it. The beam flickered as they entered.

The ground rumbled, and the opening grew wider, like a dilating pupil. Mort(e) raised the gun. But the light blinded him, forcing him to shield his eyes. The brightness of it had a warmth to it, as if the ants had harnessed the sun in this otherwise dank place. When at last he took his hand away, he faced a new chamber, round like the inside of a giant empty stomach, where the river of ants gathered into a vast, writhing pool. They made room for his feet with each step he took.

And there it was. There *she* was. The Queen. Even more vivid than the residual memories from the translator. Enormous, with a bobbing head and antennae extending out seven or eight feet like an enormous headdress. A pair of long-dead wings hung from her shoulders. Surrounding the abdomen on either side were bloated workers licking her sedentary body. A massive egg, obscenely white, sprouted from her rear. The workers nudged it toward an opening on the other side of the room, a chute that presumably went to the nursery.

A sense of déjà vu poked his brain. *I've been here*, he thought. *No, I haven't.*

"Drop your weapon," a voice said. It seemed to come from the floors and the wall. The voice was that of a human woman, very familiar. As she had in his dream, the Queen spoke with the voice of Janet. "You are welcome here," it continued. "We mean you no harm."

The entire room was some kind of translator, vibrating with the ghostly voice of his former master.

"Welcome, Sebastian," the Queen said.

The movement in the room stopped. The flow of ants on the ground came to a halt. The workers lifted their heads and faced him.

"Lower the gun, please," the Queen said, "if you wish to see your friend."

Mort(e) removed the strap and dropped the weapon. A wave of ants traveled up his right leg, making him jump.

"Remain still," the Queen said. "They are checking your belongings."

They were already inside his bag by the time she finished her sentence. Mort(e) felt the contents shift around: the canteen, the packets of beef jerky. The hand grenade.

"Please tell your daughters to be careful with the grenade," Mort(e) said. "It's very sensitive."

He felt the lump of the grenade lift out of the bag. The ants walked down his leg. They carried the gun and the grenade to the other side of the room, too far away for him to try to retrieve without the insects overwhelming him. Meanwhile, the enlarged workers returned to their incessant tongue bath.

This was not the same Queen he had encountered in the echoes of the translator. The one before him was old and tired. Unsightly cracks ran throughout her armor, to which the workers dedicated extra attention. The fissures in her skin must have been unbearably painful, littered with germs. Her face was tightly drawn in, the flesh warped and wrinkled like a rotting fruit. Her claws were weak and thin, broken sticks hanging together by the bark. If this is what her body was like, Mort(e) had to believe that her mind was similarly damaged. He pictured it as a dying ember in a room with no windows.

"Why have you come here?" the Queen asked.

"I thought you knew," he said. "I thought you planned all this."

"I want to hear it in your own words."

"I came for my friend. That's all."

"Did a voice tell you to do this?"

"No."

"The prophecy, perhaps?" she asked. "A holy book?"

"'The Warrior and the Mother,' you mean?" he asked. "No. I don't have EMSAH. I'm not a believer."

"Then what brings you here?"

"I told you. She's my friend."

The Queen tilted her head as she contemplated this. *She doesn't understand,* he thought. *She doesn't know what a friend is. Or, even worse: she* does *know, and she realizes that she can't have one herself.*

"Your quest is irrational," she said. "You want what you cannot have, and you believe you are entitled to it. This is virtually the same as EMSAH. EMSAH is the opposite of the gift we gave to you. EMSAH is a perversion of it. We wanted to see if your people could survive without succumbing to these human impulses."

"I don't care," Mort(e) said. "Is she here or not?"

The Queen tilted her head in the other direction, making the ancient antennae flop around like two stiff dreadlocks.

"I've come a long way," he said. "I'm not a philosopher. I'm a house slave who woke up one morning acting like a human."

To the Queen's left, an aperture opened. The bed of ants spread out, leaving a path from Mort(e) to the resulting doorway. He took the trail to the opening. The room inside was arranged like a human house. A green carpet extended from wall to wall, absorbing the overhead fluorescent light. A bag of laundry rested in the corner, the blue sleeve of a hoodie sticking out the top. There was a desk with a computer beside a homemade wooden shelf full of VHS tapes. An exact replica of the Martinis' basement.

He stopped and stared at the Queen. She had nothing to say.

He entered the room. A curtain hung from an exposed pipe on the ceiling. The ants had gotten every detail right, even down to the musty smell of the carpet. Mort(e) saw his hand pull the curtain to the side.

Like a dream, Sheba lay in the warm spot beside the furnace. Her tail lifted from the floor when Sebastian entered. Everything melted away. There was no fight with Daniel, no puppies, no war, no EMSAH. He was Sebastian. There was only this spot, and this friend, and this house with its square of sunlight. The outside world had never crept inside to ruin everything. He was safe.

Sheba was unchanged. Her paws still had hair. She stood up on all fours. Not a day had gone by for her, it seemed.

Mort(e) walked to her and knelt down. She let him wrap his arms around her neck. She licked his face.

I know you, she seemed to say. *Where have you* been?

Mort(e) closed his eyes and wept.

Some time passed. A rumbling began all around him. Mort(e) opened his eyes to find the shape of the room changing. The doorway widened until there was no wall between the replica of the basement and the Queen's court. The furniture and other props remained, but as the ground stretched out, these objects were pressed into a corner at the far end of the chamber. The ants swarmed about them, so that the only space in the room not covered by insects was a small circle where Mort(e) embraced Sheba.

The ants once again formed a path, this time leading to the foot of the Queen. Mort(e) took it, with Sheba hopping alongside him like a pet.

"Why hasn't she changed?" he asked. "Why isn't she like everyone else?"

"The woman found her on the road on the way out of town," the Queen said. "And when we captured the family, the child—Michael—tried to defend the dog with his life. This intrigued us, so we observed. When we tested the translator on him, we learned that you had allowed this family to live. And that you were trying to find her. I decided to keep the dog from changing. She seemed happier that way."

"And you let Michael escape?"

"Yes," she said. "The other prisoners interpreted the effects of the translator as a sign that their god had chosen him as his vessel. They formed a cult around him. So I let them flee to see how his story would affect both the remaining humans and the other animals. It did what I expected it to do. Some took advantage of it. Some embellished it. Many believed, and acted on their belief.

"All the while," she said, "we were watching you. As the humans spread their stories, we put you in a position to make a monumental decision for all life on this planet."

Mort(e) scratched Sheba's head. She pressed her skull into his stubby fingers, happy for the contact.

"Are you listening?" the Queen said.

"Yes," he said, not looking up.

"There is no excuse," the Queen said. "You have two choices. You can stay here and live in comfort with your friend. I will call off the quarantine. I will even give you a dose of the hormone that you can administer to the dog as you wish."

With that, a clump of smaller ants scurried over her left shoulder, carrying a shiny blue pellet. A pill. The Queen took it from them. Mort(e) noticed that her claws had evolved somehow, making them more like hands. The pill resembled a large jewel in the bony clasp of an old woman.

"Or," the Queen continued, "you can leave here and fulfill the false prophecy."

"You'll let me leave?"

"Yes," the Queen replied. "But once you reach the surface, you will be quarantined like all the rest. The apocalypse that your human allies have been praying for will finally be at hand. I rescued you from your gods, but there will be no second chance for your species. I have learned to accomplish extraordinary things, but I cannot remove evil from a person's heart. I cannot make a person see the truth."

"Does it matter to you that I made her a promise?" Mort(e) said. "Even if she couldn't understand it?"

"I made a promise as well," the Queen said, her tone changing from stern to soothing, the way Janet would speak when trying to calm one of the children. "I would like for you to stay. I know that you have an inquisitive mind. You would enjoy the wonders that the Colony would share with you. No one else has to die. All you have to do is make the right choice. For her and for you. For us."

"Let me talk it over with my friend here," Mort(e) said, patting Sheba on her side. He imagined that the Queen would have grimaced at this, if she had had a proper face.

He knelt on the ground, opened his pack, and removed the metal water canteen. Unscrewing the top, he held it out for Sheba to drink. He poured it while she lapped up the column of water.

Another egg dropped from the Queen's abdomen.

"You think I'm in danger of believing in some invisible human in the sky," Mort(e) said. "But it's not like that at all."

"I believe in this," he said, pointing to Sheba as she drank. "I remember my time with my friend. I realize that these things don't last. But I will fight for them."

"Maybe we have much to learn from each other," the Queen said.

The water was finished. Mort(e) shook the canteen over his free hand until a small vial dropped out. He placed the canteen on the ground. Sheba tried to probe it with her snout. He rose, the vial in his hand. The Queen's antennae extended from her head until they formed a perfect V.

"Maybe," Mort(e) said.

He threw the vial at her. The sudden movement made Sheba bark. The glass tube shattered against the Queen's face.

The movement in the room halted again. The oleic acid from the vial sent its unmistakable message to the entire court: THE QUEEN IS DEAD. PURGE. DESTROY. The marching and the licking ceased.

"Kill them!" the Queen said. But no one listened. Instead, the workers pierced her abdomen with their jaws. The room shook, echoing her agony. The smaller ants, who had covered the lower part of her body, now engulfed her thorax and head. The swarm on the ground surrounded the Queen. Together, the workers, the Alphas, and their tiny sisters forced their monarch toward the opening from which Mort(e) had entered. A pair of oversized workers tore open her egg-laying orifice and feasted on the contents inside. The creatures dragged her farther, splitting open her abdomen and allowing more eggs to spill out.

Mort(e) picked up Sheba and carried her on his shoulders. Racing past the Queen's writhing head, he climbed onto her abdomen and gripped the shell. He could feel Sheba breathing heavily into his ear. More ants from other chambers contributed to the effort. Each pair of jaws that pulled her along tore off another piece of Hymenoptera the Great. One overzealous Alpha pulled on her left antenna so hard it snapped, sending the beast tumbling backward. Unwilling to accept her fate, the Queen tried to fight them off. She gobbled up the small workers that covered her arms and claws. When an Alpha attempted to latch onto her neck, she bit viciously into the soldier's face and tore away the mandible. The other part of the Alpha's jaw flapped stupidly as she stumbled off to the side.

The wounded Alpha collapsed onto the Queen's back.

Mort(e) tried to kick her away, but the creature lunged at him with her broken jaw. Sheba barked, telling the ant to please leave them alone. Sheba was the most reasonable one here, Mort(e) thought. But then, the Alpha lurched forward to bite Sheba in half. Sheba tried to dodge her, but the monster's head slammed into her side, sending her sliding down the carapace, her paws scraping helplessly. Mort(e) shouted her name as she dropped off the side of the abdomen and disappeared into the crowd of snapping jaws and grasping talons.

All those years without Sheba, all the awful nights spooning with Tiberius in trenches and tents, all the starving, mind-numbing marches—all those years of misery and despair descended upon Mort(e) again. He'd lost her again. It was worse than watching Daniel chase her away.

And then, cutting through the earsplitting noise of the dying Colony, Sheba barked loud enough for Mort(e) to hear. *Sebastian!* she said. *I'm over here!*

That was what he heard, anyway.

Mort(e) raced to the spot in the crowd where Sheba had vanished. He was face-to-face with an Alpha. In a useless but deeply satisfying gesture, Mort(e) punched her again and again until his knuckles bled. *You hurt my friend*, he thought, *and I will KILL ALL OF YOU!* The creature snapped at him, but was too dazed by the oleic acid to hone in on her target. Mort(e) geared up for another roundhouse when Sheba barked again.

He spotted her near the replica of the Martinis' basement. There was an exit nearby, another tunnel that had opened up when the shape of the room had changed. Sheba had drawn away several soldiers, who were now regaining their senses. They surrounded her. She was on her haunches, growling, her white-and-orange fur darting about as she tried in vain to scare them off.

Mort(e) could not take on that many Alphas. Perhaps he could create a diversion to get them away from her, but Sheba would not know how to get out. Frantic, he searched the room for the weapons. He found them right where the smaller ants had left them, near the tunnel where he had first entered the room. The gun and the grenade were thirty yards away, mocking him.

Mort(e) took a running leap over the advancing horde of monsters, landing in an open space. Sheba's barking alerted one of the soldiers. The Alpha's head swiveled toward him. The mouth came at him first. Mort(e) dove to the ground. He felt the jaws catch his tail and then break away. A lightning bolt of pain shot up his spine. The last few inches of his tail were gone, leaving a bloody, mangled stump. Gritting his teeth, Mort(e) grabbed the machine gun, still covered with ants. The monster regained her footing and reared up for another strike. The other end of his tail dropped from the beast's jaws. He remembered that the gun's safety was still on. Lying prone, with the ants crawling over him to get to the Queen, Mort(e) clicked the safety with his thumb and aimed. When the Alpha dove toward him this time, she faced the barrel of a live gun. *Shoot him*, he heard the stray cats say in his mind. *Like this.*

Mort(e) pulled the trigger, crushing several ants that had lodged themselves under his finger. The muzzle flash lit up the room like a strobe light. The bullets entered the Alpha's neck and blew out the back of her skull. The creature tottered onto her abdomen, then fell over sideways.

Mort(e) got to his feet and knocked away the ants that clung to his fur. They fell and continued scurrying off to the purge. To his right, the delirious swarm tried to carry his grenade away. He plucked it from them and ran to Sheba, trying to keep his throbbing tail still.

The grenade was another one of the humans' ingenious

devices, invented far too late to make a difference in the war. Mort(e) pulled the pin, which released a burst of concentrated oleic acid. The ants surrounding Sheba spun toward the scent. Sheba continued barking at them, probably convinced that she had scared them away.

The creatures crawled toward Mort(e), their antennae seeking out the bomb, the object that must be purged. Mort(e) lobbed it into the nearby tunnel.

"Fetch," he said.

The metal pinecone bounced away into the bowels of the Colony. The ants rushed after it, stumbling over one another.

"Okay, Sheba," he said. "Let's get out of—"

Sheba sprinted past him. She, too, was chasing the damn thing. She thought they really were playing fetch.

"Sheba, no!" he said. She kept running.

Now they were all charging down the tunnel, drawn to the noise of the bouncing bomb. When he got close, Mort(e) dove to grab Sheba's tail, sliding face-first. She had the nerve to growl at him. Mort(e) got to his feet, gripped her by the scruff of the neck, and ran back the way they came. When he made it to the court, he dropped to the ground again, shielding her body and covering her ears with his hands. The bomb detonated, sending a blast of hot air and debris from the tunnel.

The explosion left his ears ringing, a noise like an army of humans yawning at once: *Awwhhhhh*. Mort(e) opened and closed his mouth to get his ear canals working properly, but the noise remained. Stumbling, he dragged Sheba to the Queen. There was a gap in the group of workers who were shoving the Queen out of the chamber. Mort(e) ran to it, tossed Sheba onto the Queen's abdomen, and climbed aboard. His wounded tail left a streak of blood on her exoskeleton. From a sitting position, he pointed the gun at all the soldiers and workers. They were not concerned with him now. Blindly, relentlessly, they pushed the hulk into the main tunnel.

The Queen's daughters had shredded her wings, clipped her antennae, and amputated all but one of her claws, which still clutched the blue pill. She had protected it. He turned to Sheba, his expression asking, *Do you see that?*

Mort(e) scrabbled up the carapace to the Queen's shoulders. He reached for the pill. It was too far away. Suddenly the Queen's head spun around.

"Let me have that pill," Mort(e) said, "and I'll help you get out of here."

They were out of the royal chamber, so she could no longer use the walls as a translator. But she understood. She extended her claw to him. He swiped the blue pill and dropped it in his backpack.

She was still facing him, waiting for his response. Mort(e) stuck the muzzle of the gun between two segments of her armor at the base of her skull. This would be her escape, to avoid seeing her own daughters destroy her. She did not resist. Her antennae went limp as she awaited this release, this unburdening. There was so much knowledge in this brain about to be destroyed. More than could be stored in all the books ever written, all the computers ever built. Billions of lifetimes. An eternity of memories, an endless treasure of visions of the future.

Mort(e) fired once. The thorax and head went stiff, then sank down. All of it was gone, obliterated by a crude weapon fashioned by poorly evolved primates. No god would have wanted it this way. Except for the Queen, who was a god herself.

They went uphill. Sheba crawled to Mort(e). He put her on his shoulders to keep her close in case he had to jump off. They made a series of turns before heading in a dead run toward an opening. Mort(e) could smell fresh air, and his whiskers pricked up when he detected salt. The ants intended to dump their mother into the ocean. Sheba gave a low whine, much like the noises she would make when her old master left her by herself. When they arrived at the exit, Mort(e) tried to get hold of the ceiling. It was too high. The overcast sky lit up the tunnel. He tasted the spray from the waves. The ants pushed the Queen halfway out of the nest. She slumped downward, her lone claw twitching as if wagging a finger at her disobedient subjects. Still holding onto the Queen's carapace, Mort(e) peered over the side to see that they were about to fall almost fifty feet to a rocky beach below. Sheba squirmed on his shoulders. Their only chance was to try to latch onto the face of the cliff. Mort(e) hesitated. There was no way to tell from here if his hands would fail him now.

Another forceful nudge from the ants caused him to snap to attention. Sheba barked impatiently. As the ants gave the Queen's body one final shove, Mort(e) jumped onto the cliff. His fingers found a sharp edge that bit into his flesh. The rock shook as the ants ejected the Queen's lumbering body from the tunnel. Seconds later, she crashed onto the stones below.

He held on. Sheba remained still. *I am not going to die because of my hands*, Mort(e) thought. He began to climb, telling Sheba to hang on, that it would be all right. Blood dripped from his wounded tail and fell down into the sea like red raindrops.

When he got close enough, he let Sheba step onto his head so she could climb onto the ledge above. He pulled himself up and rested on his stomach for a moment. His fingers were rubbed raw, but the callused skin had not broken. Examining the cliff, he figured he could climb the rest of the way.

He sat up and let Sheba place her head in his lap.

In the sky above, the first paratroopers from the *Vesuvius* began their descent.

CHAPTER TWENTY-ONE
THE BATTLE OF GOLGOTHA

ULDESAC WANTED THE soldiers to stay away from the crash site. But the new recruits gathered around the flaming wreckage like cavemen after a hunt. He shouted for them to stop. When that did not work, he ran out of the cave and emptied his pistol into the air. Several other officers did the same. Disappointed, the soldiers returned to their fortifications.

There didn't seem to be any poison gas from the crash. Besides, the humans had given up on chemical weapons years earlier because the ants were too quick to adapt. With no strategic advantage gained, Culdesac settled on this being a diversion at best, an insane example of human theatrics at worst. The Archon was praying at the end. The members of the resistance were probably running out of food in their airborne utopia, and it was possible that the Archon was another sacrifice to their bloodthirsty gods.

Then the shout went up. "There's another one!"

Culdesac whirled around. The *Vesuvius* approached from the north, cutting through the clouds. The ants shifted toward it as they retreated from the impact zone of the *Golgotha*. This second wave was no suicide mission. The *Vesuvius* meant to strafe, or bomb, or drop soldiers. Culdesac hoped that it was the latter. He wanted to collect a few of them alive.

While his officers ordered the soldiers to stand ready, Culdesac headed to the cave, keeping his eye on the approaching ship. There were objects dropping out of it, descending slowly. Parachutes. Was there no limit to the death wish these people had? Were they *this* foolish? They could not go extinct quietly. They needed an apocalypse.

The translator in his ear began to buzz. He batted it with his hand, but the noise continued, growing stronger before changing into a series of rattles and clicks. It was picking up random signals from multiple Alphas, strong enough to interfere with his antenna from afar.

The coyote walked toward him with the Alpha envoy directly behind her. "Sir," the coyote said, "we're getting a report of boats landing to the west. Should we—"

She did not get to finish her sentence. The giant ant picked her up at the waist in her viselike jaws. The coyote made a choking sound as the beast thrashed her. Culdesac pulled out his gun. The raccoon in the cave ran out with his rifle pointed at the ant.

"Shoot her!" Culdesac said, trying to reload.

The raccoon fired, drilling holes in the ant's armor plating. But instead of retaliating, the Alpha continued dragging the coyote's body across the rocky ground. His gun now loaded, Culdesac fired. The monster ignored the shots that were ripping her apart. She seemed to be possessed.

Other soldiers raced to the scene. It took four more rifles and dozens of rounds before the Alpha finally collapsed and died. The ant's leg twitched once, prompting one of the soldiers to begin firing again.

"Hold your fire," Culdesac said, waving smoke from his eyes.

He leaned over the coyote but did not bother to check her pulse. Her head was twisted almost completely around.

With all the shooting, Culdesac had not noticed that the unintelligible clicking continued from the translator. Putting his hand to his other ear, he tried to make sense of the competing signals.

"Colonel," someone said.

All his soldiers stared in the direction of the ants. There on the hilltop, Culdesac saw the visual manifestation of the gibberish clattering away in his earpiece. The ants had broken formation. They collided with one another, unable to control their bodies. Claws and mandibles locked onto each other, making it impossible to tell where one ant ended and the other began. There was the sound of scuffling feet and exoskeletons crunching and snapping. Some of the ants had been capsized, and their legs flailed helplessly as their sisters pulled them in different directions. An Alpha dragged a disembodied head and thorax in a great circle.

A wave of ants crested the ridge and began charging toward Culdesac and his soldiers.

"What's happening?" Culdesac asked. But he knew the answer before he even finished. The *Golgotha*'s air supply must have been laced with a chemical that affected the ants. Something that made them turn on one another.

He tore off the translator. "Fall back," he said to the soldiers.

They ran toward the foxholes. Behind him, Culdesac heard the unmistakable sound of a pair of jaws closing on the body of one of his soldiers. Hundreds of rifles were aimed in his direction.

"Shoot!" Culdesac screamed, knowing that he was running right into their line of fire. It was better to get shot than be torn apart. A constellation of muzzle flashes opened up before him. Bullets whizzed by his head, the sound making his ears curl. He was about to hop into the first foxhole, but he could feel the creatures right behind him. So he jumped over it instead. He heard the ants pulling the soldiers out, tossing them aside, before a hail of gunfire brought them down.

Culdesac bounded into the second row of foxholes. On either side of him, the soldiers continued firing. At his feet, a dog cowered under the lip of the trench. There was no time to discipline him, so Culdesac ripped away the dog's rifle and began shooting. The next wave of Alphas rose over the carcasses of the others and continued to advance. Some were so delirious with the poison that their tongue-like organs hung from their open mouths making them resemble giant mechanical dogs.

Culdesac drained his first clip and inserted another. He aimed for the base of the skull. Things slowed down. He pointed and fired, the muzzle flash followed by flesh and shell bursting from his target. When one creature flopped over dead, legs in the air, Culdesac lined up the sight and found another.

An Alpha attacked the trench to his left. The recruits huddled in terror as the ant straddled the foxhole. Culdesac fell backward as he shot the Alpha in her thorax and abdomen. Hot blood spilled onto the floor of the trench, but the monster kept moving. Culdesac rolled over and crawled away while the soldier behind him was snatched up.

The colonel got to his feet and broke into a run. He made it to the far end of the trench and climbed out. To the west, he spotted a fleet of old yachts and fishing boats anchored near the shoreline. A new swarm spilled out of them, made up of his own kind, other animals who fought for the humans. They splashed through the knee-deep waves, rifles raised. To him, the invaders resembled a virus taking over a host cell.

Culdesac's soldiers were in total disarray. Everything broke down into split-second snapshots: an officer shooting a private for running away; a cat holding her bloodied, amputated tail as she fled screaming from an Alpha; two dogs carrying a wounded comrade—so mutilated that the species was unclear—only to be trampled by a rampaging Alpha with her head torn off.

The Queen is dead, he thought. The Queen saw everything, but she did not see this. He was sure of it. The translator had linked him to her so intimately that he could sense her departure. Her absence created an emptiness in the universe, a void that would pull in everything he knew and believed and loved. It was not supposed to be like this. She was supposed to protect everyone, to make sure that the humans never hurt anyone ever again. He strained to hear her echo. He waited to feel the grip of her sadness around his throat, around his heart, the despair that he had the privilege of sharing with her. The burden that made him strong. He had promised to swallow her pain for her, to martyr himself so that she could be whole again. She told him that together, they *were* whole. But there was no hope now. She was gone. Culdesac, the bobcat with the forgotten name, was alone again, his people torn from the earth once more.

Someone yelled in his ear, asking what they should do next. He knew then that this would be the day he died. It was neither liberating nor frightening. It only reminded him of how much he missed the hunt.

DROPPING IN FAST from above, Wawa could see the flamethrowers as she waited to touch down. The soldiers waved the tongues of fire over the hordes of ants. Great orange snakes lashing out, gobbling up the Alphas. Some of the creatures had been driven so mad by the oleic acid that they continued to purge their sisters even while they burned.

Wawa landed hard, about fifty yards from the ant columns. She tried to remove her machine gun from its holster, but the wind flipped the parachute on top of her. The square-headed major had told her to ditch the parachute first, then worry about everything else, and she had already forgotten. By the time she untangled herself, the Black Hats were stampeding past her, each trying to get a shot at the writhing Alphas before the oleic acid wore off.

She had to run through a wall of smoke in order to find the rest of her pack. The second wave of Black Hats—armed with machine guns instead of flamethrowers—opened fire on the ants. Some of the creatures seemed to finally understand that they had been hoodwinked, but their sisters continued to pull at them, keeping them from launching a counterattack.

Of all the noises competing for her attention, there was one that Wawa could make out clearly.

Laughter.

As the ants stumbled about, mortally wounded with amputations and great bleeding punctures, the humans pounced on them. One of the men was so zealous that he leapt onto the back of a dying Alpha and shot her in the head. When the insect rolled over and pinned him to the ground, his comrades made a few jokes before helping him out from under the carcass. "What, are you hiding?" someone said.

One of the soldiers came across a decapitated ant head and kicked it toward another Black Hat. Startled, the second man shot the head, prompting the prankster to laugh hysterically. "Shut up," the second man said.

Everyone moved toward the other end of the Island, where Culdesac's forces were waiting. To advance, all the Black Hats had to do was get behind a wall of ants as the insects traced the chemical signature of the oleic acid all the way to the animals' foxholes. The marauding humans made a curious sound as they rushed ahead: "Woo! Woooo! Wahooo!" It was like dogs howling, but out of joy instead of warning or despair.

The humans climbed over the dead ants and stormed the fortifications. The animals were already in full retreat to the sea. Even though Wawa sprinted as fast as she could, she could barely get close to a living enemy. She saw a number of animals cut down from behind as they retreated. There were even a few tending to the wounded who were shot on sight. She pointed her gun in the air and fired so she could say that she was at least contributing to the ruckus. The hard ground did not sop up the blood. By the third foxhole, she appeared to be wearing red socks. But she kept running with the others, a mad avalanche bristling with guns.

Up ahead, the landing party had arrived on a nearby shore. The pitch of the yelling descended an octave, remaining in a sustained "Yeaaaaaah!" A few of the humans took a break from shooting to hold their rifles in the air with both hands in celebration. The Black Hats shouted to their incoming allies.

"Get yer ass over here!" someone yelled.

"Welcome to the party!"

Wawa could see the forces unloading from the ships, marching down gangplanks or rowing to shore in small boats. The reinforcements made their way down the beach, cutting off the only avenue of escape for Culdesac's forces.

The Black Hats came to a halt at the foot of a hill. They spread out, trying to find cover. A bullet whizzed by Wawa's head, prompting her to hide behind the abdomen of a dead Alpha. Except it wasn't dead. Still on its side, the beast turned to face her. Panicked, Wawa fell on her tail while firing madly until the ant's head dropped once more.

She got to her feet and saw that the Black Hats had surrounded a cave. There was so much gunfire coming from it that the opening itself looked like the barrel of a gun. The shooting stopped, and a few cocky humans attempted to storm the entrance. Three shots in succession took them all out. More firing ensued. The animals inside the cave were barricaded behind sandbags and had plenty of ammunition.

Wawa was about to make a run for a spot closer to the action when she felt a hand on her shoulder. She spun around to find Mort(e) staring into her eyes. "You were easy to find," he said. He held his tail, his fist colored red as it stanched an open wound. His machine gun was pocked with smashed ant carcasses. At his feet, waiting obediently, was a dog, a small female that stood on all fours. Wawa had not seen one since that night at the dog-fighting ring.

"These humans stink," Mort(e) said.

The shooting continued. The humans yelled for the animals inside the cave to surrender. Wawa wanted to join the others in the small siege. Mort(e) kept his hand on her shoulder. "Don't let him die facing his own kind," he said.

"Who?"

"The colonel. Let him go out fighting the humans."

"He doesn't have to die," Wawa said.

"Yes, he does."

She swatted his hand away and ran toward the cave. The others ordered her to take cover.

"Hold your fire!" she said.

"No, *don't* hold your fire," someone shouted back.

"Colonel!" Wawa said. "Colonel, I know you're in there!"

A bullet flew by her head. It came from inside the cave. A warning shot. A courtesy for a fellow soldier. The soldiers crouched lower behind the rocks and fortifications.

"Get down," a voice said. It was the square-headed major, down on one knee behind the severed abdomen of an Alpha soldier. A handprint tinged with mud and blood covered the left half of his craggy face.

"Colonel," Wawa said, "please surrender! They'll kill you!"

"I said get down!" the major said. Frustrated, he turned to Mort(e) and said, "Tell her to get down!"

"She doesn't listen," Mort(e) said.

"Colonel, please surrender," Wawa said. "I forgive you. We can forgive you. It's not too late."

This was what she was meant to do in this war. Culdesac had saved her. Now she would save him.

The square-headed officer ran to her, grabbed the shoulder strap of her pack, and made her kneel down with him. Another bullet zipped by. The soldiers returned fire.

"Stop!" Wawa said.

"Stay out of this," the major said.

"Give him a chance to surrender."

"He's had his chance. You're not in charge here—"

The man stopped talking when he noticed Wawa's hand resting on the handle of her pistol. The tip of the holster was pointed at the major's belly.

"You think that *house cat* is a warrior?" Wawa said. "I'm the one who'll carve you up and watch you die. Now, the Archon told me this would happen. Tell your soldiers to let the bobcat surrender."

"He's one of them."

"If you redeemed me, you can redeem him," she said. "Now let him walk."

As the man opened his mouth to respond, another barrage of gunfire drowned him out. The animals who were hiding in the cave jumped over their barricade and charged at the line of humans. There were four of them.

Wawa shoved the major away and got to her feet. "No!" she screamed.

The guns erupted. Three of the animals dropped. But one—a

bobcat—shrugged off a bullet to the shoulder, bounded over the rifle fire, and landed on top of a hapless human soldier.

"Colonel, stop! Look at me! It's me! It's—"

Culdesac tore the man open. Wawa actually *heard* it: a wet, sopping noise, like soaked fabric ripping, combined with the man gasping and choking. It was then that he spotted Wawa. Her mouth gaped. She may have been screaming. There was no way to tell with all the noise. Culdesac's eyes were like an ant's eyes, seeing in all directions but unable to focus. Even in that moment, Wawa still believed that he would remember, and understand, and accept this new world, this last chance to be a real person.

His fur now pink with blood, Culdesac lifted the corpse, trying to use it as a shield. He reared up to attack another soldier. The rifles unloaded on him. He collapsed, with one claw straining for his enemy before a final hail of bullets left him a shredded heap of fur and bone. The men and women did not cheer this time.

Mort(e) caught up with Wawa, placing his hand on her bicep and trying to turn her away from the scene. The dog was at her other side, brushing its fur against her leg, as if Wawa were the animal's master.

This was what the humans had prayed for, Wawa thought. And it had come true.

Wawa felt Mort(e)'s hand lift away. She felt nothing else.

CHAPTER TWENTY-TWO
LOVE

HE *VESUVIUS WAS* perched low in the sky, anchored by a cable tied to the Island's great tower. Below, the humans burned the bodies of their victims well into the night. The ground was too hard to bury anyone, and tossing them out to sea would only ensure that the corpses would resurface on the beach. There was talk of dropping the bodies down into the great tunnel leading to the ants' lair, on the other side of the Island, but this was dismissed. While the tunnel appeared to be inactive, the humans stayed away from it. Some day, they would have to organize an expedition into the nest to make sure that the ants were not breeding a new queen, however unlikely that may have been. For now, with Hymenoptera the Great lying dead in the Colony's trash dump, and the final quarantine canceled without her royal decree, it was time to celebrate.

Mort(e) planned to leave in the morning, having procured a small boat from a member of the amphibious assault force. "Anything for you, sir," the human owner had said. Mort(e) had no plan other than to head for the mainland and perhaps find a cabin in the mountains, far from whatever new settlements the humans and their friends were planning. If he were to find such a place, he could not say for sure if he would stay there for the rest of his life. All of that was too far into the future to worry about now. He would think about it more when the sun came up.

While the others worked, cleaning up the dead bodies and setting up a temporary base of operations, Mort(e) collected supplies for the trip. Sheba trailed behind him. Each of the incoming ships had something he needed: water bottles, food, tools, guns. A cat who also had only half a tail offered a roll of gauze for Mort(e)'s injury. A tall golden retriever who called herself Cali gave Mort(e) a Swiss army knife. She asked to take a photo with him, to which he agreed. When a woman offered him a leash for Sheba, Mort(e) told her gently but firmly to put it away and to never show it to anyone again. Scavenging—or, more precisely, collecting donations from awestruck disciples— took up a good part of the day. It kept his mind off what was in store for the planet now that the war was over.

When Mort(e) was satisfied that he and Sheba had enough supplies, he retired to a nearby hill overlooking the area where the ants had attacked one another. From there, he watched the celebration while Sheba slurped up water from a paratrooper's helmet. The humans and their animal friends had built a bonfire. The flames rose high, reflecting off the water and the silvery surface of the airship. The people danced around the carnage, holding hands, kissing, pitching their heads back with food and drink. For all these people knew, former master and ex-slave could be sharing a beer. That possibility did not seem to bother anyone.

There were bizarre works of piety among the victors. A group of female dogs wearing nun habits said prayers over the dead bodies before the soldiers carted them away. Elder Gregory led a multispecies group in song—something about how everyone had a friend in Jesus—while they hacked away at Alpha corpses with axes. The carcasses were too large to carry, so this grotesque procedure was necessary. Prisoners of war were pressed into hauling the slabs of meat to the fire. Nearby, some children from Miss Teter's class fought over a pair of amputated antennae. Two others used them for a swordfight before being corrected by an adult. But then that same adult used the antennae as drumsticks on a set of percussion instruments he had constructed from ant skulls, thoraxes, and abdomen shells.

Mort(e) could not find Wawa in the crowd. It was probably for the best. They had said all that they needed to say to each other. She was free to tell herself, along with these chanting primates who were part of her pack, that all these things had happened according to some divine plan.

Later in the day, after Mort(e) had wrapped his wounded tail, a great commotion rose up. The people were yelling so much that he at first thought something terrible had happened. But they were cheering because, for probably the first time in years, Michael was brought down from the ship and onto land. Four people carried his stretcher, with the stern bald nurse giving them orders, smacking their foreheads if they jostled the boy too much. Mort(e) suspected that she did not approve of this spectacle, but had been pressured into it by the Elders. She waved to Mort(e), probably after someone whispered to her that the messiah was observing her from a nearby hill. He waved back. For the next couple of hours, people took breaks from their labor to visit the boy and whisper prayers of thanks and mercy to their prophet. The nurse stood guard with her arms folded.

When the crowds around Michael began to thin out, Mort(e) and Sheba approached him. Michael was exhausted from the experience, his weak hands grasping at some unseen object dangling above him. The nurse patted his head, a gesture signifying love, sadness, impatience, and regret all at once. When she noticed Sheba, she leaned over and scratched the dog's ears. Sheba liked this.

"Sheba the Mother, home at last," she said. "We sang songs about you. Did you know that, girl? Yes! Yes, we did!"

Mort(e) imagined the woman with a dog of her own, in a house like the one in which he grew up.

"I'm glad that you found your friend," she said.

"Thank you."

"You know," she said, turning to Michael, "I thought this whole thing would kill him."

"Really?"

"His connection with the Queen was so strong," she said. "I was worried that he would sense her death, and then he would die, too. But he's still here, our little angel. So innocent."

She squeezed his hand. "I wish the rest of us were so innocent," she said.

Mort(e) wanted the boy to get a good look at him and Sheba, and to recognize how things had come full circle. Michael's blank stare suggested that this would never happen. So Mort(e) steeled himself to accept that he would never see this child again. At least it was easier this time. Sheba was with him.

"There's something you should know," the nurse said. "I can't tell the others. But I can tell you."

"What is it?"

"When the Queen died, Michael said something. Something she must have taught him. Or some kind of message she sent to him in her last moments."

The nurse cleared her throat and said, "Love is stronger than God."

Mort(e) turned to Sheba for a reaction. The dog merely sat on her hind legs, content. Was this the summation of all that

the Queen had learned, or some desperate acknowledgement
of the only things that her advanced intellect could never fully
comprehend? The only one who knew now was a shivering,
half-dead child who had never asked to be a part of this.

"Is that true, you think?" the nurse asked.

"We have to live like it is," Mort(e) said.

He approached Michael and reached out his hand. He stopped
suddenly, expecting the nurse to grab it once again. But she
was transfixed on the boy. Mort(e) put his palm on Michael's
shoulder, whispered goodbye, and walked away. When Sheba
lingered, he called her, and she followed.

THEY RETURNED TO the hill and ate some of the food that Mort(e)
had collected. When Sheba was finished, she rested her head
on Mort(e)'s thigh. He scratched behind her ears. The sun
went down, turning the great bonfire into the main source
of light. The flames were reflected in her tired eyes like two
wobbling orange jewels. Sheba seemed happy. He had once
told her that he was the strong one, but perhaps he had it
all wrong then, and always would have, were it not for her.
His strength began as bravery, then quickly calcified into an
impenetrable shell. An exoskeleton. Her strength was love,
always love, nothing but love. He was not strong enough to
live that way, but he wanted to be. He would try. He owed
it to both her and himself. Anything short of that would be
unworthy of all the suffering he had endured. The sadness
had no point unless he gave it one.

Mort(e) reached into his bag and fished around for the pill.
It was still there, hard and cold and small in his palm. He held
it toward the fire. Sheba sniffed and apparently liked the scent
enough to begin licking it. Mort(e) closed his fist. Sheba stared
at him in confusion, her eyes asking, *Where'd it go?* Mort(e)

wondered what she would be like. Perhaps she would not love him. Perhaps she would have EMSAH. He promised that he would still be there for her, no matter what. After all, he had carried Sheba with him for so many years. They would both be dead were it not for the other.

He opened his palm again. Delighted, Sheba gobbled up the pill. She seemed to expect another, but Mort(e) held out both hands to show that this was all he had. Sheba responded by licking his fingers. He rubbed her neck and ears.

"Sheba is alive," he whispered. It would take at least a day until the hormone began to take effect. Mort(e) was not afraid. *What more do I need?* he wondered as she nuzzled against him. Why did anyone think that they needed anything else?

He dozed off, the stars spinning above him. Sheba snorted once before falling asleep.

LATER, SHEBA WOKE Mort(e) by slobbering on his face. The sky grew brighter as it approached sunrise. The stars dimmed. Mort(e) sat up to find a more formal ceremony taking place. All the soldiers gathered near the dying fire while Elder Gregory gave a sermon and then read from his thick book. The words made as much sense to Mort(e) as his words did to Sheba.

Figuring that he was as rested as he was going to be, Mort(e) stood up and led Sheba down to the gathering. They had to walk through it in order to get to his newly acquired boat. That was okay—the EMSAH crowd had apparently been instructed to leave him alone now that he had fulfilled his role as messiah.

"And let us now sing the Prayer of St. Francis," Elder Gregory said, "the patron saint of animals." Many of the congregants turned to one another and smiled upon hearing this. "We sing this to honor this new friendship that God has ordained," Gregory added.

Sheba barked when the people broke into song. The noise prompted several people to swing their heads in her direction. They continued with the hymn.

Make me a channel of your peace.
Where there is hatred, let me bring your love;
Where there is injury, your pardon, Lord;
And where there's doubt, true faith in you.

A woman sang the line about bringing love while the top half of an ant's head was slung over her shoulder, presumably to be used as a helmet. Mort(e) tiptoed along the perimeter of the gathering until he was beside the charred, ashy rim of the bonfire.

The fire lit up the faces in the crowd. Their open mouths glistened as they belted out the lyrics about bringing light to darkness.

O Master, grant that I may never seek
So much to be consoled as to console;
To be understood as to understand;
To be loved as to love with all my soul.

The way the singers dragged out the word *soul* elicited a howl from Sheba. Mort(e) patted her side to calm her down. That was when he spotted Wawa in the second row. The St. Jude medal caught his attention. Reflecting the firelight, the medallion was a tiny yellow sun on her chest. Mort(e) kept his gaze on her until her eyes met his. She looked at the ground—not out of shame, it seemed, but out of resignation. He was another part of her past that she did not want to think about right now. She could not help him, just like she couldn't help Culdesac. She was letting go, as he had wanted her to do all along.

Make me a channel of your peace,
It is in pardoning that we are pardoned;
In giving to all men that we receive;
And in dying that we are born to eternal life.

But then he noticed Wawa lifting her eyes again, staring at Sheba, the dog who was both a relic and a ghost. The dog who, within hours, would be like her—more than an animal, better than a human. Mort(e) followed Wawa's gaze to find Sheba sniffing around the stones marking the edge of the fire pit. Then, oblivious to everything around her, Sheba squatted and urinated, sending up a small plume of ash and smoke. She did not even blink. Her eyes suggested that this course of action made perfect sense to her. The people kept singing. Nothing would take this moment away from them.

Mort(e) made his way to the boat. Sheba trotted beside him.

ACKNOWLEDGEMENTS

THERE ARE SO many people to thank, in so few pages, and this is so many years in the making. Please bear with me.

First, I have to express my gratitude to the wonderful staff at the Jean V. Naggar Literary Agency, starting with Laura Biagi. An assistant at the time, Laura fished my manuscript out of the slush and convinced her colleagues to read a book that, in her words, was about "cats, and dogs . . . and, uh, ants." Jennifer Weltz has been my tireless advocate since 2012, transforming this story from a quirky idea into a real novel. At this point, I would probably take a bullet for Jennifer. Please don't test that. I am quite serious.

Second, I must profusely thank the team at Soho Press, starting of course with Mark Doten, who took a chance on my book, and continued the long slog of reworking the story over many months. This project—and my education as a writer—owe so much to Mark's patience, experience, and optimism. I would also like to thank Bronwen Hruska, who agreed to publish a book with talking cats, along with Meredith Barnes, Paul Oliver, Abby Koski, Rachel Kowal, Amara Hoshijo, Rudy Martinez, Janine Agro, and the entire staff at the press.

It was around 2002—when I returned to the United States after living abroad—that I finally began admitting to people that I had been writing on the side for several years. Since then, numerous people have agreed to read my work and offer comments. I cringe at the stuff I made them read, and I owe each of them a special thanks for their kindness: Tom Lydon, Juliette Reiss, Sarah Kitzman, Hanh Le, Susan Calvert, Charlie Boehm, Amanda Dykstra, Ron Pacchione, Carolyn Morrisroe, Mike Paylor, Daniel Asa

Rose, Luke Crisafulli, Tony Schaffer, Troy Dandro, Cam Terwilliger, Mike McKee, Dan Fitzpatrick, Robin Fitzpatrick, Uppinder Mehan, Juan Carlos Pagan, Kelly Klein, Freddy Lopez, Dayne Poshusta, Sara Faye Lieber, Allison Trzop, Mike Sammaciccia, Grace Labatt, and Sam Trott. (I really tried to get everyone. If I missed your name, you never have to pay for a drink in my presence ever again.)

My MFA program at Emerson College saved me from spending years working on a dead-end autobiographical novel. For that, and many other things, I am very grateful. In particular, I have to thank other members of the Emerson Diaspora, especially Brian Hurley (who offered advice on this book in its larval stage), Jane Berentson, Ashley Wells, and Michael Hennessey, who have been such enthusiastic fellow travelers, and whose own work has inspired me for many years now. I also have to thank Aditi Rao, who had the misfortune of being assigned that autobiographical novel as a semester-long(!) book-editing project. And she was nice enough to edit *another* manuscript after that! I'm sorry—and yet not that sorry—to say that I got way more out of that experience than she did.

I am incredibly lucky to have such a supportive, open-minded, strange, and hilarious family, consisting of my brother, Nick; my father, Big Nick; and my mom, Loretta (Lori). When I told each of them that I had finally gotten a book deal, and that the protagonist was a cat, they all said the same thing: "Sebastian?" And when I said that the cat had a friend who was a dog, they each said, "*Sheba*?" It's hard to thank the people to whom you owe everything. So to them, and to my extended family—including Sheba's owners, the Snyders, as well as my adopted families in Grenada, Boston, and New York—I'll say this: please know how grateful I am for all the love and humor and support you've shown me over the years. And if I act otherwise, remind me for the millionth time that life is too short. That usually puts things in perspective.

Continue reading for a preview of *D'Arc*

CHAPTER ONE
THE STORY OF TAALIK

HEN THE DARKNESS passed over the water, Taalik dreamt of the temple again. A temple far beyond the seas, ruled by an ancient queen who went to war with a race of monsters. In the dream, Taalik washed ashore on a beach at nighttime. A mere fish, unable to breathe, he slapped his tail on the sharp rocks until he felt the scales cracking. His fins strained as he tried to return to the water. His lidless eye froze stiff in its socket. And then, he rose from the sand on newly formed limbs, like a crab. The claws sprouted underneath him. He opened his mouth and splayed out his gills, and the air passed through. He did not fear the light and the wind. He did not scramble back to the lapping waves, to the muted blue haze where he was born. Instead, he stood upright, no longer weightless but still strong, defying the gravity that pulled his body to the earth. He marched toward the temple—a giant mound of dirt crawling with strange creatures, each with six legs, heavily armored bodies, mouths like the claws of a lobster. Soldiers bred for killing. They worked in unison, moving as Taalik's people did, many individuals forming a whole. The creatures stood in rows on each side of him. Their antennae grazed him as he walked by, inspecting his scales, his fins. His body continued to change with each step he took. The soldiers admired his new shape, with his segmented legs, and a flexible shell that protected his spine, and tentacles that reached out from underneath, four new arms that could grasp or crush. Here, he was no mere animal, but something more, something his people would worship, something his enemies would learn to fear.

Inside the temple, he found the Queen surrounded by her children. He waited for her to speak, and soon realized that she did not have to. He had understood the message ever since that first dream, and for every dream that followed. Taalik would rule, as the Queen did. There would be a new era of peace to wash away the millennia of bloodshed. No longer would his people slip into the depths of Cold Trench while watching out for predators. No longer would they see their children snatched away. They would learn, and adapt. And one day, his people would rise from the water and find new worlds to conquer.

Or, they would die. The Queen made him understand the starkness of it. There would be no circles of life anymore. Instead, there would be one current through the dark water, leading to conquest or extinction. Life or death. And to secure life, they would not run. They would have to kill.

TAALIK KEPT HIS eyes closed as he listened for the Queen's voice rumbling through the water. Orak, his Prime, floated next to him. Ever since the first revelation, she knew to leave him alone at times like this. The Queen spoke to him only when she wanted to. Even after he opened his eyes and drifted there, Orak waited. The others hovered behind her. They followed her lead. She was the first to convert, the first to mate with Taalik, the first to follow the current with him. Orak kept the others in line, reminding them of their place, but attending to their needs as well, helping to protect the eggs and rear the hatchlings. As

Prime, she enforced Taalik's orders, even when they went against her counsel. She owed her life to Taalik. All the Sarcops did. But he owed his life to her.

Taalik and his people waited under the Lip, the vein of rock that jutted out into Cold Trench, offering shelter from the predators who swam above. This refuge would not hold forever. Their enemies searched for them, driven mad with fear of this new species. Taalik tried to make peace, even ceding territory to those who claimed it as their own. But some creatures, the sharks and other carnivores, would not relent. They would never hear the Queen's song. They would never accept that the world began, rather than ended, at the surface.

Does she speak to you today, my Egg? Orak asked.

He left her waiting too long. Even Orak's enormous patience had limits, especially with the family huddled under the Lip, the food running out. A fight had broken out the day before. Orak punished the unruly ones by ordering the soldiers to feed on their eggs. They had already uprooted the nurseries and hauled them to this desolate place. Feeding on the unborn would lighten the load, and strengthen the ones bred for war.

The Queen is silent this day, my Prime, Taalik said.

A shudder in the water. Taalik gazed into the slit above, where the Lip extended across this narrow stretch of Cold Trench. In the sliver of light he saw them, the fleet of sharks, white bellied, tails waving in unison. At the lead, fatter than the others, was the one Taalik called Graydeath. He recognized the freshly healed gash on the shark's belly, courtesy of Taalik's claw. Graydeath managed to bite it off in their last encounter. The darkness passed over the water forty times before the limb fully regenerated. The other Sarcops watched the healing in amazement, and declared that no one, not even the ocean's greatest shark, could kill the Queen's chosen one.

They smell us, Orak said.

We smell them, Taalik replied.

No enemy had ever penetrated this far into their territory, least of all an army of sharks on patrol. An act of war. It meant that the scouts Taalik dispatched had most likely been killed. He had ordered them to map the shoreline, and to find all of the shallows where his people would have the advantage. But the scouts also served as bait, drawing attention away from the Sarcops as they moved their young ones under the Lip. *They die for us, my Egg*, Orak told him later. *Now we live for them.*

Taalik watched the fleet passing overhead. He waited for the procession to end. It did not. It *would* not. Sharks of every breed crossed his line of sight, as thick as a bed of eels in some places. Mouths began where rear fins ended. In their rage, these solitary creatures banded together to fight a common enemy. The sharks baited him. They wanted the Sarcops to emerge and attack from the rear so that they could swoop around, encircle the strongest ones, and then descend upon the nest to destroy the eggs. Taalik saw it unfold in a vision planted by the Queen herself: Cold Trench clouded with blood. The torn membranes of eggs carried away by the current. Graydeath devouring the younglings while his followers waited for him to finish, not daring to interrupt his victory meal lest they become part of it.

Summon the Juggernauts, Taalik said.

Orak emitted a clicking sound, followed by three chirps—the signal that alerted the soldier caste. The Juggernauts formed their phalanx, with Orak as the tip of the spear.

Every year, when they hibernated, the Sarcops dreamt of the Queen and her empire. And when they awoke, the Queen bestowed upon them new gifts. A language. A philosophy. Until then, their entire existence revolved around fear. Fear of others, of both darkness and light, of the unknown. After the Queen's revelation, and the miracles that followed, a calm determination set in. The Sarcops would not merely react to the environment. They would reshape it as they pleased. Soon their bodies changed along with their minds, as they had in Taalik's dream. First, they sprouted limbs. Then their armored plating, making them resemble the Queen's ferocious daughters. Their mouths and throats changed. Before long, they could make sounds to match all the images and words in their rapidly evolving brains. And then, slithering from their backs, a row of tentacles that allowed them to manipulate the world around them. Only the most loyal Sarcops advanced far enough to earn the distinction of Juggernaut alongside Taalik. The rest changed in other ways. Their senses improved, their teeth sharpened, their fins became weapons. The agile Shoots could swarm their prey. The slender Redmouths could bite into their opponent and twist their bodies, pulling away flesh and bone in a whirlpool of blood. The crablike Spikes could mimic the ocean floor, setting a trap for enemies who strayed too close. Though the Juggernauts formed the vanguard, all the Sarcops knew how to fight. All would have the chance to prove themselves worthy.

Taalik told his troops that they would follow him under the Lip at full speed. They would overtake the fleet at the northern end of the crevasse, near the water's edge. There, Taalik would kill Graydeath in front of everyone. No more hiding. Today their enemies would learn what the Sarcops could do.

Taalik called for Zirsk and Asha, his third and seventh mates, who carried eggs in their pouches. When he confronted Graydeath, these two would release their eggs. Doing so would distract the sharks, who saw only the food in front of their faces. Orak watched them closely as they listened, ready to pounce on

any sign of disapproval. As a consolation for their pending sacrifice, Taalik assured them that they would recover some of the
young. *We will cut them from the bellies of dead sharks*, he
said. *The young ones will have a story to tell.*

He turned away from his soldiers and headed north, using
the rocky Lip for cover while keeping an eye on the movement
above. He felt Orak's presence, slightly behind him. She could
lead if he died. But he would live. The Queen still had so much
to show him.

Cold Trench grew shallower. The cover of the Lip gave way
to open water, where the sharks blotted out the light piercing
the surface. Taalik ascended, faster than the others, homing in
on Graydeath. He felt so tiny in the expanse. The ground rising
behind him blocked any hope of escape.

The water shivered as the sharks detected movement.
Graydeath aimed his snout at the intruder. His mouth split in
half, a red pit of jagged teeth. Scars from numerous battles left
deep divots in his skin. A severed claw still punctured his dorsal
fin, a permanent reminder of some creature that died trying to
fight the sharks.

Taalik charged at him, claws unsheathed, tentacles reaching out. They collided, a sound like boulders toppling into
the trench. Tumbling and twisting, Graydeath pulled free
from Taalik's grip and clamped his teeth at the root of one
of his tentacles. Taalik struggled to keep the mouth open, to
stop the shark from shearing off the limb at the base. Blood
leaked from the puncture wounds, driving Graydeath into a
new realm of delirium. Taalik tried to pluck out the eye, but
Graydeath squirmed his face out of reach, using his mouth as
a shield. The shark's momentum dragged Taalik away from
the battle, away from Cold Trench, and toward the shallows,
where Taalik would not be able to escape.

Taalik let him do it. Sensing victory, Graydeath thrashed again, letting go of the wounded tentacle and twisting his snout toward Taalik's head. With his claws, Taalik held the jaw open, gripping so tightly that some of the teeth broke off like brittle seashells. He pulled the shark toward land, toward the edge of the known world. They crashed onto a bed of rocks, kicking up dust and debris. A primitive creature, Graydeath nevertheless sensed the violation of the natural order that awaited him at the surface. Desperate, he tried to buck free of his opponent. A wave caught them, slamming them onto the earth. From here, Taalik could stand. And when he did, he broke free of the water. And even with the monster still trying to tear his head off, Taalik gazed at the new world, the land of the Queen—a golden patch of fine sand stretching from one end to the other, anchoring a blue dome.

Holding his breath, he dragged the shark out of the foamy waves. Taalik's body grew heavy, as if a giant claw pressed him under the water where he belonged. The shark's eyes shimmered under the piercing light, stunned at the impossibility of it all. The Queen called everyone to this place, though only a few would prove worthy. Graydeath, a king of the deep, writhed in agony. No water would rush through his gills ever again. His enormous eye caked in sand, the shark trembled as his life bled away at last.

Taalik felt as though he would burst. Unable to resist any longer, he opened his mouth, allowing the gills to flare out. Water sprayed from the two openings. The strange, weightless fluid of this place flowed through him, expanding his chest and rounding his segmented back. He released it with a choking cough. Inhaling again, deeper this time, he felt the power of it. And then he let out a roar that rattled his entire body. His voice sounded so different here, higher pitched and free to skitter away in the wind. There were no waves to muffle him. He screamed his name to announce his arrival, to shake the earth so that even the Queen, in her fortress, would hear.

This shark that lay at his feet did not have a name, save the one Taalik gave to it. Graydeath did not even understand the concept of a word, how it could rumble from the throat, and swim through the water, or float in the air, before finding purchase in someone else's mind. The Queen showed Taalik how to do this, first in his dreams, and now while he was awake.

Taalik gripped the bulging eyeball of the shark and wrenched it free of its socket. He held it aloft and said his name again and again until the blood dripped down his claw.

TAALIK TOWED GRAYDEATH to the site of the battle, where the Juggernauts overwhelmed the few sharks who remained. As Taalik expected, most of them fled when their leader disappeared. Warriors on both sides halted when they saw Graydeath with his jaw gaping, the lifeless fins flapping in the current. Detecting the scent of blood and defeat, the sharks retreated, leaving behind wounded comrades and severed body parts. Taalik immersed himself in the smell of it, the taste of it. The Juggernauts swam in great loops around him as he placed Graydeath's corpse on the ocean floor.

Orak rushed to Taalik and immediately went about inspecting his wounds. She nudged him, forcing him to rest on the ground while she licked the gashes at the base of his tentacle, keeping them free of pathogens so they could heal. Taalik knew not to argue with her. His fourth mate, Nong-wa, attended to Orak's injury, a bite mark near her left pectoral fin. The three of them watched as the others killed the stragglers from the fleet. Zirsk and Asha ordered the Juggernauts to slice open their bellies. As

Taalik promised, some of them released the eggs they had swallowed. After inspecting them, Zirsk and Asha claimed the eggs they knew to be theirs. The others cheered them on, clicking and chirping each time they ripped open one of their captives. Sometimes, the sharks would try to swallow the eggs again as the Sarcops extracted them, unaware that they died in the process.

Nong-wa, help with the eggs, Orak said.

Nong-wa got in a few more licks before swimming over to the others.

Taalik, the First of Us, Orak said. *I was afraid you would not return.*

I was afraid I would not find you when I did.

These fish cannot kill me.

No, Taalik said.

Another shark split open, but yielded no stolen eggs, only a small, undigested fish. The Shoots devoured both.

I must tell you something, Taalik said. *I fear the others are not ready to hear.*

What is it, my Egg?

I pulled that shark above the waves. The place we cannot go, from which none return.

Orak stopped licking for a second. *And yet you returned.*

Yes. The shark died. I lived.

Taalik described the enormous weight pinning him down, the thin, tasteless air that he nevertheless could breathe. He talked about the color, the brightness of it. *The Queen chose me to break this barrier*, he said. *The place above the sea holds our destiny.*

Lead us there.

We are not ready. Too many would have to be left behind.

That has not stopped us before. He knew she meant the gambit with the eggs.

There is something else, he said. He extended his claw and held out a shiny object. She reached for it with her tentacle.

What is it? she asked.

I do not know. I pulled it from the shark's fin.

She rubbed her tentacle along the curve of the object, and then gently tapped the sharp end. *A tooth? A claw, perhaps?*

No. It is some kind of weapon, forged from the earth somehow. From the rock.

Who made it?

The monsters from my dream. Enemies of the Queen. They live above the surface. They tortured the shark, and his people. I saw the scars on his hide. I felt his fear. When I pulled him from the water, he thought I was one of them.

The monsters are at war with the sharks, just like us.

They are at war with everyone, Taalik said. *They are more dangerous than the sharks. When the darkness passes over, I see millions of us, piled on the dirt, drying out under the sun. These monsters have hunted us for years. Destroyed our homelands. They hate us as much as they hate the Queen. Many of us will die if we proceed.*

Orak returned the object to Taalik. *Then we die,* she said.

She swam around to face him. Behind her, the Juggernauts held another shark while Zirsk ripped him from his gills to his rear fin. *You are the First of Us,* Orak said. *You gave us meaning and hope. But you cannot take it away. You cannot tell us what to do with it now. You gave us a choice, and we have chosen to follow you.*

She continued licking his wounds, ignoring her own injury, as was her way. He wrapped a tentacle around hers, twisting several times until the suckers latched onto one another.

They would have to abandon Cold Trench, he told her. They would not survive another hibernation period, when their enemies were sure to strike. The Sarcops would move north, following the magnetic beacon at the pole. With luck, they would find a safe haven in the ice.

Before him, Zirsk and Asha nursed their eggs. Shoots and Redmouths tugged on the corpses of their prisoners until some of the sharks split in two. Taalik observed in silence. Tomorrow, he would point them toward their future.

THE WAR WITH NO NAME RAGES ON ...

ROBERT REPINO'S COMPLETE MORT(E) SAGA CONTINUES

D'ARC   CULDESAC